"Westlake's light touch is always refreshing . . . good, clean fun."

—*Charlotte Observer*

"A showdown only Westlake could have conceived. As can be expected from this expert hand, the narrative is at once laconic and fast, the jokes constant, fresh, and funny. Dortmunder, as always, is a potent brew that makes the world look brighter."

—*Publishers Weekly*

"This is Westlake at his funniest."

—*Herald* (NH)

"This is enjoyable stuff."

—*Fort Worth Star-Telegram*

"Westlake's Dortmunder stories are among the best comic crime novels in existence, and this one is a worthy addition to the series."

—*Booklist*

By Donald E. Westlake

NOVELS

Bad News ◆ The Hook ◆ The Ax ◆ Humans ◆ Sacred Monster
A Likely Story ◆ Kahawa ◆ Brothers Keepers
I Gave at the Office ◆ Adios, Scheherazade
Up Your Banners

THE DORTMUNDER SERIES

What's the Worst That Could Happen? ◆ Don't Ask
Drowned Hopes ◆ Good Behavior ◆ Why Me
Nobody's Perfect ◆ Jimmy the Kid ◆ Bank Shot
The Hot Rock

COMIC CRIME NOVELS

Smoke ◆ Baby, Would I Lie? ◆ Trust Me on This
High Adventure ◆ Castle in the Air ◆ Enough
Dancing Aztecs ◆ Two Much
Help I Am Being Held Prisoner ◆ Cops and Robbers
Somebody Owes Me Money
Who Stole Sassi Manoon? ◆ God Save the Mark
The Spy in the Ointment ◆ The Busy Body
The Fugitive Pigeon

CRIME NOVELS

Pity Him Afterwards ◆ Killy ◆ 361 ◆ Killing Time
The Mercenaries

JUVENILE
Philip

WESTERN
Gangway (with Brian Garfield)

REPORTAGE
Under an English Heaven

SHORT STORIES

Tomorrow's Crimes ◆ Levine ◆ The Curious Facts Preceding My
Execution and Other Fictions ◆ A Good Story and Other Stories

ANTHOLOGY
Once Against the Law (coedited with William Tenn)

DONALD E. WESTLAKE

what's the
worst
that could
happen?

WARNER BOOKS

A Time Warner Company

WARNER BOOKS EDITION

Copyright © 1996 by Donald E. Westlake
All rights reserved. No part of this book may be reproduced in any form or by any electronic or mechanical means, including information storage and retrieval systems, without permission in writing from the publisher, except by a reviewer who may quote brief passages in a review.

Cover art: Copyright © 2001 by MGM Studios. All rights reserved.

Warner Books, Inc.
1271 Avenue of the Americas
New York, NY 10020

Visit our Web site at
www.twbookmark.com.

For information on Time Warner Trade Publishing's online publishing program, visit www.ipublish.com.

 A Time Warner Company

Printed in the United States of America

Originally published in hardcover by The Mysterious Press
First Paperback Printing: October 1997
Reissued: June 2001

10 9 8 7 6 5 4 3 2 1

As the I Ching says: Difficulty at the beginning
works supreme success.

This is no time for levity.
—Oliver Hardy

This is no time for levity. Hmp!
—Stanley Laurel, in agreement

what's the worst that could happen?

From the circumstances, Dortmunder would say it was a missing-heir scam. It had begun a week ago, when a guy he knew slightly, a fella called A.K.A. because he operated under so many different names, phoned him and said, "Hey, John, it's A.K.A. here, I'm wondering, you got the flu, something like that? We don't see you around the regular place for a while."

"Which regular place is that?" Dortmunder asked.

"Armweery's."

"Oh, yeah," Dortmunder said. "Well, I been cuttin back. I might see you there sometime."

Off the phone, Dortmunder looked up the address of Armweery's and went there, and A.K.A. was at a booth in the back, under the LOOSE LIPS SINK SHIPS poster where some wag had blacked out most of the Jap's teeth.

"What this is," A.K.A. said, under his new mustache (this one was gingery, and so, at the moment, was his hair), "is a deposition. A week from Thursday, 10:00 A.M., this lawyer's office in the Graybar Building. Take maybe an hour. You go in, they swear you, ask you some questions, that's it."

"Do I know the answers?"

"You will."

"What's in it for me?"

"Half a gee."

Five hundred dollars for an hour's work; not so bad. *If*, of course. Depending. Dortmunder said, "What's the worst that could happen?"

A.K.A. shrugged. "They go looking for Fred Mullins out on Long Island."

"Who's he?"

"You."

"Got it," Dortmunder said.

"There'll also be a lawyer on our side there," A.K.A. told him. "I mean, the side of the guy that's running this thing. The lawyer isn't in on what's going down, by him you *are* Fred Mullins, from Carrport, Long Island, so he's just there to see the other side doesn't stray from the program. And at the end of it, in the elevator, he gives you the envelope."

"Sounds okay."

"Easy as falling off a diet," A.K.A. said, and handed him a manila envelope, which he took home and opened, to find it contained a whole story about one Fredric Albert Mullins and an entire family named Anadarko, all living on Red Tide Street out in Carrport between 1972 and 1985. Dortmunder diligently memorized it all, having his faithful companion May deposition him on the information every evening when she came home from the Safeway supermarket where she was a cashier. And then, on the following Wednesday, the day before his personal private show was to open, Dortmunder got another call from A.K.A., who said, "You know that car I was gonna buy?"

Uh oh. "Yeah?" Dortmunder said. "You were gonna pay five hundred for it, I remember."

"Turns out, at the last minute," A.K.A. said, "it's a real lemon, got unexpected problems. In a word, it won't run."

"And the five hundred?"

"Well, you know, John," A.K.A. said, "I'm not buying the car."

Which was why, that Thursday morning at ten, instead of being in a lawyer's office in the Graybar Building in mid-town Manhattan, just an elevator ride up from Grand Central Station (crossroads of the same four hundred thousand lives every day), talking about the Anadarko family of Carrport, Long Island, Dortmunder was at home, doing his best to clear his brain of all memory of Fred Mullins and his entire neighborhood. Which was why he was there to answer the doorbell when it rang at ten twenty-two that morning, to find a FedEx person standing in the hall there.

No FedEx person had ever before sought out Dortmunder, so he wasn't exactly sure what was the protocol, but the person walked him through it, and the experience wasn't hard at all.

What was being delivered was a Pak, which was a bright red-white-and-blue cardboard envelope with something in-side it. The Pak was addressed to May Bellamy and came from a law firm somewhere in Ohio. Dortmunder knew May had family in Ohio, which was why she never went there, so he agreed to take the package, wrote "Ralph Bellamy" where the person wanted a signature, and then spent the rest of the day wondering what was in the Pak, which made for a fine distraction.

The result was, by the time May got home from the Safe-way at 5:40 that afternoon Dortmunder couldn't have told an

Anadarko from an Annapolis graduate. "You got a Pak," he said.

"I've got two entire bags. Here, carry one."

"That's not what I meant," Dortmunder told her, accepting one of the two grocery bags containing May's daily unofficial bonus to herself. He followed her to the kitchen, put the bag on the counter, pointed to the Pak on the table, and said, "It's from Ohio. FedEx. It's a Pak."

"What's in it?"

"No idea."

May stood beside the table, frowning at the Pak, not yet touching it. "It's from Cincinnati," she announced.

"I noticed that."

"From some lawyers there."

"Saw that, too. It came this morning, a little before ten-thirty."

"That's what they say they do," May agreed, "deliver everything by ten-thirty in the morning. I don't know what they do, the rest of the day."

"May," Dortmunder said, "are you going to open that thing?"

"Well, I don't know," she said. "If I do, do you think I'm liable for something?"

"Like what?"

"I don't know. Lawyers," she explained.

"Open it," Dortmunder suggested, "and if it's some kind of problem, we'll both lie, we'll say we never got it."

"Did you have to sign for it or anything?"

"Sure."

May looked at him, and finally understood. "Okay," she said, and picked the thing up. With hardly any hesitation at all, she pulled the tab along the top, reached inside, and withdrew a folded sheet of top-quality letterhead stationery and a small box, such as earrings might come in, or a kidnap victim's finger.

Putting down the Pak and the box, May opened the letter, read it, and silently passed it to Dortmunder, who looked at the five legal names and the important-looking address all in thick black across the top of the heavy expensive sheet of paper. There was also a whole string of names running down the left side, and then the typing: A heading to "Ms May Bellamy" at this apartment in this building on East Nineteenth Street, New York, New York, 10003, and

Dear Ms Bellamy:

We represent the estate of the late Gideon Gilbert Goodwin, sanguinely related to yourself. The deceased having passed away on April 1st inst., intestate except for a holograph letter to his niece June Havershaw, dated February 28, inst., requesting of her that she distribute his worldly goods to family members upon his demise as she saw fit, and Ms Havershaw having come to the conclusion that you, her sister and therefore also a niece of the decedent, should receive the enclosed from among the late G. G. Goodwin's effects, we are pleased to forward to you the late Mr. Goodwin's "lucky ring," which he considered one of his most prized possessions, and which Ms Havershaw felt you would most appreciate for its sentimental value.

Further enquiries on this matter should be directed directly to Ms Havershaw, the executrix of the G. G. Goodwin estate.

With warmest regards,

Jethro Tulley

"G. G. Goodwin," Dortmunder said.

"I remember him," May said. "At least, I think I do. He's the one smelled like horse manure, I think. He was out at the track all the time."

"You weren't all that close to him, I guess."

"I didn't want to be, the way I remember it."

"Your sister was closer to him."

"June always sucked up the grown-ups," May said. "She didn't care *what* they smelled like."

"Out to the track a lot, you say," Dortmunder said.

"He was a horseplayer, that's right."

"And yet, he didn't die broke. I notice your sister sent you the stuff with the sentimental value."

"Uncle Gid wouldn't have left much," May said. "He was also married a lot of times. Women he met out at the track."

"I'm surprised he had anything at all, then. What's this ring look like?"

"How do I know?" Shrugging, May said, "It's still in the box, isn't it?"

"You mean, you don't remember it?" Dortmunder was baffled. "I figured, sentimental and all, there was some connection between you and this ring."

"Not that *I* know of," May said. "Well, let's have a look."

The box wasn't wrapped or sealed or anything; it was just a black box with a spring inside to keep the lid shut. May opened it, and they both looked in at a cloud of white cotton. She shook the box, and something in it thumped, so she turned it upside down over the table and the cotton fell out, and so, separately, did the something that thumped.

A ring, as advertised. It was gold-looking but it wasn't gold, so it was probably brass at best. The top was a flat five-sided shape, like the shield around Superman's big *S* on his uniform chest. Instead of an *S,* though, the ring displayed on its flat surface three thin lines of tiny stones—chips, really—that were diamondy looking, but were not diamonds, so they were probably glass. At best. The top line was discontinuous, with a blank section in the middle, while the other two were complete. It looked like:

▬▬▬▬   ▬▬▬▬

▬▬▬▬▬▬▬▬▬

▬▬▬▬▬▬▬

Dortmunder said, "Which sentiment exactly does this represent?"

"No idea," May said. She slipped the ring onto the middle finger of her left hand, then held that hand with fingers downward over her right palm, and the ring fell into the palm. "I wonder if he found it in a cereal box."

"That was the lucky part," Dortmunder suggested.

"The whole purpose of sending me this," May said, as she slipped the ring onto the middle finger of her right hand, "is that June wants *me* to call *her*."

"Are you going to?"

May held her right hand over her left palm, fingers downward. The ring fell into the palm. "Not a chance," she said. "In fact, I'm not even going to answer the phone for a while." Turning the ring this way and that in her fingers, she said, "But it isn't a bad-looking thing, really."

"No, it's kind of restrained," Dortmunder agreed. "You don't expect that in a horseplayer."

"Well, it doesn't fit *me*," she said, and extended a hand toward Dortmunder, the ring lying in the palm. "Try it."

"It's yours," Dortmunder objected. "Your uncle G.G. didn't send it to *me*."

"But it doesn't fit. And, John, you know . . . Umm. How do I phrase this?"

"Beats me," Dortmunder said. He had the feeling he wasn't going to like what came next no matter how she phrased it.

"You could use a little luck," May said.

"Come on, May."

"Skill you've got," she hastened to assure him. "Adaptability you've got, professionalism you've got, good competent partners you've got. Luck you could use a little. Try it on."

So he tried it on, sliding it onto the ring finger of his right hand—a ring of any kind on the ring finger of his left hand could only remind him of his unfortunate marriage (and subsequent fortunate divorce) many years ago to and from a nightclub entertainer in San Diego who operated under the professional name of Honeybun Bazoom and who had not been at *all* like May—and it fit.

The ring fit perfectly. Dortmunder let his right arm hang at his side, fingers loose and dangling downward as he flapped his hand a little, but the ring stayed right where he'd put it, snug but not tight. It felt kind of good, in fact. "Huh," he said.

"So there you are," she said. "Your lucky ring."

"Thanks, May," Dortmunder said, and the phone rang.

May gave it a look. "There's June now," she said. "Wondering did I get the package, do I love the ring, do I remember the good old days."

"I'll take it," Dortmunder offered. "You aren't here, but I'll take a message."

"Perfect."

But of course this didn't necessarily have to be May's sister calling, so Dortmunder answered the phone in his normal fashion, frowning massively as he said into the thing, with deep suspicion, "Hello?"

"John. Gus. You wanna make a little visit?"

Dortmunder smiled, so May would know it wasn't her sister on the phone, and also because what he had just heard was easily translated: *Gus* was Gus Brock, a longtime associate in this and that, over the years, from time to time. A *visit* meant a visit to a place where nobody was home but you didn't leave empty-handed. "Sounds possible," he said, but then caution returned, as he remembered that Gus had described it as a *little* visit. "How little?"

"Little trouble," Gus said.

"Ah." That was better. "Where?"

"A little town out on Long Island you never heard of, called Carrport."

"Now there's a coincidence," Dortmunder said, and looked at Uncle Gid's lucky ring, nestled on his finger. Seemed as though the luck had already started. "That town owes me one."

"Yeah?"

"Doesn't matter," Dortmunder said. "When do you want to make this visit?"

"How about now?"

"Ah."

"There's a seven twenty-two train from Grand Central. We'll make our own arrangements, coming back."

Even better. The location of the visit should include a vehicle of some sort, which could be made use of and then turned into further profit. Nice.

Seven twenty-two was an hour and twelve minutes from now. "See you on the train," Dortmunder said, and hung up, and said to May, "I like your Uncle Gid."

"This is the right distance to like him from," she agreed.

3

If Caleb Hadrian Carr, whaler, entrepreneur, importer, salvager, sometime pirate, and, in his retirement, New York State legislator, could see today the town he'd founded and named after himself on the south shore of Long Island back in 1806, he'd spit. He'd spit brimstone, in fact.

Long Island, a long and narrow island east of New York City, has taken as its standard Bishop Reginald Heber's famous maxim, "Every prospect pleases, and only man is vile." Once a pleasantly wooded landmass of low hills and white beaches, well-watered by many small streams, populated by industrious Indians and myriad forest creatures, Long Island today is a Daliscape of concrete and ticky-tack, all its watches limp.

Far out the island's south shore, beyond the blue-collar gaud of Nassau County but not all the way to the trendy glitz of the Hamptons, lies Carrport, an enclave of newish wealth in a setting that looks, as the entranced residents keep pointing out to one another, exactly like an old-fashioned New England whaling village which, of course, except for its not technically being in New England, is exactly what it is.

These current residents of Old Carrport are mostly drop-ins for whom the shingled Cape Cod is a third or fourth or possibly fifth home. They are people who don't quite qualify for the "old" money fastnesses of the Island's north shore ("old" money means your great-grandfather was, or became, rich), but who have more self-esteem (and money) than to rub elbows with the sweaty achievers to their east. To sum them up, they would never deign to have anything to do with a person from show business who was not at least a member of Congress.

The residents of Carrport had not always been such. When Caleb Carr built his first house and pier at Carr's Cove (he'd named that, too), it was mostly as a place to keep his wife and family while at sea, and to sort and store his fish, salvage, and loot when ashore. Other crew members eventually built little homes around the cove for their own families. An enterprising second-generation youngster who suffered from seasickness stayed on land and began the first general store.

By the time Caleb Carr died, in 1856 (his last act was an anti-Abolitionist letter to the *New York Times,* which ran in the same issue as his obituary), he was rich in honors, rich in family, rich in the esteem of his fellow Americans, and rich. His seven children and four of his grandchildren all had homes in Carrport, and he could look forward from his deathbed to a solid community, ever carrying his name and prestige and philosophy onward into the illimitable reaches of time.

And yet, no. For half a century Carrport dozed, growing slowly, changing not at all, and then . . .

Every generation, New York City produces another wave of nouveaux riches, and every generation a giddy percentage of these head east, out to Long Island, to establish yet another special, trendy, in, latest, au courant, swingin weekend hot spot. Carr's Cove got its invasion in the twenties, young Wall Streeters with Gatsby self-images and faux flapper wives, who loved the frisson that came from the sight of those ships' lights offshore; smugglers! The booze the weekenders would drink next Friday was gliding shoreward right now, through the deep ocean black. (In truth, those passing lights were mostly fishermen, homeward bound, and the booze the Carrporters would consume next weekend was being manufactured at that moment in vats in warehouses in the Bronx.)

Whatever is in will be out. The Gatsbys and their flappers are long gone, dustbinned by their children as "square." The faint air of Carrport raffishness so beloved by the weekenders of yore is now replaced by an air of moneyed fastidiousness. Housing for those in the service trades and some commuters has ringed the original town with a wimple of the standard Long Island sprawl. (All suburbs look like paintings from before the discovery of perspective.) The alleged Fredric Albert Mullins and his neighbor, the dubious Emmaline Anadarko, all of Red Tide Street, lived or had lived out there. But the big old sea-captain houses, shingled, ample, dormered, well-porched, white-trimmed, still ring the cove as they always did, facing out to the unchanging sea, today owned mostly by corporate types and, in a few instances, by corporations themselves.

Today's recurrent Carrporters are for the most part business lions for whom the beach house is merely an adjunct to the pied-à-terre penthouse in Manhattan. These people actually live in London and Chicago and Sydney and Rio and Gstaad and Cap d'Antibes and Aspen and— Well. Don't ask them where "home" is. They'll merely shrug and say, "Sorry, only my accountant knows the answer to that."

At the moment, six of the big old houses around the cove are owned by corporations rather than persons, and are used—according to those same accountants—for "meetings, seminars, client consultations, and focus groups." They are also oases of rest and recuperation for the senior executives of those corporations, should one of them find himself forced to be in Boston or New York or DC with a sunny weekend coming up.

One of these latter houses, number Twenty-Seven Vista Drive, is carried on the books of Trans-Global Universal Industries, or TUI as it's known on the Big Board, or Max Fairbanks, as it's known in the world of palpable rather than corporate reality. Max Fairbanks, a billionaire media and real-estate baron, owns much of the planet and its produce and people, through various interlocking corporations, but the threads, for those who can follow them—and no one but the previously mentioned accountants can begin to follow them—all lead eventually back to the parent corporation, TUI, which is corporeally incorporated in the person of Max Fairbanks.

Who had been having a bad year. A few business deals had come unstuck, a few politicians in various precincts around the world had come unbought, and a few trends promised by the specialists had not come through at all. Cash flow was brisk, but in the wrong direction. Downsizing had been done when times were good, so now, when there was need to cut the fat, there was no fat left to remove. Max Fairbanks was far from poor—several light-years from poor, in fact—but his financial problems had forced him into an uncomfortable corner and he—or his accountants, those guys again—had at last taken action.

4

"He's in Chapter Eleven," Gus Brock said.

"Is this a person," Dortmunder asked, "or a book?"

They were on the 7:22 Long Island Railroad commuter train out of Grand Central, running eastward across the suburbs, surrounded by workaholics *still* focused on their Powerpaks. Gus, a blunt and blocky guy with a blunt and blocky mustache that seemed to drag his face downward as though it were woven of something heavier than hair, said, "It's a bankruptcy."

"This guy is bankrupt?" Dortmunder frowned at his coworker's sagging profile. "This guy is broke, and we're on our way to rob him? What's he got left?"

"Zillions," Gus said. "What falls outta Max Fairbanks's pockets every day is more'n you and me see in a lifetime."

"Then how come he's bankrupt?"

"It's a special kind of bankrupt they have for people that aren't supposed to get hurt," Gus explained. "Like when countries go bankrupt, you don't see an auctioneer come in and sell off the towns and the rivers and stuff, it just means a court takes over the finances for a while, pays everybody eight cents on the dollar, and then the country can go back to what it was doing before it screwed up. This guy, he's that kinda rich, it's the same deal."

Dortmunder shook his head. *All* of finance was too much

for him. His understanding of economics was, you go out and steal money and use it to buy food. Alternatively, you steal the food. Beyond that, it got too complex. So he said, "Okay, it's just one of those cute ways rich guys have to steal from everybody without having to pick locks."

"You got it."

"But so what?" Dortmunder asked. "If he's still got everything he had, and he had zillions, what do we care what chapter he's up to?"

"Because," Gus said, "this place out in Carrport, it belongs to the corporation, and so the court has jurisdiction over it now, so nobody's supposed to use it."

Dortmunder nodded. "It's empty, you mean."

"Right."

"Okay. If that's all."

"That's all," Gus agreed. "Max Fairbanks is in Chapter Eleven, so the house his corporation owns in Carrport is under the control of the bankruptcy court, so nobody's supposed to go there, so it's empty."

"So *we* go there," Dortmunder said. "I get it."

"Piece of cake," Gus said.

5

"Max Fairbanks," Max Fairbanks said, "you're a bad boy." The milky blue eyes that gazed softly back at him in the bathroom mirror were understanding, sympathetic, even humorous; they forgave the bad boy.

Max Fairbanks had been in the business of forgiving Max Fairbanks, forgiving his indiscretions, his peccadilloes, his little foibles, for a long long time. He was in his midsixties now, having been born somewhere and sometime—somewhere east of the Rhine, probably, and sometime in the middle of the nineteen thirties, most likely; not a good combination—and somewhere and sometime in his early years he'd learned that a gentle word not only turneth away wrath, it can also turneth away the opponent's head just long enough to crush it with a brick. Smiles and brutality in a judicious mix; Max had perfected the recipe early, when the stakes were at their highest, and had seen no reason for adjustment in the many successful years since.

As with so many self-made men, Max had begun by marrying money. He wasn't Max Fairbanks yet, not back then, the century in its fifties and he in his twenties, but he'd long since stopped being his original self. Had there ever been loving parents who had given this child a name, their own plus another, no one by the 1950s knew anything about them, including Max, who, having found himself in London, called himself Basil Rupert, and soon made himself indispensable to a brewer's daughter named Elsie Brenstid. Brenstid *père*, named Clement for some reason, had found young Basil Rupert far more resistable than his daughter had, until Basil demonstrated just how the Big B Brewery's company-owned pubs could be made to produce considerably more income with just the right applications of cajolery and terror.

The marriage lasted three years, producing twin girls and an extremely satisfactory divorce settlement for Basil, Elsie being by then ready to pay anything to get away from her husband. Basil took this grubstake off to Australia, and by the time the ship landed he had somehow become a native Englishman called Edward Wizmick, from Devon.

Success stories are boring. On that basis, Max Fairbanks was today the most boring of men, having piled success upon success over a span of four decades covering five continents. The occasional setback—no, not even that; *deceleration* was the word—such as the current Chapter Eleven nonsense in the United States hardly counted at all, was barely a blip on the screen.

And it was certainly not going to keep Max from enjoying himself. In his long-ago childhood, he had come too close to being snuffed out too many times, in too many squalid alleys or half-frozen marshes, to want to deny himself any pleasure that this life-after-(near)death might offer.

For instance. One minor irritation within the minor irritation of the Chapter Eleven was that Max was not supposed to avail himself of the beach house in Carrport. The cleaning staff could still come in once a week to maintain the place, but other than that it was supposed to be shut off and sealed until the Chapter Eleven arrangement had been satisfactorily concluded. But in that case, what about Miss September?

Ah, Miss September; Tracy Kimberly to all who love her. The minute Max saw her pubic hair in *Playboy* he knew he had to have her for his own, temporarily. The problem, of course, was Mrs. Fairbanks, the fair Lutetia, Max's fourth and final wife, the one he would grow old with (slowly), the one who had several hundreds of millions of dollars in Max's assets in her own name, for reasons the accountants understood. Lutetia could be counted on to act with discretion so long as Max acted with discretion, which meant there were only certain specific venues in which he could hope to run his fingers through that soft and silky hair, one of them *not* being the apartment in Manhattan. But Tracy Kimberly, in avid pursuit of a career as an entertainment journalist, lived in Manhattan, and it would be even less discreet for Max to travel great distances with her; for instance, in airplanes.

Hence, the Carrport house, in the bathroom of which, in postcoital warmth, Max Fairbanks yet again forgave himself all; the adultery, the breaking of the Chapter Eleven pact, everything. (Had a judge not refused him access to his own beach house, Max might very well have taken the pneumatic Tracy and her feathery hair to a nice West Fifty-ninth Street hotel, in a suite overlooking Central Park, with room service to provide the champagne. But when one was supposed to have been dead and discarded and forgotten by the age of ten, when one had been intended by fate to be a brief flicker, no more than another minor piece of roadside litter on the highway of history, then there was no greater pleasure in this afterlife than doing what you've been told specifically not to do. What were they gonna do? Kill him?)

Because of the legal situation, and also because it was more sentimental, Max and Tracy were getting by with minimal illumination this evening. "I wanna learn Braille," he had said, in his colloquial and unaccented English, as he'd first leaned over her in the living room downstairs. Later, upstairs, the hall light that automatically switched itself on every evening as a deterrent to burglars had been their only source of light, and it had been enough. And now, ready to leave the bathroom, he first switched off its glittery lights before opening the door and reentering the smooth dimness of the master bedroom, where Tracy lay like an éclair atop the black silk sheet. "Mmm," he murmured.

Tracy moved, smiling, her teeth agleam in the gloaming. "Hi," she breathed, and moved again.

Max put one knee on the bed—silk is surprisingly cold,

and not as romantic as many would like to think—and leaned forward, smiling at the charming brooch of Tracy's navel. Then he stopped. His head lifted. He listened.

"Honey, I—"

"Ssshh."

She blinked. She whispered, "What is it?"

"A sound."

The éclair became a snowbank: "A wife?"

"A burglar, I think," Max whispered, and reached for the bedside drawer where he kept the gun.

6

There are many ways to bypass or otherwise defeat a burglar alarm. On the walk through town from the railroad station in the evening dark, Dortmunder and Gus discussed the possibilities, learning they had different favorite methods, depending on the manufacturer of the alarm. "I'll let you handle it," Dortmunder finally agreed. "My fingers slip sometimes."

"Mine don't," Gus said.

The house was as Gus had described it; large and rich and dark, except for that usual upstairs hall light people leave on to tell burglars there's nobody home. Gus looked at the front door and then went around to consider a couple of windows, and then went back to the front door and on into the house, pausing only briefly to give the alarm a little attention on the way by.

Inside, the place had the anonymous good looks of any corporate milieu; a lot of beige, a lot of good but uninteresting furniture, nothing quirky or individual. Nobody had actually lived in this house for many years, and it looked it.

But that was okay; Dortmunder and Gus didn't plan to move in either. And corporate types do tend to throw the money around when they're spending company cash on their own perks, so there should be more than one item of interest in this place.

Beginning with the large dining room, an imposing space

with a table that could seat sixteen, four pairs of French doors leading out to the wraparound porch and the view of Carr's Cove, and a long heavy mahogany sideboard containing a whole lot of first-rate silver. "Nice," Gus said, lifting a cake server. A winter scene with horse and sleigh was engraved on its wide flat blade.

Dortmunder looked into the drawer Gus had opened, and yes, indeed, that was all silver in there. Not silverplate; silver. Antique, probably. "I'll get some pillowcases," he said, and while Gus explored the sideboard further, Dortmunder went back to the front hall, found the broad staircase, and was halfway up the stairs when the lights came on.

A whole lot of lights. Dortmunder stopped. He looked up, and at the head of the stairs was a bulky older man in a white terry-cloth robe. The telephone in the man's left hand didn't bother Dortmunder nearly as much as the gun in his right.

"Um," Dortmunder said, as he tried to think of an explanation for his presence on this staircase at this moment that didn't involve him having broken, or intending to break, any laws. Hmmmm.

"Freeze," the man said.

Freeze. Why does everybody say freeze anymore? Whatever happened to "hands up"? With "hands up," you had a simple particular movement you could perform that would demonstrate to one and all that you weren't making any trouble, you were going along with the armed person, no problem. What are you supposed to do with "freeze"? Teeter on one foot? Maintain a stupid expression on your face? "Freeze" is for television actors; in real life, it's demeaning to all concerned.

Dortmunder ignored it. The gun was taking most of his attention, while the telephone the man was dialing one-handed took the rest. (Except for his faint awareness of a soft and sibilant swooshing sound from the dining room, as a French door was gently opened, and as gently closed. Gus Brock, bless his heart, was outta here.) So, rather than freeze, Dortmunder put a hand on the banister, rested his weight there in gloomy patience, and tried to think.

Well. When the going gets hopeless, the hopeless keep going. "Mister," Dortmunder said, *knowing* this was a waste of breath, "I'm prepared to just go home, you know? Forget the whole thing. Nothing's hurt, nothing's taken."

"If you move," the man said, as he lifted the phone to his ear, "I will shoot you in the kneecap and you will walk with a limp for the rest of your life. I am a very good shot."

"You would be," Dortmunder said.

7

The town of Carrport boasted the fourth-highest-paid municipal police force in New York State. The boys and girls in blue enjoyed that status, and their jobs, and saw no reason to agitate for an increase to Number Three. Crime in Carrport was low, drug use discreet and limited for the most part to the more affluent residents in the privacy of each other's homes, and the risk of injury or death on the job was much lower than in, oh, say, certain precincts of New York City. It was true that local rents were high, even on a well-paid cop's salary, and local supermarkets charged gourmet prices for normal crap, but so what? COLAS were written into the police contract; they wouldn't suffer. All in all, "Service With A Smile" might have been a better slogan for the Carrport Municipal Police Department than the "To Protect, To Serve, To Uphold And To Honor" thought up by some long-forgotten alderman and squeezed onto every CMPD car door, just under the shield.

The CMPD's equipment was also up to snuff, modern and well maintained, though of course not what the police forces of Los Angeles or Miami would consider the state of the art. When money had to be spent, the town fathers preferred to spend it on the personnel rather than on cute toys that would never be needed. (Besides, if the demand for a cute police toy ever did arise, they could always call on the Suffolk

County cops, who were also well paid, but who in addition were equipped grandly enough to enable them to invade Syria, if the overtime could be worked out.)

The call that evening to Suffolk County 911 was logged in by the emergency service staff in HQ at Riverhead, at eleven minutes past nine, then rerouted to the CMPD, where the duty sergeant took down the information, understanding at once everything implied by that address, Twenty-Seven Vista Drive, numbers that even in a police report would always be spelled out. He immediately called one of the two cars on patrol duty this evening, manned (and womanned) by Officers Kebble and Overkraut. Kebble was driving this shift, so Overkraut took the squeal: "Overkraut."

"Prowler captured at Twenty-Seven Vista Drive. Householder is armed and has the suspect in custody. Householder is a Mr. Fairbanks."

The name was known to Kebble and Overkraut, of course, but neither commented. In the old days, there would have been some badinage on the radio at this point, while Kebble sped them toward Vista Drive, but not any more. These days, recordings are made, and kept, of every damn thing. Creativity has been throttled in its crib. "On our way," Overkraut told the sergeant and the tape and God knows who else, adding no remark about the richness or famousness of the householder called Fairbanks, and no disparagement voiced about householders packing heat. "Over and out," Overkraut said, put the mike away, and made his comments unsupervised to Officer Kebble, who commented back.

There was no need for either the rooflights or the siren, not in Carrport on a quiet spring Thursday evening at quarter past nine. And not if the householder were already holding a gun on the intruder. So Officer Kebble drove swiftly but unobtrusively across town and stopped in the driveway at Twenty-Seven Vista, where the house was lit up like a NASA launch. The officers donned their hats and stepped out of their vehicle. Officer Kebble paused to adjust her equipment belt around her waist—it always rode up when she was in the car—and then they proceeded to the front door, which opened just as they reached it, and an astonishingly beautiful young woman with tousled hair, wearing a white terry-cloth robe, greeted them, saying in a husky whisper, "Oh, good, here you are. Max is in the parlor with *him*."

Why, Officer Overkraut asked himself, as they thanked the young woman and moved into the house in the direction she'd indicated, just why can't Officer Kebble look more like *that*?

The parlor. Beige furniture. Gray-green wall-to-wall carpet. Large stone fireplace, with no ashes and irritatingly shiny brass andirons. Prints of paintings of Mediterranean village streets. Lamps with *large* round pale shades. And Max Fairbanks standing in the middle of the room in another white terry-cloth robe, plus a small dark S&W .38 clamped in his right fist, pointed unswervingly at the burglar, a slope-shouldered defeated-looking fellow in dark clothing and thinning hair, who had an air of such dejection and collapse there seemed no need to point anything at him more threatening than a banana.

"Evening, Mr. Fairbanks," Overkraut said, moving toward the burglar, bringing out his handcuffs, being sure not to get in the line of fire.

"Very prompt response time," Max Fairbanks said. "Very good."

"Thank you, sir."

The burglar humbly extended his wrists to be cuffed. Overkraut had meant to cuff him behind his back, but the gesture was so meek, so pathetic, that he hadn't the heart to make things worse for the guy, so he went ahead and squeezed the metal rings onto those bony wrists, while the burglar sighed a long and fatalistic sigh.

While Overkraut frisked the burglar, surprised to find him weaponless, Kebble said, "Any idea how many of them broke in, Mr. Fairbanks?"

"Only this one, I think," Fairbanks answered. "Looks like he did something cute to the front-door alarm."

Officer Kebble shook her head, while the extremely attractive young woman in terry-cloth robe number one came in and stood by the door to watch. "If only," Kebble said, "they would turn those talents to good. But they never do."

Overkraut said, "You won't need that pistol any more, sir."

"Right." Fairbanks dropped the S&W into his terry-cloth pocket.

Kebble said, "Had he taken anything, sir, before you found him?"

"I don't think so, he was just—" But then Fairbanks stopped and frowned at the burglar and said, "*Just* a minute."

The burglar lifted his head. "What," he said.

"Let me see those hands," Fairbanks demanded.

"What? What?"

"Show Mr. Fairbanks your hands," Overkraut said.

"I got nothing in my hands." The burglar turned his hands over as best he could with cuffs on, to show his open palms.

"No," Fairbanks said. "That ring."

The burglar stared. "What?"

"That's my ring!"

The burglar covered the ring with his other hand. "No, it isn't!"

"That son of a bitch took my ring! I left it on the kitchen sink, and—"

"It's *my* ring!"

"Quiet, you," Overkraut said, and meaningfully touched the nightstick on his belt.

"But—"

"Officers, I want that ring."

"But—"

"I don't want you to impound it as evidence, or any of that nonsense, I want my ring back, and I want it now."

"It's my ring!"

Overkraut faced the agitated burglar. "Unless you want *real* trouble, mac," he said, "you'll take that ring off this second, and you won't give me any lip."

"But—"

"That's lip."

"I—"

"And that's lip," Overkraut said. He slid the nightstick out of its loop on his belt.

The burglar breathed like a bellows, very nearly producing more lip, but managed to control himself. Bobbing on his heels like somebody who needs badly to go to the bathroom, he at last pulled the ring off the finger of his right hand and dropped it into Overkraut's left palm. "This isn't right," he said.

Ignoring him, Overkraut turned to drop the ring into Fairbanks's palm, saying, "Glad you spotted that, sir."

"Oh, so am I, Officer." Holding the ring up, smiling on it, he said, "There you are, you see? The symbol of twee. I based my whole corporation on this."

If that was an insider tip, Overkraut didn't get it. "Well, I'm glad you got it back, anyway, sir," he said.

Sounding mulish, the burglar said, "It isn't right. I'll go along with some things, but that isn't right."

"Officers," Fairbanks said, as he slipped the ring onto the third finger of his own right hand (he had a wedding ring on the left, though the attractive young woman over by the door didn't, Overkraut noticed), "officers, I have to say, although I'm grateful for your presence, and I'm glad we captured this fellow and got my ring back—"

"*My* ring."

"—I have to admit, there's a certain embarrassment involved here, and— I'm not sure how to say this, particularly in front of the, uh, what do you call him? Perpetrator?"

Kebble said, "Why don't I put him in the car, and call in to the station that we got him, and, sir, you can talk to my partner."

"That's very good, Officer, thank you so much."

Kebble herded the burglar out of the room, the man throwing many sullen looks over his shoulder on the way, and once they had gone, Fairbanks said to Overkraut, "Officer, I'm now going to explain to you why, although your capture of this felon this evening is creditable and indeed newsworthy, my own presence here, and Miss Kimberly's, are, for a variety of reasons, best left out of the picture."

"Mr. Fairbanks," Overkraut said, "I'm all ears." Which was in fact almost accurate.

8

Dortmunder was very very *very* angry.

To be arrested was one thing, to be convicted, sent to prison, given a record, made to wear ill-fitting denim, forced to live in close proximity to thoroughly undesirable citizens, listen to lectures, take shop, eat slop, all part of the same thing, all within the known and accepted risks of life. But to be made fun of? To be humiliated? To be *robbed . . .* by a *householder*?

To have May's ring stolen, that was what hurt. That was what changed the whole situation, right there. Until that point, facing the householder and the householder's gun— and so much for all those chapters the householder was supposed to be away in—and then facing the local law, Dortmunder had fully expected to go forward from here in a normal fashion, through the program, all hope gone, three times and you're in, throw away the key, okay, ya got me, I'll never live on the outside again.

But when the son of a bitch stole the ring, that's when it changed. That's when Dortmunder knew he could no longer play by the rules. He was *going* to get that ring back. Which meant, he was going to escape.

The woman cop with the lard ass walked him out to the cop car in the driveway and put him in the backseat, then hit the button that locked both rear doors and raised the thick wire mesh divider between front and back seats, imprisoning him in there. Then she sat up front, behind the wheel, to use her radio.

All right. He was going to escape, that was a given. Which meant he had to do it before they reached the local police station, where they would not only have sturdy cells to lock him into but would surely take his fingerprints at once, so that even if he escaped after that they'd still know who he was, and it would be much more difficult, henceforward, to live a normal life. So it had to be now, in this car, before they got where they were going.

A workman thinks first of his tools. What did he have, besides these handcuffs, which all they did was restrict his movements? (His movements would be even more restricted were the cuffs holding his wrists behind his back, but Dortmunder had undergone the process of arrest once or twice before in his life, and he'd learned, particularly with a younger or fairly inexperienced cop, that if one humbly extended one's wrists and looked hangdog, often one got the more comfortable option of being cuffed in front. It had worked this time, too, so he didn't have to do the Houdini thing of climbing through his own arms, like squirming backward through a barrel hoop.)

Tools, tools, tools . . . He had a belt, with a buckle. He had shoes, with shoelaces. His pants had a zipper, and the zipper had a pull tab, the metal piece you grasp when opening or closing the zipper. The pull tab was not attached to the zipper slide but was held to it by a tooth extending inward from the tab into a groove on each side of the slide. Dortmunder, watching the back of the woman cop's head, reached down to the front of his pants. Grasping the pull tab in one hand and the slide in the other, he twisted them in opposite directions, and the pull tab came off in his fingers. A tool.

The rear doors of the cop car were shut and locked, but were otherwise ordinary automobile doors, except there were no buttons or cranks to open the windows, just little blank shiny metal caps where the buttons or cranks would normally be. The inside panel beneath each shut window was held in place by a whole lot of Phillips-head screws.

Dortmunder slid over to the left, behind the woman cop. His right hand moved under his left hand, as he reached down between his hip and the door and inserted a top corner of the pull tab into the X in the head of the nearest screw. He applied pressure, but nothing happened, so he stopped, took a breath, gripped the pull tab more tightly, and gave a sudden jerk. Resistance, resistance; the screw turned.

Fine; loose is all we need right now. Dortmunder moved on to the next screw, up near his left elbow. Same resistance, same sudden jerk, same abrupt victory. The third screw, though, had to be jerked twice before it quit fighting.

Dortmunder had loosened five of the screws, with at least that many still to go, when the male cop with the dirty hat came out, got into the passenger seat up front, gave one casual glance back at his slumped and oblivious prisoner, tossed his hat onto the floor (no wonder it was dirty), and said, "Okay, we can take him in."

"What did he want to talk to you about back there?"

The male cop laughed. "Wait'll you hear," he said, and Dortmunder loosened the sixth screw.

The female cop drove, Dortmunder worked on the screws, and the male cop told the story about Max Fairbanks and the bankruptcy court. Fairbanks—so that son of a bitch who'd copped Dortmunder's ring was the guy himself, the head cheese—had given the cop a capsule version of his legal situation, and it came out exactly the way Gus had described it to Dortmunder, except with the added wrinkle that Max Fairbanks was in violation of the court order in re that house there, and didn't want anybody to know about it.

Isn't that a nice one? Max Fairbanks is breaking the law, he's going against an order from a judge, and he asks this meatheaded cop with the dirty hat to aid and abet him in his crime, and the cop does it! Is life unfair, or what?

It's unfair. The cop had agreed that, since Max Fairbanks wasn't supposed to be there, and since in addition he certainly wasn't supposed to be there with that particular young

woman, it was the two cops who had noticed a light on in the
house they knew was supposed to be empty, and had entered,
and captured the burglar themselves.

"That's better for you, too," the male cop said, turning his
head to look back at Dortmunder through the wire mesh. "If
there's nobody in the house, it's simple burglary, but if
there's somebody home when you break in it's robbery, and
you'll do heavier time for that. So you luck out, you see?"

"Thank you," Dortmunder said, and popped the last screw.

Carrport is an early town, and on weeknights not much of
a happening town, not since the Gatsbys and the flappers
faded away. The streets are lined with many more leafy trees
than streetlights, so there was rarely enough light to make its
way inside the police car as it drove steadily from the resi-
dential area surrounding the cove and headed uptown and
uphill toward the main business district, where the police station stood. The darkness was fine for Dortmunder as he removed all those screws, pocketing them so they wouldn't
make noise rolling around on the floor, and as he silently
popped the panel out at last and leaned it against the rear of
the front seat, behind the female cop, carefully smearing fingerprints away with his palms. But then the darkness got to
be a little too much of a good thing, because Dortmunder
needed to see the machinery inside the door before he could
go on to phase two.

And here's the business district, such as it is; real-estate
agents and video stores. Most places call this section downtown, but in Carrport it's uphill to here from the cove, the
businesses placed up and away from the more valuable real
estate down around the water, so the locals call it uptown,
and when they need anything they go somewhere else.

Still, there were more streetlights here, and fewer leafy
trees, so now Dortmunder could see the layout inside the
door. This bar goes across here, this elbow goes this way, and
if you pull this pin out here—

Thunk. The window dropped like a guillotine into the
doorwell.

"What was that?" cried the male cop, and the female cop

slammed on the brakes, which was good, because Dortmunder, headfirst, pulling and then pushing himself with his handcuffed hands, was going *out* the window, kicking himself away from the car as he fell, ducking his head down and hunching his shoulders up, landing on his curved upper back, then rolling out flat, faceup, then spinning to the right several times because of his remaining momentum from the car. And *then,* bruised, battered, manacled but free, he staggered to his feet while the cops were still trying to get their vehicle stopped over there, and ran for the nearest darkness he could find.

9

Max's eyes glittered under the porch lights as he watched the sparkly police car move away down the brightly illuminated asphalt and on past the gateposts to the outer darkness, bearing off that hapless burglar with the hangdog look. And without his ring. Find a job you're better suited to, my friend, that's my advice.

Was there a better feeling than this? Not only to have won, but to have rubbed your enemy's nose in his defeat. The ring twinkled on Max's finger, still warm from the burglar's hand.

This was why he was a winner, a winner against all the odds, and always would be. Luck followed the bold. And look what it had brought him this time.

When he'd first decided to take the ring, Max hadn't as yet looked closely at it, hadn't realized it actually *did* belong to him, in an odd and delightful way. The taking had been merely an amusing fillip to an already enjoyable evening; to cap it all by robbing the robber. After all, what's the worst that could happen?

And now it turned out it *was* his, had been spiritually his all along. What a surprise, when the police officer had handed him the ring and he'd turned it over, to see it there: TUI.

The ring itself was nothing, an undistinguished plain cheap band, except for that symbol on its face. The broken line above two solid lines: *Tui*, his own personal trigram. He'd even named his umbrella corporation for that symbol, once he'd become wealthy enough to need an umbrella corporation. *Trans-Global* represented the broken line at the top, while *Universal* and *Industries* were the two solid lines, and the initials on the Big Board are TUI. That's me. This ring *is* mine, I was more right than I knew.

He even showed it to the rather slow-witted policeman, though the fellow could have had no idea what he was talking about: "There you are, you see? The symbol of *Tui*. I based my whole corporation on this."

Have to throw the coins, very soon. But first, time to rid oneself of the woman. And protect oneself from whatever danger might grow out of this breach of the bankruptcy court order. "Dear," Max said, as he stepped back into the house, switching off most of those exterior lights, "in the kitchen."

She looked alert, and still fetching, in the terry cloth: "Yes?"

"Next to the phone, you'll find the number of a local car service. Give them a call, dear."

She looked prettily confused: "We're leaving the car?"

Meaning the Lamborghini they'd driven out here in, at the moment in the multicar garage attached to the house. "I'll have to stay on a bit longer," Max explained. "Because of this incident."

She didn't like it, but what was she to do? Off she went to make the call, while Max hurried upstairs to dress. Soon she joined him, making a few perfunctory little seductive moves while changing into her own street clothes, but he had no interest any more. Partly, she was now a known quantity—no; a known quality—but mostly he just wanted to be alone, with his new ring.

Soon, they made their way downstairs, while their terry-cloth robes remained behind, crumpled in wanton embrace in the hamper. Out front, a dark blue Lincoln town car purred discreetly on the drive. Max absently kissed Miss September's cheek and patted her other cheek, and sent her on her way. Then he moved briskly through the house, switching off lights as he went.

The library. Deep tan leather armchairs, green glass globed reading lamps, books bought by a decorator by the yard. But among them, The Book, and on the marble mantel over the seldom-used fireplace a small Wedgwood mustard pot containing three shiny pennies.

So. There was time to throw the coins only once before he'd have to vacate these premises, and they gave him a seven, a nine, an eight, and three consecutive sevens, producing:

Fantastic. The Creative above, and his own trigram, Tui, the Joyous, below. But only one moving line, the nine in the second place.

Max flipped the pages of The Book. Hexagram number ten: "Treading (Conduct)." The Judgment: "Treading upon the tail of the tiger. It does not bite the man. Success."

Yes, yes, yes. Wasn't that true? Wasn't that his entire life story? Treading on the tail of the tiger, getting away with it, and finding success through his rashness.

Which was just what he'd done tonight, seeing the ring, suddenly wanting it, seeing the joke, seeing the triumph, thinking *what's the worst that could happen?* and saying, "That's my ring!"

Nine in the second place: "Treading a smooth, level course. The perseverance of a dark man brings good fortune."

That's me. The dark man, overflowing with good fortune. Max smiled as he put away the pennies and The Book.

Soon the house itself was dark again, and Max was at the wheel of the black Lamborghini, driving the empty Southern State Parkway toward the city. The ring glinted on his finger in the dashboard lights, and Max smiled on it from time to time. I love this ring, he thought. My lucky ring.

10

Dortmunder had never felt more sure of himself in his life. He'd stripped that door panel and jumped from that moving car as though he'd been practicing those jukes for a week. When the alley he'd run into, behind and parallel to the main drag, happened to go past the rear of the local hardware store, he'd paused, hunkered down by that back door lock, and caressed it with fingers grown masterful with rage. The door eased open and he slid inside, shutting and relocking it just before the thud of heavy police brogans sounded outside. And yes, they did try the knob.

Happily, this was another place that left a light on for burglars, so they wouldn't hurt themselves tripping over things in the dark. Skirting the range of that light, Dortmunder made his way to the front of the shop, settled down there on a can of grout with his chained hands crossed on his knees, and watched through the big plate-glass front window as the search for him ebbed and flowed outside.

He'd thought it would take half an hour for officialdom to decide he'd managed to get clear of this immediate area, but in fact it was fifty minutes before the police cars—Suffolk County, as well as local—and the cops on foot stopped going back and forth out there.

When at last there was quiet again in Carrport, and Dortmunder rose from the grout can, it was to find he was very stiff and sore; and why not? Working his shoulders and legs and torso, moaning softly, he made his way slowly to the rear of the store, where a vast array of tools awaited him, wanting only to help him get rid of these cuffs.

Easy does it. Many screwdrivers and other small hand tools offered themselves for insertion into the keyhole in the middle of the cuffs. Something will pick this lock, something, something . . .

Ping. The cuffs fell to the floor, and Dortmunder kicked them under a nearby roach poison display. Rubbing his wrists, which were chafed and sore, he moved around the aisles of the store, choosing the tools he wanted to take with him. Then at last he went out by the same back door, and continued on down the same alley.

Carrport wasn't that hard to learn. If you walked downhill, you'd eventually reach the cove, and if you turned left at the cove, sooner or later you'd reach Twenty-Seven Vista Drive. Of course, if you were hiding from police cars and foot patrols along the way, it would probably take a little longer than otherwise, but still and all, eventually there would be the house, dark again except for the lying burglar light in the upstairs hall. No police around, no reason not to visit.

Dortmunder's method for bypassing the front-door alarm worked just as smoothly as Gus's had, maybe even more smoothly, but this time Dortmunder didn't merely saunter on in. This time, he knew the house was occupied—this was robbery, not burglary, important to keep that distinction in mind—and he knew the occupant had a gun and a telephone (and a ring he didn't deserve, damn his eyes), and he was not at all interested in a dead-on repeat of their previous encounter. So he sidled, he slunk, he stopped many times to listen and to peer at the murky dimness of the upstairs hall, and after all that, the place was empty.

Empty. You try to be a burglar, and you're a robber; then you try to be a robber, and turns out you're a burglar. God *damn* it to hell!

Dortmunder tromped around the empty rooms, room after room after room, and it became clear that Max Fairbanks and his girlfriend hadn't actually been living here at all, had just dropped in to complicate the life of a simple honest housebreaker, and once their bad deed for the day was done, they'd decamped. Yes, here are their terry-cloth robes, in the hamper. Been and come . . . and gone.

Dortmunder ranged through the empty house, turning lights on and off with abandon, knowing the cops now believed Max Fairbanks was in residence, knowing they would never for a second believe this particular escapee had returned to the scene of the crime.

But would Fairbanks have left his ill-gotten loot behind, possibly on that kitchen counter he'd mentioned? No; it was gone, too, just as gone as Fairbanks himself. Probably on the bastard's finger.

I'm going to get that ring back, Dortmunder swore, a mighty oath, if I have to chew that finger off. Meantime, finishing his interrupted journey from earlier, he went upstairs again for some pillowcases.

Half an hour later, Dortmunder stepped through the side door to find a long garage with spaces for five cars, three of the spaces occupied. The nearest vehicle was a twelve-passenger Honda van, good only for bringing middle management here from the railroad station. The farthest was a little red sports car, the Mazda RX-7, meant for upper-echelon executives when they wanted to take a spin around the cove. And the one in the middle was a gleaming black four-door Lexus sedan; trust corporate America to buy all its cars from Asia.

The Lexus was Dortmunder's choice. He loaded the back seat with eight full and clanking pillowcases, then found the button that opened the overhead door in front of his new transportation, and drove on out of there, pausing like a good houseguest to push the other button that switched off the garage lights and reclosed the door, before he drove away from Twenty-Seven Vista Drive, possibly forever.

There were a lot of police cars out and about at the moment, roaming here and there in the world, but none of them were concerned with a nice new gleaming black Lexus sedan. Dortmunder found the Long Island Expressway, switched on the stereo to an easy-listening station, and enjoyed a very comfortable ride back to town.

Where he had two stops to make before going home. The first, on the West Side in Manhattan, was to drop in on a fella named Stoon, who was known to exchange cash for items of value; Stoon liked the stuff in the pillowcases. And the second was to drop the Lexus off at the rear of a place called Maximilian's Used Cars in Brooklyn. The lot was closed at this hour, of course, but Dortmunder put the Lexus keys into an envelope with a brief and enigmatic note, tossed the envelope over the razor wire for the dobermans to sniff, and then took a cab home, where May was still up, watching the eleven o'clock news. "I always look at that," she said, gesturing at the set, "just in case they might have something to say about you."

"I'm sorry, May," Dortmunder told her, as he dropped twenty-eight thousand dollars in cash on the coffee table. "I've got bad news."

11

Dortmunder walked into the kitchen around nine the next morning, yawning and scratching and blinking his eyes a lot, and Andy Kelp was there, smiling, seated at the kitchen table. "I don't need this," Dortmunder said.

May was also present, already making his coffee, having heard him ricochet around the bedroom and bathroom the last quarter hour. "Now, John," she said, "don't be grumpy. Andy came by to say hello."

"Hello," Dortmunder said. He sat at the table already half-covered by Andy's elbows and reached for the Cheerios, on which he liked to put a lot of sugar and a lot of milk.

Andy, a bony cheerful guy with a sharp-nosed face, sat smiling like a dentist as he watched Dortmunder shovel on the sugar. "John," he said, "why have an attitude? May said you scored terrific last night."

"She did, huh?"

May, bringing his coffee—a lot of sugar, a lot of milk—said, "I knew you wouldn't mind if I told Andy."

You think you know a person. Dortmunder hunched his shoulders and ate.

Andy said, "So, if you scored and you're home free, what's the long face?"

May said, "John, the ring isn't that important."

"It is to me," Dortmunder said.

Andy looked alert, like a squirrel hearing an acorn drop. "Ring?"

Dortmunder gave them both a look. To May he said, "That part you didn't tell him, huh?"

"I thought you'd want to."

"No," Dortmunder said, and filled his mouth with enough Cheerios to keep him incommunicado for a week.

So it was May who told Andy about the FedEx Pak and the sentimental value gift ring from the semi-unknown uncle, and about it fitting John's finger (at least she didn't make a point about his allegedly needing some extra luck, he was grateful for that much), and about how when he went out to the Island last night a householder stole it from him.

Dortmunder had been hunched forward, grimly chewing, staring into the bowl of Cheerios, through the whole recital, and when he looked up now, damn if Andy wasn't grinning. "Mm," Dortmunder said.

Andy said, "John, is that what happened? The guy boosted the ring right off your finger?"

Dortmunder shrugged, and chewed Cheerios.

Andy *laughed*. What a rotten thing to do. "I'm sorry, John," he said, "but you gotta see the humor in it."

Wrong. Dortmunder chewed Cheerios.

"I mean, it's what you call your biter bit, you see? You're the biter, and you got bit."

Gently, May said, "Andy, I don't think John's quite ready to appreciate the humor."

"Oh? Oh, okay." Andy shrugged and said, "Let me know when you're ready, John, because it's really pretty funny. I hate to say it, but the guy's kinda got style."

"Nn mm nn," Dortmunder said, which meant, "And my ring."

"But if you don't want to talk about it yet," Andy said, "I can understand that. He made you look foolish, humiliated you, made fun of you—"

"Andy," May said, "I think John is going to stab you with his spoon."

"*But*," Andy said, shifting gears without losing a bit of

momentum, "the reason I came over, there's a little possibility I heard about you might be interested in, having to do with a shipment of emeralds out of Colombia, smuggled, you know, that this ballet troupe is supposed to have, and they're coming to bam, and I figure—"

May said, "Andy? Coming to bam what?"

"No no," Andy said, "they're coming to BAM, the Brooklyn Academy of Music, over in Brooklyn, a lot of shows go there that aren't quite right for Broadway because they don't use smoke machines, but they're too big for off Broadway, so this ballet troupe—"

Andy went on like that for a while, describing American culture, the history of ballet in the New World, and the prominence of emeralds in the Colombian economy, until at last Dortmunder rinsed down his Cheerio cud with a lot of coffee and said, "No."

Andy looked at him. "No what?"

"No emeralds," Dortmunder said, "no ballet, no bam, no wham, no thank you, ma'am."

Andy spread his hands. "Why not?"

"Because I'm busy."

"Yeah? Doing what?"

"Getting my ring back."

May and Andy both looked at him. May said, "John, the ring is gone."

"Until I get it back."

Andy said, "John? You're going after this billionaire, this Max guy?"

"Fairbanks. Yes." Dortmunder lifted another mountain of Cheerios toward his mouth.

"Wait!" Andy said. "Don't eat yet, John, bear with me."

Dortmunder reluctantly returned the mountain to the bowl. "And."

"And billionaires got guards, security, all these people, you can't just waltz in and say hello."

"I did last night."

"From what May tells me," Andy said, "that's because last

night the guy was doing a little something off the reservation. Had some kinda girl with him, didn't he?"

"I'm just saying."

"But most of the time, John, he'll be *on* the reservation, you know? I mean, even if you knew where the reservation was. I mean, how do you even find this guy?"

"I'll find him."

"How?"

"Somehow."

"All right, look," Andy said. "This emerald business can hold a few days, they're still coming up out of South America, dancing in Cancún right now, wherever. If you want, I would work with you on this ring thing and—"

"Never mind."

"No, John, I *want* to help. We'll take a swipe at the ring, see what happens, then we'll talk emeralds."

Dortmunder put his spoon down. "I don't care about emeralds," he said. "The guy took the damn ring, and I want it back, and I'm not gonna think about anything else until I *get* it back, and I didn't know the guy was an Indian, but that's okay, if he lives on a reservation I'll *find* the reservation and—"

"That's just a saying, John."

"And so is this," Dortmunder said. "I'm gonna find the guy, and I'm gonna get the ring. Okay?"

"Fine by me," Andy said. "And I'll help."

"Sure," Dortmunder said, taking a stab at sarcasm. "You got Max Fairbanks's address?"

"I'll call Wally," Andy said.

Dortmunder blinked, his attempt at sarcasm dead in the dust. "What?"

"You remember Wally," Andy said, "my little computer friend."

Dortmunder gave him a look of deepest suspicion. "You aren't trying to sell me a computer again, are you?"

"No, I gave up on you, John," Andy admitted, "but the thing about Wally is, he can access just about any computer anywhere in the world, go scampering around in there like a bunny rabbit, find out anything you want. You need to know where a billionaire called Max Fairbanks is? Wally will tell you."

May smiled, saying, "I always liked Wally."

"He moved upstate," Andy said. He looked alertly at Dortmunder. "Well, John? Do I give him a call?"

Dortmunder sighed. The Cheerios in the bowl were soggy. "You might as well," he said.

"See, John," Andy said, happy as could be, taking somebody's cellular phone out of his pocket, "already I'm a help."

12

It was raining over Maximilian's Used Cars. Actually, it was raining over this entire area, the convergence of Brooklyn and Queens with the Nassau County line, the spot where New York City at last gives up the effort to go on being New York City and drops away into Long Island instead, but the impression was that rain was being delivered specifically to Maximilian's Used Cars, and that all the rest was spillage.

Dortmunder, in a raincoat that absorbed water and a hat that absorbed water and shoes that absorbed water, had walked many blocks from the subway, and by now he looked mostly like a pile of clothing left out for the Good Will. He should have taken a cab—he was rich these days, after all—but although it had been cloudy when he'd left home (thus the raincoat) it hadn't actually been raining in Manhattan when he left, and probably still wasn't raining there. Only on Maximilian's, this steady windless watering-can-type rain out of a smudged cloud cover positioned just about seven feet above Dortmunder's drooping hat.

One thing you could say for the rain; it made the cars look nice. All those !!!CREAMPUFFS!!! and !!!ULTRASPECIALS!!! and !!!STEALS!!! shiny and gleaming, their rust spots turned to beauty marks, their many dents become speed styling. Rain did for these heaps and clunkers what arsenic used to do for over-the-hill French courtesans; gave them that feverish glow of false youth and beauty.

Plodding through these four-wheeled lies, Dortmunder looked like the driver of all of them. As he approached the office, out through its chrome metal screen door bounded a young guy in blazer and chinos, white shirt, gaudy tie and loafers, big smile and big hair. He absolutely ignored the rain, it did not exist, as he leaped like a faun through the gravel and puddles to announce, "Good morning, sir! Here for wheels, are we? You've come to the right place! I see you in a four-door sedan, am I right, sir? Something with integrity under the hood, and yet just a dash of—"

"Max."

The young man blinked, and water sprayed from his eyelashes. "Sir?"

"I'm here to see Max."

The young man looked tragic. "Oh, I am sorry, sir," he said. "Mister Maximilian isn't here today."

"Mister Maximilian," Dortmunder said, "has no place to be except here." And he stepped around the young man and proceeded toward the office.

The young man came bounding after. Dortmunder wished he had a ball to throw for the fellow to catch, or a stick. Not to throw. "I didn't know you were a friend of Mister Maximilian's," the youth said.

"I didn't know anybody was," Dortmunder said, and went into the office, a severe gray-paneled space where a severe hatchet-faced woman sat at a plain desk, typing. "Morning, Harriet," Dortmunder said, as the phone rang.

The woman lifted both hands from the machine, the right to hold one finger up toward Dortmunder, meaning I'll talk to you in just a minute, and the left to pick up the telephone: "Maximilian's Used Cars, Miss Caroline speaking." She listened, then said, "You planted a bomb here? Where? Oh, that's for us to find out? When did you do this? Oh, yes, yes, I know you're serious."

Dortmunder moved backward toward the door, as the

gamboling youth entered, smiled wetly, and crossed to sit at a much smaller desk in the corner.

Harriet/Miss Caroline said, "Oh, last night. After we closed? Climbed the fence? And did you change the dogs' water while you were here, were you that thoughtful?" Laughing lightly, she hung up and said to Dortmunder, "Hi, John."

Dortmunder nodded at the phone. "A dissatisfied customer?"

"They're all dissatisfied, John, or why come *here?* And then they call with these bomb threats."

Jerking a thumb over his shoulder, toward the cars outside, Dortmunder said, "Those are the bomb threats."

"Now, John, be nice."

Dortmunder seemed to be doing a lot of gesturing; this time, it was toward Peter Pan in the corner. "I see you got a pet."

"My nephew," Harriet said, with just a hint of emphasis on the word. "Have you met?"

"Yes. Is Max in?"

"Always." Picking up the phone again, she pressed a button and said, "Max, John D. is here." She hung up, smiled, started typing, and said, "He'll be right out."

And he was. Through the interior door came Maximilian himself, a big old man with heavy jowls and thin white hair. His dark vest hung open over a white shirt smudged from leaning against used cars. For a long time he'd smoked cigars, and now, after he'd given them up, he continued to look like a man smoking a cigar; a ghost cigar hovered around him at all times. Chewing on this ghost in the corner of his mouth, he looked left and right, looked at Dortmunder, and said, "Oh, I thought she meant John D. Rockefeller."

"I think he's dead," Dortmunder said.

"Yeah? There goes my hope for a dime. What can I do you for?"

"I dropped a car off the other night."

"Oh, that thing." Max shook his head; a doctor with bad news for the family. "Pity about that. A nice-looking car, too. Did you notice how it pulled?"

"No."

More headshaking. "The boys in the shop, they figure they can probably do something with it, they can do anything eventually, but it's gonna be tough."

Dortmunder waited.

Max sighed. "We know each other a long time," he said. "You want, I'll take it off your hands."

"Max," Dortmunder said, "I don't want you to do that."

Max frowned: "What?"

"I don't want you to load yourself up with a lemon," Dortmunder said, while Harriet stopped typing to listen, "just on account of our friendship. I wouldn't feel right about it. The thing's that much of a turkey, I'll just take it away, and apologize."

"Don't feel like that," Max said. "I'm sure the boys can fix it up."

"It'll always be between us, Max," Dortmunder said. "It'll be on my conscience. Just give me the keys, I'll see can I get it started, I'll take it off your lot."

This time Max scowled. "John," he said, "what's with you? Are you *negotiating?*"

"No no, Max, I'm sorry I dumped this problem in your lap, I didn't realize."

"John," Max said, beginning to look desperate, "it's worth *something.*"

"For parts. I know. I'll take it to a guy can strip it down, maybe I'll get a couple bucks off it. Harriet got the keys?"

Max stepped back, the better to look Dortmunder up and down. "Let's change the subject," he decided. "Whadaya think a the weather?"

"Good for the crops," Dortmunder said. "Harriet got the keys?"

"You met Harriet's nephew?"

"Yes. *He* got the keys?"

"I'll give you twelve hundred for it!"

Dortmunder hadn't expected more than five. He said, "I don't see how I can do that to you, Max."

Max chewed furiously on his ghost cigar. "I won't go a penny over thirteen fifty!"

Dortmunder spread his hands. "If you insist, Max."

Max glowered at him. "Don't go away," he snarled.

"I'll be right here."

Max returned to his inner office, Harriet returned to her typing, and the nephew opened a copy of *Popular Mechanics*. Dortmunder said, "Harriet, could you call me a cab?"

The nephew said, "You're a cab."

Harriet said, "Sure, John," and she was doing so when Max came back, with an old NYNEX bill envelope stuffed with cash, which he shoved into Dortmunder's hand, saying, "Come back when it's sunny. Rain brings out something in you." He stomped back into his office, trailing ghost cigar smoke.

Dortmunder read an older issue of *Popular Mechanics* until his cab arrived. Then, traveling across the many micro-neighborhoods of Queens, he reflected that he'd just done much better with Maximilian's Used Cars than ever before. Was it because Max happened to have the same first name as the guy who stole May's uncle's lucky ring, and this was a kind of revenge to beat down all Maxes everywhere? Or was he just on a roll?

That would be nice. He'd never been on a roll before, so he'd have to pay attention to what it felt like, if it turned out that's what this was. Eight hundred fifty dollars more than he'd dared hope for; so far, it felt good.

Home, he unlocked his way into what should have been an empty apartment, since May would be off at work at the supermarket, and there was Andy Kelp in the hall, walking toward the living room from the kitchen, a can of beer in one hand and a glass of orange juice in the other. "Hi, John," he said. "Where you been?"

Dortmunder looked at his apartment door. "Why do I bother to lock this thing?"

"Because it gives me a challenge. Come on in. Wally's got your rich guy pinned to the wall."

13

Ah hah. So this was the moment of decision. Press on, or not?

The real fury that had driven Dortmunder on the eventful night, that had fueled his brilliance and expertise in escaping from those cops, was gone now; you can't stay white-hot mad at somebody forever, no matter what they did. Between the stuff he'd sold to Stoon, and the unexpectedly large return on the car, he'd cleared almost thirty grand from his encounter with Max Fairbanks, which was probably about three thousand times what the ring was worth. So did he really still want to pursue this vendetta, chase down some jet-setting billionaire who, as Andy had pointed out, would usually be surrounded by all kinds of security? Or was he ahead now, enough ahead to forget it, get on with his life?

Well, no. Having seen Andy Kelp's reaction, and in a more muted way May's reaction, to what had happened to him, he could see now that most people would look at the story in a way that made it seem like he was the goat. Also, given Andy's big mouth, it was pretty certain that in no time at all everybody he knew would have heard about the ring incident in Carrport. They might laugh to his face, like Andy did, or they might laugh behind his back, but however they handled it, the point was, Max Fairbanks would come out of it the hero and John Dortmunder the jerk.

Unless he got the damn ring back. Let him walk around with that ring on his finger, on this personal finger right here, and *then* who's the goat?

Okay. Max Fairbanks, here I come.

Which meant, first, Wally Knurr here I come, so Dortmunder walked on into the living room and there he was, Wally Knurr, looking the same as ever, like a genial knish. A butterball in his midtwenties, his 285 pounds, devoid of muscle tone, were packed into a ball four feet six inches high, so that he was at least as wide as he was tall, and it seemed arbitrary in his case that the feet were on the bottom and the head on top. This head was a smaller replica of the body, as though Wally Knurr were a snowman made of suet, with blue jellybean eyes behind thick spectacles and a beet for a mouth. (The makers presumably couldn't find a carrot, so there was no nose.)

Dortmunder was used to Wally Knurr's appearance, so he merely said, "Hey, Wally, how you doing?"

"Just fine, John," Wally said. When he stood from the chair he'd been perched on, he was marginally shorter. The orange juice stood on the end table beside him. He said, "Myrtle and her mother say hello."

"And back at them," Dortmunder said. This having exhausted his social graces, he said, "You found my guy, huh? Sit down, Wally, sit down."

Wally resumed his chair, while Dortmunder crossed to the sofa. To the side, Andy sat at his leisure in the overstuffed chair, smiling upon Wally as though he'd created the little fella himself, out of instant mashed potato mix.

Wally said, "Finding Mr. Fairbanks wasn't the problem. He's kind of everywhere."

"Like bad weather," Dortmunder said. "Wally, if finding him wasn't the problem, what *was* the problem?"

"Well, John," Wally said, swinging his legs nervously under his chair (his feet didn't quite reach the worn carpet when he was seated), "the truth is, the problem is you. And Andy."

Laughing lightly, Andy said, "Wally thinks of us as crooks."

"Well, you are," Wally said.

"I am," Dortmunder agreed. "But so is Fairbanks. Did Andy tell you what he did?"

Andy said, "I just said he had something of yours. I figured, you wanted Wally to know the details you'd rather tell him yourself. Put your own spin on it, like they say."

"Thanks," Dortmunder said, and to Wally he said, "He's got a ring of mine."

Wally said, "John, I don't like to say this, but I've heard you tell fibs about rings and things and this and that and all kinds of stuff. I like you, John, but I don't want to help you if you're going to do felonies, and after all, that's what you do."

Dortmunder took a deep breath and held it. "Okay," he said, "here it is," and he gave Wally the full story, including the Chapter Eleven stuff and the house supposed to be empty—and yes, it was a felony he and an unnamed partner, not Andy, planned in that supposedly empty corporate-owned building that night—and when he got to the theft of the ring he got mad all over again, and it didn't help when he saw Wally—Wally!—hiding a smirk. "So that's it," he finished, sulky and feeling ill-used.

"Well, John, I believe you," Wally said.

"Thanks."

"Nobody would tell a story like that on themselves if it wasn't true," Wally explained. "Besides, when I looked for Mr. Fairbanks, I read all about the Chapter Eleven bankruptcy, and I even remember something about the house in Carrport."

"So there you are," Dortmunder said.

"You told that very well, John," Andy said. "There was some real passion in there."

"But if you do meet with this Mr. Fairbanks again," Wally said, "how are you going to get him to give you your ring back?"

"Well," Dortmunder said, "I thought I'd use a combination of moral persuasion and threats."

"You aren't going to hurt anybody, are you?"

There's only so much truth a person should tell in one day, and Dortmunder felt he might already have overdosed. "Of course not," he said. "You know me, Wally, I'm one hundred percent nonviolent."

"Okay, John." Smiling, animated, Wally said, "You know, finding Mr. Fairbanks was very interesting, very different from other stuff I do."

"Oh, yeah?"

"Usually, if you're looking for somebody," Wally explained, "you go through the airline computer systems, probably United Airlines, most of the others run through that. And you go to the big hotel chain computers, like Hilton or Marriot or Holiday Inn. And the car rental companies, and like that. But not with Mr. Fairbanks."

"Oh, no?"

"He doesn't travel the way other people do. He has all kinds of offices and homes all over the world, and they're all tied together with fax lines and phone lines and protected cables and all kinds of stuff, so he doesn't stay in hotels. And when he goes someplace, he doesn't take a commercial flight. He travels in one of his own airplanes—"

"One of," Dortmunder echoed.

"Oh, sure," Wally said. "He's got five I know about, I mean passenger airplanes, not cargo, and I think there may be some more over in Europe he isn't using right now."

"Uh huh," Dortmunder said.

"So I have to track him with the flight plans his pilots give the towers."

"Uh huh."

"And this," Andy said, "is the guy you're gonna hunt down like a wounded deer, am I right, John?"

"Yes," Dortmunder said. To Wally he said, "Tell me more."

"Well, they send out his schedule," Wally said. "His staff does, to his different homes and offices. Just a rough schedule of where he's going and what he's doing. They fax it, mostly, and they fax the changes to it, he's always changing it, so everybody knows where he is and how to get in touch with him."

"That's one nice thing, John," Andy said. "Here you've got a guy, he tells the *world* where he's gonna be."

"Good," Dortmunder said. "Then he can tell me. Wally, where is he?"

There was a manila envelope on the floor beside Wally's chair. Stooping now, with many grunts and false starts, Wally picked up this envelope and took from it two sheets of paper, as he said, "You just want for the rest of May, I guess."

"Sure," Dortmunder said.

"Okay." Wally studied the papers. "Well, today," he said, "he's in London."

"That's fast," Dortmunder said. "He was on Long Island last Thursday."

"Wait for it," Andy said.

Wally said, "He got to London this morning."

"How long is he gonna be there?" Dortmunder asked, thinking he really didn't want to have to go all the way to London to get his ring back.

"Day after tomorrow," Wally said, "he's going to Nairobi."

"Nairobi." Dortmunder didn't like the sound of that. "That's in Africa someplace, isn't it?"

"Uh huh."

"Is he ever coming back to the States?"

"Saturday," Wally said, "because he's going to testify at a congressional hearing next Monday, a week from today."

Andy said, "What you've got there, John, you've got your basic moving target."

Dortmunder said, "London, Nairobi, Washington, all this week. He's going to Washington on Saturday?"

"On Monday. He's going to spend the weekend at Hilton Head, in South Carolina."

"Nice for him," Dortmunder said. "How long's he gonna be in Washington?"

"Until Wednesday. Then he goes to Chicago for two days, and then Sydney for the next—"

"Sydney? That's a person."

"Sydney, Australia, John, it's a city. And then the Monday after that he flies back and goes to Las Vegas, and then he—"

Dortmunder said, "Are we still in May?"

"Oh, sure, John," Wally said. "The schedule says he'll be in Las Vegas two weeks from today."

"I'm almost feeling sorry for this guy," Dortmunder said.

"I think he likes it," Andy said.

"Well, I'm not gonna chase him around London and Africa, that's for sure," Dortmunder said. "I can wait till he comes back this way. Washington isn't so far, where's he stay in Washington? Got another house there?"

"An apartment," Wally said, "in the Watergate."

"I've heard of that," Dortmunder said. "It's some kinda place."

Wally and Andy looked at one another. "He's heard of it," Andy said.

Wally said to Dortmunder, "It's a great big building over by the Potomac River. It's partly offices and partly hotel and partly apartments."

"Apartments are harder," Dortmunder said. "Doormen, probably. Neighbors. Could be live-in help there, a guy like that."

Grinning, Andy said, "John? You planning a burglary at the Watergate?"

"I'm planning to get my ring back," Dortmunder told him, "if that's what you mean."

Andy still had that little crooked grin. "No big deal," he suggested. "Just a little third-rate burglary at the Watergate."

Dortmunder shrugged. "Yeah? So? What's the worst that could happen?"

"Well," Andy said, "you could lose the presidency."

Dortmunder, who had no sense of history because he had no interest in history because he was usually more than adequately engaged by the problems of the present moment, didn't get that at all. Ignoring it as just one of those things Andy would say, he turned to Wally. "So he's gonna be there next Monday night? A week from today."

"That's the schedule," Wally agreed.

"Thank you, Wally. Then so am I."

14

Already it had become a habit, a ritual, a pleasant little meaningless gesture. While he was in conversation or in thought, the fingers of Max's left hand twiddled and turned the burglar's ring on the third finger of his right hand. The cool touch to his fingertips, the feel of that flat shield-shape with the *Tui* symbol on it, the memory of that spur-of-the-moment *mal geste*, served to strengthen him, encourage him. How unfortunate that it was too good a joke to tell.

All day Monday, as he was chauffeured in a British-division TUI Rolls from meeting to meeting, he twirled the ring. Monday evening, as he attended Cameron Mackenzie's latest, *Nana: The Musical*, with another aspiring entertainment journalist (this one, English, was named Daf), he twirled the ring. (He'd already seen the New York production of *Nana,* of course, but enjoyed the original London version even more, if only for how reflexively the British despise the French.) And Tuesday morning, in his suite at the Savoy, he fondled the ring as the managers of his British newspaper chain presented their latest rosy predictions—no matter what they did, he knew, no matter how many contests they launched, no matter how many football hooligans they espoused, no matter how many breasts or royals they exposed, they would still be read only by the same four hundred thousand mouthbreathers—when Miss Hartwright, his London secretary, deferentially entered to say, "B'pardon, Mr. Fairbanks, it's Mr. Greenbaum."

Greenbaum. Walter Greenbaum was Max's personal attorney in New York City. He would not be phoning for a frivolous reason. "I'll take it," Max decided, and while the newspaper managers withdrew into their shells of politeness within their baggy suits he picked up the phone, pressed the green-lit button, and said, "Walter. Isn't it early for you?" Because New York was, after all, five hours behind London; it would be barely six in the morning there.

"Very," Walter Greenbaum's voice said, surprisingly close. "But it's also very late. When can we talk?"

That sounded ominous. Max said, "Walter, I'm not sure. I'm due at the Ivory Exchange Bank in Nairobi tomorrow, I don't think I'll be back in the States till—"

"I'm here."

Max blinked. "Here? You mean in London?"

"I Concorded last night. When are you free?"

If Walter Greenbaum were troubled enough by something to fly personally to London rather than phone, fax, or wait, Max should take it seriously. "Now," he said, and hung up, and said to the managers, "Good-bye."

= =

Walter Greenbaum was a stocky man in his fifties, with deep bags under his eyes that made him look as though he spent all his time contemplating the world's sorrows. Once, when a friend pointed out to him that the removal of such bags was the easiest trick in the plastic surgeon's playbook, he had said, "Never. Without these bags I'm no longer a lawyer, I'm just a complainer." And he was right. The bags gave his every utterance the gravity of one who has seen it all and just barely survived. And yet, he was merely doing lawyer-talk, like anybody else.

"Good morning, Walter."

"Morning, Max."

"Coffee? Have you had breakfast?"

"There was a break-in at the Carrport facility on Long Island last weekend."

I am hearing this for the first time, Max reminded himself. Sounding mildly concerned, he said, "A break-in? That's what comes from leaving the place empty. Did they get much?"

"Perhaps a quarter million in silver and other valuables, plus a car."

Max's mouth dropped open. His mind stalled. He couldn't think of a single response to pretend to have.

Walter smiled thinly into the silence he'd created, and said, "Yes, Max. He went back. He escaped from the police, and he went back to the house."

"Back? Back?" What does Walter know?

They were standing in the white-and-gold living room of the suite, with views of the Thames outside the windows, where black birds tumbled in a strong wind beneath plump hurrying clouds. Neither of them gave a thought to the view, as Walter gestured at a nearby white sofa, saying, "Why don't you sit down, Max? Before you fall down."

Max sat. Walter pulled a white-and-gold Empire chair over near him, leaving tracks in the white carpet. Seating himself in front of Max like a sorrowing headmaster, he said, "I'm your attorney, Max. Try to tell me the truth."

Max had now regained control of himself. So; the burglar had escaped from those incompetent policepersons, had gone back to the house (in search of his ring?), had stripped the place, and then had stolen a car to transport his loot away from there. And somehow, as a result, Max's own participation in the evening's events had become known. Not good.

He said, "Walter, I always tell you the truth. If there's something I don't want to tell you, I simply don't tell you. But I don't lie."

"You should have told me," Walter said, "that you meant to violate the orders of the bankruptcy court."

"You would have insisted I not do it."

"Who was the woman?"

"With me, in Carrport?" Max shrugged. "Miss September." But then another awful thought struck. "Does Lutetia know?"

"Not yet."

"Walter, this is not something for a wife to hear, not now, not ever. You *know* that, Walter."

"I certainly do," Walter agreed. "Which is another reason I wish you'd mentioned your plans before acting on them."

"I don't see . . . why . . . why . . ." Max ground to a halt, took a deep breath, and started again: "How did it come out? About *me*?"

"Apparently," Walter told him, "the officers originally meant to cover up for you, but once their prisoner slipped out of their hands they could no longer do that, they didn't *dare* do it, they were in too much trouble as it was. There was also the fact you made the 911 call."

"I can't believe— Walter, if you'd *seen* that fellow, that burglar, you wouldn't— How on earth did they manage to lose him? He was as docile as a cow!"

Walter shook his baggy head. "Don't trust those who are docile as cows, Max."

"I can see that. So he went back," Max mused, rubbing the ring against the point of his chin. "Looking for the ring, I suppose."

"The what?"

"Nothing, nothing."

"Max," Walter said, leaning back in his chair so it made a noise like a mouse, "you know better than this. You're supposed to *confide* in your attorney."

"I know, I know, you're right." Max wasn't used to feeling embarrassment in the presence of other human beings, and he didn't like it; soon, he'd start to blame Walter. He said, "I'm just not sure you'll think it funny."

Walter raised his eyebrows, which made his bags look like udders. "Funny? Max? I'm supposed to find something in this situation funny?"

Max grinned a little. "Well, in fact," he said, "I stole the burglar's ring."

"You stole . . ."

"His ring." Max held up his hand, to show it. "This one. You see? It has the trigram on it, and—"

"You just happened to be holding a gun on him anyway, so you thought—"

"No, no, after. When the police came."

"You stole the burglar's ring, with the police standing there?"

"Well, they suggested I look around, see if he'd taken anything, and it was a spur-of-the-moment thing, I said, that ring on his finger, right there, that's mine. And they said, give Mr. Fairbanks back his ring." Max beamed. "He was furious."

"So furious," Walter pointed out, "that he then escaped from the police and came looking for you, and found a quarter million dollars worth of loot instead."

"Not a bad trade, from his point of view," Max said, and held his hand up to admire the ring. "And I'm happy as well, so that's the end of it." Dropping his hand, he shrugged and said, "And the insurance company will certainly pay. We own it."

"And the judge," Walter said, "will ask questions."

"Yes, I suppose he will," Max agreed, as a faint cloud darkened his satisfaction. "But we can limit the damage, can't we? What I mean is, I can surely say I merely went out there to get some personal items that are *not* a part of the Chapter Eleven, and I happened upon the burglar just as he was breaking in, lucky thing I was there and so on, and we needn't mention Miss September. Which is to say, Lutetia. *That's* where there could be trouble, if we're not careful."

"It doesn't look good to the court," Walter said, "you leaving the country immediately after."

"It wasn't *immediate*, Walter, and this trip has been planned for months. Every move I make is planned *well* ahead, you know that."

Walter said, "I've been on the phone with the judge."

"And?"

"My most difficult job," Walter said, "was to get him to

agree to begin with a private conversation in chambers, rather than a session with all parties in open court."

"A session in court? For what?"

"Oh, Max," Walter said, exasperated. "For violating the terms of the Chapter Eleven."

"For God's sake, Walter, everybody knows that's just a dance we're all doing, some folderol, not to be taken seriously."

"Judges," Walter said, "take everything seriously. If you are making use of assets that are supposed to be frozen, he can if he wishes reopen the negotiation, bring in the creditors' representatives—"

"*Those* miserable—"

"Creditors."

"Yes, yes, I—"

"Including the IRS."

Max grumbled. He didn't like to be crowded, he didn't like it at all. Feeling ill-used, he said, "What do you want me to do?"

"Put off Nairobi."

"Walter, that's very difficult, they—"

"You can do what you want, and you know you can, at least on that front. Put off Nairobi, fly back to New York with me tomorrow, meet with the judge in chambers at one on Thursday afternoon."

"And?"

"And look penitent," Walter said.

Max screwed his face around. "How's that?"

"You can work on it," Walter said. "On the plane."

15

"The thing is," Dortmunder said.

"Washington," May suggested.

"That's it. That's it right there."

They were walking home from the movies in the rain. May liked the movies, so they went from time to time, though Dortmunder couldn't see what they were all about, except people who didn't need a lucky ring. When those people in the movies got to a bus stop, the bus was just pulling in. When they rang a doorbell, the person they were coming to see had to have been leaning against the door on the inside, that's how fast they opened up. When they went to rob a bank, these movie people, there was always a place to park *out front*. When they fell off a building, which they did frequently, they didn't even bother to look, they just held out a hand, and somebody'd already put a flagpole sticking out of the building right there; nice to hold onto until the hay truck drives by, down below.

Dortmunder could remember a lot of falls, but no hay trucks. "Washington," he said.

"It's just a city, John," May pointed out. "You know cities."

"I know *this* city," Dortmunder told her, pointing at the wet sidewalk between his feet. "In New York I know what I'm doing, I know where I am, I know *who* I am. In Washington I don't know a thing, I don't know how to *go*, to do this, to do that, I don't know how to *talk* there."

"They talk English in Washington, John."

"Maybe," Dortmunder said.

"What you need," May said, "is a partner, somebody who knows that place, can help you along."

"I dunno, May. What do I give him? Half the ring?"

"This Fairbanks is very rich," May pointed out. "A place he lives, there's got to be other stuff around. Look how much you got from his place on the Island."

"Well, that's true," Dortmunder said. "But on the other hand, who do I know in Washington? Everybody I know is from around here."

"Ask," May suggested.

"Ask who?"

"Ask everybody. Start with Andy, he knows a lot of people."

"The thing about Andy," Dortmunder said, as May unlocked them into their apartment building, "is he *likes* knowing people."

They went up the stairs in companionable silence, Dortmunder thinking about a nice glass of bourbon. Spring rains are warm, but they're still wet.

May unlocked them into the dark apartment. Switching on the hall light, Dortmunder said, "Andy isn't here. Think of that."

"Andy isn't here *all* the time."

"He isn't?"

May concentrated on relocking the door. Dortmunder said, "You want some bourbon? A beer?"

"Tea," she said. "I'll make it." Probably something she'd picked up in one of the magazines she was always reading.

"I'll stick to bourbon," Dortmunder decided. "And I'll make it."

They headed to the kitchen, switching on lights along the way, and Dortmunder made himself a bourbon on the rocks that just *looked* warm; even with the ice cubes floating around in there, you knew that drink would warm your insides.

May was still waiting on her tea. "I'll be in the living

room," Dortmunder said, and left the kitchen, then turned back to say, "Here he is. I told you, remember?"

Not looking up from her tea, May called, "Hi, Andy."

Andy, just entering, shut the hall door and called, "Hi, May."

Dortmunder headed again for the living room, saying to Andy, "You might as well come along."

"Long as I'm here."

"That's it."

Andy was carrying some kind of leather shoulderbag with a flap, like a scout on horseback in a western movie. Dortmunder wasn't positive he really wanted to know what was inside that bag, but he was pretty sure he'd be finding out. In the meantime, Andy shifted this bag around on his shoulder, indicating it was fairly heavy, and said, "I'll just get a beer first."

Dortmunder thought. He looked at the glass in his own hand. Rising with some difficulty to the responsibilities of host, he said, "You want a bourbon?"

"Thanks for asking, John," Andy said, "but I'll just stick to beer."

So they went their separate ways, Dortmunder settling himself into his own chair in his living room, tasting the bourbon, and finding it every bit as satisfying as he'd hoped. Then Andy came in with his beer, sat on the sofa, put the beer and the shoulderbag on the coffee table, reached for the shoulderbag's flap, and Dortmunder said, "Before you do that, whatever it is, lemme ask you a question."

"Sure," Andy said. His hand, en route, made a left turn and picked up the beer instead.

"Who do you know in Washington?"

Andy drank beer. "The president," he said. "That senator, whatsisname. An airline stewardess named Justine."

Dortmunder tasted bourbon; *that* was still good, anyway. "Who do you know," he amended, "that isn't a civilian?"

Andy looked alert. "You mean, somebody in our line of work? Oh, I see, to be the local for when you do the Watergate."

"May says, probably there'll be enough stuff in the guy's place to make it worth somebody's while."

"That's true, judging from last time. Lemme think about it," Andy decided, and leaned forward, putting down his beer. "In the meantime," he said, reaching again for the shoulderbag, "here's the reason I'm here."

"Uh huh." Dortmunder held tight to his bourbon.

Andy flipped back the shoulderbag's flap, and pulled out a smallish black metal box with a telephone receiver on one side of it. "I'm gonna have to unplug your phone for a few minutes," he said.

Dortmunder glared at the box. "Is that an answering machine? I told you before, Andy, I don't want—"

"No no, John, I told you, I gave up on you with technology." Grinning in an amiable way, Andy shrugged and spread his hands, saying, "I understand you now. The only reason you're willing to travel in cars is because there's no place in an apartment to keep a horse."

"Was that sarcasm, Andy?"

"I don't think so. What this is," Andy said, "is a fax. You've seen them around."

Well, that was true. A fax was something you picked up and carried to the fence. In the straight world, they were yet another way to tell people things and have them tell you things back. Since telling people things and hearing what bad news *they* had to impart had never been high among Dortmunder's priorities, he didn't see where the fax figured into his own lifestyle. If he had a fax, who would he send a message to? What would it say? And who would send a message to *him*, that they couldn't send by telephone or letter or over a beer at the O.J. Bar & Grill on Amsterdam Avenue?

Andy carried this black box of his over to the telephone on its end table, hunkered down beside it, and briskly unhooked the phone from the wall outlet so he could hook up his fax instead, while Dortmunder said, "Why do I have this, all of a sudden? And how long am I gonna have it?"

"The thing about a fax, John," Andy explained, "it's harder to bug. It isn't impossible, the feds got a machine that can pick up a fax and it still goes on to the regular party, without anybody being the wiser, but it isn't *routine*, not yet, not like a phone call. Just a minute." Andy picked up the phone part of the fax and started tapping out a number.

Dortmunder said, "Is that a local call?"

"No, it isn't." Andy listened, then said, "Hi, it's Andy. Go ahead," and hung up.

"Don't mind me," Dortmunder said. His bourbon glass was almost empty, except for ice.

Hunkering beside the fax, Andy swiveled around to Dortmunder and said, "Wally called me. He's got news, but none of us wants him to tell me on the phone. So he's—"

The phone rang. Dortmunder said, "Get that, will you? You're right there."

"No, no, this is Wally," Andy said, and the phone rang a second time, and May appeared in the doorway with a mug of tea. She looked around at everything and saw the black box and said "What's that?" just as the box suddenly made a loud, high-pitched, horrible noise, like a lot of baby pigeons being tortured to death all at once. May's eyes widened and the tea sloshed in her mug and she said, "What's *that?*"

The pigeons died. The box chuckled to itself. Dortmunder said, "It's a fax. Apparently, this is the only way Wally likes to talk now."

"Here it comes," Andy said.

Dortmunder and May watched in appalled fascination as the box began slowly to stick its tongue out at them; a wide white tongue, a sheet of shiny curly paper that exuded from the front of the thing, with words on the paper.

Andy smiled in paternal pleasure at the box. "It's like a pasta machine, isn't it?" he said.

"Yes," Dortmunder said. It was easier to say yes.

The white paper, curling back on itself like a papyrus roll, kept oozing from the box. Then it stopped, and the box made a bell *bing* sound, and Andy reached down to tear the paper loose. Straightening, he went back to the sofa, sat down, took some beer, unrolled the fax—he looked exactly like the herald announcing the arrival in the kingdom of the Duke of

Carpathia—and said, "Dear John and Andy and Miss May." Smiling, he said, "What a polite guy, Wally."

"He's a very nice person," May said, and sat in her own chair. But, Dortmunder noticed, she didn't sit back and relax, but stayed on the edge of the chair, holding the mug of tea with both hands.

Andy looked back at his proclamation, or whatever it was. "I just picked up an internal memorandum of Trans-Global Universal Industries, which is Max Fairbanks's personal holding company, and his plans have changed. Instead of going to Nairobi, he's coming to New York—"

"Good news," Dortmunder said, with some surprise, as another person might say, *Look! A unicorn!*

"He's going to be arriving tomorrow night—"

"Wednesday," May said.

"Right. —because he has an appointment with his Chapter Eleven judge on Thursday. Then he'll leave for Hilton Head on Friday and go back to the schedule the way it was before."

"He's going to be *here*," Dortmunder said, tinkling the ice in his empty glass. "Staying here. Two nights. Where?"

"We're coming to that now," Andy said, and read, "In New York, Fairbanks stays with his wife Lutetia at the N-Joy Theater on Broadway. I hope this is a help. Sincerely, Wallace Knurr."

Dortmunder said, "The what?"

"N-Joy Theater on Broadway."

"He stays at a *theater*?"

"It isn't Washington, at least, John," May pointed out. "It's New York. And you know New York."

"Sure, I do," Dortmunder said. "The guy lives in a theater. Everybody in New York lives in a theater, am I right?"

16

Although the two pillars upon which TUI had always stood were real estate (slums, then office buildings, then hotels) and communications (newspapers, then magazines, then cable television), the corporation had also from the beginning spread horizontally, like crabgrass, into allied businesses. In the last few years, the real estate and communications sides of the firm had grown more and more useful to one another, combining their specialties to create theme parks, buy a movie studio, and carve tourist centers from the decayed docksides and crumbled downtowns of older cities. And now, most recently and most triumphantly, they had come together to construct, house, and operate a Broadway theater.

The center of Manhattan Island is the absolute zero point of the triangulation of entertainment and real estate in the capitalist world. Here, millions of tourists a year from all around the planet are catered to in and around buildings constructed on land worth hundreds of thousands of dollars a foot.

Max Fairbanks had long wanted an obvious presence in New York City, mostly because there were already a few other prominent billionaires with obvious presences in New York City, and one doesn't become a billionaire in the first place without some certain degree of competitiveness in one's nature. The profit motive was there as well, of course—the N-Joy complex was expected to do for New York City what Disney World had done for Orlando; put it on the map—but merely a strong second after self-aggrandizement, which was why the name of the theater: the N-Joy Broadway, for Max's symbol, *Tui*, one of the characteristics of which, in The Book, was the Joyous.

The N-Joy Broadway was a legitimate stage theater, suited most particularly for revivals of beloved musicals, but it was much much more than that. Girdling the theater was the Little Old New York Arcade, shops and boutiques recreating an earlier and cleaner version of the scary city outside; no longer would the tourists have to brave the dangers of the actual Fifty-seventh Street, farther uptown.

Above the theater—a state-of-the-art extravaganza replete with spinning platforms, hydraulically lifted and lowered stages, computerized files, built-in smoke machines and Dolby sound under every seat—rose a forty-nine-story granitelike tower, containing a few floors of offices—show business, architecture, a few of Max Fairbanks's enterprises—and then the N-Joy Broadway Hotel, whose four-story-high lobby began on the sixteenth floor. On an average day, eighty-two percent of the twelve hundred rooms above the N-Joy Broadway Hotel lobby were occupied, but the residents of these of course were all transients, rarely remaining as long as a week. Like the Paris Opera, the N-Joy Broadway contained only one permanent resident, and her name was Lutetia.

Lutetia Fairbanks her name was, most recently, and now Lutetia Fairbanks forever. A tall and handsome woman, with striking abundant black hair, she moved with a peculiarly deliberate walk, a heavy but sensual thrusting forward and bearing down, as though she were always seeking ants to step on. The regal, if slightly Transylvanian, aspect this gave her was enhanced by her predilection for swirling gowns and turbanned headgear.

Lutetia's home, for the last sixteen months and on into the foreseeable future, was a twelve-room apartment carved into the brow of the N-Joy, above the marquee and below the hotel lobby. Her parlor windows, of soundproof glass, looked out at the world's most famous urban vista through the giant white neon O of the building's emblazoned name. Her frequent guests—she was quickly gaining local prominence as one of the city's premier hostesses—were whisked up to her aerie in a manned private elevator just off the theater entrance. Hotel staff serviced the apartment. The same climate control equipment that micromanaged the ambiance of both theater and hotel lobby purified and tempered the atmosphere in the apartment. The furnishings were antiques, the servants well trained in other nations, the living easy. So long as Max didn't fuck up, everything would keep on coming up roses.

It seemed to Lutetia that Max was, or had been, fucking up. He had that look in his eye, that childish glint of guilty pleasure, risking it all to throw just one spitball at teacher.

They had met here in the ballroom late on Wednesday afternoon, where Lutetia was overseeing the preparations for this Friday's dinner, at which the guests of honor were to be Jerry Gaunt, the latest superstar reporter from CNN, and the Emir of Hak-kak, an oil well near Yemen. Max had sought her out here, she having far more important things to do than chase after some errant husband.

That depending, of course, on just how errant he was being. "What have you been up to?" she demanded, once they'd repaired to the farther end of the ballroom, away from the busily place-setting servants.

"Nothing, my darling," Max said, blinking those oh-so-innocent eyes of his. "Nothing, my pet."

"You're in trouble with the bankruptcy, that's why you're back in New York."

"*And* to see you, my sweet."

"Bull," she told him. "What were you doing in Carrport? Who were you there with?"

"*Nobody*, precious. I needed, I merely needed, to get away from it all, out where no phones would ring, no messengers would descend, no *problems* would have to be dealt with."

"That last part didn't work so well, did it?"

Max spread his hands, with his oh-so-sheepish smile. "How was I to know some dimwit crook would choose that night to attack the place?"

"If he'd only known you were there," Lutetia pointed out, "he would surely have left you alone, if only out of professional courtesy."

"You *are* hard, Lutetia, very hard."

"Max," Lutetia said, stalking around him with that boots-of-doom stride, "two things you are not permitted to bring into my house and my life. Scandal, and disease."

"Pet, I wouldn't—"

"Scandal is worse, but disease is bad enough. I will *not* be humiliated, and I will not be put at risk of a disgusting death. I won't have it, Max. We both know what *my* lawyers could do, if they wished."

"But why would they wish? Love petal, why would *you* wish?"

"I'm busy here, Max," she informed him. "I will not have my schedule destroyed by some overgrown boy playing hooky."

"You'll hardly know I'm here, my sweet."

"Hardly."

"Will we dine together, love?"

"Not tonight," she said, to punish him. She *knew* he'd had a woman out there on the Island, she could feel it in her antennae; on the other hand, she didn't really and truly want to know the miserable details, not for sure and certain, because then she *would* have to do something drastic, if only to satisfy her pride, as powerful and overweening as his. "I'm dining out tonight," she announced. "With friends." Then, relenting a bit, she said, "Tomorrow night we could have dinner, if you have any appetite after your meeting with the judge."

"I *know* I'll have an appetite then," he said, and smiled his oh-so-roguish smile at her, adding, "Will I see you *later* tonight, my lotus blossom?"

She was about to refuse, just on general principles, but the gleam in his eye snagged her. He was, as she well knew, as rascally in bed as out, which was sometimes wearing but sometimes fun. "We'll see," she said, with half a smile, and permitted him to bite her earlobe before he scampered off and she returned to the servants, to inform them that they would be wanting the *coral*-colored napkins on the tables, as any fool could tell from the centerpieces, not the peach.

17

"I don't think I like this much," Dortmunder said.

"Why not?" Andy asked, and pointed at the bright color photo of the main reception room, with its working marble fountain and deep maroon plush sofas. "I think it's snazzy."

"I don't mean the look of it," Dortmunder said. "I mean the getting into it."

"Oh, well," Andy said. "Sure, that."

Years ago, Dortmunder and his friends had discovered what a great help in their line of work the architectural magazines could be, with their glossy photos of rich people's residences, room after room of what would or would not be worth the picking, plus blueprints of houses *and* gardens, plus visible in the backgrounds of many of the pictures this or that exterior door, with its hardware in plain sight.

The Max and Lutetia Fairbanks apartment in the new N-Joy had been given this treatment, of course, several months back, in one of the high-toned interiors magazines, and Andy had found a copy at a used-magazine store this afternoon and brought it over to Dortmunder's place, where they sat with beers side by side on the sofa, the magazine open on the coffee table in front of them, turning back and forth over the six pages of photos and copy. And Dortmunder didn't like what he saw. "The problem is," he said, "time."

"Not much lead time," Andy said.

"You could say that."

"I did say it."

"He's gonna be there tonight," Dortmunder said, "and he's gonna be there tomorrow night, and then he's going down to somebody's head."

"Hilton Head, it's an island down south."

"An island down south I'm not even gonna think about. So it's tonight or tomorrow night, if we're gonna get him at home in New York, and it sure as hell isn't gonna be tonight, so that leaves tomorrow night, and that isn't very much lead time."

"Like I said," Andy pointed out.

"And first," Dortmunder said, "there's the question of how do you get in. A private elevator from inside the theater lobby that doesn't go anywhere except to that one apartment, that's how *they* get in."

"And it has an operator," Andy said, "a guy in a uniform inside the elevator there, that pushes the button. Suppose we could switch for the operator? Take his place?"

"Maybe. Not much time to set that up. What if we bought tickets and went into the theater? It doesn't say here, but don't you figure they've got some window or something, they can look out and see the stage, watch the show if they feel like it?"

"Well, the problem there is," Andy said, "I went by the place this morning, and it's got some musical playing there, and it's sold out for the next seven months."

"Sold out?" Dortmunder frowned. "What do you mean, sold out?"

"Like I said. It isn't like going to the movies, John, it's more like taking an airplane. You call up ahead of time and say this is when I wanna fly, and they sell you a ticket."

"For seven months later? How do you know you're gonna feel like going to some particular show seven months from now?"

"That's the way they do it," Andy said, and shrugged.

"So switch the elevator operator," Dortmunder said. "Except the ushers and people in the theater probably know the real guy."

"Probably."

"Lemme think," Dortmunder said, and Andy sat back to let him think, while Dortmunder read through the article in the magazine all over again, the round sentences about volumes of space, and tensions between the modern and the traditional, and bold strokes of color, all rolling past his eyes like truck traffic on an interstate. "Says here," he said, after a while, "the apartment is serviced by the hotel staff. That'd be maids and like that, right?"

"Right," Andy said.

"Hotel maids, with those big carts they have, clean sheets, toilet paper, soap, all that stuff, and the dirty laundry they take away. Are they gonna go down to the lobby with all that and take the elevator from there up to the apartment?"

"They'd look kind of funny," Andy agreed, "pushing one of those hotel carts around a theater lobby."

"And a hotel lobby," Dortmunder said. "And the street, because the hotel and the theater are different entrances. So that's not the way they do it, is it?"

"A service elevator," Andy said.

"Has to be. An elevator *down* from somewhere in the hotel. Probably one of the regular service elevators, except the elevator shaft goes down those extra floors."

"And it won't have any operator," Andy guessed. "The maids can push those buttons for themselves."

Dortmunder at last reached for his beer, then quickly straightened it before much spilled. "We've got today and tomorrow," he said. "When May comes home, we'll pack some stuff and go check in at the hotel. I'll have to go over to Stoon's place and buy a credit card, something that's good for a few days."

"Once you're in," Andy said, "you give me a call and tell me what room you're in."

"And you come over late—"

"Around one in the morning, right?"

"And we toss the hotel."

"And we find the elevator."

"And I get my ring."

"And a couple other little items along the way," Andy said. Smiling at the photos in the magazine, he said, "You know, a fella could just take a truckload of that stuff there and go downtown to Bleecker Street somewhere and set up an antique shop."

Dortmunder drank beer. "You do that," he said. "And I get my ring."

18

The concept of horizontal expansion in the corporate world is that the elements, if carefully chosen, will increase one another's business and therefore profit. It was estimated that 23 percent of the guests registered at the N-Joy Broadway Hotel took in the show at the N-Joy Broadway Theater while they were in town, and that in fact 67 percent of those had chosen that particular hotel because they'd come to New York expressly to see that specific show. Conversely, 19 percent of non-hotel-guest theatergoers chose to dine in the hotel's main dining room before or after seeing the show, a respectable number, but one which management thought could be increased. They had a good show, a good hotel, and a good restaurant; the combination had to be a winner.

As for that show, it was *Desdemona!*, the feminist musical version of the world-famous love story, slightly altered for the modern American taste (everybody lives). Hit songs from the show included "Oh, Tell, Othello, Oh, Tell," and "Iago, My Best Friend" and the foot-stomping finale, *"Here's* the Handkerchief!"

There were statistics also, known to management, as to how many Europeans stayed at the hotel and/or attended the show, how many South Americans, how many Japanese, how many Canadians, how many Americans, and (show attendance only) how many New Yorkers (eleven, so far). There were statistics about income levels and education levels and number of family members in party, and all of that stuff, but so what? What it came down to was, the N-Joy had, according to plan, quickly established itself as a destination for amateurs, vacationers, not very worldly world travelers of moderate income and education. Except for TUI employees, who had no choice, the hotel got almost no business trade, a market they wouldn't be starting to tap into until five years down the line, when the top-floor conference center was completed. In the meantime, they knew their customers and were content with their customers, and business was ticking along pretty much as anticipated.

Of course, not every customer exactly matched the statistics and the demographics. For instance, most hotel guests who arrived by taxi had come from one of New York's three principal airports or possibly one of its two railroad stations or even, more rarely, it's one major bus depot; none had ever come here from Third Avenue and Nineteenth Street before, as John and May Williams with a home address in Gary, Indiana, had done, late on the afternoon of Wednesday, May 10; though of course there was no way for the scarlet-uniformed doorman to know where this particular taxi had come from nor what a short journey had been taken by that scuffed and mismatched luggage Mr. Williams was wrestling the bellboy for until Mrs. Williams kicked Mr. Williams a mean one in the ankle.

Most of the hotel's guests lived more than a hundred miles from New York City, whereas the Williamses, who had never been in Gary, Indiana, in their lives, actually lived a mile and a half from the hotel, downtown and then across to the east side. Most hotel guests used credit cards, as did Mr. Williams, but usually they were the guests' own cards, which had not recently been stolen, ironed, altered, and adjusted. And most hotel guests used their own names.

"Mr. and Mrs. Williams, enjoy your stay at the N-Joy," the desk clerk said, handing Dortmunder two of the magnetized cards they'd be using instead of room keys.

"We will," Dortmunder said. "I'm sure of it."

"New York!" breathed May, with a dazzled smile. She gazed around at this lobby in the sky, a four-story-tall Greek temple to the goddess of costume jewelry. "So this is New York!"

Dortmunder thought she was overdoing it, but the desk clerk seemed pleased.

19

Andy Kelp was disappointed. He'd come to the N-Joy
early, hoping to pick up an item or two en passant, since John
and May would have luggage with them anyway and you
might as well put something in it, but there was just nothing
here to attract his acquisitive eye.

Not that there weren't shops, stores, boutiques. The lobby
was ringed by them, like a necklace of paper clips, each with
its own display windows to show the enticements within, each
with the names of other cities in gold letters down at one corner of the display window, to suggest that this shop had
branches in those cities. But why? Why have a store full of
this stuff in Milan, in London, in Paris, in Beverly Hills? Well,
okay, Beverly Hills. But in those other cities, what these cita-
tions must mean is that they've got a shop like this in a *hotel*
like this in those cities. So the argument was, why travel?

With the shops closed and foot traffic in the lobby sparse,
Kelp eased himself into boutique after boutique, hoping there
might be something toward the rear of the place different
from what was visible through the window, but it was always
more of the same, and the key word was *shiny*. Shiny leather,
shiny men's watches, shiny furs, shiny pink glass vases,
shiny covers of shiny magazines, shiny purses, shiny shoes,
shiny earrings. It was like being in a duty-free shop for mag-
pies.

Midnight, and no score. Kelp knew John and May didn't like him to burst in unexpectedly, and he might maybe have been doing it a little too often lately, so he would definitely not go to their room before the 1:00 A.M. appointment, which meant, what now? Whereas the New York City outside this building was still jumping, just getting into its evening surge, the N-Joy was down and dark, all except for the cocktail lounge, tucked away in a far corner. So Kelp went there.

The cocktail lounge was a long low-ceilinged lunette curved around a massive bar. The principal color was purple, and the principal lighting was nonexistent. The candles that guttered on every table were encased in thick red glass. The main light source, in fact, was the shiny black Formica tops of the round tables, each of them surrounded by vast low overstuffed armchairs that to sit in would be like trying to sit in a jelly donut. Three of the tables were occupied, by murmuring, whispering, muttering couples, all dressed up with nowhere to go, drinking stingers or something worse. At the bar were two women, one of them a waitress in a black tutu, the other a customer with her elbows on the bar, her lumpy old shoulderbag on the stool next to her, and a tall glass in front of her that, judging by her bleak expression, was definitely half-empty and not half-full.

The bar stools were tall and wide, with soft purple vinyl tops. Kelp took one equidistant from both women, put one forearm on the bar, and watched the bartender, a dour workman with a mustache, finish building two stingers. The waitress took those drinks away, and the bartender turned his attention to Kelp. "Yes, sir," he said, sliding a paper napkin onto the bar.

"Bourbon," Kelp said.

The bartender nodded and waited, but Kelp was finished. Finally, the barman said, "And?"

"Oh, well, a glass, I guess. And an ice cube."

"That's it?" A faint smile appeared below the mustache. "We don't get much call for that kind of thing here," he said.

"You've got bourbon, though," Kelp suggested.

"Oh, certainly. But most people want something with it.

Some nice sweet vermouth? Maraschino cherry? A twist?
Orange slice? Angostura bitters? Triple sec? Amaretto?"

"On the side," Kelp said.

"You got it."

The bartender went away, and the woman to Kelp's left
said, "Hello."

He looked at her. She was probably in her midthirties, attractive in a way that suggested she didn't know she was attractive and therefore didn't try very hard. She was not in a
holiday mood. The sound of her voice when she'd said hello
had made it seem as though she hadn't particularly wanted to
speak but felt it was a requirement and so she'd gone ahead
and done it. "And hello," Kelp said.

The woman nodded; mission accomplished. "Where you
from?" she asked.

"Cleveland, Ohio. And you?"

"Lancaster, Kansas. I'm supposed to go back there . . .
sometime."

"Well," Kelp said, "if that's where you live."

"I believe my husband has left me," she said.

This was unexpected. Kelp didn't see a second glass on
the bar. He said, "Maybe he's in the men's room."

"I think he left me Monday," she said.

Ah; today being Wednesday. Kelp thought about that
while the bartender placed a glass and an ice cube and some
bourbon on the paper napkin in front of him. "Thanks," he
said, and said to the woman, "Here in New York? Just disappeared?"

"Not disappeared, left me," she said. "We came here Sunday, and on Monday he said, 'Anne Marie, it isn't working
out,' and he packed his bag and went away."

"That's rough," Kelp said.

"Well," she said, "it's rough because it's *here*. I mean, he's
right, it *isn't* working out, that's why I've been having an affair with Charlie Petersen for three years now, and is *he*
gonna turn white as a sheet when he hears the news, but I do
wish he'd done it, if he was gonna do it, I do wish he'd done
it in Lancaster and not here."

"More convenient," Kelp said, and nodded to show he sympathized.

"What it was," she said, "this trip was our last try at making the marriage *work*. You know how people say they wanna make the marriage *work*? Like they wanna give it a paper route or something. So we came here and we got on each other's nerves just as bad as we do at home in Lancaster, only here we only had one room to do it in, so Howard said, it isn't working out, and he packed and took off."

"Back to Lancaster."

"I don't believe so," she said. "He's a traveling salesman for Pandorex Computers, you know, so he's all over the Midwest anyway, so he's probably with some girlfriend at the moment."

"Any kids?"

"No, thank you," she said. "This damn glass is empty again. What's that you're drinking?"

"Bourbon."

"And?"

"And more bourbon."

"Really? I wonder what that's like."

"Barman," Kelp said, "I think we got a convert. Another of these for me, and one of these for the lady, too."

"Yes, sir."

"I hate to be called the lady."

"Sorry," Kelp said. "My mama told me pronouns were impolite."

"The lady sucks."

"That's good news," Kelp said. "From now on, I'll refer to you as the broad. Deal?"

She grinned, as though she didn't want to. "Deal," she said.

The barman brought the drinks, and the broad sipped hers and made a face. Then she sipped again, tasted, and said, "Interesting. It isn't sweet."

"That's right."

"Interesting." She sipped again. "If you get tired of calling me the broad," she said, "try Anne Marie."

"Anne Marie. I'm Andy."

"How you doing?"

"Fine."

"You see, what it is," she said, "it's a package, a tour, we paid for everything ahead of time. I've got the room until Saturday, and I got breakfast until Saturday, and I got dinner until Friday, so it seemed stupid to go back to Lancaster, but in the meantime what the hell am I doing here?"

"Holding up the bar."

"I certainly don't want to get drunk," she said. "I've been pacing myself." She frowned at the half-empty glass in front of her. "Will this get me drunk?"

"Probably not," Kelp said. "Unless you're one of those rare people with the funny chemistry, you know."

She looked at him as though she might begin to doubt him soon. She said, "How long are you here for?"

"Oh, for a while," he said, and sipped from his own half-full glass.

She thought about that. "You like this hotel?"

"I'm not staying here," he said.

She was surprised. "Why would you come in here," she asked, "if you're not staying here? You couldn't have been just passing by."

"I've got an appointment in the neighborhood," he told her, and looked at his watch, and said, "pretty soon. So I'm killing time here."

"So we're ships passing in the night," she said.

"Possibly," Kelp said. "In this hotel, do they have that little refrigerator in the room full of stuff?"

"Beer," she said, "and champagne, and macadamia nuts and trail mix."

"That's the one. Does it have bourbon?"

She considered, then pointed at her empty glass. "This stuff? I'm not sure."

"I could come around later, take a look," Kelp suggested.

"I figure, my appointment, I'm probably done by three, maybe earlier, something like that."

"That's some late appointment," she said.

"Well, you know, New York," he said. "The city that never sleeps."

"Well, *I* sleep," she said. "Though not so much, actually, since Howard left. I suppose he isn't coming back."

"Doesn't sound it," Kelp said.

"I'm in 2312," Anne Marie said. "When your appointment's done, you know, you could try, knock on the door. If I'm awake, I'll answer."

20

When Dortmunder woke up, he had no idea *where* the hell he was. Some beige box with the lights on and faint voices talking. He lifted his head, and saw an unfamiliar room, with a TV on, all the lights on, himself sprawled on his back atop a king-size bed with its thick tan bedspread still on it, and May slumped asleep in a chair off to his left, one of her magazines on the floor beside her. On the TV, people covered with blood were being carried to ambulances. Wherever it was, it looked like a real mess. Then, as Dortmunder watched, the people and the ambulances faded away and some candy bars began to dance.

Dortmunder sat up, remembering. The N-Joy Broadway Hotel. Max Fairbanks. The lucky ring. The service elevator. Andy Kelp coming by, later; one in the morning.

There was a clock radio bolted to the table beside the bed; its red numbers said 12:46. Dortmunder moved, discovering several aches, and eventually made it to his feet. He sloped off to the shiny bathroom, where he found his own personal toothbrush and toothpaste, plus the hotel's soap and towels. When he finally came back out of the bathroom, feeling a little more human and alive, May was stirring in her chair, looking for her magazine, coming awake just as fuzzily as he had. Seeing him, she said, "I fell asleep."

"Everybody fell asleep."

They'd checked in late in the afternoon, hung around the room for a while to unpack and think things over, then had a pretty good dinner down in the hotel's restaurant. Then May had gone back to the room to read while Dortmunder did a preliminary walk-through of the hotel, getting to know the lay of the land, then went back to compare what he'd seen with the floor plan placed on the inside of the room door in case of fire. "You Are Here." "Use Staircase A." "Do Not Use Elevator." Still, they were marked, the elevators, on the floor plan.

The layout was simple, really. The hotel was basically a thick letter U, with the base of the U on Broadway and the arms of the U on the side streets. The space in the middle was occupied, down below, by the theater and by the hotel lobby, with a glass roof at the top of that lobby on the sixteenth floor. The U started with floor seventeen and went on up that way, so all the hotel rooms could have windows.

"I don't sleep well in chairs," May said, getting to her feet.

"Well, you didn't mean to," Dortmunder said.

"Doesn't help," she decided, and went off to the bathroom, while Dortmunder crossed to the room's only window and drew the heavy drapes open partway. The window wouldn't open, so he pressed his forehead against the cool glass in order to look as straight down as possible.

They had an inside room, meaning no city vistas but also no traffic noise, and the view below, just visible with your forehead flat against the windowpane, was the glass roof of the lobby. Earlier this evening, that glass dome had been very brightly lit, but now it was dim, as though some sort of fire had been banked down there.

12:53.

Dortmunder crossed to the door to once again study the floor plan in its little frame. He leaned in close, peering, figuring it out.

The floor plan was mostly little rectangles of numbered rooms, with a central corridor. In the middle of each of the three sides was a cluster of service elements: staircase, elevators, ice machine, and unmarked rooms that would be storage for linens and cleaning supplies. Of course, Max Fairbanks's apartment didn't show on this simple floor plan, but Dortmunder already knew it was above the theater and below the hotel and that it faced onto Broadway. So the service cluster on the Broadway side must be the one that contained the special elevator. Dortmunder's room was around on the south side, so when Andy got here they'd—

The door whacked Dortmunder sharply on the nose. He stepped back, eyes watering, and Andy himself came in, saying, "I hope I'm not early."

"You're not early," Dortmunder said, massaging his nose.

Andy peered at him, concerned. "John? You sound like you got a cold."

"It's nothing."

"Maybe the air-conditioning," Andy suggested. "You know, these buildings, it's all recycled air, it could be you—"

"It's nothing!"

May came out of the bathroom, looking more awake. "Hi, Andy," she said. "Right on time."

"Maybe a minute early," Dortmunder said. His nose was out of joint.

May said, "A minute early is right on time."

"Thank you, May."

Dortmunder, seeing no future in remaining irritated, let his nose alone and said, "We got this little floor plan here," and showed Andy the chart on the door. He explained where they were, and where the service elevator to the apartment should be, and Andy said, "Can it be that easy?"

"Probably not," Dortmunder said.

"Well, let's go look at it anyway," Andy said.

May said, "John, where's the control?"

"The what?"

"For the TV," she said. "The remote control. I thought I'd watch television while you're away, but I can't find the control."

"Maybe it's in the bed," Dortmunder said.

"Maybe it's *under* the bed," Andy said.

They all looked, and didn't find it. May said, "This is only one room and it isn't that large a room and it doesn't have that many things in it. So we have to be able to find the control."

Andy said, "Are you sure you ever had a control?"

"*Yes*. That's how I turned it on in the first place. And, John, you were changing channels one time."

"So it ought to be in the bed," Dortmunder said.

"Or under the bed," Andy said.

They all looked again and still didn't find it, until Andy went into the bathroom and said, "Here it is," and came out with the control in his hand. "It was next to the sink," he said.

"I'm not even going to ask," May said, taking it from him. "Thank you, Andy."

"Sure."

Dortmunder, who didn't believe he was the one who had carried the control into the bathroom in the first place, but who saw no point in starting an argument, said, "Can we go now?"

"Sure," Andy said, and they left.

The corridor was long, not too brightly lit, and empty. Here and there, room service trays with meal remnants waited on the floor. Dortmunder and Andy went down to the end of the corridor, turned right, and here was another identical corridor, with identical carpeting and lighting and room service trays. Midway along, an illuminated green sign on the right, up near the ceiling, said EXIT. "Down there," Dortmunder said.

Halfway along the corridor, under the green exit sign, were the elevators, on the right, the inner side of the building, away from the street. Next to the elevators on their left was the staircase, and next to them on their right was the room containing the ice machine. Opposite the elevators was a blank wall decorated with a mirror and a small table and a chair with wooden arms. Opposite the staircase was an unmarked door.

Unmarked and locked. Andy spoke to it, gently, and soon it opened, and they stepped through into a square room filled with rough wooden shelves on which were piled stacks of linen, of toilet paper, of tissue boxes and boxes containing soap and shampoo and body lotion. To their left was an open space in front of two sets of elevator doors.

"One of these," Dortmunder said, nodding at the elevator doors. "Ought to be, anyway."

"Maybe the one that's coming," Andy said.

Dortmunder listened, and could hear the faint buzzing whirr of an elevator moving upward through its shaft. "Not to this floor, though," he said.

"Well, maybe," Andy said. "Let's wait back here."

Dortmunder followed him, and they faded back into the rows of supplies, just as the whirring stopped and they heard the elevator doors open. Andy lifted an eyebrow at Dortmunder—*see?*—and Dortmunder lowered an eyebrow at Andy: *yeah, I see.*

Looking through mountains of clean towels, they watched a guy in a black-and-white waiter outfit push an empty two-tiered gray metal cart out of the elevator. Its doors closed behind him as he opened the door to the main corridor, pushed the cart through, and disappeared.

Speaking softly, Andy said, "Gone to pick up those trays."

"So we've got a few minutes."

They left the supplies, went over to the elevators, and Andy pushed the up button. The elevator that had brought the waiter was still there, so its doors immediately opened. Andy held them open while he and Dortmunder studied the simple control panel inside. It was just black buttons with numbers on them, 31 the highest number (they were at the moment on 26) and 17 the lowest number, with two more buttons below 17, marked KITCHEN and LAUNDRY.

"So it must be the other one," Andy said.

"Or," Dortmunder said, contemplating the control panel, and thinking about how his luck tended to run, "we didn't figure it right."

"What else could it be? So we'll hang around here till the waiter comes back through, and then we'll bring up the other one."

"We'll see what happens," Dortmunder agreed.

They released the elevator door and went back to the stacks of towels. "It probably won't be just a button," Dortmunder said. "I mean, if we're right about it. It'll probably be a key, for the security."

"Sure. You can go to any other floor in that elevator, but you can't go to *that* floor unless you've got the key."

The waiter opened the door from the hall and pushed in the cart, now piled high with trays and dishes and utensils. He maneuvered the cart, which was apparently unwieldy when full, around to the elevator, thumbed open the doors, pushed the cart aboard, pushed a button inside, and disappeared.

Immediately, Andy went out and pushed the up button. There were no lights or indicators to say whether or not the other car was coming; they could only wait and see.

"Of course," Dortmunder said, following, "they might have the other one shut off at night."

"Why? They got a lot of stuff to do all night long. And you know? Come to think of it, maybe we should duck back in there again."

"What for?"

"Well, just in case," Andy said, "when the elevator gets here, and the door opens, there's somebody aboard."

"Right," Dortmunder said.

So they went back to the towels and waited, and soon the other elevator did arrive, and when its doors opened, it was empty. Andy hurried to it before the doors could shut again, and he and Dortmunder studied the control panel, which was identical to the first one. "Naturally," Dortmunder said.

"They've gotta clean," Andy insisted. "Somehow, they've gotta clean. Rich people clean a lot, they hire whole companies to clean."

"Let's take a look on seventeen," Dortmunder said.

═ ═
═

The corridor on seventeen had almost the same colors of walls and doors and carpet as the corridor on twenty-six, but not exactly, so that your first idea was that something had gone wrong with your eyes. On that floor, Dortmunder and Andy checked out all three service clusters, north, west, and south (west being the one that should be above the Fairbanks apartment), and found nothing they hadn't already seen on twenty-six. Sighing, Andy looked at his watch and said, "And it was gonna be so simple."

"It is simple," Dortmunder said. "We can't get in."

"There's *gotta* be a way. Do they keep a maid chained up in there? How does she get new soap? How does she get rid of the old sheets?"

They were standing in the public corridor again, near the public elevators in the middle section. The Fairbanks apartment should be directly beneath their feet. Dortmunder looked up and down the corridor and said, "We need another door. A door without a number on it."

"Sure," Andy said.

They moved southward down the corridor, and by the time they'd got to the turn they'd found three unmarked locked doors, unlocked them all, and found first a room full of maids' carts and vacuum cleaners, then a room full of television sets and lamps, and then a bathroom, probably for staff. So they turned and went the other way, and north of the elevators they found a locked and unmarked door that opened to a great tangle of pipes; heat or plumbing or both. And the next door they opened was an elevator, with a maid's cart in it.

"Well, look at that," Andy said.

"Somebody coming," Dortmunder said, having heard the public elevator stop, down the hall. Moving as one, like a very small flock of birds wheeling in the air, they stepped into this new hidden elevator and let the door snick shut behind them.

Now it was dark. They both patted walls until Andy found the light switch, and then it was okay again.

This was an elevator like the service elevators, simple and rectangular and painted industrial gray. Its control panel was even simpler: two buttons, neither of them marked. And just to remove any last vestige of doubt, the maid's cart contained boxes of stationery marked, in fussy lettering, MF or LF.

There was a keyhole in the control panel, just above the buttons. Andy stooped to study it, then straightened again and said, "No."

Dortmunder looked at him. "No?"

"This is not your ordinary lock," Andy said.

"No," Dortmunder agreed. "It wouldn't be."

"Your ordinary lock I shrug at," Andy explained. "But not this. And I suspect," he went on, "that it probably has an alarm in there behind it, to go off in some security office somewhere if anybody sticks a bobby pin or anything in that keyhole."

"Wouldn't surprise me," Dortmunder said.

"In fact," Andy said, "it would be my opinion that it would be safer to go through the floor and shinny down the cable or climb down the rungs, if there's rungs, than to fool around with this lock here. If we turn the screws there and there and there and there to take the face off the control panel, just to see what's what and how come, *that* could send a signal to security."

"I don't doubt it," Dortmunder said.

"So let's take a look at this floor here."

They moved the cart as far back as possible, then got down on hands and knees and looked at the floor. It was plywood, four large sheets of plywood, screwed down and painted gray. They rapped the plywood with their knuckles, and the sound was flat, not echoing. They looked at each other, on all fours, like dogs meeting at the neighborhood fire hydrant, and then they got to their feet and Andy said, "Steel underneath."

"I noticed that," Dortmunder said.

"No trap door for access to the machinery or anything."

"That's right."

"So the machinery's probably up above."

They looked upward, at the plain gray-painted roof of the elevator, and in the rear right quadrant were the clear outlines of a trap door. And in the trap door was a keyhole. "They're beginning to annoy me," Dortmunder said.

"Us guys don't give up," Andy said.

"That's true," Dortmunder said, "though I sometimes wonder why."

"When the going gets tough," Andy said, "the tough get an expert. I know when a lock is beyond my simple rustic skills. What we need is a lockman."

"You want to bring somebody in?"

"Why not? What we pick up in that place down there we split three ways instead of two. You don't care anyway, you just want your ring."

"That's also true," Dortmunder admitted. "But a little profit would be nice."

"I'll see if Wally Whistler's around," Andy said, "or Ralph Winslow, they're both good. I'll show them the pictures in that magazine, they'll *pay* us to come along."

"I wouldn't hold out for that," Dortmunder said, and looked at the damn keyhole in the damn control panel. "Here we are, right here and all," he said, "and the ring right down there underneath us. I can *feel* it."

"We'll get it," Andy assured him, and looked at his watch and said, "But not tonight. Tomorrow night." He turned to unlock the door to the corridor. "Tonight I kinda got an appointment, I wouldn't want to be late."

Dortmunder frowned at him. "An appointment? This time of night?"

"Well, New York, you know," Andy said, and opened the door cautiously, and stuck his head out just a bit to see if the coast was clear, and nodded back at Dortmunder, "the city that never sleeps."

Dortmunder followed him out to the corridor, and behind him the unmarked door snicked shut. "New York, the city with insomnia," he said. "Is that a good idea?"

"See you tomorrow," Andy said.

21

Most of the guests staying at the N-Joy Broadway Hotel, when they got up in the morning, went out sight-seeing, but not the Williamses. They got up and went out, like everybody else, but Mrs. Williams then became May Bellamy and went to work at the supermarket downtown, while Mr. Williams reverted to one John Dortmunder, who went home to East Nineteenth Street, where he did what he usually did at home all day long, which wasn't much.

It had been agreed that Dortmunder and May would get together back at the hotel at six, to add another hotel meal to the credit card tab they were running up, and then wait for Andy Kelp and X Hour to arrive, which they figured to be midnight; this evening, they'd try not to fall asleep. So at about five-thirty, Dortmunder left the apartment, and when he opened the street door downstairs who was coming up the stoop but Gus Brock. "Hello," Dortmunder said.

"Hello," Gus said, and stopped there on the steps.

Dortmunder said, "This is not a coincidence, am I right?"

Gus scrinched up his eyes. "What isn't a coincidence? I came over to see you."

"That's what I meant. I'm walking uptown."

"Then so am I."

They started walking together, and after they made the turn onto Third Avenue and headed uptown Gus said, "I read in *Newsday* where we scored pretty good out on the Island last week."

"Oh, yeah?"

"That *was* us, wasn't it? Took all that stuff from that big house in Carrport?"

"Us?" Dortmunder asked. "How do you figure 'us'?"

"Well, you know, John," Gus said, "you didn't know about that place, I did. You didn't know about the Chapter Eleven and all that, and I did."

"Except the guy was there," said Dortmunder. "So much for all your chapters."

"It was *our* little job, John," Gus said. "I'm just asking you to consider the situation and you'll see it would be fair I should get a piece of this. Maybe not *half*, I'm not a greedy guy, but—"

Dortmunder stopped, on the sidewalk. People and traffic went by in all directions. He said, "Gus, you and I went out there to make a little visit and it *didn't happen*. You went away—"

"John, don't fault me," Gus said. "You would've went away, too."

"Absolutely," Dortmunder said. "And I wouldn't come to you afterward and say we did this and we did that."

"Sure you would," Gus said. "Can we walk, John? Where are we walking anyway?"

Dortmunder started walking again, and Gus kept pace. "Uptown," Dortmunder said.

"Thank you. About us sharing—"

"No, Gus," Dortmunder said. "That little visit *stopped*. You went away, and I was arrested."

"Yeah, I read about that," Gus said, and shook his head with empathetic concern. "Wow, that was a close one."

"It wasn't a close one," Dortmunder said, "it was a direct hit. I was *arrested*."

People going by looked at them, but kept going. Gus said, "You don't have to shout about it, John, it isn't like hitting the lottery or something."

Patiently, calmly, Dortmunder said, "After I was arrested, I escaped. Nobody helped me, and especially you didn't help me, I just—"

"Come on, John."

"—escaped. And after I escaped I went back to that house, and that was a completely different visit, that didn't have one thing to do with you. You were gone, and I was escaped, and it was a whole new start. So what I got was what *I* got and not what *we* got."

They walked half a block in silence, Gus absorbing the philosophy of Dortmunder's concept, and then he sighed and said, "John, we been friends a long time."

"I would say," Dortmunder said, "we've been associates a long time."

"Okay, a little more precise, fine. I understand your position here, I'd be a little aggrieved at my partner, too, if the circumstances were reversed, but John I'm asking you to put yourself in *my* position for a minute. I'm still the guy that found the score, and I still have this like empty feeling that the score went down and I didn't get bupkis for it."

"You should've stuck around," Dortmunder said, unsympathetically. "We could've escaped together."

"John, you're usually a reasonable kind of a guy."

"I'm trying to break myself of that."

"So that's how you want to end it. Bad feelings all around."

Again, Dortmunder stopped in the flow of pedestrian traffic to turn and frown at Gus, studying him, thinking it over. Gus faced him, being dignified, and finally Dortmunder said, "Did you hear about the ring?"

Gus looked bewildered. "Ring? What ring?"

I'm going to tell him the story, Dortmunder decided, and if he laughs that's it, let him walk away. "It's the reason I went back to the house," he said.

"Which I thought, when I realized what must have happened," Gus said, "was a very gutsy thing to do."

"It was a very necessary thing to do," Dortmunder told him, "given what happened."

"Something happened?"

"After I was arrested, the cops asked the guy, did he take anything? And the guy said, he took my ring, he's wearing my ring. And it was *my* ring, that May gave me, and the cops made me take it off and give it to the guy."

Gus's jaw dropped. "He stole your *ring*?"

Dortmunder watched him like a hawk. "That's what happened."

"Why, that bastard!" Gus cried, and pedestrians made wider detours around them as they stood there. "That son of a bitch, to do a thing like that!"

Dortmunder said, "You think so?"

"They've already got you caught," Gus said, "they've got you arrested, you're facing heavy time, and he has to rub your nose in it? What a crappy guy!"

Dortmunder said, "Let's walk."

"Sure."

They started walking, and Gus said, "I can't get over it. I never heard such a nasty thing to do. Kick a guy when he's down."

"That's why I had to escape," Dortmunder said. "I had to go back there and try to get my ring back, only the guy was already gone. So I took all that other stuff instead."

"I get ya," Gus said.

"But I still want my ring," Dortmunder said.

"Naturally," Gus said. "Me, I'd chase the son of a bitch around the world if I had to."

"It was looking like that was exactly what I was gonna have to do," Dortmunder told him, "only now it turns out, he's at another of his places, right here in New York."

"No kidding," Gus said.

"*Also* got a lot of nice stuff in it," Dortmunder said.

"I bet it does."

"We're going in there tonight," Dortmunder said, "try to get my ring, pick up whatever else's around."

"We?"

"Andy Kelp and a lockman, I don't know who yet, and me. You wanna make it four?"

Gus thought about that. "You mean, forget the Carrport thing, and come in with you on this one."

"That's it."

"Deal me in," said Gus.

22

Max was furious. To be talked to like that, to be *chastised*, by some pip-squeak stooge, was intolerable. Max was shaking when he finally left Judge Mainman's chambers at two-thirty—an hour and a half with that moron!—shaking with frustration and rage, ready to commit a personal murder with his own two hands for the first time in years and years. "That—that—that—"

"I wouldn't say it, Max," Walter Greenbaum advised, walking beside him. Walter, Max's personal attorney with the heavy bags under his eyes, could even make a statement like that sound like profundity.

"At least not until we're out of the building," said John Weisman, walking on Max's other side.

John Weisman was another attorney, yet another of Max's attorneys. It seemed to Max sometimes that he had attorneys the way Chinese restaurants have roaches. Every time you turned on the light, there were more of them. This one, John Weisman, was a specialist, Max's bankruptcy attorney. The man devoted his life to bankruptcy cases, and charged an arm and a leg, and lived very well indeed off bankruptcy, proving either that you *can* get blood from a turnip, or a lot of those things claiming to be turnips were lying.

In any event, Weisman didn't have Walter's solonic majesty, so that his not-till-we're-outside crack merely sounded like a not-till-we're-outside crack. A compact lean man in tip-top physical condition, Weisman apparently spent all his spare time in rugged pursuits, hunting, camping, hiking, mountain climbing, you name it. Max personally thought it showed great restraint on Weisman's part not to come to court in a camouflage uniform.

Although today it was Max who might have been better in camouflage. Judge Mainman, a fat-faced petty inquisitor, had treated him with such *disdain*, such *contempt*, as though there were something wrong with a successful man wishing to avail himself of the benefits of the law. Why would successful men buy legislators, if they weren't to make use of the resulting laws? But try to tell that to Judge Mainman.

"I can't do it, you know," Max said, as they left the court building, down all those broad shallow steps that irritatingly forced you to *think* about every step you took—rather appropriate for a courthouse, actually—and across the sidewalk full of scruffy *people* in Max Fairbanks's *way*, to the waiting limousine, whose waiting chauffeur in timely fashion opened the rear door.

The attorneys waited until everybody was inside the limo and the door shut, and then Walter said, "Can't do what?" while Weisman said, "Sorry, Mr. Fairbanks, you have no choice."

Walter looked at Weisman: "Has no choice in what?"

"Selling the house."

"I can't do it," Max said. The limousine pulled smoothly and silently away from the rotten courthouse. "It's a personal humiliation. It's a humiliation within my own company! In front of my own employees!"

"Still," Weisman said, "we do have the order."

The order. Judge Mainman, the puny despot, had been fuming when they'd entered his chambers, petulant that anyone would treat his magnificent decisions lightly. He didn't believe Max's *sworn* statement that he'd only gone out to Carrport to pick up some important papers, and he'd made his disbelief insultingly obvious. He was so affronted, this minor little pip-squeak of a judge, he was *so* affronted, he spoke at first with apparent seriousness about reopening the entire Chapter Eleven proceeding, a move that could only improve his creditors' prospects and cost Max who knows how much more money. Millions. Actual money; millions.

So it had been necessary to *grovel* before the son of a bitch, to apologize, to promise to take the bastard's orders *much* more seriously from now on, and then to *thank* the miserable cretin for backing off from an entire junking of the agreement, backing off to a mere order to *sell the Carrport house.*

Yes. Sell the house, put the proceeds from the sale into the bankruptcy fund, and let it be dribbled away into the coffers of the creditors. And every single TUI employee in middle management and above, every last one of them who had ever spent a night, a weekend, a seminar *afternoon*, out at the Carrport house, would understand that the boss had lost the house to a miserable bankruptcy judge.

"There's got to be some way out of this," Max said. "Come on, one of you, think of something."

Walter said, "Max, John's right. You have to put the property on the market. The best you can do is hope it isn't sold between now and the time we're finished with this adjustment."

"Well, no," Weisman said. "The house has now been placed in the category of assets to be disbursed, there's nothing we can do about that."

"Hmmmmm," said Walter. Even his hmmmmms sounded wise.

Max said, "If I put it on the market at some outlandish price? So no one will *ever* buy it?"

"Then you're in contempt of court," Weisman said. "You have to offer the house for sale at fair market price, and I have to so represent to the court. There's nothing else to be done."

Bitter, brooding, Max twisted his new ring around and around and around on his finger. He wasn't even conscious of that gesture any more, it had become so habitual so soon. "I've lost the goddam house," he said.

"Sorry, Mr. Fairbanks," Weisman said, "but you have."

Walter said, "Max, you'll just have to put this behind you, and look ahead." Even Walter, though, couldn't make *that* twaddle sound like anything but twaddle.

Max said, "I can go out there one more time?"

"So the court has ordered," Weisman said. "After apprising the court, you're permitted one final overnight visit, to gather and remove personal and corporate possessions and to make a last inventory."

Miss September. Maybe that goddam burglar will be there again; this time, I'll shoot him. "It's a hell of a small silver lining," Max grumbled, "for such a great big fucking cloud."

23

"Don't look now," May said, "but that's Andy."

So of course Dortmunder *did* look, and it was Andy all right, across the restaurant, having dinner and a nice bottle of red wine with an attractive woman with a nice smile. The woman caught Dortmunder looking at her, so Dortmunder faced his own meal again, and said, "You're right."

"I told you not to look," May said. "Now she's staring at us."

"She'll stop after a while," Dortmunder said, and concentrated on his lamb chop.

May said, "Andy doesn't want to know us at the moment, or he'd come over, or wave, or something."

Dortmunder shifted lamb to his cheek: "I've had moments, I felt the same way about him."

"I wonder who she is," May said.

Dortmunder didn't wonder who she was, or have anything else to add on the topic, so conversation lapsed, and they both continued to eat the pretty good food.

It was just after eight o'clock in the evening, and the restaurant in the N-Joy Broadway Hotel was thinning out, most tourists eating early because they ate early at home, or because they were going to a show afterward, or because they were exhausted and wanted to go to bed. May was having wine with dinner but Dortmunder was not, partly because he generally didn't drink before going to work and partly because May would be going home after dinner and it would be up to Dortmunder to keep himself awake until midnight.

They'd talked it over this evening, upstairs, before coming down to dinner. There was a possibility there would be complications tonight, since it was impossible to know ahead of time just what they would meet when the maid service elevator doors opened down below at the apartment level. If they met trouble of some kind, and if the law got involved, and if the law came to understand that the interlopers had descended from the hotel, it would probably not be a good idea for May to be asleep somewhere in that same hotel under a false name, riding on a false credit card. So after dinner she would pack up a small amount of her stuff, leaving her large suitcase for Dortmunder with any luck to fill later with items once belonging to Max Fairbanks, and she would take a taxi home, hoping to hear from Dortmunder in person in the morning rather than via the morning news.

Dortmunder hadn't known Andy Kelp intended to be in the hotel this early in the evening, nor that he'd be with a woman. Was she the lockman? There were some very good female lockmen, with slender and agile fingers, but in taking that one look over his shoulder Dortmunder didn't think he'd recognized her as anybody he'd ever seen before. And if she were the lockman, wouldn't Andy bring her over and introduce her, so maybe they could all have dinner together? So she was probably a civilian, which made it less than brilliant for Andy to have brought her here, but who knew why Andy did what he did?

"Probably," Dortmunder said, finishing his lamb chop and dabbing his mouth with his napkin, "she's an undercover cop and he doesn't know it."

May looked over that way, past Dortmunder's shoulder. *She* could look, but he wasn't supposed to. "I doubt it," she said. "Are we going to have dessert?"

"I always did before," Dortmunder said.

The waiter came over, at his signal, and it turned out there wasn't an actual dessert menu, nor even one of those dessert carts they wheel around so you can point at what you want. Instead, what the waiter had was all the desserts memorized, and he was so proud of this accomplishment he was happy to reel them off as many times as the customer wanted. Unfortunately, he had them memorized in order, so if you said, for instance, "The third one, with the butterscotch on top. Was that chocolate or vanilla underneath?" he didn't know. All he could do was reel off *all* the desserts again, and go more slowly when he got to the third one.

But eventually Dortmunder got them all memorized in his own mind as well, and then he could choose, the pecan swirl vanilla cake with the raspberry sauce, and May could have the rocky road ice cream, and they could both have coffee, and the waiter went away, and Dortmunder wondered how long it would be before he could clear his head of all those desserts. It was worse than the Anadarko family of Carrport, Long Island.

He wondered if the Anadarkos were related to Max Fairbanks. Probably not.

"Don't look now," May said, "but they're leaving."

So naturally Dortmunder looked, and when he turned around of course the woman was facing in this direction anyway, standing beside the table, and she noticed his movement, and she looked him straight in the eye for the second time in one meal. Dortmunder blinked like a fish and faced front, and May said, "I told you don't look."

"If you don't want me to look," he pointed out, "don't tell me what they're doing."

May looked past his shoulder again. "They're walking away now," she said. "He has his arm around her waist."

"I don't even care," Dortmunder said.

It took his entire dessert to get him back in a good mood.

24

Dinner at the Lumleys'. Lutetia enjoyed the Lumleys because, although they'd been rich for more than one generation, they still liked to talk about money. Harry Lumley was in commercial real estate in various cities around the globe—at the moment, briskly withdrawing himself from Hong Kong *and* Singapore—while Maura Lumley was in cosmetics, specializing in strangely colored lip and nail treatments for high school girls. "There are *millions* in those little idiots," Maura liked to say. "All you have to do is *draw* it out of them."

They were ten tonight at the Lumleys', in their Fifth Avenue penthouse duplex overlooking Central Park just north of the Metropolitan Museum. The other three couples were also rich, of course, the gentlemen being captains of industry, or at least captains of stock shares, and their wives being extremely attractive in that lacquered way required of women who have married recent money. The conversation ranged over politics and taxes and dining experiences around the globe. It was all very pleasant, very ordinary, very reassuring, and it wasn't until the sorbet that Lutetia noticed Max wasn't saying anything.

Now what? Managing Max was a full-time job, and not always an easy one. Lutetia didn't mind the work, she knew she was good at it, but there were times when she wished he had come with an owner's manual. Usually at an evening like this, Max would be very much an element of the party, full of gossip, full of jokes about politicians, full of ethnic humor and racial humor and class humor and economic humor, but tonight he was merely being attentive, smiling at other people's humor, eating distractedly, adding nothing to the occasion, looking at his watch from time to time.

He's a million miles away, Lutetia thought, but in which direction?

From that point, through the rest of the meal and on to the brandy or port on the terrace afterward, Central Park a great black sleeping beast stretched out below them, Lutetia did her best to *involve* Max, stimulate him, make him enter into the spirit of the occasion. She even went so far as to remind him of two or three of his favorite stories, asking him to regale the group with them; something she *never* did. And the worst of it was, he readily agreed, only to produce an amiable but mechanical recital, without his usual clever dialects and mischievous facial expressions, so that his efforts—or hers, through him—produced only mild laughter, merely polite.

He wasn't *sullen*, he didn't appear to be *angry*, his manner wasn't what you could call *worried*, there was nothing *hostile* about him. He just wasn't Max, that's all. Lutetia began to be afraid.

It wasn't until they were in the limo, going through dark Central Park on their slightly roundabout way home, that the penny, or the shoe, or whatever it was, dropped. Lutetia had resolved not to raise the subject, not to pose any questions, not to do a thing except watch Max with extreme care, ready to jump at the slightest unexpected sound, so he was the one who at last broached the topic: "The judge," he said.

She looked at him, alert, wary. "Yes?"

"He apparently has . . . I've apparently given him *power* over me beyond . . . It's certainly not what I thought this legal square dance was all about."

"He displeased you."

"If he were crossing the road ahead of us," Max said, gesturing at the winding blacktop road in the dim-lit leafy park, "I'd have Chalmers run him down."

Chalmers was the driver. Mildly, Lutetia said, "Do you think Chalmers would do it?"

"If I told him to, he'd damn well better."

"What did the judge do, my dear?"

There were really quite a few lights in the park. Max's face was now plain, now in shadow. It seemed to Lutetia his expression was pained. "He humiliated me," he said.

Oh, dear. Lutetia well knew there was little short of death you could do to Max Fairbanks worse than that. She herself might argue with him, defy him, even sneer at him, but she would make damn sure she was out of the country first, if she ever decided it had become necessary to humiliate him; by divorce, for instance, or a public affair with a poor person. Sympathizing, grateful to Max for having shared his pain with her, she took his hand in both of hers and said, "You give these little people power, Max, they don't always use it well."

In the next passing streetlight, she could see his grateful smile, and smiled back. She said, "Tell me what he did."

"First he threatened to open the entire Chapter Eleven again, which would cost us millions. Literally, millions. Walter and that other fellow, Weisman, groveled at the bastard's feet while I sat quietly in the background—"

"Good."

"And at last he agreed to a compromise. And even *that* I didn't understand until afterward, when the lawyers explained it to me."

They were out of the park now, driving down the well-lit Seventh Avenue, and Lutetia could see Max plain. What he had been covering back at the Lumleys', hiding with a veneer of polite good humor, was a haggard vulnerability, an uncharacteristic self-doubt. Still holding his hand in both of hers, she said, "What was it? What did he do?"

"He took away the Carrport house."

This was so unexpected she very nearly laughed, but realized in time that Max would not put up with being laughed at over this matter. Swallowing her amusement, she said, "What do you mean, took it away?"

"It has to be sold, and the proceeds added to the Chapter Eleven pot."

Lutetia studied him, not understanding. "I don't see— That's annoying, of course, but why does it hit you so *hard*?"

They were stopped at a traffic light. He shook his head, angry with himself, and looked out at busy midtown, just before midnight. "I suppose I've made a fetish of that house," he said. "I enjoyed— You were never there."

"You never wanted me there."

"You never wanted to be there."

That was true. The Carrport house was a part of Max's corporate business, and nothing to do with her. It was used for corporate matters of various kinds, which would bore her, and also, she suspected, for hanky-panky, about which she didn't want to know. "I wasn't interested in a suburban house on Long Island," she acknowledged. "But why was it so important to you?"

"*I* was the host out there," he said. "The master, the thane. I enjoyed that, bringing management out, being, I don't know, lord of the manor or some such thing. That was the only place where I was physically the commander of my armies, all gathered around me. Feudalism, I suppose. It may sound foolish . . ."

"As a matter of fact," she told him, "it sounds quite real. Not something you would have normally told me."

"That's true enough." Max shook his head. "Not something I'd even told myself before. I never understood how important Carrport was to me."

"So this judge," Lutetia said, "he didn't merely take away a corporate asset, he stole a part of your pleasure in who you are."

"Irreplaceable," he said.

"Oh, no, my dear," she assured him. "You'll get over it, and you'll find some other symbol. It was only a symbol, re-

ally, not actually *you*. Some other house, a plane, a ship—
Have you thought about a ship?"

He frowned at her, as though she might be making fun of
him. "A ship? What are you talking about, Lutetia?"

"A number of men," she said carefully, "financial giants,
somewhat like you, have found comfort in commanding a
yacht. You could dock it here in New York, travel all sorts of
places in it, have your management meetings aboard it, do all
the things you used to do in Carrport."

He looked at her with growing suspicion. "You don't like
ships. You don't like being on the water."

"I was never interested in Carrport either, remember? This
would be *your* place. Even better than Carrport, I should
think. Master of your own ship, on the high seas."

Really suspicious now, he said, "Lutetia, why are you so
good to me?"

"Because, my dear," she told him, with absolute truth,
"you're so good to me."

The car had stopped now in front of the theater. The show
inside—*Desdemona!*—had broken nearly an hour ago, and
the lobby was half-lit, visible through its bank of glass doors.
Arthur, their doorman/lift operator, came out of the lobby,
crossed the broad sidewalk still rich in pedestrians, and
opened the rear door for them. Lutetia emerged first, and just
heard Max, behind her, say to Chalmers, "Wait."

They crossed the sidewalk together, following Arthur,
Lutetia saying, "You told Chalmers to wait? Are you going
out again?"

"I'm going to Carrport."

Arthur held the lobby door, and they stepped through,
Lutetia staring at Max, saying, "Are you mad? You just told
me the judge took it away from you!"

"I'm permitted one last visit," he explained, as Arthur
opened the elevator doors and they boarded. "To remove my
personal possessions, inventory that shouldn't be sold with
the property. One overnight."

"*Now?* It's nearly midnight!"

"When else am I going to do it?"

The elevator sped upward and Max gave her the open frank and honest look she mistrusted so. "I have to leave tomorrow in any event, then I'm in Washington, then Chicago, then Sydney, then Nevada, on and on. The place has to be put on the market right away."

The doors opened at their reception room. "Wait," Max told Arthur, as Lutetia clapped the apartment lights on.

As they crossed the reception room, Lutetia said, "So you won't come back here tomorrow, but go from Carrport straight to Kennedy and fly south."

"That makes the most sense," he said. "I'll just grab the papers I need, and my overnight bag. I'll be out there by one, sleep, have most of the day tomorrow to do my inventory, say my . . . good-byes, to the house."

And have it off with some tootsie, Lutetia thought. Her antennae were always very good. Following him into the bedroom, she said, "I'll come with you."

He stopped, as though he'd run into a glass wall. Turning, he said, "You will not."

"But I really should," she said. "And I want to. You're right, I never did see the place out there, and this will be my last chance. Now that I know it means so much to you, I feel I should be with you when you say your farewells." Resting a loving hand on his forearm, she said, "I want to feel close to you, Max, you know that. I want to be a help to you."

"But you don't want to— You have so much to do *here*."

"As a matter of fact, no," she said, and smiled her sunniest smile. "The next two days, my calendar is absolutely empty. I can't think of anything nicer to do, anything more romantic, than to be driven out to your thane's castle with you for your final night there, to spend the night with you, there, in the symbol of your inner self. There must be fireplaces. Tell me there are fireplaces."

Trying for a friendly smile, nearly accomplishing it, he said, "Love petal, you don't want to do that. An unfamiliar house, you'll be uncomfortable, away from everything you care for, stuck in—"

"But *you* are everything I care for, dearest," she assured

him, and then allowed slight doubt to color her features as she said, "Unless . . . You don't have any *other* reason for going out there by yourself, do you?"

"Of course not, sweet minx," he said, and spontaneously hugged her, and let her go. "You know me better than that, my warm bunny."

"Then it's settled," she announced, innocent and happy. "Off we go!"

"Off we go," he echoed, less exuberantly. He looked as though the dinner he'd eaten at the Lumleys' might be disagreeing with him. He sighed, and his next smile was a brave one. "I'll just get my . . . things."

25

The lockman was not the woman from the restaurant at dinner. The lockman was Wally Whistler, and Andy Kelp didn't mention the woman at dinner, or dinner itself, or anything about that entire scene. Which was okay with Dortmunder. No sweat off his nose. He didn't mind if Andy Kelp wanted to snub him at dinner and have secrets. Didn't matter to him.

Since Gus Brock had already showed up, a couple minutes early, the arrival of Wally Whistler and Andy Kelp meant the gang was all here. Wally Whistler was a cheerful guy and a first-rate lock expert, whose only flaw was a certain absent-mindedness. He'd once spent a period of time in an upstate prison merely because, visiting the zoo with his kids, he'd absentmindedly fiddled with a lock, and the resulting freed lion had made everybody upset and irritated until the tranquilizer dart had made it possible to put the lion back in his cage. Another time, Wally had been helping some people one night at a Customs warehouse on the Brooklyn docks—people who hadn't wanted to encumber Customs with a lot of documents and forms—and he was, as usual, playing absent-mindedly with locks, and when he realized he'd somehow unlocked his way from the warehouse into the bowels of a cargo ship, the ship had already sailed, and he hadn't managed to get off the thing until Brazil, which was unfortunate, because Brazil and the United States don't have an extradition treaty. Wally Whistler, like some other of Dortmunder's friends, liked to travel by extradition, which meant, when overseas, they'd confess to a crime in America they knew they could prove they hadn't done, be extradited back home, produce the proof of innocence, and walk. Without extradition from Brazil, it had taken Wally a long time indeed to get home, but here he was at last, as good as ever, and just as absentminded.

"This is our room here, that's somebody else," Dortmunder pointed out, seeing Wally drift in the direction of the connecting door to some other room.

"Oh, right," Wally said.

Gus said, "Open sesame."

They looked at him. Dortmunder said, "What?"

"We're going to Aladdin's Cave, aren't we?" Gus asked. "So why don't we do it."

Everybody agreed that was a good idea, so they trooped on out of the room. Wally carried a few small tools in his pockets, but none of the others had brought along anything special. They were prepared to wait and see what they found when they got down to the apartment. It was true Max Fairbanks had to be approached with care, since he was known to carry heat—a memory Dortmunder would retain for a good long time—but they expected that the element of surprise, plus their force of numbers, would be able to deal with that problem.

They took the public elevator down to seventeen, then walked around to that unmarked door in the center section, which Wally went through even more quickly and laconically than Andy had. The four crowded inside—with the maid's cart already there, it was a tight fit—and Wally hummed a little tune as he hunkered down in front of the control board. "Very nice," he commented. "The lockmakers are getting smarter and smarter. *Look* at this stuff."

Dortmunder said, "Is it gonna be a problem?"

For answer, the elevator started down.

"I guess not," Andy said.

The ride was short and smooth, and at the end of it was a closed wood door just like the one up above, except that this one, when Wally tried the knob, wasn't locked. "Less work for mother," Wally said, and cautiously opened the door.

They looked out at hallway, a cream-colored wall decorated with fine Impressionist paintings and faux Roman electric sconces. Wally was about to stick his head out a little farther, look to left and right along this hall, when they all heard the voices.

"Somebody coming," Dortmunder hissed, and Wally eased backward into the elevator, allowing the door to close almost completely, leaving just a hair's breadth through which they could hear the voices as two people walked past the door.

A woman: "—a good night's sleep."

A man (Max Fairbanks! Dortmunder recognized his irritating voice, here sounding rather bitter): "I'm looking forward to it."

Andy whispered, "They're going to bed."

Gus whispered, "Perfect."

Dortmunder visualized himself, in half an hour or so, tiptoeing into that bedroom, the ring in sight at last, gleaming on Fairbanks's sleeping finger, getting closer and closer.

Meanwhile, the woman, her voice receding down the hallway, was saying, "And in the morning, I'll go with you to the airport, and then . . ."

And then she receded out of hearing range, and Wally slowly pushed the door open once more, and the four of them crept out to the gleaming art-filled hallway, with gleaming rooms visible at both ends.

They were about to move when the woman's voice was heard again, distinctly saying, "We're ready, Arthur." So she was one of those people who spoke more loudly to servants. And then she was heard saying, "And you can go home now, I won't be back till tomorrow afternoon."

Dortmunder said, "What?" He turned toward the sound of the voice, while the other three reached out to restrain him.

"Oh, wait," said the woman's voice, and then there was a loud single clapping sound and the lights went out.

Pitch blackness. The sound of an elevator motor, whirring somewhere nearby. "They *left*!" Dortmunder cried.

"Hush! Ssshhh! Hush!" everybody cried, and Andy half-whispered, "There could be other people here."

"In the dark?" Dortmunder demanded. "They're *gone*, goddamit."

Gus said, "How do we get these lights on?"

"Oh, there's nothing to that," Dortmunder snapped. "The point is, we got here *just* too late. The son of a bitch is gone, and you *know* he's got my ring on his goddam fat finger."

The sound of the elevator stopped. The son of a bitch and his woman had reached street level.

Gus said, "What do you mean, there's nothing to that? You know how to turn on the lights?"

"Sure," Dortmunder said. "But we should wait until they get away from here, just in case they happen to look up, that son of a bitch with my ring on his finger."

There was a little silence at that, until Andy said, "*I* don't know how to turn on the lights. You mean there's some trick?"

"No, it's very easy," Dortmunder said, and clapped his hands together once, and the lights came on.

Everybody blinked at everybody else. Gus said, "You clap for the lights to go on?"

"And off," Dortmunder said. "Didn't you hear the sound when they left? It's a stunt kind of electric thing people do, I've run into it a few times. You're going along, minding your own business, you make *just* the wrong noise, the lights come on. People do it in their living rooms, wow their friends. I never saw it in a whole apartment before."

Gus said, "What if they turn on the television, and there's applause?"

"Probably," Dortmunder said, "they get migraine. But the point is, Max Fairbanks and my ring are *gone*."

Aggravated, disconsolate, he turned away and went down to the end of the hall and turned right, and there was the door to the other elevator, over there across the reception room.

Two minutes. Two minutes earlier, and he'd have had Max

Fairbanks in his grip, he'd have gotten his ring back, no question. No question.

No, not even two minutes. Step out of the elevator when the son of a bitch is going by, grab him right then, yank the goddam ring off his finger, and then let the scene play out however it wants. But, no. Cautious, that was his problem. Too goddam cautious, hide in the elevator until it's too late.

"John."

Dortmunder turned, glowering, and there was Gus, who didn't even notice the expression on Dortmunder's face. The expression on Gus's face was one huge beaming smile. In his right hand he held a gold bracelet, and in his left a small but exquisite Impressionist drawing. "John," he said, "about that Carrport deal. I just want you to know. We're square."

"I'm happy for you," Dortmunder said.

26

The maid's cart. Its original cargo of linen and cleaning supplies having been left in a heap on the apartment hallway floor, it was loaded with paintings, jewelry, and other nice tchotchkas, then rolled back into the elevator, and ridden up to the hotel.

Floor seventeen. Gus and Andy went off to snag a regular public elevator, while Dortmunder and Wally waited with the loot. Andy then held that elevator while Gus went back to the turning in the hall to signal that the coast was clear. Then Dortmunder and Wally pushed the very heavy cart down the hall, around the corner and to Andy in the elevator. Then they all went up to twenty-six, where once again Gus stood chickee while the others trundled the cart down to Dortmunder's room. He unlocked them in, Gus joined them, and they emptied the cart onto the bed. Then they reversed the route, took the cart back down to the apartment and loaded it up a second time.

If anybody in the public halls had noticed them on any of their several journeys, things might have gotten somewhat sticky, since none of them actually looked very much like a hotel maid, despite the cart they were pushing, nor were they even in hotel maid uniform, but the N-Joy Broadway Hotel was not a lively place at two and three in the morning, so they remained undisturbed.

Once everything was transferred to Dortmunder's room,

they were all quite pleased by their harvest; except Dort-munder, of course. But the other three had stars in their eyes as they looked around at all this treasure, or possibly dollar signs in their eyes. Sparkly, anyway.

The plan now was, Andy and Gus and Wally would leave, one at a time, each carrying a single small bag plus as much extra little stuff as their pockets would hold. Dortmunder had already put in a wake-up call for 6:00 A.M., at which time he would rise and check out, with these four large suitcases here. "Kennedy Airport," he would loudly tell the cabdriver who took him away from the N-Joy, but a few blocks later he would change the destination to the address of Stoon the fence, about twenty blocks north of the N-Joy on the West Side, where the other three would meet up with him, and where the night's takings would be swapped for cash.

They did their packing, made their preparations, and then Wally left first, fumbling with the room's doorknob as he grinned around at them, saying, "Call me any time, fellas."

"Leave the door alone," Dortmunder said.

"Sorry," Wally said, and left.

Gus was next. "It's true what they say," he announced. "You do good for somebody, it comes right back atcha."

"Mm," said Dortmunder.

"See you around," Gus said, and left, jingling.

Then Andy. Hefting his little bag, he said, "John, don't be so downhearted. *Look* at all the stuff we got."

"Not the ring," Dortmunder said. "The point was to get the ring back. As far as I'm concerned, the son of a bitch can have all this other stuff right now, as long as I get my ring."

"The rest of us don't feel that way, John."

"The rest of you didn't get your ring stolen."

"That's true."

"So you know what this means," Dortmunder said.

"No," Andy admitted. "What does it mean?"

"Washington," Dortmunder said, as gloomy as a man can be in a room full of treasure. "I gotta go to Washington, DC. What do I know about Washington, DC?"

Andy considered, then nodded. "Use your phone?"

Dortmunder shrugged, but couldn't help saying, "Local call?"

"Very local. In the hotel." Andy nodded again and said, "It's time you met Anne Marie."

27

Anne Marie Carpinaw, nee Anne Marie Hurst, didn't know what to make of the fellow she knew as Andy Kelly. In fact, she wasn't sure he was somebody you could make into a thing at all. Maybe he was already made and set, and unalterable.

Different, anyway. In Anne Marie's experience, men were sweaty creatures, harried and hurried, hustling all the time, tiptoeing over quicksand ever, never comfortable in their own minds, in their own skins, in their own circumstances. Her recently decamped husband, Howard Carpinaw, the computer salesman, was definitely of that breed, scrambling from sale to sale, always talking big, always producing little. Her father, the fourteen-term congressman from Kansas, had been the same, had spent twenty-seven years running for reelection, had never devoted a minute of his life to actually calmly *occupying* the position he kept running for, and finally ended his career with a heart attack at yet another rubber chicken Kiwanis luncheon down on the hustings.

Somehow, Andy Kelly wasn't like that. Not that he was disinterested or turned off or bored, he just didn't *try* too hard. For instance, he'd made it plain in their first meeting that he'd like to go to bed with her, but it had also been plain he wouldn't kill himself if she turned him down, whereas most men, in her experience, claimed they *would* kill themselves if she turned them down, and then reneged.

It was sensing something of that difference that had first attracted her attention in the cocktail lounge. She'd already rebuffed three husbands—*obvious* husbands, their wives asleep upstairs reflected in their guilty eyes—and when this other fellow had come in she'd been prepared to rebuff him, too. But then he didn't sit too close to her, didn't smile at her, didn't say harya, didn't acknowledge her existence in any way. And then he got into some amusing conversation—amusing for them, apparently—with the bartender, so it was somewhat in the manner of a person shaking a birthday present to try to guess what's inside the giftwrap that she'd poked out that first word: "Hello." And the rest was becoming history.

So, despite the laconic manner, she knew he was definitely interested in her, but it was plain she wasn't the end of the world. So far, he acted as though nothing was the end of the world. To be around a man for whom life was *not* perpetually at third down and long yardage; what a relief.

On the other hand, she couldn't figure out what he did for a living, and it's still important to know what a man does for a living, because economic and social class are both determined by occupation, and Anne Marie, free spirit though she might be, was not free spirit enough to want to spend time with a man from the wrong economic and social class. Andy seemed to have all the money he needed, and not to worry about it (but then, he didn't worry about anything up till now, that was the charm of the guy). Still, his clothing and manner didn't suggest inherited wealth; this was not some main stem pillar slumming in the N-Joy. She'd hinted around, hoping some occupation would emerge, some *category*, but nothing yet.

Not a lawyer, certainly not a doctor, even more certainly not an accountant or banker. An airline pilot? Unlikely. Not a businessman, they're the sweatiest of them all. Maybe an inventor; was that possible?

She was afraid, the more she thought about it, that what

Andy Kelly was most like was a cabdriver who'd learned not to get aggravated by bad traffic. But would a cabdriver be this cool, in this situation? Intrigued, more so than she'd expected to be, she awaited his return tonight from another "appointment."

Appointments after midnight, two nights in a row. Was that a clue? To what? They weren't appointments with some other woman, she was pretty sure of that, based on his behavior with her afterward. But what appointment could you have that late at night, lasting an hour or two?

Maybe he's a spy, she thought. But who is there to spy on any more? All the spies are retired now, writing books, reading each other's books, and beginning to wonder what the point had been, all those years, chasing each other around in their slot-car racers while the real world went on without them. More of the desperate men, those were, hustling to keep up, falling a little farther behind every day. Nope, not Andy Kelly.

So here it was Thursday night, becoming Friday morning, and on Saturday she was supposed to fly back to KC and then drive across the state on home to Lancaster, and of course that's what she was going to do, it was part of the package, but Andy Kelly was suddenly the wild card in the deck, and she couldn't help asking herself the question: What if he says *don't go*?

Well, most likely he wouldn't say any such thing, why should he? And whoever or whatever he might turn out to be, she did already know for certain he was definitely a New Yorker and never a Lancastrian, so he wouldn't be coming home with her, so either he asked the question or he didn't. And however unlikely it was that he'd ask, she felt she ought to be ready with the answer just in case, so what was the answer?

She didn't know. She was still thinking about it, and she still didn't know, at ten minutes to three in the morning when the phone rang.

She was seated on the bed at the time, back against the headboard, watching an old movie on television with the sound turned off, as an aid to thought, so now she reached out to the phone on the bedside table, kept looking at the people on horseback on the television screen, and said, "Hello."

"Hi, Anne Marie, it's Andy."

"It better be," she said, "or I don't answer the phone at this hour."

"I'm a little late. My appointment took longer than I thought."

"Uh huh."

"But that was okay, because it was very successful."

"Good," she said, wondering, what are we talking about?

"But here's the thing," he said. "There's a friend of mine."

Uh oh, she thought. "Uh huh," she said. Group gropes, is this where we're headed?

"He's got a problem," Andy said, "and I think you're the perfect person to talk to him."

Her voice very cold, Anne Marie said, "And you want to bring him over now."

"That's right, a few minutes talk and— Whoa. Wait a minute. Back up here."

"That's right," she said. She was more disappointed in him than she would have thought possible. "Back *way* up."

"Anne Marie," he said, "get that thought out of your head this second. There are some things in life that are team efforts, and there are some things in life that are solos, you see what I mean?"

"I'm not sure."

"My friend," Andy said, "needs to have a conversation about Washington, DC, and then—"

"Why?"

"He'll explain. He'd like to come talk, maybe five minutes at the max, and then he goes away, and if there's more to it he'll give you a phone call sometime, but at least now you know who he is."

"Who is he?"

"A friend of mine. I'd like to bring him over. Okay?"

She looked around the room. Do I trust Andy? Do I trust

my own instincts? The bed was a mess, clothes were strewn around, the TV was on, though silent. "How soon would you get here?" she asked.

"Two minutes."

Surprised, she said, "Where are you? In the bar?"

"Closer. Be there in two minutes," he said, and hung up.

Two minutes later, the bed was made, the clothes were put away, the TV was off, and there was a knocking at the door. Anne Marie still wasn't sure exactly what was going on here, but Howard was gone, her New York week was winding down, the future was completely unknowable, and her new slogan might as well be Caution To The Winds. So she opened the door, and there was Andy, smiling, and his friend, not smiling.

Well. This new guy wasn't somebody to be afraid of, though at first glance he didn't look right to be Andy's friend. He was not chipper, not at all chipper. He was closer to the kind of men she already knew, except he was down at the end of the struggle, after all the hustling has failed, all the energy has been spent on futile struggle, and the exhaustion of despair has set in. He looked to be in his midforties, and what a lot of rough years those must have been. He was the picture of gloom from his lifeless thinning hair through his slumped shoulders to his scuffed shoes, and he looked at her as though he already knew she wasn't going to be any help.

"Hello," she said, thinking how complicated life could get if you merely kept saying hello to people. She stepped aside, and they came in, and she shut the door.

"Anne Marie," Andy said, "this is John. John, my friend Anne Marie."

"Harya," said John, in a muted way, and stuck his hand out.

She took the hand, and found he was in any event capable of a firm handshake. "I'm fine," she said. "Should we . . . sit down on something?" One bed and one chair; that was the furniture, except for stuff with drawers.

"I'm not staying," John said. "Andy says you grew up in Washington."

"There and Kansas," she acknowledged. "We had homes both places. Usually I went to school in Kansas, but college in Maryland, and then lived mostly in Washington for a few years. With my father and his second wife, and then his third wife."

"The thing is," John said, apparently not that fascinated by her family, "I gotta go to Washington next week, I got a little something to do there, but I don't know the place at all. Andy figured, maybe you could fill me in, answer some questions about the place."

"If I can," she said, doubtful, not knowing what he had in mind.

"Not now," he said. "I know you're busy. But I could like make up a list, my questions, give you a call tomorrow. Now you know who I am."

No, I don't, she thought. She said, "What is it you have to do in DC?"

"Oh, just a little job," he said.

This was not a good answer. She was starting to wonder if she should be worried. What had she got mixed up with here? Terrorists? Fanatics? She said, "It wouldn't involve anything blowing up, would it?"

He gave her a blank look: "Huh?"

Andy said, "Anne Marie, it isn't anything like—" But then he saw the expression on her face, and he shook his head and turned to his friend, saying, "John, the best thing, I think, is level with her."

John obviously didn't think that was the best thing at all. He stared at Andy as though Andy had asked him to change his religion or something. He said, "Level? You mean, level level? On the level?"

Andy said, "Anne Marie, just as a hypothetical, what would you say if I told you we weren't entirely honest?"

"I'd say nobody's entirely honest," she said. "What kind of not honest are you?"

"Well, mostly we pick up things," he said.

John said, "Right. That's it. Pick up things."

She shook her head, not getting it, and Andy said, "You know, like, we see things lying around and we pick them up."

Anne Marie felt her way through the maze of this locution. She didn't quite know how to phrase her next question, but went ahead anyway: "You mean . . . you mean you're thieves?"

Beaming, happy she'd got it, Andy said, "Personally I prefer the word *crook*. I think it's jauntier."

"You're crooks."

"See? It is jauntier."

"These appointments, late at night . . ."

"We're out picking up things," he said. "Or planning it. Or whatever."

"Picking up things." Anne Marie struggled to find firm ground. First tonight she'd thought Andy was slightly enigmatic but fun, then she'd thought he was sexually kinky and maybe dangerously kinky, and then she'd thought he was a homicidal terrorist, and now it turned out he was a thief. Crook. Thief. Too many lightning transformations. Having no idea what she thought of this most recent one, she said, "What did you pick up tonight?"

John, grumbling, said, "Not what I was looking for."

"But a lot of nice things," Andy said. "I would say tonight was one of our more profitable nights, John. In a *long* time."

"Still," John said. He seemed very dissatisfied.

So she turned her attention to John, saying, "What was it you wanted that you didn't find?"

He merely shrugged, as though the memory were too painful, but Andy said, "Tell her, John. She'll understand. I don't know Anne Marie that long, but already I can tell you, she's got a good heart. Go ahead and tell her."

"I hate telling that story, over and over," John said. "It's got the same ending every time."

"Do you mind, I tell it?"

"It'll still come out the same," John said, "but go ahead."

John ostentatiously looked at the blank TV screen, as

though waiting for a bulletin, while Andy said, "What happened, about a week ago John and another fella went to a place that was supposed to be empty—"

"To pick up some things," Anne Marie suggested.

"That's it. Only it wasn't empty, after all, the householder was there, with a gun."

"Ouch," Anne Marie said.

"John's feelings exactly," Andy said. "But that's what we call your occupational hazard, it's all in the game. You know. But what happened next wasn't fair."

John, watching the nothing on TV, growled.

Andy said, "The householder called the cops, naturally, no problem with that. But when the cops got there the householder claimed John stole a ring and was wearing it. Only it was *John's* ring, that his best close personal friend, her name is May, you'd like her, she gave him. And the cops made him give it to the householder."

"That's mean," Anne Marie said, and she meant it. She also thought it was kind of funny, she could see the humor in it, but from the slope of John's shoulders she suspected she would be wiser not to mention that side.

"Very mean," Andy agreed. "So John, after he got away from the police—"

Surprised, she said, "You escaped?"

"Yeah." Even that memory didn't seem to give him much pleasure.

"Oh," she said. "I thought you were out on bail or something."

"No," Andy said, "he got away clean. But he's been looking for the householder ever since, because he wants his ring back. It's got sentimental value, you know."

"Because his friend gave it to him," Anne Marie said, and nodded.

"Because," John said, "he made a fool outta me. I'm gonna feel itchy and uncomfortable until I get that ring back."

"This householder is a very rich householder," Andy said.

"I mean, he didn't *need* the ring. Also, he's got a lot of houses, including one in this very building."

"So last night . . ." she said.

"You know the phrase," he told her. "Last night, we cased the joint."

"Of course."

"And tonight we went there," Andy said, "and we just missed the guy, he was just going out the door. So John did not get his ring."

"Again," John said.

"But we *did* get a lot of other stuff," Andy said. "Nice stuff. As long as we were there."

Anne Marie said, "And this man is going to Washington?"

"Next week. He's got a house there, too. John figures to pay him a visit."

"And this time," John said, "he'll be there."

Anne Marie said, "Where's this house exactly?"

"Well, it's an apartment, is what it is," Andy said. "In the Watergate."

This time she felt she could show her amusement, and did. "John? You want to pull a burglary at the Watergate? A little third-rate burglary at the Watergate?"

Andy said, "I already tried that on him, and it didn't work. John isn't much of a history buff."

Anne Marie said, "So that's why you'll have some questions about DC. You want to get in there, and get your ring, and get out again, and not get into trouble along the way."

"That's it," Andy said.

John, the recital of his tale of woe at last finished, turned away from the TV screen and said, "So if it's okay with you, I'll give you a call here tomorrow, sometime, whenever you say. I'll have some questions figured out."

"Sure," Anne Marie said. "Or . . ." And she allowed a pause to grow, while she lifted an eyebrow at Andy, who gave her a bright look but no other response. So she said to John, "Did Andy tell you my own situation at the moment?"

"He didn't tell me anything," John said, "except you knew Washington."

"Well, my marriage seems to have hit an underwater stump and sunk," she said. "Theoretically, I'm supposed to go home on Saturday, but I'm not sure I think of it as home any more. I'm not sure *what* to think, to tell you the truth. I'm at kind of loose ends here."

"Anne Marie," Andy said, "I wouldn't have hoped to even ask this, but I'm wondering. Do you mean that you think you could stick around some, give us advice along the way?"

"It's been awhile since I've been in DC," she said.

John's head lifted. He damn near smiled. He almost looked normal. He said, "Yeah?"

Andy, with all evidence of delight, said, "Anne Marie! You'd come along?"

"If I wasn't in the way."

"In the way? How could you be in the way?" Andy looked at John, and they grinned at each other, and Andy said, "John? Is Anne Marie in the way?"

"Not in *my* way," John said.

Andy looked back at Anne Marie, and grew more serious. He said, "Is it gonna bother you? You know, us picking up things, here and there, along the way? I mean, that's what we *do*. Is that gonna be a problem?"

Anne Marie smiled, and shook her head. She had no idea what she was doing, or why, or what was going to happen next, but there was no other door in her life right now she could think of opening that had even the prospect of fun behind it. "I'm a politician's daughter, Andy," she said. "Nothing shocks me."

28

Fortunately, just before they'd left the apartment in the N-Joy, Max had managed to sneak a cellular phone into the bathroom and call Miss September to tell her do *not*, repeat *not*, come out to Carrport tonight, we'll get together soon, my little fur muffin, I'll call the next time I'm in the northeast, do *not* come to Carrport. And off he went, willy-nilly, with Lutetia.

But then it wasn't so bad. The old love in a new setting, an invigorating change of pace. And the memory of Miss September so recently on this black silk sheet—laundered since; ah, well—could only add to the spirit of the occasion.

Max was feeling so pleased with himself, and with life, and with the success of his maneuvering, and with his recent decision that TUI should replace the Carrport house with a corporate yacht, that next morning, over bran muffins and coffee, he showed Lutetia his new ring, his pride and joy, and explained its history.

She was amused and appalled, exactly the response he'd been hoping for. "Max, what a terrible person you are!" she cried, laughing at him across the breakfast table. "To treat that poor fellow that way."

"You should have seen the expression on his face," Max said. "It was priceless. He looked like a basset hound."

"You'd better hope," she told him, "he never gets to see *your* face again."

"Somehow I don't think," Max said, comfortably twirling the ring on his finger, "we travel in the same circles."

After breakfast, Max went through the house one final time, finding very little in it he cared about. All this safe bland decorating, good for the corporate image but not exactly hearty, nothing that stuck in the mind or created a yearning for possession. Leave it, leave it all, sell the stuff. The damn burglar got everything of value, anyway.

Lutetia found a squat brown vase she liked. "It reminds me of you," she said, "when you've been bad and you're afraid you'll be caught."

"Oh, my sweetness," Max said, pursing his mouth and trying to look like Sydney Greenstreet in a pet, "how you talk to me."

"I'll put dried flowers in it," she decided, holding the vase up to see it better in the light. "It will fit in wonderfully at the apartment. The place is almost perfect as it is, so carefully put together—*you* wouldn't notice a thing like that—but occasionally one still finds something to add to the effect."

"Take it," Max said, magnanimous to a fault. "If it shows up on some inventory somewhere, we'll say the burglar got it."

"Of course he did," Lutetia said. "He has a very good eye, your burglar."

"Especially for rings," Max said, with a malicious little leer.

Lutetia laughed, and clucked her disapproval, and went away to put the vase in her overnight bag, while Max went to the library to get the only thing he actually cared about in this building. The Book, his guide, the source of his self-image and strength, the home of *Tui*, the Joyous. It was called the I Ching, and it was the soul of the wisdom of the East, and Max put it in his bag.

Then they were ready to go. They had sent Chalmers and the limo back to the city last night. The burglar had made off with the Lexus, of course, leaving in the garage the Honda van for the transportation of middle management in manageable groups, and the Mazda RX-7, the very paradigm of the little red foreign sports car. (Little red foreign sports cars used to be Italian or French, but times change, times change.) The Chapter Eleven judge could have the Honda, and be damned to him, but the Mazda would stay with Max, definitely, and no arguments.

It was without a backward glance that Max left the Carrport house for the last time, at the wheel of the little red Mazda, Lutetia beside him, his mind full of plans for the yacht—to be called *Joyous*—as he also idly wondered where they'd stop for lunch. Somewhere on the water, for preference.

A lovely day, all in all, whizzing around Long Island in the little red car, finding an acceptable seafood restaurant with a view southward over the Atlantic, chatting and joshing with Lutetia, the two of them in a jolly mood. It was, in fact, delightful to Max, that in his uxorious moments, at those times when, out of necessity or conviction, he wanted to be a husband, he had found for the role such a wife as Lutetia. (The I Ching had helped him choose her, of course, from the then-available herd.)

Then at last they made their way to Kennedy Airport for Max's midafternoon flight. He would enplane to Savannah, to be met there by the car that would take him to Hilton Head, while Lutetia drove the Mazda back to the city and stashed it in the basement garage at the N-Joy.

"I have a few stops to make along the way," she told him. "Antique shops and whatnot, you'll probably get to the island before I make it home. I'll phone you when I get there."

She did, too.

29

Dortmunder was under the bathroom sink when the phone rang. He was down there, with hammer and screwdrivers and pliers and grout, because of the responsibility of having money all of a sudden. Before this, the space behind the top drawer in the bedroom dresser had always been enough for whatever stash he had to tuck away, but not now.

It was rolling in, all at once, just rolling in. First the twenty-eight grand for the stuff he took out of the house in Carrport, then the thirteen fifty for the Lexus that also came from the same house, and now twenty-four and a half large was his share of the proceeds from the last visit to the N-Joy Broadway Hotel night before last, where it turned out Mrs. Fairbanks's taste was both exquisite and expensive. Even after spending a little on himself and May, Dortmunder still had over fifty thousand dollars American in his kick. A lot to take care of.

So that's why he was under the sink, constructing a new bank down there, when the phone rang. It's Andy, he thought, struggling backward out from under the sink. Ouch! Dammit! That hurt. I know it's Andy.

Only it wasn't. "Hey, John," said a hearty voice to Dortmunder's surly hello. "Ralph here."

Ralph. Dortmunder knew a couple of Ralphs; which one was this? "Oh, yeah," he said. "How you doing?"

"Just fine," said Ralph, and faintly in the background ice cubes could be heard, clinking against a glass.

Oh. So this was Ralph Winslow, another lockman, the one Andy would have gone to if Wally Whistler had been unavailable. Unless working on a particularly complex safe, Ralph Winslow at all times had a glass of rye and water in his hand, ice cubes clinking.

Was this another visit somewhere? If so, he'd have to turn it down. Max Fairbanks was a full-time occupation. "What's up?" Dortmunder asked.

"Well, I'm just calling," Ralph said, "to tell you I'm with you one hundred percent."

This sentence didn't seem to have any content. Dortmunder said, "Thanks, Ralph."

"I heard about the business with the ring," Ralph explained.

Dortmunder's eyebrows came together at the middle of his nose. "Oh, you did, did you?"

"And I want you to know," Ralph said, "it coulda happened to any one of us."

"That's right," Dortmunder said, full of belligerence.

"And whoever it might have happened to," Ralph went on, "it was a shitty thing the guy did."

"Right again," Dortmunder said, softening a bit.

"And I wish ya the best with gettin it back."

"Thanks, Ralph," Dortmunder said. "I appreciate that."

"Any time, if there's anything I can do," Ralph said, "help out a little, just let me know."

"I'll do that."

"He can't treat us that way, you know what I mean?"

Us. Dortmunder almost felt like saluting. "I know what you mean," he said, "and thanks, Ralph."

"That's all," Ralph said. "I gotta go. See you around."

"Sure," Dortmunder said, and went back under the sink, feeling a little better about life, not even much minding the little nicks and bloodlettings that were a part of his carpentry, and five minutes later the phone rang.

"Now, *that* one's Andy," Dortmunder muttered, backing

out from under the sink. "Ouch. Why doesn't he just come over, he's got so much to say? Come over and help."

But this one wasn't Andy either: "John? Fred Lartz here."

"Oh, yeah, Fred. How you doing?"

Fred Lartz was a driver, or at least he used to be a driver, and the unspoken agreement among his friends was that he still was a driver, though the truth was he'd lost his nerve ever since that unfortunate afternoon, coming back from a cousin's wedding on Long Island, when he happened to take a wrong turn on the Van Wyck Expressway—there had been alcohol at this wedding—and wound up on taxiway 17 at Kennedy Airport, with an Eastern Airlines flight, just in from Miami, coming fast the other way. After he got out of the hospital he was never quite the same, but he was still Fred Lartz the driver, the guaranteed best getaway specialist in the business. Only these days it was his wife, Thelma, who did the actual driving, while Fred sat beside her to give advice. The two of them still only got one split, so nobody minded. (And though nobody would ever say so, Thelma was better than Fred had ever been.)

Now, Fred said, "I'm doing fine, John. I just wanted to tell you, Thelma and me, we heard about your trouble, and we just want to say, it was a rotten thing to happen, and you don't want to let it get you down."

"Oh," said Dortmunder. "You mean the, uh, the, uh, the ring, uh . . ."

"That's it," Fred said. "Thelma and me, we feel for you, John, and if there's anything either of us can do, any way we can help out, you just give us a call."

"Well, thanks, Fred."

"Will you do that?"

"Count on it," Dortmunder said, and they said their good-byes, and five minutes later the phone rang.

"I think I'm getting too much sympathy," Dortmunder told his hammer, put it down, backed out from under the sink—ouch—and this time it was Jim O'Hara, a general purpose workman like Gus Brock or Andy Kelp, and he too had heard about the stolen ring and wished to offer his condolences and expressions of solidarity. Dortmunder thanked him, and hung up, and decided not to try going under the sink for a while. Instead, he got himself a beer and sat in the living room by the phone, and waited.

Somebody had been doing a lot of gossip; Gus, maybe, or Wally Whistler. Or both. Or everybody by now.

In the next half hour, he heard from five more guys, all associates in the job, all expressing their best wishes in his troubles. It was like being in the hospital, only without the flowers. He was gracious, within his limitations, and had two more beers, and decided not to work on the bank under the sink at all today. Until tomorrow, the money could stay where it was, in a brown paper supermarket bag, closed with masking tape and shoved up against the wall behind the sofa where Dortmunder sat.

Again, the phone rang. Dortmunder answered, in his new gracious voice, saying, "Hi."

"Hello, John, it's Wally."

Wally? Wally Whistler? Why would Wally Whistler call to offer sympathy, when they'd already been through all this together at the N-Joy? "Hello, there, Wally," Dortmunder said.

"I just wanted to tell you," Wally said, sounding as though he had a cold or something, "your friend isn't at Hilton Head any more."

Wally. In Dortmunder's mind, Wally now morphed from Wally Whistler, the lockman, to Wally Knurr, the computer genius who was tracking Max Fairbanks for him. Catching the sense of what this Wally had just said, Dortmunder lunged upward, wide-eyed. "What? Where is he?"

"Don't know," this Wally said. "A fax just went out to his people that he's unavailable from now, Saturday, until Monday morning."

"And where's he gonna be Monday morning?"

"Oh, that doesn't change," Wally said. "He still has to appear before that committee, so from Monday morning his schedule's the same. It's just over the weekend."

"Thanks, Wally," Dortmunder said, and hung up, and sat brooding at his empty beer can. This didn't change anything, since he'd never for a second had it in mind to attack an island off the South Carolina coast—piracy was not part of his job description—but it was still confusing, and maybe worrisome.

Unavailable? Max Fairbanks unavailable? To his own people, Max Fairbanks was *never* unavailable. So what's going on? What's happened?

And where is Max Fairbanks?

"I'm not even supposed to *be* here," Max complained to the detective. Running distraught fingers through rumpled hair, he said, "I'm supposed to be preparing for my testimony before Congress on Monday. I have to *talk to Congress* on Monday. I don't see what I'm accomplishing here at all. I don't see it at all. What am I accomplishing? I'm not accomplishing anything here, I'm not even supposed to *be* here."

The detective calmly but disinterestedly waited for Max to run down. He was a thirtyish chunky fellow with bushy black hair and a long fleshy nose, and he had introduced himself as Detective Second Grade Bernard Klematsky. He didn't look much like a detective of any grade, but more like a high school math teacher, with his rumpled gray suit and rumpled blue tie. But he was the detective in charge of the burglary at the N-Joy apartment, he was laconic as hell, and he just had a few questions to ask.

Well, for that matter, so did Max. What the hell *happened* here? It's as though a tornado had been through, and cleaned the place out. Nothing large had been taken, not the grand piano or the antique armoire in the master bedroom or the medieval refectory table here in the reception room, or anything like that. But everything, everything, every item of any value at all small enough to fit into the overhead bin or under the seat in front of you was *gone*. Stripped clean, the one night Lutetia wasn't home.

Well, thank God she wasn't home, come to think of it. Horrible that would have been, to be actually present when they came breaking in. As it was, Lutetia was now asleep in her bedroom—or, rather, unconscious—and had been so for many hours, heavily sedated by one of her doctors, leaving Max alone in the denuded reception room to deal with this rather thick-witted detective, who didn't seem to realize who he was dealing with here.

Max couldn't quite bring himself to utter the words *Do you know who I am?* but he was close. In fact, probably the main consideration keeping him from voicing that question was the suspicion that this slow-moving blunt-minded bored detective more than likely already had a smart-aleck answer waiting on the shelf.

Nevertheless, though, this was ridiculous, to sit here hour after hour at the whim of some *detective*. Certainly, when Lutetia's screaming voice on the telephone last night had at last managed to communicate to him something of the enormity of what had occurred, he had at the earliest opportunity this morning reversed his travel—car to Savannah, private plane to JFK, limo to the N-Joy—to be with her in this traumatic situation. And certainly he'd been happy to see this detective, Bernard Klematsky, happy to answer his questions, happy to help in any way he could, happy to see the man so obviously earnest in his work, but enough was enough.

There should by now have come a point at which Max could shake the detective's hand, wish him well, give him a telephone number where Max could be reached if necessary, and leave. Back to Hilton Head, back to the extremely attractive secretary waiting there to help him prepare his testimony before Congress on Monday, back to his normal life.

Instead of which, this fellow Klematsky, this roadshow Columbo, was *holding* him here. Gently, yes; indirectly, yes; but nevertheless, that was what was happening.

"If you'll just give me a little of your time, Mr. Fairbanks.

I'm expecting some phone calls, then you can help me with one or two little details."

"Why don't I help you with those details now, so I can leave?"

"I wish we could to it that way, Mr. Fairbanks," Klematsky said, not even trying to look sympathetic, "but I've got to wait for these phone calls before I know exactly what it is I need to ask you."

So here he was, hour after hour, all of Saturday going by, Saturday evening coming up, Lutetia unconscious in the other room, the apartment raped, and Detective Klematsky as bland as an ulcer diet—which Max would be needing, if things kept on like this.

But what could he do? He'd called his New York office, told them to hold all messages for the weekend—nothing else in his business life could possibly matter between now and Monday—and he remained hunkered down in this place, waiting, and every time the phone rang, which it did from time to time, it was for Klematsky. Who lives here, anyway?

But now at last Klematsky, having come back from yet one more phone call, seemed ready to get on with it. He'd always taken his calls in some other room, so Max could hear nothing but murmuring without words, so he had no idea what all this hugger-mugger was about, but he was glad that finally they might be getting down to it. Ask the bloody questions, and let me go. It's my plane, and my pilot, and he'll fly whenever I say, whenever I get there, so let me *get* there.

And here came the first question: "Your wife, Lutetia, lives in this apartment?"

"Well, we both do," Max said, "though this isn't my legal residence, and I suppose she's here more than I am. Business keeps me traveling a great deal."

"She's here more than you are."

"Yes, of course."

"She's here almost all the time, isn't she, Mr. Fairbanks?" Klematsky had some sort of notebook, was riffling through it, looking at little handwritten notes in it. "She's something of a hostess in New York, isn't she?"

"My wife entertains a great deal," Max said. And what was the point of all this?

"But Thursday night she wasn't here."

"No. Thank God for that, too."

"You and she went away together?"

"Yes."

"Just for the one night?"

"That was all the time I had, as I say, I'm supposed to be in Washington—"

"And where did you go?"

"My corporation owns—well, it did own, we're giving it up, selling it—a house out on Long Island, we've used for management sessions, that sort of thing. I suppose we were saying good-bye to it. Sentimental; you know how it is."

"You were sentimental about giving up the house on Long Island."

"We'd had it for some years, yes."

"And your wife was sentimental about giving it up."

"Well, I suppose so," Max said, trying to find his way through the obscurity of these questions, not wanting to compromise himself with an outright lie either. "I suppose she felt about it much the same way I did."

"So you were saying good-bye to the house."

"Yes."

"And your wife was also saying hello to it, wasn't she?"

Max gaped. "What?"

"Wasn't that the first time your wife had ever been in that house, the first time she'd ever *seen* it?"

How on earth had the fellow found that out, and what in hell did it have to do with this burglary? Max said, "Well, as a matter of fact, she's always wanted to get out there, but her own schedule, you know, so that was the last opportunity."

"Before you sold the house."

"That's right."

"Why are you selling the house, Mr. Fairbanks?"

Be careful, Max told himself. This man knows the most

unexpected irrelevant things. But why does he cáre about them so much? "It's part of a court settlement," he said. "A legal situation."

"Bankruptcy," Klematsky said.

Ah hah; so he did know that. "We're in," Max said, "part of my holdings are in a Chapter Eleven—"

"Bankruptcy."

"Well, it's a technical procedure that—"

"Bankruptcy. Isn't it bankruptcy, Mr. Fairbanks?"

"Well . . . . . . yes."

"You're a bankrupt."

"Technically, my—"

"Bankrupt."

Sighing, Max conceded the point: "If you want to put it like that."

Klematsky flipped a page. "When did you and your wife decide to make this sentimental journey to Carrport, Mr. Fairbanks?"

"Well, I don't know, exactly," Max said. He was beginning to wonder if he should have an attorney present, any attorney at all, perhaps even a couple of them. On the other hand, what essentially did he have to hide from this fellow? Nothing. He's here to investigate a burglary, nothing more. God knows why he's going into all this other stuff, but it doesn't *mean* anything. "The sale of the house was decided . . . recently," he said. "So our going out there had to be a recent decision."

"Very recent," Klematsky said. "There's nothing about it in your wife's datebook."

"Well, she doesn't put *everything* in her datebook, you—"

Klematsky, surprised, said, "She doesn't? You mean there's even *more* stuff she does than what's in there?"

"I have no idea," Max said, getting stuffy with the fellow, wondering if he dared just stand up and walk out on him, yet still curious as to what all this was about. "I don't make a habit," he said, "of studying my wife's datebook."

"I have it here, you wanna see it?"

"No, thank you. And, to answer your question, I think the decision to go out there was quite spur of the moment."

"It must have been," Klematsky said. "Thursday night you had dinner with people named Lumley and some other people at the Lumleys' apartment uptown."

"You *are* thorough," Max said, not pleased.

Klematsky's smile was thin. "That's why I get the big bucks."

"You're going to say," Max suggested, "that Lutetia didn't mention to anyone at the dinner party that we were going out to Carrport later that night."

"Well, no," Klematsky said. "I was going to say your wife told Mrs. Lumley she felt overtired, felt she'd been doing too much, and was looking forward to a good night's sleep that night here in her own apartment."

Max opened his mouth. He closed it. He opened it again and said, "We made the decision in the car, coming downtown."

"I see. That's when you talked to her about it."

"We talked about it."

"Who brought the subject up?"

"Well, I suppose I did," Max said.

Klematsky nodded. He turned to another page in his damn notebook. He read, nodded, frowned at Max, said, "Wasn't there a little something else about the house at Carrport recently?"

"Something else? What do you mean?"

"Wasn't there a robbery there?"

"Oh! Yes, of course, in all this I'd completely forgotten—"

"Funny how memory works," Klematsky said. "You were out there during the robbery, weren't you?"

"Well, no," Max said. "Just before. He broke in again after I left. The police caught him once, when I was there, but then he escaped from the police and went back to the house, after I'd left."

"You mean the two of you were in the house—"

Good God, he even knows about Miss September. "Yes,

yes, all right, the two of us were there, for perfectly innocent reasons—"

Klematsky stared at him. "You and the burglar were there for perfectly innocent reasons?"

Max stared, lost. "What?"

Klematsky spread his hands, as though all this were obvious. "The two of you were there, we agreed on that."

"Not me and the— Not me and the *burglar*! I thought you were talking about— Well, I thought you meant someone else."

"And the police," Klematsky went on, as though Max hadn't spoken at all, "came in because the house was supposed to be empty and they saw it was occupied, and—"

"Not at all, not at all," Max said. "I *called* the police. I captured the burglar, I held a gun on him, and I called the police. Check their records."

"Well, I did," Klematsky said, "and they're very confusing. These small-town cops, you know. First there's a report that the police found a burglar and nobody else there. Then there's an amended report that the police found the burglar and *two* other people there, you and somebody else. And after that, there's another amended report that the police found the burglar and *one* other person there, meaning you. And there's also a 911 call, originally said to be by you, and then said to be by somebody else."

Now Max had truly had enough. Much of this was embarrassing, some of it was less than forthcoming, but none of it had anything to do with what had happened in this apartment right here on Thursday night. "Detective," he said, putting on his stern manner, the manner that usually preceded somebody being fired, "I applaud your enterprise in digging up all this irrelevant material, but that's what it is. Irrelevant material. Somebody broke into *this* place Thursday night. They took well over a million dollars' worth of property. I'm not sure yet *how* much they took. Why isn't *this* your concern? Why do you keep going on and on about *Carrport*?"

"They're both burglaries, aren't they?"

"Burglaries take place all the time! Are you saying these two are *connected*? That's absurd!"

"Is it?"

Suddenly a suspicion entered Max's brain. The burglar; the ring. Could it be the same man, come back looking for his ring, following Max around? Was that, in his bumble-footed fashion, what this clown of a detective was getting at? Max said, "You think it's the same people."

"I don't think anything yet," Klematsky said. "I see all sorts of possible scenarios."

He doesn't know about the ring, Max thought, that much he can't know about. So he doesn't know about the burglar, and *could* the burglar be chasing me, chasing the ring? It seemed impossible, ridiculous. Distracted, he said, "Scenarios. What do you mean, scenarios?"

"Well, here's a scenario," Klematsky said. "You're bankrupt."

That again? "I'm technically—"

"Bankrupt."

Max sighed. "Very *well*."

"There's a house full of valuable possessions, that you're not supposed to be in, and you *are* in, while there's a burglary going on."

Is it possible the burglar could be hanging around *now*, somewhere nearby? A man batting too many gnats, Max said, "Before. I was there before."

"Before, during, after." Klematsky shrugged. "You're all around it. And now we come here, and at the last second you talk your wife into leaving this apartment, when she didn't want to, and all of a sudden the coast is clear."

"Coast? What coast? Clear? *Wait* a second!"

The absurdity of Klematsky's suspicions, now that Max finally understood what they were, was *so* extreme that no wonder it hadn't occurred to him what horsefeathers filled the Klematsky brain. His own wealth and, in this instance, comparative innocence, combined with the distraction of thoughts about the burglar, had kept him from grasping Klematsky's implications before this. Now, astounded, horrified, amused, pointing at himself, Max said, "Do you think *I* committed these burglaries? Hired them done? For the *insurance?*"

"I don't think anything yet," Klematsky said. "I'm just looking at the scenarios."

"You should be looking at a padded cell," Max told him. "You think because I'm in *bankruptcy* court—? Do you really believe I'm *poor?* You— You— I could buy and sell a thousand of you!"

"Maybe you could buy and sell a thousand," Klematsky said, unruffled, "but they wouldn't be me."

"From here on," Max said, getting to his feet, "you may speak to me through my attorney, Walter Greenbaum. I'll give you his phone number, and a number where you can reach me if you have anything sensible to say."

As calm as ever, Klematsky turned to a fresh page in his notebook. "Fire away."

Max gave him the numbers and said, "You've wasted far too much of my time, when you should have been out looking for the people who actually *did* this. Unless you think you have cause to stop me, I am now going back to Hilton Head."

"Oh, I have no reason to hold you, Mr. Fairbanks," the unflappable Klematsky said. "Not at the moment. Is your Congress thing going to be on C-Span?"

"Perhaps the congressmen were my partners in crime," Max said, sneering. "Perhaps they're the ones who did the actual breaking in."

"Wouldn't surprise me," Klematsky said.

31

The first thing they couldn't agree on was how they were going to get to Washington. Dortmunder wanted to take the train, Andy wanted to drive, and May and Anne Marie both wanted to fly. As Andy had earlier suggested, May and Anne Marie hit it off right from the start, liked each other fine, and were in complete agreement about taking the plane to Washington, DC. "It's a hop and a skip," Anne Marie said, and May said, "See? Not even a jump. It's over before you know it, and you're *there*."

"Where?" Dortmunder demanded. "In some farmer's field fifty miles away, at an *airport*, with *taxis*, and another hour before you get anywhere. I don't wanna go to Washington by taxi. The train is door to door."

This conversation was taking place Saturday evening in Dortmunder and May's apartment, and now Andy stood and went over to the living room archway to look down toward the apartment entrance and say, "Door to door? John? You got a train runs down the hall out there?"

"Downtown to downtown," Dortmunder said. "You know what I mean. It's not even a hop and a skip, it's just a hop from here over to Penn Station, take the train, you're right there in Washington, right where you want to be."

"Well, no," Anne Marie said. "Where you are is at Union Station over on Capitol Hill. The Watergate is way across town by Foggy Bottom, the other side of *everything*. All of the monuments, all of the official buildings, all of the tourists, *everything* is inbetween Union Station and the Watergate."

Which is where they were headed, of course. Since the Watergate was all things to all people—a hotel *and* an apartment building *and* a shopping mall *and* an office building, and probably also backup guitar in a garage band on weekends—it had been decided they might as well all stay right there in the hotel part while Dortmunder and Kelp visited Max Fairbanks in the apartment part. The Williams credit card that Dortmunder had used in the N-Joy surely having crashed and burned by now, he'd bought another card from Stoon the fence that had caused him to make his telephone reservation at the hotel—1-800-424-2736—in the name of Rathbone, Mr. and Mrs. Henry Rathbone. Andy and Anne Marie, while in Washington, would be the Skomorowskis.

Anyway, "I still like the train," Dortmunder grumbled, although this local expert's report on the inconvenience of the Washington depot for their particular plans did have to be taken into account, and did dampen his enthusiasm a bit.

Which Andy now tried to dampen even more, saying, "John, you don't want the train. The train's Amtrak, am I right?"

"So?"

"And Amtrak's the government, right?"

"And?"

"And the government's Republicans right now, right?"

"Yeah?"

"And Republicans don't believe in maintenance," Andy explained. "Cause it costs money."

"Well," Dortmunder said, "I can't wait for the Democrats to get back in."

"Wouldn't help," Andy said. "The Democrats don't know how to run a business. Forget Amtrak. I'll get us a nice car, comfortable, an easy ride, we travel at our own pace, stop when we want for a meal or whatever, first thing you know, we're there."

The local expert chimed in again at that, saying, "Andy, you don't want to drive in Washington. The traffic's a mess, there's no place to park—"

"Who's gonna park?" Andy said. "When we get there, we leave the car someplace, when we go back I'll get another one."

Anne Marie frowned at him. "You're talking about rental cars, aren't you?"

"Not exactly," Andy said.

"Oh," Anne Marie said.

"So we're gonna leave tomorrow morning," Andy said. "I'll pick us up a really nice car, I'll go over to First Avenue, where the hospitals are."

Anne Marie said, "Hospitals?"

"The thing is," Andy explained, "when I feel I need a car, good transportation, something very special, I look for a vehicle with MD plates. This is one place where you can trust doctors. They understand discomfort, and they understand comfort, and they got the money to back up their opinions. Trust me, when I bring you a car, it'll be just what the doctor ordered, and I mean that exactly the way it sounds."

Looking dazed, Anne Marie said, "You people are going to take a little getting used to."

"What I do," May told her, sympathetically, "is pretend I'm in a bus going down a hill and the steering broke. And also the brakes. So there's nothing to do but just look at the scenery and enjoy the ride."

Anne Marie considered this. She said, "What happens when you get to the bottom of the hill?"

"I don't know," May said. "We didn't get there yet."

Andy said, "So it's settled. Ten in the morning, in a first-rate grade-A automobile, some model good for highway touring, Anne Marie and I will come by, pick you two up, we'll head south."

"And I'll get my ring," Dortmunder said.

"And more towels," May said. Smiling at Anne Marie, she said, "One nice thing about John following this man Fairbanks around is, we get a lot of very good hotel towels."

32

The Saab not only had MD plates, they were Connecticut MD plates, the very best MD plates of all. Here, said these plates, we have a doctor with a stream on his property, running water. A tennis court? You bet. Walk-in closets. Music in every room. When you traveled in this forest-green Saab with the sunroof and the readout on the dashboard that told you the temperature *outside* the car, you weren't just traveling in an automobile, you were traveling in a lifestyle, and a damn good one at that.

Andy Kelp explained all this to Anne Marie Sunday morning, as they drove across town to pick up Dortmunder and May. Anne Marie nodded and listened and learned and, following May's advice, spent most of her time looking out the Saab's window at the scenery.

She was in it now, and not just in the Saab, either. In the Rubicon, maybe. She hadn't so much crossed the Rubicon as dived straight into that turbulent stream fully dressed. Her stay at the N-Joy—enlivened toward the end by a massively intrusive but amusing police investigation—was over now, her room occupied by some other transient. Her return ticket to KC was dead; having been a special fare, it was nontransferable, and had ceased to exist when she'd missed that Saturday plane. Nobody she knew could have any idea where she was. Friends and family back in Kansas, even Howard, should Howard decide to change his mind about their marriage, none of them could find her now. On the other hand, and this was a bit unsettling to realize, there was nobody she could think of who would try really really hard to track her down.

So maybe this wasn't such an insane mistake, after all, sitting here in a freshly stolen mint-condition Saab. Maybe this was a good time to start over, start fresh. These might not be the most rational people in the world with whom to begin this new life, but you can't have everything. And, for the moment at least, hanging out with these strangers was rather fun.

Since last night, she was living in Andy's apartment in the West Thirties, though who knew for how long. Also, she wasn't the first woman who'd ever lived there, as various evidences had made clear. When she'd asked him about those previous occupants he'd looked vague and said, "Well, some of them were wives," which wasn't an answer that would tend to prolong the conversation.

Play it as it comes, she thought. Don't worry about it. Watch the scenery.

"Be right down," Andy said, when he'd double-parked in front of the building where Dortmunder and May lived.

"Right," Anne Marie said.

The scenery wasn't moving at the moment, but she went on watching it, the scenery here being mostly sloppily dressed people in a hurry, a lot of battered and dirty parked cars, and grimy stone or brick buildings put up a hundred years ago.

Am I going to like New York? she asked herself. Am I even going to stay in New York? Am I actually going to become involved in a crime, and probably get caught, and wind up on Court TV? What would I wear on Court TV? None of the stuff I brought with me.

That was a strange thought. Most of her clothing, most of her possessions, were still at home at 127 Sycamore Street, Lancaster, Kansas, a modest two-story postwar wooden clapboard home on its own modest lot, with detached one-car

garage and weedy lawns front and back and not much by
way of plantings. Anne Marie and Howard had bought the
house four years ago—another of their flailing attempts to
unify the marriage—with a minimum down payment and a
balloon mortgage, which meant that at this point the house
belonged about 97 percent to the bank, and as far as Anne
Marie was concerned the bank was welcome to it. And
everything in it, too, especially the VCR that never did work
right. All except the dark-blue dress with the white collar; it
would be nice if the bank were to send her that. It would be
perfect for Court TV.

=

Two hundred fifty miles between New York City and
Washington, DC, give or take a wide curve or two. Through
the Holland Tunnel and then New Jersey New Jersey New
Jersey New Jersey Del Maryland Maryland Baltimore Baltimore Baltimore Baltimore Maryland lunch Maryland outskirts of Washington outskirts of Washington outskirts of
Washington, and now it was up to Anne Marie to be the har-
bor pilot who would steer them to their berth.

They had run along two kinds of highway. One was country highway, with green rolling hills and leafy trees and a
wide grassy median between the three northbound and the
three southbound lanes, and it was all pleasantly pretty every
time you looked at it, and it was all the *same* pleasantly
pretty every time you looked at it, and the goddam green
hills were *still* there every time you looked at it. And the
other was city highway, where the lanes were narrower and
there was no median strip and the traffic was full of delivery
vans and pickup trucks and there were many many exits and
many many signs and the road's design was a modified roller
coaster, elevated over slums and factories, undulating and
curving inside low concrete walls, sweeping past tall sooty
brick buildings with clock faces mounted high on their fa-
cades that always told the wrong time.

"Suitland?" May and John in the backseat had been looking at maps, just for fun, and now May looked up, looked around at the scenery, and said, "There's a place next to Washington called Suitland?"

"Oh, sure," Anne Marie said. "That's very close in, over near District Heights."

"The whole place should be called Suitland," John said.

May said, "Are we going by there?"

"No," Anne Marie told her, "we're taking the Beltway the other way around, through Bethesda."

Andy, driving with the nonchalance of somebody who didn't much care if this car picked up a dent or two, said, "I'm on the Beltway? Or inside the Beltway? Or what?"

"You're on the Beltway," Anne Marie told him. "Pretty soon you'll cross the river and then turn off—"

"What river?" Andy asked.

Anne Marie, surprised, said, "The Potomac."

"Oh, right. The Potomac."

"I've heard of that," John said, from the backseat.

"I'm going to take you into the city from the south," Anne Marie explained. "That's the quickest way to get to the Watergate area. So we'll be crossing the Potomac twice."

John said, "Andy, you got to introduce this person to Stan Murch."

Andy said, "I was just thinking the same thing." Seeing Anne Marie's raised eyebrow, he explained, "That's a friend of ours that takes a particular interest in how you get from point A to point B."

Anne Marie said, "Doesn't everybody?"

"Well, Stan kind of goes to extremes," Andy said. "Is this your river?"

"Yes," Anne Marie said. "You want the exit to the George Washington Memorial Parkway."

"The George Washington Memorial Parkway? They really lean on it around here, don't they?"

"After a while, you don't notice it," Anne Marie assured him. "But it is a little, I admit, like living on a float in a Fourth of July parade. Here's our turn."

There was a lot of traffic; this being Sunday, it was mostly tourist traffic, license plates from all over the United States, attached to cars that didn't know *where* the hell they were going. Andy swivel-hipped through it all, startling drivers who were trying to read maps without changing lanes, and Anne Marie said, "Now you want the Francis Scott Key Bridge."

"You're putting me on."

"No, I'm not. There's the sign. See?"

Andy swung up and over, and there they were crossing the Potomac again, this time northbound, the city of Washington spread out in front of them like an almost life-size model of itself, as though it were all still in the planning stages and they could still decide not to go ahead with it.

From here, things got sudden. "Route 29, the Whitehurst Freeway."

"Who was Whitehurst?" Andy asked, making the turn.

"President after Grover," Anne Marie said. "Stay with 29! Don't take any of those other things. And especially don't take 66."

"Get your kicks on Route 66," Andy suggested.

"Not this time. Sixty-six goes *under* the Watergate. Don't take Twenty-fifth Street, it goes the wrong way, you want the next one, down there, Twenty-fourth Street."

"I thought that might be the next one," Andy said.

"It isn't always," Anne Marie told him. She watched as Andy made the turn, and said, "That street that goes off at an angle there, that's New Hampshire, you want that."

"If you say so."

They got stopped by a light and Andy peered at the street signs. "Is that One Street?"

"No, I Street. Sometimes they spell it like your eye, but it's the letter. All the north-south streets are numbers, and all the east-west streets are letters."

"We're on New Hampshire. What's that?"

"A spoke of the wagon wheel."

Andy nodded. "I bet there's even some way that that makes sense," he said, and the light turned green and he drove on over I and down past H, saying, "I thought it was gonna be J."

"Turn right on Virginia," Anne Marie said.

"Another spoke of the wagon wheel?"

"Different wheel," Anne Marie said.

"Some time," Andy said, stopping at another red light, "you'll have to tell me all about it."

"You can turn right on red in Washington," she told him, as the light turned green. "Or on green, for that matter."

Andy made the turn and said, "Somehow, I have a feeling I'm going in circles here."

"In a way," Anne Marie said. "That's the Watergate across the street there. Can you get over there?"

"Well, that depends," Andy said, "on how much all these other people care about their cars."

Fortunately, they all cared.

＝＝

Fifteen minutes later, there was a knock on Anne Marie's door. She was in a very nice room, the largest hotel room she'd ever seen, on the fifth floor of the Watergate Hotel, with large potted shrubs flanking the broad glass door leading to the balcony and a long view out over the Potomac to Virginia on the other side. She quit looking at that view to go over to the door and let Andy in. He'd dropped them at the hotel entrance and then driven away to, as he'd said, "deal with" the car, and now he was back. "All set," he said, coming in.

She shut the door. "What did you do with the car?"

"Well, I drove away from here," he told her, crossing to the bed where his big battered canvas bag had been placed by the bellboy, "and I came to a stop sign, so I stopped."

"And then what?"

"I came back here," he said, and zipped open the bag.

She moved around until she could see his face. "You left the car at a stop sign? Just got out and left it there?"

"Wiped the steering wheel first." The others, before getting out of the car, had also smeared any place they might have left fingerprints.

Anne Marie stared at him. "But . . . why? Why make a mess with the traffic?"

"Well, you know," Andy said, "I feel a certain responsibility to the doctor."

"I'm not following this," Anne Marie admitted.

Andy changed clothes while he explained. "Well, let's say I found a parking space and left the car there."

"There are no parking spaces in Washington."

"So that's another consideration. But say I did find something like that, it could be weeks before the cops notice anything and the doctor gets his car back. This way, the cops have already noticed the situation by now, they're probably phoning the doctor this minute, he could be reunited with that nice vehicle before sundown. How do I look?"

Andy was now wearing a short-sleeve white dress shirt open at the collar with a half-dozen pens in a white pocket protector in the shirt pocket, plus khaki pants and tan workboots and dark-framed eyeglasses with clip-on sunglasses angled up toward his forehead and a yellow hardhat. In his left hand he held a clipboard. Work gloves protruded from his right hip pocket. "Different," Anne Marie decided.

"Good."

"What's going to happen now?"

"Well, you and May can do some sight-seeing or shopping or whatever, figure out where we'll eat dinner, stuff like that. And John and me," Andy said, hefting the clipboard as he crossed to the phone, "are gonna go case the joint. What's his room number?"

33

The Watergate *is* a complex, not one building but six, all of them odd-shaped and dropped at random onto a triangular chunk of land next to Kennedy Center, flanked by the Potomac on the west, Virginia Avenue on the northeast, and New Hampshire Avenue (with the Saudi Arabian embassy a giant gray toolbox across the street) to the southeast. The beret-shaped building at the apex of the triangle is Watergate East, a co-op apartment building divided into two addresses: Watergate East, North and Watergate East, South, which should not be confused with Watergate South, a boomerang-shaped building, also a co-op, behind Watergate East, South. The final co-op is a riverboatlike trapezoid at the angle between Virginia Avenue and the river and, in a burst of creative nomenclature, it is called Watergate West.

We're not done. Sorry, but we're not done. There are also two office buildings, famous in the Nixon administration. (The Democratic National Committee is no longer headquartered there.) These are called Watergate 600 and Watergate 2600, and behind the latter is the 235-room Watergate Hotel. Lest we forget, there's also the Watergate Mall, tucked in behind Watergate East, full of all kinds of shopping opportunities. And finally, there's an ornamental pool in the middle of the complex (probably called the Watergate Water), surrounded by the kind of landscaping usually associated with model railroad sets; trees made of cotton balls dipped in green ink, that sort of thing.

The complex is open and closed at the same time, the mall absolutely open to pedestrians (any one of whom could be a shopper), the office buildings and hotel having normally minimal security, and the apartment houses primarily guarded by security men and women in blue blazers who sit at counters in the lobbies and buzz in the acceptable arrivers while presumably rejecting the unclean.

It was in Watergate East, North that TUI maintained a two-bedroom two-bathroom fourth-floor apartment, where Max Fairbanks was scheduled to spend Sunday and Monday nights, while appearing before a congressional committee on Monday afternoon. And it was here, in that apartment, where John Dortmunder intended to find Max Fairbanks and relieve him of a certain ring.

≡

Sunday afternoon. Dortmunder and Kelp, invisible in their engineers' drag, prowled the complex, making notations on their clipboards and saluting the occasional security person by touching their pens to their temples. (The first time he did this, Dortmunder touched the wrong end of his pen to his temple, but after that he got it right.)

Wandering, roving, they found the two-level garage beneath the apartment building and saw that here, too, access to the elevators was monitored by building staff, but very loosely. Then they found the truck ramp that descended beneath the building and on out to the back, giving access for deliveries to the boutiques in the mall. A person could move between the truck ramp and the upper level of the garage through a door with a laughable lock.

They went on through the mall, unseen, and out to the promenades that connected all the buildings. The hotel was down to their right, the Watergate Water dead ahead. The buildings all around them were thoroughly balconied, to take advantage of the river views, and the balcony railings were

composed of rows of spaced vertical white concrete stan-
chions, looking from the distance like very serious teeth, so
that from down here the buildings were stacks of sharks'
jawbones, one atop the other, all those teeth sticking straight
up.

Kelp looked up at the balconies of Watergate East, North
and said, "Hey."

Dortmunder looked up. "What?"

"She's gone now."

"Who?"

"There was a woman up there, leaning over the balcony,
gotta be right near where we're going tonight, she looked
like Anne Marie."

"Couldn't be," Dortmunder said. "The hotel's over there."

"I know. She just looked like. Well . . . from this distance."

"And you probably don't really know her looks yet," Dortmunder pointed out, and added, "She's a good sport, isn't
she."

"I sure hope so," Kelp said. "Let's look at that garage
some more."

====

A little after three, they got back to Dortmunder's room,
and May wasn't there. "Maybe they're both in my room,"
Kelp said, and phoned, but there was no answer. So they sat
down at the round table near the balcony and the view—
from here, up close, the teeth looked like a highway divider—and went over the notes they'd taken, the kinds of
locks they'd seen, the internal TV monitors they'd noted, the
posts and routes of the security personnel. They didn't have
information, of course, about the actual apartment and the
lay of the land up there, but that would come later, when they
went in.

About fifteen minutes after they'd arrived, May and Anne
Marie came in, grinning, and Kelp said, "Hey, there. Have a
good time?"

"Pretty good," Anne Marie said, and May dropped on the round table in front of them a bunch of Polaroid pictures.

Kelp picked up one of the pictures and looked at it. A curving hall with round nearly flush ceiling lights. Gray patterned wallpaper, shiny brown wood doors, a kind of mauve carpet with a big complex medallion on it every ten feet or so. A red-lettered exit sign some distance away around the curve. Kelp said, "What's this?"

"The hall outside the apartment where you're going," May told him, and pointed. "That's the door to it right there."

Anne Marie touched a couple of other pictures, saying, "This is an apartment just like the one where you're going, only it's two floors down. But it's the same layout."

Dortmunder and Kelp went through the pictures. Interiors, exteriors, balcony shots, elevator shots. Kelp said, "What *is* all this?"

"We thought it might help," May said.

Anne Marie said, "We weren't doing anything else, so what the heck."

Kelp said, "So that *was* you, up on the balcony."

"Oh, did you see me?" Anne Marie smiled. "You should have waved."

Stunned, Dortmunder said, "May? How did you do this?"

"Turns out," May said, "there's only certain special real estate agents are permitted to list the apartments here, because it's all co-ops. So every Sunday afternoon, between noon and three, there's open house."

"It's over now," Anne Marie said.

"The way it works," May explained, "you go to the desk downstairs and check in—"

"I used my real name and ID," Anne Marie said.

"There didn't seem to be any harm in it," May said. "Anyway, after a couple minutes a real estate agent comes and gets you and rides up in the elevator with you and tells you what's available, and asks what you're interested in."

"There's a lot of people at this open house," Anne Marie said. "I got the idea a bunch of them are people already liv-

ing there in that building, they just want to snoop around in
their neighbors' apartments."

"So after you've looked at a couple places," May went on,
"you just tell the real estate agent thank you, I can find the
elevator on my own, and you leave. And it's okay because
she's got half a dozen other people she's showing around."

"So then you take the stairs," Anne Marie continued, "and
go wherever you want. If we knew how to pick locks, we
could have gone right into that apartment you fellas want,
and took pictures all over the place."

Dortmunder and Kelp looked at each other, their mouths
open. "If I'd known," Dortmunder said, "I could have gone in
there, done what they said, got into the apartment, and just wait
for that son of a bitch to show up."

"That would have been very nice," Kelp agreed.

"It's over now," May said. "It's after three."

Anne Marie said, "But they do it every Sunday."

"Next Sunday," Dortmunder said, "Fairbanks isn't gonna
be here, and neither are we." He sighed, then more or less
squared his shoulders. "Okay," he said. "No use crying over
spilt blood. We can still get in, no problem."

"When?" Kelp asked him.

"Early," Dortmunder said. "If he isn't there yet, we'll wait
for him. We'll have an early dinner, the four of us, then you
and me'll go in. Nine o'clock. We'll go in at nine."

34

Sunday, 9:00 P.M. Max should have left hours ago for DC, but he was restless, troubled in his mind. So many things had gone so badly lately. Two burglaries. The loss of the Carrport house. The added complications of the bankruptcy, difficulties he had never anticipated. The insane detective in New York who so clearly believed that Max had arranged to burglarize his own homes, and who seemed perfectly capable of rooting around in Max's affairs until he did find something illegal that Max might have done. It was all as though some black cloud were hovering above his head, confusing him, keeping him off-balance.

Nine P.M. The Hilton Head condo was dark and empty, except for himself in the spacious living room, seated on the broad canvas sofa, the table lamps on both end tables the only illumination. The secretary who had been here to help him with his statement before the congressional committee tomorrow, among other things, had come and gone, leaving him alone in the house. In a guest cottage half a mile away, a nameless chauffeur awaited his call, already well overdue. Here in the condo air-conditioning hummed, and beyond the broad uncurtained front windows stretched the wide porch, the regular narrow pickets of the porch rail, and then the Atlantic, extending far out eastward under a pale moon and a black sky, the sea's black surface glinting here and there and over here, as though tiny men in black armor were creeping ever closer.

Open on the glass coffee table in front of him was The Book, the I Ching. He'd been reading it, dipping in here and there, hoping for general guidance, somehow reluctant to open the door to his own particular situation. But why? He'd never been afraid to know his destiny before. That destiny, whatever by way of destiny he might still have out ahead of himself, was all lagniappe anyway, a treat from the master of the house, an extra serving of dessert, a long and delicious overtime following the brief harsh course he was supposed to have led. So why be afraid now?

I'm not, he decided, and reached for the three shiny pennies on the glass coffee table, and six clattering tosses later—loud, the copper pennies on the glass—he had his current reading, this moment in his life, and there was Tui! His own Joyous trigram, in the upper half of the hexagram, with the only moving line at the base of it, the nine in the fourth place. The lower trigram was Chên, the Arousing, Thunder, and the number of the hexagram was 17, and its name was Following.

Following? Max had never seen himself as following, as being a follower. Could it mean those who followed Max? And if so, was it for good or for ill? Could the follower be the New York detective, Klematsky? Could it be that hapless burglar? Could it be the damn bankruptcy judge, dogging his tracks?

Max bent over The Book, studying its words. Following, the Judgment: "Following has supreme success. Perseverance furthers. No blame."

Yes, yes, he knew The Book well enough by now to furnish the words it would customarily elide. What the judgment meant was, no blame would accrue to Max if he persevered, but in this situation (whatever this situation was) perseverance was linked with the concept of following, and it was only in understanding the link between the two that he could succeed.

Maybe the Image would clarify things:

The Image
Thunder in the middle of the lake:
The image of FOLLOWING.
Thus the superior man at nightfall
Goes indoors for rest and recuperation.

Hmmm. The Book often spoke of the superior man, and Max naturally assumed it was always referring to himself. When it said the superior man takes heed, Max would take heed. When it said the superior man moves forward boldly, Max would move forward boldly. But now the superior man goes indoors? At nightfall? It *was* nightfall, and he *was* indoors.

Max read on. The explications given by the editors of The Book, sometimes very helpful, seemed to him this time merely reductive. Following and its image, they suggested, merely meant that in life one time followed another time, and when it was the appropriate time to stop working and get some rest the superior man would stop working and get some rest. But here was Max at Hilton Head, where he'd been romping quite successfully with a compliant secretary. Did he need to be told, at this moment, to stop working and get some rest?

Or was The Book simply pointing out his present situation, like a map mounted in a public space, featuring an arrow with the notation YOU ARE HERE? If so, then the moving line would be the significance. Nine in the fourth place:

Following creates success.
Perseverance brings misfortune.
To go one's way with sincerity brings clarity.
How could there be blame in this?

Oh, well, really, what's all that supposed to mean? A minute ago, perseverance furthered. Now the editors say this line means the superior man should see through sycophants, which was hardly Max's problem.

In another part of The Book, there was more about the meaning of the lines, first quoting a bit of the line and then glossing it:

"Following creates success": this bodes misfortune.
"To go one's way with sincerity": this brings clear-sighted deeds.

And what do the editors have to say about this, when success is equated with misfortune? Max read, and pondered, and began to see what they meant, and he didn't like it at all.

What The Book was saying to him was that he had succeeded in getting somebody to follow him that he didn't *want* following him; the line is in the wrong place. There's danger in being followed this way, all kinds of trouble, and the way to avoid it is to see clearly. To see the follower clearly.

Who? Detective Klematsky sprang to mind. Should Max try to exert pressure at the NYPD, have Klematsky replaced by somebody less insane? Or would that just make more trouble than before? And what if the follower isn't Klematsky after all, but is, for instance, the bankruptcy judge, Mainman?

How could he see the follower clearly if he didn't know which follower it was? Max had *known* he felt beleaguered, and now he knew why. He was being trailed somehow, followed by somebody, and he could feel it, sense it. But who?

This isn't enough information, Max decided, and tossed the coins again. You could approach The Book two or three times in a row this way, before the information would reduce to gibberish. And this time he got—wait a minute, Tui again, his own trigram, but now at the bottom of the hexagram. And once more the other trigram was Chên, the Arousing, Thunder, this time on the top. The previous hexagram had come back to him, inverted, with again only one moving line, this time the nine in the second position.

The number of the hexagram was 54, and its name was the

Marrying Maiden, and Max felt a chill go up his back, and thought about turning down the air-conditioning.

The Marrying Maiden. He'd never been led to that hexagram before, but in his reading of The Book he'd come across it several times, and he'd noticed how unpleasant it was, and he'd always been glad when 54 had not come up.

But now it had. Hexagram 54, what are you?

The Judgment
THE MARRYING MAIDEN.
Undertakings bring misfortune.
Nothing that would further.

Good God. It was some undertaking of his, something he had done, that had brought about this mess. What was it? What had he done? The Carrport visit? Was it that damn judge after all?

With fingers that now trembled a bit, Max turned the page to read the image of this hexagram:

The Image
Thunder over the lake:
The image of THE MARRYING MAIDEN.
Thus the superior man
Understands the transitory
In the light of the eternity of the end.

The eternity of the end! Wait, wait, wait a minute here. Why bring death into this? Yes, of course, Max had always laughed at death, had always said, and always believed, because of course it was true, that his own life was an afterthought, a joke, a cosmic error, that he was supposed to have been snuffed out long ago, lifeless in the first dew of his youth, but that didn't mean, that doesn't mean, that doesn't mean he wants to *die*. What *is* this, all of a sudden?

What exactly is he being warned about here? Is there actually an assassin following him? Has some enemy—there are enemies, oh, God, there are enemies—hired a killer to stalk him? But we're all businessmen here, aren't we, all rational people? Our weapons of choice are attorneys and accountants, not assassins. Still, could it be that someone was driven too close to the edge, has someone's sanity snapped, *is there a murderer coming?*

That window ahead of him, with its black view of the black ocean, how exposed it is. How exposed he is, here in this double halo of light from the lamps flanking this sofa, like two shotgun barrels firing at once.

What an image! Max ducked his head, blinked at the page of The Book, tried to concentrate, tried to read the editors' comments, tried to find the loophole.

So hard to concentrate, so hard to read. And *what* namby-pamby is this from the editors? It might as well be out of Ann Landers. No, worse, Joyce Brothers. *They* say, these Hallmark-level editors, *they* say this terrifying image of the superior man understanding the transitory in the light of the eternity of the end, they say it simply means friends should avoid misunderstandings that will make their relationships turn sour.

Oh, please. How can they say such a thing? Max read and read, time going by, the pages turning this way and that, and finally he calmed enough to realize that the hexagram of the Marrying Maiden was at its literate level simply about the ways in which a girl adapts herself to her bridegroom's household, the difficulties and delicacies of being low woman on the totem pole in a traditional Chinese family.

Still, even though that was the literal meaning of what he'd just read, the whole point of the I Ching was to adapt the concrete imagery of its hexagrams to the specifics of one's own life. Max Fairbanks was no blushing bride, cowed by her new mother-in-law. So what could this mean? Somehow, he had entered into a relationship the way a bride enters into a relationship with her new husband's family, fraught with peril. Once she accepts the ring—

No. It can't be.

Max stared at The Book, stared at the pennies, stared at the window, which had become opaque with a rise in humidity outside, a passing mist, so that what he saw was his own startled self, squat on the sofa.

The burglary at the N-Joy.

He *returned* to the Carrport house.

He knows where I am. Well, of course he does, everybody knows where I am, the newspapers know where I am. And he's following me, because he wants this ring.

He can't have it. Max looked at the ring, glinting and winking on his finger. It felt so good there, so warm, so right. This is *my* trigram!

The Watergate apartment. He expects me to be there, next.

I could still be wrong, he thought, trying to soothe himself. It could still be something else, anything else. There's still more to the answer, there's the one moving line that I haven't consulted yet, the nine in the second place. That could change everything.

Max turned the page. He bent his head over The Book. He read the two sentences, then read them again, then looked up at himself in the window.

It's about him. The Book has done it again, and I can't argue. First it described me, as I am at this moment. Then it described the situation that was coming closer to me. Then it pointed to the person who had caused that situation. And now it says what that person is doing:

Nine in the second place means:
A one-eyed man who is able to see.
The perseverance of a solitary man furthers.

He's coming to get me.

35

"John! Ssshhh! John! Wake up! Pssst! John! Ssshhh!"

"I'm awake, I'm awake," Dortmunder grumbled, and opened his eyes to look at a color-deprived room with the lights on dim.

Andy was leaning over him, still jostling his shoulder. "You fell asleep, John," he said.

"What gives you that idea?" Dortmunder sat up to put his feet over the edge of the bed, and looked around. It was a big bed with a big soft spread on it. His shoes were on the tan wall-to-wall carpet. The room looked like it should be in the Carrport house. "What time is it?"

"A quarter to five. He isn't coming, John."

"Sure he's coming," Dortmunder said. "He's got to talk to Congress tomorrow. Today. You don't stand up Congress."

"He isn't coming here at quarter to five in the morning, John. You want a cup of coffee?"

"Yes."

"You want some breakfast?"

"Yes."

Andy went away at last, and Dortmunder got up from the bed, creaking a lot, and went over into the bathroom, where there was a fresh toothbrush in the medicine chest, along with many other little amenities.

This was some apartment. Two large bedrooms, each with

its own full bath, plus a long living room, a pretty good compact kitchen, a smallish dining room, and a half bath off the hall between living room and bedrooms. Also off the living room was one of those balconies with all the concrete teeth, providing a view of Virginia's low hills over the river. The design throughout was like the inoffensive design at Carrport, except this was much more basic and minimal, without the antiques and little fineries that would fit so nicely into the pocket of a passing wayfarer. There was damn-all here to steal, if it came to that. Unless you felt like roaming the halls with a television set in your arms, which they didn't at all feel like doing, you could leave this place starved for a sense of accomplishment.

The lights had been on all over the apartment, turned low, when they'd arrived, so they'd left them like that. It made it easy to move around the place, and wouldn't startle Fairbanks when he arrived. Except the son of a bitch wasn't arriving.

In the dining room, also dimly lit, Andy had set a nice spread at one end of the table, toast and jam and butter and orange juice and milk and coffee. "Looks good," Dortmunder admitted, as he sat down.

"There was Cheerios," Andy said, "but it had little bugs in it."

"No," Dortmunder agreed.

"I figured," Andy said, "one thing you don't want your food to do is walk."

Dortmunder filled his mouth with toast and butter and jam and said, "I wonder where the hell Fairbanks is."

Andy looked at him. "What?"

So Dortmunder chewed for quite a long while, and swallowed coffee with the toast and the other stuff, and said, "Fairbanks."

"I wonder where the hell he is," Andy said.

"Me, too," Dortmunder said.

"He was supposed to be as regular, this guy," Andy said, "as a person full of bran."

Dortmunder said, "Things started going wrong when all of a sudden he's off the radar screen for the weekend."

"Maybe he knows you're after him," Andy said, and grinned to show he was kidding.

Nevertheless, Dortmunder took the idea seriously, but then shook his head. "No way. He can't know there's *anybody* looking for him, not yet. And even if he did, the last time we saw each other, I didn't look like somebody was gonna go *after* anybody."

"I'm sure that's true," Andy said, and he might have been smiling in an unacceptable way, but before Dortmunder could be sure one way or the other, Andy'd covered his mouth with his coffee cup.

Dortmunder chewed some more jam and butter and toast, and thought about things. He drank coffee. "Maybe there's something on television," he said.

Andy looked at him. "You mean a movie? Watch a movie?"

"No. Maybe there's something about Fairbanks."

Andy didn't get it. "Why would there be something about Fairbanks on television?"

"Because," Dortmunder said, "the guy is rich and famous, and Congress is pretty well known itself, so maybe when the one goes to see the other, there's something about it on television."

"Huh," Andy said. "I never would of thought of that. Could be you could be right."

"Thank you, Andy," Dortmunder said, with dignity.

After breakfast—they left the dishes in the dining room for the maid service—they went into the living room, where there was a television set you wouldn't *want* to carry around the halls. It was as big as a drive-in movie, a huge screen almost up to the ceiling that made everything look slightly gray and grainy; not out of focus, exactly, but as though it were a copy of a copy of a copy.

At 5:30 in the morning, there were things being broadcast on this giant TV that maybe didn't look as scary at normal size. Dortmunder and Kelp watched a number of programs with disbelief before they found a news channel—not CNN, some other one—that promised a morning update of "congressional activities," which conjured images of congresspeople playing volleyball and Ping-Pong, so they settled down to watch the giant people of that station on this giant screen, who just kept on promising the congressional activities update while showing countless commercials of grown-ups eating candy bars intermixed with noncommercials of grown-ups shooting at each other. It was nearly forty minutes before the blond lady with the bionic teeth said, "And now the congressional update," and then another nine minutes of posturing and flapdoodle from other active congresspeople before paydirt was finally struck:

Appearing before the subcommittee on entertainment tax reform this morning will be media mogul Max Fairbanks, chief executive officer of the giant entertainment and real estate conglomerate called Trans-Global Universal Industries, better known as TUI. Mr. Fairbanks's appearance is scheduled for eleven o'clock, when he is expected to tell a sympathetic committee that only by the removal of the World War II–era entertainment luxury tax will the American film and television and multimedia industry be able to compete in the global markets of tomorrow, by producing the top-quality artistic and entertainment production which the industry, with a solid financial base, would be able to provide, were it not for this onerous tax.

"Whadaya bet," Andy said, "this station here is one of the things he owns?"

"Pass," Dortmunder said.

So what now? Would Fairbanks be here tonight or not? He was *supposed* to, but on the other hand he was supposed to have been here last night, too. Figure he's got this 11:00 A.M. thing with these sympathetic congresspeople, where he's asking them to let him keep more of the money. Afterward, won't he take some of them to lunch or something? Or maybe they take him to lunch, at taxpayers' expense, just to help out the poor guy. Then after that he's not supposed to do anything till tomorrow, when one of his private planes would take him to Chicago.

So won't he come here in between, change his clothes, have a nap, kick back, chill out; whatever chief executive officers do?

On the other hand, will he maybe show up here with a mob, a whole lot of people that two unarmed visitors from New York might not be able to deal with too well? That's another possibility.

"What it comes down to is," Dortmunder said, "I don't wanna lose this guy again."

"Agreed," Andy said.

"Washington's bad enough. I don't wanna have to do Chicago."

"Absolutely," Andy said.

"So we gotta lie in wait for him, but so *we* get *him* and not the other way around."

"Exactly," Andy said.

Which meant, after all, they would have to do the breakfast dishes. They needed to restore the place to exactly the condition it had been in before they got here, which meant not even taking any of the few minor valuables they'd noticed along the way, because the plan now was, they'd leave here but keep an eye on the place. Sooner or later, unless Fairbanks had changed his plans radically, he would show up, and they could return, and then they'd see what was what.

Housecleaning took about twenty minutes, and at the end of it they took a cleaning rag from under the kitchen sink, carried it out to the balcony, and draped it over one of the teeth there. That way, they'd be able to tell from down below, down in that landscaped area there, which ones were Fairbanks's windows. They also left the glass balcony door slightly open, which would screw up the air-conditioning, just enough to be noticeable. That way, when Fairbanks finally arrived here, they would be able to see from down below when the apartment lighting changed, and when the balcony door was shut. The theory behind it all was, Fairbanks would assume the open door and the cleaning rag were the results of a sloppy maid service.

It was just after seven o'clock when they finished tidying up and leaving their signals to themselves, and they were about to depart when the phone rang. They didn't want to open the door with a phone ringing in the apartment, just in case there was somebody going by out there whose attention might be attracted, so they stood impatiently by the front door, waiting, and the phone rang a second time, and then after a while it rang a third time, and then a male voice with no inflection, one of those imitation voices used by computers, said a phone number and then said, "You may leave your message now."

Which the caller did. This was a human voice, male, the sound of a young staff aide, eager, trying to be smoothly efficient: "Mr. Fairbanks, this is Saunders, from Liaison. I'm supposed to come over there this morning to pick up the pack packs, but I'm told you're in residence at the moment because of this morning's hearing. I didn't want to disturb you, so, uh . . ."

Dead air, while Saunders tried to figure out what to do, then did: "I'll come over around eleven, then, when you'll be on the Hill. So I'll pick up the pack packs then, that'll be early enough." Click.

Andy said, "Pack packs?"

Dortmunder said, "Maybe it's something to do with Federal Express."

Andy raised a brow. "You'll have to explain that," he said.

"When I first got the ring," Dortmunder told him, "it came from Federal Express, and it was in what they called a pack, only they spelled it different, like P-A-K. So maybe this is a Pak pack for Federal Express."

"A Pak pack of what?"

"How should I know?"

"Maybe," Andy said, "we should look for it."

Dortmunder considered that. "We do have time," he said.

The object they were looking for didn't take long to find. At the back end of the living room, away from the balcony and the view, was a small office area, being a nice old-fashioned mahogany desk with an elaborate desk set on it featuring two green-globed lights. There were also a swivel chair, nicely padded, in black leather, and a square metal wastebasket, painted gold. In the bottom right drawer of this desk, which wasn't even locked, they found a big fat manila envelope on which was handwritten in thick red ink

PAC

"Here it is," Andy said.

Dortmunder came over to look. "And *another* way to spell pack," he said. "These people must have all flunked English."

"No, no, John," Andy said. "Don't you know what a Pac is?"

"How do you spell it?"

"This way," Andy said, gesturing to the manila envelope. "It's a legal bribe."

"It's a what?"

"It's how Congress figured it out they could get bribed without anybody getting in trouble," Andy explained. "Like, for instance, say you wanted to give a congressman a bunch of money—"

"I don't."

"Okay, but for instance. As a hypothetical. Say you got, oh, I don't know, some lumber, and you want to cut it down and you're not supposed to cut it down, but if you give this congressman some money they'll cut you a loophole. But if you just give him the money, flat out, boom, here's the money, chances are, he might go to jail and you could be embarrassed. So they invented these things, these Pacs, the letters stand for something . . ."

"That's more than you can say for the congressmen."

"Wait a minute," Andy said. "I'm trying to remember."

"Well, the *P,*" Dortmunder said, "probably means 'political.' "

"Right! Political Action Committee, that's what it is. You give the money to this committee, and *they* give it to the congressman, and then it's legal."

"They launder it," Dortmunder suggested.

"Right. I think they learned it from some people in Colombia."

"So this is the Pac pack the guy on the phone was talking about."

"Must be."

"Andy," Dortmunder said, "does this mean that envelope's full of money?"

They both looked at the envelope. They looked at each other. They looked at the envelope. Reverently, Andy took it out of the drawer and put it on top of the desk. Dortmunder closed the drawer. Andy turned the envelope over, squeezed the metal tabs together so he could lift the flap, lifted the flap, and then lifted the envelope slightly so he could look inside. "It's full of white envelopes," he said.

"And what are *they* full of?"

Andy looked at Dortmunder. His eyes were shining. "John," he breathed, "nobody ever gave me a bribe before."

"The envelopes, please," Dortmunder said.

Andy shook the white envelopes out onto the desk. They were all pudgy, they were stuffed really full. They all had acronyms written on them, in the same thick red ink. There was PACAR and IMPAC and BACPAC and seven more. Ten envelopes.

"I think," Dortmunder said, "we have to open one."

So Andy did. There was a very nice leather-handled letter opener included in the desk set; Andy took it and slit open IMPAC and out came the green paper, and they were fifty hundred-dollar bills, crisp and new.

"Five thousand dollars," Andy said.

Dortmunder prodded another of the envelopes, like a cook checking the bread dough. "Five grand in each? Try another one."

PACAR: Five thousand dollars.

Andy said, "John, what we have here is fifty thousand dollars. In cash."

"God damn it," Dortmunder said. "What a shame."

Andy frowned at him. "A shame? What's a shame?"

"I just stopped to think about it," Dortmunder said. "Saunders is gonna come pick this stuff up at eleven o'clock. We've gotta leave it here."

"*John*, this is fifty big ones!"

"If Saunders comes here and it's gone," Dortmunder pointed out, "Saunders calls the cops. Or at the very least he calls Fairbanks. And we can forget it when it comes to getting in here when Fairbanks comes home."

"John," Andy said, "are we going to let fifty thousand dollars get away from us because of one *ring?*"

"Yes," Dortmunder said.

"No," Andy said.

Dortmunder said, "Andy, don't give me trouble on—"

"Just a minute here," Andy said. "Let me think."

"Sure. Think."

"We already opened these two envelopes, you know."

"There's more envelopes, and right there's the red pen they use. We can put it all back together same as it was."

"That would be a shame and a pity and a total waste," Andy protested. "Go away, John, amuse yourself while I think."

"I don't want to screw up getting the ring."

"I *know*, John, I never seen such a one-track mind in my life. Lemme think, willya?"

"I'm just saying," Dortmunder said, and at last walked away to the other end of the living room, by the slightly open door to the balcony. He stood there and looked out at the cleaning rag draped on a tooth, and beyond it at the early morning view. In the view at the moment were a number of people running, in the green landscape just this side of the river. These were running people who weren't in any hurry to get anywhere and who in fact weren't going anywhere in particular, and the kind of running they were doing was called jogging. So far as Dortmunder was concerned, that was the biggest misuse of time and energy anybody ever thought of. Think of all the better ways you could spend your time; sitting, to begin with.

"Okay, John."

Dortmunder looked over at Andy, who was now seated at the desk with something else on the desktop in front of him. "Okay?" he said. "What's okay?"

"Come take a look."

So Dortmunder went over, and Andy had taken a sheet of TUI letterhead stationery out of the desk, and using the same red pen he'd written,

> Saunders,
> My secretary dealt with the PAC pack.
>
> Fairbanks
>
> PS: Take this note with you.

Dortmunder said, "Take this note with you?"

"Well, he can't leave it here."

"Isn't he gonna wonder why he's supposed to take it with him?"

"Wonder?" Andy seemed bewildered by the idea. He said, "Why would a guy like Saunders wonder? He's a young white-collar employee, he's not paid to wonder, he's paid to fetch. Now, if I told him, *burn* this note, that's going too far. But I say, 'Take this note with you,' that just means carry a piece of paper. John, that's what Saunders *does.*"

Dortmunder studied the note. He frowned at the big manila envelope, now again containing its ten fat smaller envelopes. He said, "It might work."

"Of course it'll work, John," Andy said. "What's the worst that can happen? We hang around outside until after the cops come and go. Besides, we gotta take the chance, you *know* that. We cannot leave this money here."

Dortmunder thought about it, and at last he shrugged and said, "You're right. Every once in a while, you gotta take a chance."

"Now you're talking," Andy said, and when he stood up the manila envelope was under his arm.

—— ——
——

The women were both in May's room, so that's where Dortmunder and Andy went. When they walked in, May and Anne Marie were up and dressed, watching the *Today* show on television. The faces they turned toward Dortmunder and Andy were both expectant and relieved. But then May looked at Dortmunder's hand and said, "You didn't get it."

"He never showed up," Dortmunder said.

Andy said, "But we got a plan." Dropping the manila envelope on the bed, he said, "We also made out a little. There's fifty big in there."

Anne Marie said, "Does that mean what I think it means?"

"It was Pac money," Andy told her.

Anne Marie apparently knew what *that* meant, because she went off into peals of laughter. "At last," she said, when she could say anything again, "the trickle-down theory begins to work."

May said, "John? Tell us everything."

So Dortmunder did, with interpolations from Andy and questions from Anne Marie, and when he was finished he said, "So we stay over one more night, and *tonight* I finally meet up with Max Fairbanks and get my ring back. But just to be on the safe side, I think I ought to call Wally."

Andy said, "Who, Wally Knurr?" To Anne Marie he explained. "He's our computer guy, with the access to everything." To Dortmunder, he said, "How come?"

"Fairbanks was supposed to be in that apartment last night and he wasn't," Dortmunder said. "I guess he'll do his talking to Congress this morning, but what else is he doing I'm not sure any more I know. And he did that news blackout over the weekend. So what's he up to? What's going on? I feel like I could use an update from Wally." He looked over at the bedside clock and said, "Is seven minutes after eight too early to call him?"

"They're early risers up there in Dudson Center," Andy assured him.

So Dortmunder made the call, and first he had to have a pleasant civilian conversation with Myrtle Street, Wally's lady friend, which he did reasonably well, and then Wally came on and said, "John! I've been trying to call you!" He sounded out of breath, or even more out of breath than usual.

"Hell," Dortmunder decided. "I knew it. What's gone wrong, Wally?"

"I don't know," Wally said, "but something sure has. Fairbanks has sent the word out that there will be *no* information given out as to his whereabouts from now on. If people want to reach him, they should make contact through his corporate headquarters in Wilmington, Delaware, a place he's *never* been to, not even when they laid the cornerstone for the new building."

"Well, goddamit," Dortmunder said. "Why's he doing all that?"

"I don't know, John," Wally said. "I'm sorry. I do know he still plans to have his two business meetings in Chicago, but I can't find out where he'll be staying or when he'll get there or when he'll leave. Then he'll definitely be somewhere in Australia on the days he's supposed to be there—"

"Which doesn't help a lot."

"Oh, I know, John. And the next time he's willing to have his whereabouts known is next Monday, a week from now, when he gets to Las Vegas."

"Vegas doesn't change?"

"I guess because everything was all set there already, so it's too late to keep it secret. But *after* Las Vegas, there isn't a word on what he's gonna do or where he's gonna be. Not a word."

"But Vegas is still what it was."

"So far, anyway," Wally said. "He'll be at the Gaiety Hotel, Battle-Lake and Casino two nights next week, Monday and Tuesday, after he gets back from Australia."

"Unless he changes his mind again."

"I'm sorry, John," Wally said. "I know I said I could track

him for you. But this is very unusual for Max Fairbanks. Maybe the IRS is after him or something."

"Somebody's after him, don't worry about that," Dortmunder said. "Thanks, Wally. If there's any change—"

"Oh, I'll let you know, you or Andy, right away. Or probably Andy, he's got an answering machine."

"Right."

"Tell him, there's about four messages from me on his machine."

"About this conversation we're just having right here."

"Oh, sure."

"I'll tell him," Dortmunder said, and immediately forgot. "So long, Wally."

When he hung up, everybody wanted to know what the other, more interesting, half of the conversation had been, so Dortmunder repeated Wally's bad news, and Andy said, "So we don't get the ring. I'm sorry, John. Not this trip."

"Damn it to hell," Dortmunder said. He was really angry. "We come all this way, and what do we get? A lousy fifty thousand dollars!"

36

For some reason, this time, when Max told the story, it seemed less funny. Maybe it was the fault of this particular audience.

Which was certainly a possibility. For this go-round of the retailing of the story of his theft of the burglar's ring, Max had an audience of just one: Earl Radburn, chief of security of TUI, the man whose job it was to see to it that nobody stole anything *anywhere* within the sovereign domain of TUI, within the Max Fairbanks fiefdom. Telling his anecdote once more, this time under the ice-blue gaze of Earl Radburn, Max couldn't help but feel that somehow the man disapproved of him.

Well, so be it. Who was boss here, anyway? If Earl Radburn can't see the humor, that's Earl Radburn's loss.

Anyway, Earl was not a man noted for much sense of humor. A compact, hard-muscled ex-marine probably in his fifties, he had a pouter pigeon's chest and walk—or strut—a sand-colored nailbrush mustache, and stiff orangey hair cropped so close to his tan scalp he looked like a drought. His clothing was usually tan and always clean, creased, starched, and worn like a layer of aluminum siding. If he had a home life nobody knew it, and if he had a sorrow in his existence it was probably that this job didn't come with a license to kill.

Max, having left DC immediately after a quite successful

congressional hearing—what a nerve the government has, taxing decent citizens—had had himself driven over highways put down some time ago by the government up to his corporate headquarters here in Wilmington, Delaware, choosing this place because everybody knew he never came here, had never been here before, and was in fact pleasantly surprised when he first laid eyes on the industrial park encircling TUI's glass-sheathed, modern-architected, low, broad-based main building. While driving up, he'd phoned Earl Radburn in Earl's security office in New York, and Earl had driven down to meet him.

Now they were alone together in a bright and airy conference room, with greensward as neat as a golf course outside the large windows, their sofas comfy, their soda water bubbly, and Earl as much fun to tell an anecdote to as an Easter Island head. Nevertheless, this is the fellow to whom he must once again recount the lark of stealing a burglar's ring.

"In any event," he said, when he had finished and Earl had made absolutely no response at all, "there you have it. That's what happened."

Earl said, "Sir," which was his way of saying he'd stored the information he'd been given so far and was ready to receive more. Get on with it, in other words.

So Max got on with it. "Before the local police managed to bring the man to their station, he escaped."

Earl's lip curled slightly.

"He went back to the house," Max said. "Fortunately, we'd, I'd, left by then. He ransacked the place."

"I've read that report," Earl said.

"I thought that was the end of it."

"But now," Earl suggested, "you think he's the one broke into your place in New York."

"I *know* it," Max said.

Earl's expression didn't change, but his skepticism was palpable. "Sir," he said, "you can't *know* it. You can suspect it, but—"

Max held up his right hand, palm toward himself, displaying the ring. "He wants this ring. He wants it back. He's going to come after me again, I know he is."

Earl looked at the hand. "You wear the ring, sir?"

"Absolutely! It's mine. I stole it fair and square, and I'm going to keep it. Don't you see my corporate symbol on it, right there?"

"A coincidence," Earl assured him.

"Of *course* it's a coincidence! A wonderful coincidence! That's why I'm going to keep this ring."

"There could be more than one coincidence in the world, sir," Earl pointed out. "The robbery in New York could have been done by anybody."

"It was *him,* I tell you," Max insisted, though he couldn't quite bring himself to acknowledge to Earl that the reason he knew with such assurance was that the I Ching had told him, through the hexagram for the Marrying Maiden. He said, "I can feel him out there, I know he's there. That's why I've insisted on a complete blackout of my movements from now on."

"Which complicates all our jobs, sir," Earl said.

"It's temporary, and it's necessary. I have a plan, Earl."

Earl waited, a rough-hewn statue awaiting a pedestal.

Max said, "The only place I'm going that I haven't made a secret, the only place in *this* country, is Las Vegas, because that was set up and the news distributed some time ago. I'll be there a week from now, next Monday and Tuesday, and I'm sticking to it. So that's the only place he can try for me again. With your help, Earl, we'll set a little trap for this burglar."

"You'll be the bait, you mean."

"Use as many people as you need," Max told him. "Think of me as being under your command."

Earl's eyebrow flickered minimally.

Max said, "In this situation only, of course."

"Sir."

"He'll know I'm going to be in Las Vegas. He'll know when, and he'll know where. And it's the *only* time and place he'll be sure of knowing where I am. He won't be able to re-sist it."

"If he's pursuing you, sir," Earl said, as the phone on the conference table rang, "then you're undoubtedly right."

The phone rang again. Max said, "You take that, Earl. I'm not here."

"Sir."

Earl rose from his sofa, crossed to the conference table, picked up the phone, spoke into it: "Radburn." Listened; spoke: "What time did you leave the message?" Listened; spoke: "What time did you go there?" Listened; spoke: "Did you mention your name in the message?" Listened; spoke: "Mr. Fairbanks will make arrangements for a second package." Listened; spoke: "Well, it's too late, then." Listened; spoke: "Someone will call you." Hung up; turned and spoke to Fairbanks: "Sir, you're right."

What now, Max thought. He said, "Something happened?"

"He was in the Watergate apartment," Earl said. "Your burglar. He got away."

"I *knew* it! That's why I didn't go there! What, did he steal the ashtrays?"

"A bit more than that, sir. There were some Pac contributions—"

"No! That was fifty thousand dollars!"

"Yes, sir. Your man Saunders phoned there this morning, not wanting to disturb you, but wanting to pick up the contributions, and left a message on the answering machine. When he arrived later, the package was gone and a note addressed to him by name and signed by you said your secretary had taken care of the contributions."

"Saunders wouldn't fall for a thing like that."

"Well, he did, sir," Earl said. "A short time ago, however, a woman from IMPAC phoned Saunders asking after the donation. He checked around to your secretary and some of the other recipients, discovered the truth, and called my office. They put him through to me here."

"That son of a bitch," Max said. "Fifty thousand dollars."

"One of the committees," Earl went on, "refused to accept Saunders's explanation and apology, insisting the delay was another expression of corporate arrogance and a power play. BACPAC, I believe he said it was. Saunders said they told him you can no longer count on their senator."

Hell. Hell and damnation. Max *did* count on that goddam senator. There were a couple of banking bills . . . What a mess *that* could turn out to be.

And all because of one stupid seedy small-time burglar.

"Las Vegas," Max growled. He could not remember ever having been this angry, not even during his first marriage. "We'll get that son of a bitch in Las Vegas," he snarled, "and personally I will tear him limb from limb."

"Yes, sir," Earl said. "My people and I will be happy to deliver him to you."

37

Detective Second Grade Bernard Klematsky, currently assigned to the Fairbanks burglary at the N-Joy, knew all kinds of people. It was useful to him in his work to maintain connections with a great variety of persons, because you never knew when somebody might have just the one fact you needed to get your job done quickly and successfully. And Klematsky liked to be quick almost as much as he liked to be successful.

Among the variety of Bernard Klematsky's acquaintances there were even some who spent their time on the opposite side of the law from the side where Klematsky dwelled, and among those latter was a light-fingered fellow named Andrew Octavian Kelp. From time to time, this Kelp provided a bit of information here, a kernel of knowledge there, of benefit to society generally and to Klematsky particularly, so it was an association worth cultivating.

Not that Kelp was a stoolie; unfortunately, the man would not turn in, up, or on his friends. But he did have a certain underworld expertise that Klematsky could from time to time call upon, and the reason he could do so was because, as it turned out, from time to time Kelp, in the course of his own nefarious doings, also had need of information, which he could get nowhere except from his old friend on the force, Bernard Klematsky. There was a narrow range within which they could be useful to one another, since Klematsky would not knowingly abet a criminal enterprise any more than Kelp would turn rat, but still it was possible for them on occasion to be useful to one another. Besides which, they enjoyed one another's company.

All of which was why, on Sunday, May 14, in pursuit of a certain theory he found promising, Bernard Klematsky called Andy Kelp, found him not at home (he was on his way to Washington, DC), and left a message on his answering machine. He left another message Monday morning, and then went out on another part of his caseload, and when he got back to the precinct Kelp had left a message for him. So he called Kelp, got the machine again, and left a message. Later, he went home, and on Tuesday morning when he got to the precinct there was a message waiting from Kelp. So he phoned, got the machine, and left a message. Some time later, he was about to go out to lunch, and in fact was halfway down the stairs, when another detective came out to the landing and called, "Somebody's on the phone, says you want to talk to him."

Klematsky was hungry, as he often was. His mind was on lunch. Still, he turned around and called up to the other detective, "Ask him if his name is Kelp."

The detective went away, and Klematsky listened to his stomach make rumbling noises until the detective came back and called down the stairs, "He says, who wants to know?"

"That's Andy," Klematsky said, and smiled. "Tell him I'll be right there."

— —
=

They had lunch together in a place of Andy's choosing, since Bernard was this time the one seeking information; Andy would pick the lunch, and Bernard would pay for it. Andy chose Sazerac, a New Orleans–influenced (but not slavishly so) neighborhood joint at the corner of Hudson and Perry streets in the West Village, down the block from the Sixth Precinct. They were supposed to meet at one o'clock, but Bernard got held up by a couple last-minute things at the precinct, so it was twenty after before he walked down Hudson and into the place, which was about average for him.

A narrow glass-walled porch wrapped around the two exterior walls of Sazerac, and that was where Andy was seated, looking out the windows at the cops going to and from the Sixth Precinct. Bernard put his hat on a hook—he'd taken to wearing a jaunty Tyrolean hat lately, with a feather, believing it made him seem more devil-may-care—and sat across the table, his back to the Sixth Precinct, saying, "Hello, there, Andy. You look well."

"I like your hat," Andy told him.

"Why, thanks."

"I saw you coming down the street there, I thought it was Peter O'Toole or somebody."

"I think he's taller than I am."

"Okay, his brother."

The waitress came by to ask her question and Andy said, "I believe I'll have an Amstel and the crab cakes."

Because he was paying for this meal, Bernard said, "Beer? Andy, you're going to have a drink at lunch?"

"That's because I feel safe, with the precinct right there," Andy told him.

Bernard looked at the menu and decided he'd have the jambalaya because it looked as though it would be filling without being expensive; then he decided what the heck, he'd have an Amstel, too. The waitress went away, and Andy said, "You see the taxi garage on the corner?"

Behind him, in other words. Bernard twisted around and looked, and directly across the street was a red brick taxi garage, the yellow cabs going in and out. The precinct was half a block beyond it. Twisting back, he said, "Yeah?"

"Does it look familiar?"

"Why not?" Bernard asked. "I've seen it before, when I come down to the Six."

"You've seen it on television," Andy told him.

"I have?"

"They used that for the outside of the garage in the show *Taxi.*"

"No kidding." Bernard skewed around for another look, then faced the table and said, "It looked cleaner on TV."

"Oh, well, you know," Andy said. "TV."

"Well, that's true."

The waitress brought their Amstel beers and they sipped companionably, and then Bernard said, "I haven't been hearing much about you lately."

"Good," Andy said.

"I'd hate to think you've reformed or retired or something," Bernard said.

"I did all of those things," Andy said, and began to blink like mad. "I gave up a life of crime because I discovered that crime doesn't pay. So now I'm legit and I'm happy—"

"And you're blinking," Bernard said. As they both knew, Andy blinked a lot whenever he was telling lies, which was unfortunate in a man of his profession.

Andy took a breath. He stopped blinking. He said, "So how are things with *you,* Bernard?"

"Very interesting," Bernard said. "We've been nabbing the bad guys left and right."

"Oh, yeah?"

"That's right. Filling up the prisons so fast they're out there building *more* prisons, and we're filling *them* up."

"I been noticing," Andy said, "how crime is down, and the streets are safe, and the insurance companies aren't hardly paying any claims at all any more. So that's why, huh? The good work you and the guys are doing."

"We help," Bernard said, and they smiled at each other, and the food came.

They were both serious about food, so they didn't do much conversation until the thoroughly empty plates were taken away. Then, over Bernard's dish of ice cream and Andy's second Amstel, Bernard said, "There *are* crimes still, here and there."

"I'm sorry to hear that, Bernard, after all your effort."

"Funny you should mention insurance companies."

"Did I? Oh, yeah, I remember."

"Because there's one kind of crime," Bernard said, "that really gets me. Nonviolent crime, I mean. Violent crime is something else."

"Absolutely."

"You were never violent," Bernard pointed out, "back before you reformed and retired, that was one nice thing about you."

"Thank you, Bernard."

"*The* one nice thing about you."

"Okay."

"But among nonviolent crimes," Bernard said, "the one that really gets my back up is insurance fraud."

Andy looked surprised. "You care that much about insurance companies?"

"I don't give a damn about insurance companies," Bernard told him, "they'd cheat their own mothers, if they had mothers. No, what gets me about insurance fraud is, the crook is using *me.*"

"Ah."

"Oh, Mr. Detective," Bernard said, imitating a fluttery householder of indeterminate sex, "somebody broke in and stole all my goodies and here's my list of what they took and please give me the docket number to give my insurance company, and then you can go away and run in circles trying to solve a crime that never happened."

"Straight citizens, you're talking about," Andy suggested.

"They're supposed to be straight," Bernard said. "Sometimes, though, they get themselves professional assistance, you know?"

"You mean," Andy said, "these are people that like hire a couple guys of the type I used to hang with before I—"

"Reformed and retired."

"And all that. Hires them to do what they do anyway, only they bring the stuff back after the insurance is paid?"

"I think they get a cut," Bernard said, "or maybe a flat fee. I don't know how it works. Would you?"

"Not me," Andy said, blinking.

"I suppose you've forgotten all that stuff," Bernard agreed.

"If I ever even knew it. Are you looking for somebody that helped an honest citizen steal his own goods, Bernard? Is that what this is about?"

"Absolutely not, Andy," Bernard said. "I know you wouldn't give me a friend of yours."

Nodding, Andy said, "We respect one another, Bernard. That's why I was surprised."

"Who I'm after," Bernard said, "who I really and truly want, is not the guys that waltzed out of the place with the stuff, but the owner that set it up."

"Because he's making you part of his scam."

"Exactly. And him I'll get on my own." Bernard ran his spoon around his empty bowl six or seven times, hoping to find more ice cream, then said, "But I want to be fair."

"Of course you do."

"Maybe this guy *didn't* set it up. I admit, I feel a prejudice against him."

"That's big of you, Bernard."

"He just gets my back up," Bernard said. "But if he didn't set up the job, I don't want to waste my time on him, spinning my wheels, letting the real bad guys get away."

"You want to conserve your energy," Andy suggested.

"That's exactly it. So I'm not asking names or anything like that, I'd just like to know in a theoretical kind of way, did any of your former associates from the bad old days, did they recently say anything about a fake burglary in midtown."

"In midtown," Andy echoed, frowning slightly.

"That new theater place on Broadway," Bernard told him, "with the hotel next to it and everything. Called the N-Joy."

"And there was a burglary in there recently?" Andy asked. "That you think it doesn't smell right?"

"And I could be wrong, I admit that. But I was wondering," Bernard said, "if the arrogant son of a bitch bankrupt bum that owns the place didn't maybe set it up himself."

"And you'd like to know," Andy said, "if I heard from

anybody that any kind of scam like that was going down anytime recently."

"That's it."

Andy looked solemnly at Bernard. His eyes blinked steadily, like a metronome. He said, "I never heard a word of anything like that, Bernard. Not a word."

Bernard looked at those blinking eyes. "Thanks, Andy," he said, "I appreciate it." And he waved for the check.

38

W hen Dortmunder walked into the O.J. Bar & Grill on Amsterdam Avenue at three minutes before ten on Tuesday night, Rollo the bartender, a tall meaty balding blue-jawed guy in a dirty long-sleeved white shirt and dirty white apron, was kneeling on the shelf inside the left front plate-glass window, installing a new neon beer sign. "With you in a minute," he said, nodding to Dortmunder, his hands full of neon tubes, electric cords, and lengths of chain for hanging the thing.

"Right," Dortmunder said, and moved toward the bar, where the regulars were discussing those black lines that's on everything you buy now that make the cash register go beep.

"It's a code," the first regular was saying. "It's a code and only the cash registers can read it."

"Why do it in code?" the second regular asked him. "The Code War's over."

A third regular now hove about and steamed into the conversation, saying, *"What?* The *Code* War? It's not the Code War, where ya been? It's the *Cold* War."

The second regular was serene with certainty. "Code," he said. "It was the Code War because they used all those codes to keep the secrets from each other." With a little pitying chuckle, he said, "Cold War. Why would anybody call a war *cold?"*

The third regular, just as certain but less serene, said,

"Anybody's been *awake* the last hundred years knows, it was called the Cold War because it's always winter in Russia."

The second regular chuckled again, an irritating sound. "Then how come," he said, "they eat salad?"

The third regular, derailed, frowned at the second regular and said, "Salad?"

"With Russian dressing."

Dortmunder leaned on the bar, off to the right of the main conversation, and watched Rollo in the backbar mirror. The barman also had several screwdrivers, a hammer, pliers, and a corkscrew, and was using them all, one-handed, while holding up the beer sign with the other.

Meanwhile, the conversation was continuing, as the first regular rejoined it, saying, "Code. That's what I'm talking about, the black lines. It's some kinda conspiracy, that's all *I* know."

A fourth regular, who until now had been using the bottles on the backbar as a kind of impromptu eye test, now reared around, righted himself, and said, "Absolutely. A conspiracy." Closing one eye to focus on the other regulars, he said, "Which conspiracy you mean?"

"The little black lines on everything you buy," the first regular said, bringing him up to speed.

The fourth regular considered that, closing first one eye and then the other: "That's a conspiracy?"

"Sure. It's in code."

"Like the war," said the second regular, with a smirk at the third regular.

The fourth regular nodded, closed both eyes, clutched the bar, opened both eyes, closed one eye, and said, "Which conspiracy?"

The first regular was affronted by this question. "How do *I* know? It's in code, isn't it? That's what makes it secret. If it wasn't in code, we'd know what it was."

The third regular suddenly slapped the bar and said, *"That's* what it is. Now I remember."

The others all swiveled around on their stools to consider

Mister Memory. The first regular said, carefully, "That's what what is?"

"The Code War," the third regular told him. "That's what they call those little black lines, on accounta that's what they're for. When they have price wars."

"The *Code* War," the second regular announced, incensed that his definition had been taken from him, "was the war between *us* and *Russia* that's *over* now."

"Wrong," the third regular said, showing his own brand of serenity.

The first regular said, "I think everybody's wrong," and called, "Rollo! What's the name of that code, all the black lines on everything you buy?"

"Bar," Rollo answered, dropping some pliers and a screwdriver.

"*There's* a one-track mind for you," said the first regular, and all the regulars chuckled, even the fifth regular, who was asleep with his head pillowed by a copy of *Soldier of Fortune* magazine.

"*This* is a bar, Rollo," the third regular called, and they all chuckled again, as Andy Kelp walked in, shared a hello with Rollo, and walked over to join Dortmunder.

The first regular was saying, "There *is* a name, though, for those black lines, I know there is."

Andy said, "We the first?"

The second regular, doubt in his voice, said, "Morse?"

"Yes," Dortmunder said.

The third regular, blossoming with scorn like time-lapse photography, said, "Morse! Man, do you get things haywire. Morse code is what they put on those little notices they stick on the bottom of the furniture that you're not supposed to take off. It's a federal law, and it's named after Senator Morse."

"Civil," said the fourth regular, with both eyes open.

The third regular turned to repel this new attack. "We're *bein* civil," he announced. "All except somebody I don't feel I wanna mention."

"Civil *code*," said the fourth regular, being civil. "That's what they call the black lines."

A quick *bzt* sound came from the general direction of Rollo, followed by a curse, and the dropping of a lot of tools.

"No," the first regular said, "it is not the civil code, which is something to do with the subways. It's called something else. I'd know it if I heard it."

Still on his knees, Rollo backed away from the window, then stood.

"Area?" suggested the fourth regular.

"No no no," the first regular said, "area codes is another word for zoning."

Rollo picked up his tools and the neon sign and headed for the bar.

"Zip?" suggested the fourth regular.

The other regulars all looked down at their pants.

Rollo made his way around the end of the bar, dropping his tools onto the shelf there.

"A zip is a *gun*," the first regular said.

Rollo approached Dortmunder and Kelp, dropping the neon sign into the trash barrel along the way. "Nobody likes foreign beers anyway," he explained. "They're made with foreign water."

"Well, when you put it like that," Kelp said.

Rollo nodded. "You want the back room, right?"

"Yeah," Dortmunder said. "There'll be five of us." It had long been a tenet of his that if you couldn't accomplish a task with five men you shouldn't try it at all. He'd seen exceptions to that rule, of course, just as there are exceptions to all rules, but as a general guide of thumb, so to speak, he still went with it.

"I'll send them back," Rollo said. "Who's coming?"

Understanding Rollo's idiosyncracy, that he knew his customers by their drink, which he felt gave him some kind of marketing advantage, Dortmunder said, "There'll be the vodka and red wine."

"Big fella," Rollo said, who was no slouch himself.

"That's him," Dortmunder agreed. "And the rye and water."

Rollo considered. "Lotta ice? Clinks a lot?"

"Right again. And the beer and salt."

"Him," Rollo said, with a downturn of the mouth. "What a boon to business *he* is."

Kelp explained, "Stan's a driver, you see, ne's got himself used to not drinking too much."

"I'd bet my money," Rollo said, "he's got a black belt in not drinking too much."

"So that's why the salt," Kelp went on. "He gets a beer, he sips it slow and easy, and when the head's gone he adds a little salt, pep the head right back up again."

"What I like to pep up," Rollo said, "is the cash register. But it takes all kinds. I'll get your drinks."

Rollo turned away, and pulled out a tray, while down at the other end of the bar the regulars had segued in a natural progression into consideration of cold cures. At the moment, they were trying to decide if the honey was supposed to be spread on the body or injected into a vein. Before they'd solved this problem, Rollo had put ice into two glasses, put the glasses on the tray, and taken down from the shelf a fresh bottle of some murky dark liquid behind a label reading AMS-TERDAM LIQUOR STORE BOURBON—"OUR OWN BRAND." With the bottle also on the tray, Rollo turned and slid the whole thing toward Dortmunder, saying, "Happy days."

"It's feed a *cough*," said the first regular.

"Thanks, Rollo."

Dortmunder took the tray and followed Kelp past the regulars, who were now all demonstrating various kinds of cough, and on back beyond the bar and down the hall past the two doors marked with dog silhouettes labeled POINTERS and SETTERS and past the phone booth, where the string dangling from the quarter slot was now so grimy you could barely see it, and on through the green door at the very back, which led into a small square room with a concrete floor. All the walls were completely hidden floor to ceiling by beer and liquor cases, leaving a minimal space in the middle for a battered old round table with a stained felt top that had once been pool-table green, plus half a dozen chairs. The room had been dark, but when Kelp hit the switch beside the door the scene was illuminated by a bare bulb under a round tin reflector hanging low over the table on a long black wire.

Kelp held the door while Dortmunder carried in the tray and brought it around to the far side of the table and put it down. The chairs facing the door were always the most popular ones, and tended to be taken by the earliest arrivals.

Dortmunder sat in the chair facing the door head-on, while Kelp, to his right, stood a moment to pick up the bottle, study its top, and with admiration say, "Boy, they do a good job. Looks just like a government seal, and you could swear the cap was never opened."

"My ice cubes are melting," Dortmunder commented.

Kelp looked in both glasses, then said, "Well, John, you know, they would anyway."

"But not alone. My ice cubes don't like to melt alone."

"Gotcha." Kelp opened the bottle, poured murky liquid over the ice cubes in both glasses, placed the glasses on pre-existing circular stain marks on the felt, and put tray and bottle on the floor between their chairs. Then he sat down, as the door opened again, and a stocky open-faced fellow with carroty hair came in, carrying a glass of beer in one hand and wearing a salt shaker in his shirt pocket. He looked at Dortmunder and Kelp, seemed dissatisfied, and said, "You got here ahead of me."

"Well, we said ten o'clock," Dortmunder said. "It's ten o'clock."

"Hi, Stan," said Kelp.

"Yeah, hi, Andy," said the newcomer, who still seemed dissatisfied. His name was Stan Murch, and when things had to be driven, he was the driver. Taking the seat next to Kelp, so he'd have no worse than his profile to the door, he said, "They're tearin' up Sixth Avenue again. Would you believe it?"

"Yes," Dortmunder said.

Stan lived in the depths of Brooklyn, in Canarsie, with his

cabdriver mother, so plotting the ramifications and combinations of travel between his place and anywhere in Manhattan was his ongoing problem and passion. Now, sipping in an agitated way at his beer, taking the salt shaker from his pocket and putting it on the table, he said, "So I took the Brooklyn Battery Tunnel, right? This time of night, what else would you do?"

"Exactly," Kelp said.

"From there it's a straight shot," Stan explained. "Up Sixth Avenue, into the park, out at Seventy-second, over to Amsterdam, wham, bam, I'm here."

"That's right," Dortmunder agreed. "You're here."

"But not this time," Stan said darkly.

Dortmunder looked again, but he'd been right; Stan was definitely here. He decided to let that go.

Stan said, "This time, I get up into the Twenties, *there* it is again, those big lumber pieces painted white and red, *half* of Sixth Avenue all torn up, backhoes and bulldozers and who knows what all inside there, we're down to no lanes. And you know something else?"

"No," Dortmunder said.

"It's always the left side! They go along, a year, two years, the left side of Sixth Avenue all tore up, and then finally they repave it, they take all the barriers away, you figure, now they're gonna do the right side. But no. Nothing happens. Four months, six months, and then *bam*, they're tearin up the left side again. If they can't do it right, why don't they just quit?"

"Maybe it's a political statement," Kelp suggested, and the door opened, and in came a hearty heavyset fellow in a tan check sports jacket and open-collar shirt. He had a wide pleasant mouth and a big round pleasant nose, and he carried a glass full of ice cubes that clinked pleasantly as he moved. This was Ralph Winslow, the lockman, who was taking Wally Whistler's place this time because Wally, since their work together at the N-Joy, had fallen upon a mischance. He'd been waiting for a crosstown bus and hardly even noticing the armored car parked there, in the bus stop because it was also in front of the bank, and when the armored car's alarm went off he hadn't at first realized it had anything to do with him, so he was still standing there when the guards came running out of the bank, all of which he was still explaining to various officials deep in the bowels of authority, which meant Ralph Winslow had been phoned and was free.

"Whadaya say, Ralph?" Kelp said, and Ralph stood a moment, glass in hand, ice cubes tinkling, as though he were at a cocktail party. Then, "I say, evening, gents," he decided, and closed the door.

"Now," Dortmunder said, "all we need is Tiny."

"Oh, he's outside," Ralph said, coming around to sit to Dortmunder's left, where he too could watch the door.

"What, is he getting a drink?"

"Tiny? He's got his drink," Ralph said. "When I came back, he was explaining to some fellas there how you could cure a cold right away by squeezing all the air out of a person."

"Uh oh," Dortmunder said.

"Bad air out, good air in, that's what he was saying," Ralph explained.

Standing, Kelp said, "I'll go get him."

"Good," Dortmunder said.

Kelp left the room, and Ralph said, "I understand this one's out of town."

"Vegas," Dortmunder told him.

Nodding, Ralph said, "Not a bad place, Vegas. Not as good as the old days, when they were going for the high rollers. Back then, you could put on a sheet and be an oil billionaire and unlock your way through half the safes in town. These days, they've gone family, family oriented, mom and pop and the kids and the recreational vehicle. Your best bet now, out there, is be a midget and dress like a schoolkid off the bus."

"I don't think," Dortmunder said, "it's gone entirely Disneyland."

"No no," Ralph agreed, "they still got all the old stuff,

only it's adapted. The ladies on the stroll are all cartoon characters now. Polly Pross, Howdy Hooker."

"And the twins," Stan said, "Bim and Bo."

"Them, too," Ralph agreed, and the door opened, and Kelp came in, looking a little dazed. "They're layin around on the floor out there," he said, "like a neutron bomb."

"Uh huh," Dortmunder said.

Kelp continued to hold the door open, and in came a medium range intercontinental ballistic missile with legs. Also arms, about the shape of fire hydrants but longer, and a head, about the shape of a fire hydrant. This creature, in a voice that sounded as though it had started from the center of the earth several centuries ago and just now got here, said, "Hello, Dortmunder."

"Hello, Tiny," Dortmunder said. "What did you do to Rollo's customers?"

"They'll be all right," Tiny said, coming around the table to take Kelp's place. "Soon as they catch their breath."

"Where did you toss it?" Dortmunder asked.

Tiny, whose full name was Tiny Bulcher and whose strength was as the strength of ten even though his heart in fact was anything but pure, settled himself in Kelp's former chair and laughed and whomped Dortmunder on the shoulder. Having expected it, Dortmunder had already braced himself against the table, so it wasn't too bad. "Dortmunder," Tiny said, "you make me laugh."

"I'm glad," Dortmunder said.

Kelp, expressionless, picked up his glass and went around to the wrong side of the table, where he couldn't see the door without turning his head.

"You should be glad," Tiny told him. "So you got something, huh?"

"I think so," Dortmunder said.

"Well, Dortmunder," Tiny said, "you know me. I like a sure thing."

"Nothing's sure in this life, Tiny."

"Oh, I don't know about that," Tiny said, and flexed his arms, and drank, so that for the first time you could see that he had a tall glass tucked away inside that hand. The glass contained a bright red liquid that might have been cherry soda, but was not. Putting this glass, now half empty, on the table, Tiny said, "Lay it on us, Dortmunder."

Dortmunder took a deep breath, and paused. The beginning was the difficult part, the story about the goddam ring. He said, "Does everybody know about the ring? The ring I had?"

"Oh, sure," Stan said, and Ralph said, "I called you, remember?" and Stan said, "I called you, too," and Tiny, who had not called, *laughed*. This was a laugh, full-bodied and complete, the real thing, a great roaring laugh that made all the cartons around the walls vibrate, so that he laughed to a kind of distant church bell accompaniment. Then he got hold of himself and said, "Dortmunder, I heard about that. I wish I could've seen your face."

"I wish so, too, Tiny," Dortmunder said, and Tiny laughed all over again.

There was nothing to be done about Tiny; you either didn't invite him to the party, or you indulged him. So Dortmunder waited till the big man had calmed himself down—caught his breath, so to speak—and then he said, "I been trying to get that ring back. I tried out on Long Island, and I tried here in the city, and I tried down in Washington, DC. Every time I missed the guy, so I never got the ring, but every time I made a profit."

"I can vouch for that," Kelp said, and glanced over his shoulder at the door.

"But by now," Dortmunder said, "the problem is, all the stuff I lifted from this guy, he knows I'm on his tail."

Kelp said, "John? Do you think so?"

"The fifty thousand we took from the Watergate," Dortmunder said. "I think that's the one that did it."

Tiny said, "Dortmunder? You took fifty G outta the Watergate? *That's* no third-rate burglary."

Once again, Dortmunder let that reference sail on by, though by now he was coming to recognize its appearances, like Halley's Comet. He said, "I think the guy was suspicious before that, when we cleaned out his place in New York—"

"Dortmunder," Tiny said, "you have been busy."

"I have," Dortmunder agreed. "Anyway, after that, the guy changed his MO. Before then, he was very easy to track, he's this rich guy that tells his companies where he's gonna be every second, and Wally— Remember Wally Knurr?"

"The butterball," Tiny said, and smiled in fond recollection. "He was amusing, too, that Wally," he said. "Could be fun to play basketball with him."

Not sure he wanted to know exactly what Tiny meant by that, Dortmunder went on, "Well, anyway, Wally and his computer tracked the guy for us, until all of a sudden—the guy's name is Max Fairbanks, he's very rich, he's an utter pain in the ass—he went to the mattresses. Nobody's supposed to know where he is, nobody gets his schedule, he shifted everything around, Wally can't find him no matter what."

"You got him scared, Dortmunder," Tiny said, grinning, and gave him an affectionate punch in the arm that drove Dortmunder into Ralph, to his left.

Regaining his balance, Dortmunder said, "The one place he's still scheduled for that everybody knows about is next week in Vegas."

Ralph said, "That's the only exception?"

"Uh huh."

Ralph tinkled ice cubes. "How come?"

"I figure," Dortmunder said, "it's a trap."

Kelp said, "John, you don't have to be paranoid, you know. The Vegas stuff was set up before he went secret, that's all."

"He'd change it," Dortmunder said. "He'd switch things around, like he did in Washington and like he's doing in Chicago. But, no. In Vegas, he's right on schedule, sitting out there fat and easy and obvious. So it's a trap."

Tiny said, "And you want to walk into it."

"What else am I gonna do?" Dortmunder asked him. "It's my only shot at the guy, and he knows it, and I know it. If I don't get the ring then, I'll never get it. So I got to go in, saying, okay, it's a trap, how do I get around this trap, and I figure the way how I get around this trap is with the four guys in this room."

"Who," Tiny said, "you want to amble into this trap with you."

Ralph said, "This won't be a Havahart trap, John."

Stan said, "What do I drive?"

"We'll get to that," Dortmunder promised him, and turned to Tiny to say, "We go into the trap, but we *know* it's a trap, so we already figured a way out of it. And when we come out, I got my ring, and you got one-fifth of the till at the Gaiety Hotel."

Tiny pondered that. "That's one of the Strip places, right? With the big casino?"

"It makes a profit," Dortmunder said.

"And so will we," Kelp said, looking over his shoulder.

Tiny contemplated the proposition, then contemplated Dortmunder. "You always come up with the funny ones, Dortmunder," he said. "It's amusing to be around you."

"Thank you, Tiny."

"So go ahead," Tiny said. "Tell me more."

39

The wood-cabinet digital alarm clock on the bedside table began to bong softly, a gentle baritone, a suggestion rather than a call, an alert but certainly not an alarm. In the bed, Brandon Camberbridge moved, rolled over, stretched, yawned, opened his eyes, and smiled. Another perfect day.

Over the years since he'd first arrived out here, Brandon Camberbridge had tried many different ways to rouse himself at the appropriate moment every day, but it wasn't until his dear wife, Nell, had found this soothing but insistent clock on a shopping expedition to San Francisco that his awakenings had become as perfect as the rest of his world.

At first, long ago, he had tried having one of the hotel operators call him precisely at noon each day, but he hadn't liked it; the prospect of speaking to an employee the very first thing, even before brushing one's teeth, was unpleasant, somehow. Later, he'd tried various alarm clocks of the regular sort, but their beepings and squawkings and snarlings had made it seem as though he were forever coming to consciousness in some barnyard rather than in paradise, so he'd thrown them all out, or given them away to employees who were having trouble getting to work on time; the gentle hint, before the axe. Then he'd tried radio alarms, but no station satisfied; rock music and country music were far too jangling, and religious stations too contentious, while both E-Z Lisnen and classical failed to wake him up.

Trust Nell. The perfect wife, in the perfect setting, off she went into the wilds of America to come back with the perfect alarm clock, and again this morning it bonged him gently up from Dreamland.

Responding to its unaggressive urge, up rose Brandon Camberbridge, a fit and tanned forty-seven, and jogged to the bathroom, then from there to the Stairmaster, then from there to the shower, then from there to his dressing room where he fitted himself into slacks (tan), polo shirt (green, with the hotel logo: ▔▔), and loafers (beige), and then from there at last out to the breakfast nook, where, along with his breakfast, there awaited his perfect secretary, Sharon Thistle, and the view out from his bungalow to his perfect paradise, the Gaiety Hotel, Battle-Lake and Casino, here in sunny *sunny* Las Vegas.

"*Good* morning," he cried, and seated himself before half a grapefruit, two slices of crispy dry toast, a glass of V-8 juice, and a lovely pot of coffee.

"Good morning," Sharon said, returning his smile. A pleasantly stout lady, Sharon combined the motherly with the quick-witted in a way that Brandon could only think of as perfect. She had her own cup of coffee before her at the oval table placed in front of the view, but she would have had her real breakfast hours ago, since she still lived the normal hours that Brandon had given up seven years back when he'd taken over this job as manager of the Gaiety. The life of the hotel was centered primarily in the evening hours, spilling both backward to the afternoon and forward to late night, and it seemed to Brandon that the man responsible for it all should be available when activity in his realm was at its height. Thus it was that he had trained himself to retire no later than four every morning, and spring back out of bed promptly at noon. It was a regimen he had come to relish, yet another part of the perfection of his paradise.

The view before him as he ate his breakfast was of his life, and his livelihood. From here, he could see over manicured lawns and plantings and wandering asphalt footpaths to the swimming pool, already filled with children no doubt shrieking with joy. (In this air-conditioned bungalow, with the double-paned glass in every window, one didn't actually hear the shrieking, but one could see all those wide-open mouths, like baby birds in a nest, and guess.)

Beyond the pool and some more plantings rose the sixteen-story main building of the hotel, sand-colored and irregularly shaped so as to give every room in the hotel a view of some other part of the hotel, there not being much of anything beyond the hotel that could reasonably have been called a view.

To the left he could just glimpse the tennis courts, and to the right a segment of the stands circling the Battle-Lake. Above shone the dry blue sky of Las Vegas, a pale thin blue like that of underarm stick deodorant. From the trees, had the windows been open and the children in the pool silenced, one could have heard the recorded trills of bird song. Who could ask for anything more?

Not Brandon. Smiling, happy, he ate a bit of grapefruit—the boss's grapefruit was always perfectly sectioned, of course—and then said, "Well, what have we today?"

"Nothing much," Sharon told him, leafing through her ever-present steno pad, "except Earl Radburn."

"Ah."

Earl Radburn was head of security for all of TUI, which meant he was technically in charge of the security staff here. But their own chief of security, Wylie Branch, was a very able man, which Earl understood, so Earl, except for the occasional drop-in, more or less left Wylie alone to do the job. So Brandon said, "Just touching base, is he?"

"I don't think so," Sharon said, surprisingly. "He wants to meet with you."

"*Does* he? And what do you suppose that's all about?" But even as he asked the question, Brandon realized what the answer must be, so he amended his statement, saying, "Oh, of course. The big cheese."

"Yes, I suppose so," Sharon said, with her understanding smile. The rapport between Brandon and Sharon, it sometimes seemed to him, was almost as perfect as that between himself and his dear wife, Nell, who at the moment was away on another of her shopping expeditions into the wilds of America, this time to Dallas.

Brandon picked up his toast and said, "Has he arrived?"

"Flew in from the East this morning," Sharon reported. "We had a cottage open."

"Good," Brandon said, and bit off some toast, and ruminated on the state of his world.

For instance, of *course* they had a cottage open. In the old days, the six cottages around the Battle-Lake were almost always completely booked, with clients ranging from oil sheiks to rock stars, but since the shift in emphasis all over this city to a family trade, and the shift of those splendid high rollers of yesteryear to other oases of relaxation, mostly outside the United States, the cottages—two and three bedrooms, saunas, whirlpools, satellite TV, private atria, *completely* equipped kitchen, private staff available on request, all *far* beyond the budget of the average family—were empty more often than not, and were used these days mostly by TUI executives and other businesspersons having some relationship with TUI. In fact, when the big cheese himself, Max Fairbanks, arrived next Monday, he too would be put in one of the cottages—the best one.

But here was Earl Radburn already, on Wednesday, a full five days in advance of the big cheese, which did seem like overdoing it a bit. Swallowing a smooth taste of coffee, Brandon said, "Have you set up an appointment?"

"Three P.M.," the irreplaceable Sharon told him, consulting her steno pad. "With Wylie Branch, in cottage number one."

Where the big cheese would stay. "Ah, well," Brandon said. "Into every life a little boring meeting must fall. We've survived worse."

Outside, the silent children shrieked.

— —
— —

Not since the glory days of Versailles, with its completely artificial cross-shaped great canal on which gondolas took palace guests for outings, sham battles were fought by real ships, and musical extravaganzas by torchlight were presented on great floating barges, had the world seen the like of the Battle-Lake at the Gaiety Hotel, Battle-Lake and Casino on the Strip at Las Vegas. The recirculated waters of the lake housed thousands of fish imported from all five continents, gliding sinuously together through the plastic lily pads near the concrete shores o'erhung with plastic ferns and miniature plastic weeping willows.

At the hotel end of the lake yawned a great cave opening, closed by barred gates at all times except when the ships came out. These were great sailing ships, men-o-war and frigates, one-half life-size replicas of such famous seagoers as John Paul Jones's *Bon Homme Richard*, Captain Kidd's *Adventure*, and Sir Francis Drake's *The Golden Hind*. Radio-controlled, these ships wheeled and ran, regardless of wind, their sails flapping every which way as they fired loud and smoky broadside after loud and smoky broadside, sometimes at one another, to the cheers of the crowds in the stands ashore. Some ships were even equipped with masts that would suddenly flop over and dangle, having presumably been severed by a musketball from somewhere or other.

These sea battles took place twice a day, at 4:00 P.M. and again half an hour after sunset, the earlier one being devoted mostly to wheeling and racing, while the evening show featured gaudy broadsides and at least two ships catching spectacularly afire.

The sound effects for all the battles came from speakers in the trees spaced around the lake, the same speakers that produced birdcalls at other times of the day, so that the effect was truly stereophonic, meaning you couldn't tell exactly where any particular sound came from, but a loud boom occurring at the same instant that a ship out on the lake released a great puff of white smoke led most observers to conclude that the boom and the smoke were somehow connected.

The lake ranged from four to nine feet deep, and tourists were not encouraged to throw coins into it, but many of them did anyway, which meant a problem with the homeless, three of whom had so far drowned in their efforts to harvest some of the cash stippling the Gunite bottom. Still, the Battle-Lake was a major tourist attraction, at *least* as popular as that other place's volcano, and so the occasional loss of a homeless person (who by definition was not a paying customer, after all) was a not unreasonable price to pay.

What a way to go, here in Paradise, your hands full of coins, your lungs full of recycled water.

≡

When Brandon entered the spacious living room of cottage number one at three that afternoon, Earl Radburn in his knife-crease tan clothing stood at the picture window, with its view out over the Battle-Lake, at the moment peaceful, with the tall Moebius shape of the hotel beyond it. Hearing Brandon enter, Earl turned and said, "I don't like that lake."

"Most people speak well of it."

"Most people don't have to protect a fellow with ten billion dollars."

How do you respond to a statement like that? Brandon looked around, and over in the conversation area he saw Wylie Branch sprawled in the angle of the sofas, one arm thrown out over the sofa-back on each side, one cowboy-booted foot up on the glass coffee table. His tan chief of security uniform was its normal neat self, but next to Earl Radburn's air-brushed display even Wylie looked sloppy. And when he sat all casual and easy-going like that, like the rancher he would have been if his daddy hadn't played too many tables too long here in Vegas—at other people's joints, needless to add—when he seemed completely relaxed and amiable like this, it almost always meant he was utterly riled about something. Looked as though Earl had already put Wylie's nose out of joint.

And now the damn man was trying the same thing with Brandon, who would not rise to the bait. Nodding at the lake, he said, "Well, Earl, if you're worried about submarines coming up out of there to kidnap Mr. Fairbanks and take him away to Russia or someplace, make your mind easy. The lake has no outlet, and nobody with a submarine is currently registered at the hotel."

Ignoring that, Earl came away from the window toward the conversation area, saying, "We got a very specific problem here this time."

"Which us boys," Wylie explained, smiling broadly the while, "ain't up to handling by ourself."

Earl, who really could be obtuse, took that statement at face value: "We'll bring in whatever additional manpower we decide we need," he said. "Wylie, of course, your people will be at the center of our defensive structure, since they already know the terrain."

Wylie's smile grew as broad as that cave mouth over there. "Us dogs will surely appreciate that bone, Earl," he said.

Which snagged Earl's attention for just a second or two, Brandon could see the faint loss in the man's momentum, but Earl's capacity for narrow concentration could sail past bigger boulders than Wylie Branch's irritation. Almost immediately back on track, Earl seated himself at catty-corners to Wylie (but out of arm's reach, Brandon noted) and said, "Sit down, Brandon, let me tell you about it."

No point getting annoyed at Earl; he was who he was. So Brandon merely sat down, some distance from both of them, and Earl said, "Mr. Fairbanks played a little joke a while back that he's beginning to regret."

Ah. Although Brandon himself had never seen this side of the big cheese's character, there had always been rumors throughout TUI that Max Fairbanks had an antic element within him that could suddenly erupt in messy or embarrassing ways. He waited eagerly to hear what the man had done this time, and Earl went on, "There's a corporate house out on Long Island, off New York City—"

"I've been there," Brandon assured him. "On several retreats and seminars."

"Well, Mr. Fairbanks was there," Earl said, "a few weeks ago, and he caught a burglar."

Wylie made a surprised laugh, and said, "Well, good for him."

"*If,*" Earl answered, "he'd left well enough alone. But he didn't. He had to go ahead and steal a ring from the burglar."

Brandon said, "He did— He *stole* from the *burglar?*"

With a low chuckle, Wylie said, "That happens, yeah," which gave Brandon an unexpected look into the workings of the Gaiety's security force.

Earl said, "The burglar escaped from the police, small-town cops, and he's been after Mr. Fairbanks ever since, either trying to get his ring back, or revenge, who knows."

"He must," Brandon said, "have felt a certain humiliation."

"It got him sore," Earl agreed, "we're sure on that much."

Brandon said, "But what do you mean, he's been *after* Mr. Fairbanks? A man like Mr. Fairbanks, nobody could be *after* him."

"This one is," Earl said. "Went back to the Long Island house soon as he escaped, but fortunately Mr. Fairbanks was already gone. So he got some kind of gang together, this fella did, and they broke into Mr. Fairbanks's house in New York City. Missed him again, but both places they stole a lot of valuable stuff, antiques and like that. Then Mr. Fairbanks went to Washington, but he didn't go to the apartment where he'd usually go, and damn if the fella didn't show up again and steal some *more* stuff. Alone this time, or with others."

Wylie said, "Persistent."

"He's making too much trouble," Earl said. "That's why Mr. Fairbanks put a secrecy order on all his movements."

"I saw that," Brandon said. "And I noticed, I wondered about it, the only exception is when he's here."

"That's right," Earl said.

Wylie laughed. "You're gonna set a bear trap, huh?"

Brandon, wide-eyed, said, "What? In my hotel? Earl, I protest! We have children here! Families!"

Earl was unfazed. "The fella's coming this way," he said. "Nothing we can do about that, Brandon, we know he's on his way. It's our job, protect Mr. Fairbanks and nab this burglar once and for all."

"Here," Brandon breathed, his voice hollow, his chest suddenly full of skittery nerve endings. "Here at the Gaiety."

Wylie said, "Brandon, I know how you feel, and you know I

got to feel the same way. Our first job is, protect the hotel, and the guests—"

"Of course!"

"—but at the same time," Wylie insisted, "Mr. Max Fairbanks *is* the owner of this place, *and* our boss. If he's in trouble, and this is the only way we can help him out, then that's our duty."

Earl said, "I knew I could count on you, Wylie."

Wylie *likes* this, Brandon thought, in horror. He can spout all the pious claptrap he wants about protecting the hotel and the guests, but the truth is, he smells a war coming and he likes it. Hand grenades among the slot machines. Mortars in the wading pool.

Submarines in the Battle-Lake.

Earl was saying, "Wylie, from this point on, we'll want a check on every single guest that comes in here, to be sure they are who they say they are."

"And," Wylie said, "I'll infiltrate some of my people among the guests, in civvies, keep them moving around on the paths outside, watch for interlopers."

Wylie's forgotten his snit, Brandon realized. Earl has brought Wylie a war, and Wylie has forgiven him everything.

Brandon looked over toward the big window, and the view out over the Battle-Lake at his Paradise. Near him on the sofas, the two mercenaries put their heads together to continue their discussion. Weapons. Stakeouts. Lines of fire. Lines of defense. Perimeter patrols.

Oh, my.

40

T he phone started ringing a little before one on Wednesday afternoon. At least this time Dortmunder wasn't under the sink; this time, he was trying to pack.

The meeting last night at the O.J. had been shorter than such meetings usually went, because he didn't yet have a detailed plan, but on the other hand it had been longer than necessary, because none of the other four could believe he didn't have a detailed plan, and they wanted to keep talking about it.

"You must have an *idea*," Andy Kelp had said at one point, for instance, but that was the whole problem. Of course he had an idea. He had a whole lot of ideas, but a whole lot of ideas isn't a plan. A plan is a bunch of *details* that mesh with one another, so you go from this step to this step like crossing a stream on a lot of little boulders sticking out, and never fall in. Ideas without a plan is usually just enough boulders to get you into the deep part of the stream, and no way to get back.

So, while he was packing, he kept thinking about his ideas. Or trying to. For instance, the one in which Andy had a heart attack on top of a dice table and Stan and Ralph were the EMS medics and Tiny was a rent-a-cop, and while they were knocking over the cashier's cage Dortmunder was waiting outside the cottage for the security forces there to be rushed over to cover the robbery. Lots of missing boulders in *that* stream.

Or the one where they knocked out the power lines, having first drawn trails in fluorescent paint to the places they wanted to reach; like the middle of the stream.

Or the bomb scare.

Or the one where they stole the tiger from the zoo—Wally Whistler would be better than Ralph Winslow at that part, actually—and released it into the casino.

Or the one . . .

Well. The point was, the details would have to wait, that's all, until Dortmunder got to Vegas, which would be tonight, on the late flight out of Newark, if he could ever get finished packing here.

But, no. The phone had to keep ringing. Briefly, that first time, he considered not answering it, but it could be May from the supermarket; since she wasn't coming along on this trip, she might have some last-minute thing she wanted to say. Or it could be any of the other four guys in the caper, with a problem; people sometimes have problems. So every time the phone rang he answered it, and every time it was the same thing, and what it was was, everybody wanted in.

The first was Gus Brock: "John, I thought we were pals again."

"I got no problems with you, Gus," Dortmunder admitted.

"So how come I'm included out?"

"Oh, you mean, uh . . ."

"I mean the little visit to Vegas," Gus said. "Andy Kelp just happened to mention it."

"Mention should be Andy Kelp's middle name," Dortmunder said.

"My lady and his lady and him and me," Gus said, "knocked back a little omelette for lunch, and the subject come up, and my question is, where am I in this thing?"

"Gus," Dortmunder said, "it isn't that we aren't pals, you know that, but for what I need—"

"You're talking an awful lot of security," Gus said, "a place like that."

"I know I am," Dortmunder agreed, "but I've always said, if you can't do a task with five guys, you—"

"I want aboard, John," Gus said. "And this time, it isn't for the percentage, you know what I mean?"

"No," Dortmunder said.

"I want to be there," Gus told him, "when you get the ring. Okay? I wanna help. Just solidarity, like."

"Well, say, Gus," Dortmunder said, extremely uncomfortable, "that's, uh, that's pretty, uh . . ."

"Don't worry about it," Gus said. "I'll ride along with Andy."

"Okay, Gus," Dortmunder said. He felt unexpectedly pleased and cheerful and buoyed up, and at the same time he was thinking he could always alter the plan a little, do different details when it came time to do the details, and Gus would probably be a useful addition to the crew anyway, and the five man rule wasn't written in stone, so what the heck. "See you there," he said, and hung up, and went back to his packing, and barely had a drawer open when the phone rang.

This time, it was Fred Lartz, the one-time driver whose wife, Thelma, these days did the actual driving. "John," he said, "I was talking to Ralph Winslow this morning, I hear you're gonna get that ring back."

"I hope I am."

"The way Ralph describes it," Fred said, "you're gonna need more than one driver. I mean, you got Stan, am I right?"

"More than one driver? Why would I—"

"You're gonna have vehicles comin into town," Fred said, "and goin out of town. Think about it, John."

"You mean, you want in."

"Thelma and me," Fred said, "we haven't had a vacation out west in a long time. Nice driving out there. We'd like to do our bit with you, John. Thelma and me. We talked it over, and that's what we think."

So Dortmunder agreed that Fred and Thelma should take part, and this time he wasn't even back in the bedroom when the phone rang, and it was another longtime associate, with the same story, and no way to tell the guy no.

It went on like that, phone call after phone call. And then there came a phone call from A.K.A., who said, "John, I hear you're gonna make a trip."

"And you want to come along."

"John, I really would if I could," A.K.A. said. "But you know me, I always got these little stews on the fire, stews on the fire, you gotta stick around those little stews if you got them goin, you know."

"I remember," Dortmunder said. "Fred Mullins of Carrport told me about that."

"And wasn't that a shame, John?" A.K.A. asked. "I remember that whole thing like it was yesterday."

"So do I," Dortmunder said. "Some of the names are fading, though."

"What I feel," A.K.A. said, "is I owe you a little something for things that didn't work out, here and there, now and again, once and a while."

"It's good of you to feel that way," Dortmunder assured him.

"So do you remember," A.K.A. asked, "a guy named Lester Vogel? Used to be in the luggage business, making luggage, you know."

"I don't think I do," Dortmunder said.

"Went to jail for a while, some time back."

"For making luggage?"

"Well, you know," A.K.A. said, "Lester liked to put his initials on his luggage, expression of pride and all that, and turns out, with the initials on, and the designs and so on, his stuff looked an awful lot like some other stuff that had the edge on him in terms of getting there first. There was this talk of counterfeit and all this, and these other people had the inside track with the law, you know, so Lester went inside, carrying his goods in a pillowcase, nobody's initials on it."

"Same thing," Dortmunder said, "happened to a guy I know, making watches. He called them Rolez."

"These things happen," A.K.A. said, "and you'd expect a

little understanding from the competition, mistakes can come along to anybody, but there you are."

"Uh huh," Dortmunder said. "Where am I?"

"Lester's out," A.K.A. told him. "Got out a year or so ago."

"I'm glad," Dortmunder said.

"Moved out west for his health," A.K.A. said. "Moved to a place in Nevada called Henderson, near Vegas."

We might be getting to it now, Dortmunder thought, and said, "Oh, yeah?"

"Has a little factory there."

"Back in the luggage business?"

"No no, he's in the household cleaner business now," A.K.A. said. "Little stuff to make the house look shiny and nice."

"Spic and Span," Dortmunder suggested.

"Well, I think his is Spin and Span," A.K.A. said. "Same color box, though. But his big seller is Clorex."

"Ah," said Dortmunder.

"Sells pretty well there in the southwest," A.K.A. said, "across the border into Mexico, down along the Caribbee. One way and another, you know, he undercuts the competition pretty good."

"I bet he does."

"I could give him a call," A.K.A. suggested, "tell him you might drop by."

"Yeah?"

"The thing is," A.K.A. said, "Lester's got employees, he's got buildings, he's got trucks, it could be he could be of use to you, you know what I mean? A lot more than if *I* came along, even if I could. I mean, what do *I* know about out west?"

A sudden boulder in the stream, right there. And another. And another. This is a new idea, it uses all those volunteers keep calling on the phone. Dortmunder, remembering an interesting fact about Las Vegas, said, "This business, your friend, this is chemicals, am I right?"

"Cleaning products," A.K.A. said. "We're not talking drugs here, John, controlled substances, nothing like that."

"No, I understand," Dortmunder said. "And maybe I will get in touch with your friend. You wanna give me a number?"

A.K.A. did, and said, "I'll call him now, say you're on the way."

"A guy like this," Dortmunder said, "the business he's in, he's probably got industrial gas, wouldn't he?"

"You could ask him," A.K.A. said, "but I should think probably, yeah. All that Tex-Mex stuff they eat down there, I should think they *all* got industrial gas."

41

It was an unexpected complication for Andy Kelp when it turned out Anne Marie wanted to come along. "Don't tell me you know Las Vegas, too," he said.

"Never been there in my life," she assured him. "Politics was all the gambling we ever did in my family."

This conversation was taking place in a cab headed uptown, late Wednesday afternoon. They'd had lunch with Gus and Gus's friend Tillie, and then they'd taken in a movie down in the Village, and now they were on their way back uptown to what until recently had been Kelp's apartment but which was now rapidly becoming "their" apartment, and here it turned out Anne Marie wanted to come along on the caper in Vegas. This was enough to cause Kelp to undergo a major reappraisal of the relationship right here in the taxi, with bright-eyed Anne Marie studying his profile the whole time.

Over the years, Andy Kelp had had a number of relationships with persons of the opposite sex, some of them solemnized by the authorities in various rites and rituals, others not. He didn't divide these relationships by the degree of their solemnity, however, but by their length, and in his experience there tended to be two kinds of interpersonal intergender relationships: (1) short and sweet, and (2) long and bitter.

Kelp knew this wasn't everybody's experience. John and

May, for instance, and others he could think of. But for himself, up until now, it had always been true that every new pairing started off on a happy high, which gradually ebbed, like the tide. Short relationships, therefore, tended to leave a residue of nostalgia, a semihappy glow in which the rough spots were gauzed over and the highlights highlighted, while longer relationships tended to come to a close with bitterness and recrimination, bruised egos and unresolvable disputes, so that only the wens and warts remained outstanding in the memory.

So the question he had to ask himself, Kelp thought, riding there in the taxi beside the expectant Anne Marie, was how did he want to remember her. Did he want to remember her warmly and sweetly, or coldly and bitterly? If she was important enough to him so that he would want the memory of her to be golden—and she was, she definitely was—then wasn't it about time to let memory begin its useful work, by saying good-bye, Anne Marie, good-bye?

On the other hand, he had to admit, he was somehow finding it difficult to think about life after saying good-bye to Anne Marie. He enjoyed her, and he knew she enjoyed him. And in one significant way, she was different from every other woman he'd ever met, and a very pleasant significant difference it was. In essence, she just didn't seem to give a damn about the future.

And that, so far as Kelp was concerned, was unique. Every other woman he'd ever met, when she wasn't being worried about her appearance, was being worried about what was going to happen next. They were all of them fixated on the future, they all wanted assurance and reassurance and something in writing and a *plan*. For Kelp, who lived his life with the philosophy that every day was another opportunity to triumph over the unexpected—or at least not get steamrollered by the unexpected—this urgency to nail down tomorrow was completely inexplicable. His reaction was: Say, you know, it isn't even that easy to nail down *today*.

(Of course, that this very philosophy might be the cause of the nervousness in his woman friends that made them fret more than they otherwise might about events to come, had not as yet occurred to him. However, since all his days were brand new, since he wasn't stuck to a predetermined pattern, it was a thought that could still occur; nothing is precluded.)

Still, the point was, Anne Marie was different. She took the unexpected in stride and didn't seem to worry much about anything, and particularly not about whatever might be coming down the pike. This made her very easy for a guy like Andy Kelp to hang out with, and maybe it's also what made it easy for her to hang around with him. Here today, and who knows about tomorrow, right? Right.

The cab was approaching *their* apartment. Anne Marie waited, a little half-smile on her lips, a bright look in her eye. *She* isn't worried about what's gonna happen next, Kelp realized, so why should I? I don't want to break up with her today, I know that much.

"If you came along," he said, knowing that even to start a sentence with the word *if* was an acknowledgment that she was going to get her way, "if you did, what would you do with yourself?"

She beamed. "I'll think of something," she said. "We'll think of something together."

42

Wylie Branch always stood with one hip cocked and arms akimbo and head back, eyes slightly lidded, as though about to go for a quick draw; except that the holster on his right hip contained a walkie-talkie instead of a six-gun. He held that stance now, neat enough in his tan chief of security uniform, and looked out the picture window of cottage number one at the Battle-Lake, where tourists stood around with their mouths open, imitating the fish in the water, and watched one another throw perfectly good coins into the lake's shallow depths. "Well," he said, "Earl Radburn may have his brains in his hindquarters, but he's right about that effin lake."

Behind him, Brandon Camberbridge had been roving restlessly around the cottage, fussy and picky, not only a nellie but a nervous nellie, his reflection flickering across the glass in front of Wylie like the ghost of Franklin Pangborn, but now he came forward to present his fretful profile to Wylie as he also looked out at the lake. "Oh, Wylie," he said. "We can't disturb the lake."

"It's a dang security nightmare," Wylie told him.

"But it's so beautiful," Brandon said. "It's a perfect part of paradise."

"Sooner or later," Wylie said, "it's gonna have to get shut down for a while anyhows, drained, cleaned out, spiffed up.

So why not do it now? Anybody asks, it's just regular maintenance."

"Thursday," Brandon said, counting days on his fingers, starting with today, progressing from there, "Friday, Saturday, Sunday, Monday. The big cheese isn't going to get here for four more days, Wylie. You want that beautiful lake turned into a dry quagmire for a *week?*"

"Quagmires aren't dry," Wylie said.

"You know what I mean."

"You mean you want everything pretty," Wylie accused him. "You mean you don't care if the head cheese, or whatever you call him—"

"Big cheese, Wylie, *please.*"

"You don't care if the big boss comes here and gets robbed or wounded or worse, just so's your little kingdom stays pretty."

"That's unfair, Wylie," Brandon said, and he looked briefly as though he might cry. "You *know* I'm doing everything in my power to see to it the big cheese is protected, but I do not see how draining our beautiful lake is going to do one single thing to help in that way at all."

Wylie sighed, and shifted position, to stand with the other hip cocked. Earl Radburn, head of security for the entire TUI and a tightass pain in the butt if there ever lived one, had been and come and gone and went, leaving Wylie in charge of security for Max Fairbanks's upcoming visit. He'd also left beefed-up security behind him, in the form of a bunch of beefed-up security guards, extra ones from other parts of the TUI empire, now temporarily under Wylie's orders, so that Wylie knew for sure and certain, if anything *did* happen to go wrong during the Fairbanks stay, it would be his own head that would roll as a result and not Earl Radburn's, and certainly not this goddam faggot next to him.

Wylie didn't particularly want his head to roll. He liked it here. He liked his job, he liked the authority he held over other employees, he liked the first-rate salary he hauled in, he liked banging the boss's wife—that Nell, whenever she wasn't away on one of her eternal shopping and shagging trips all over these United States of America, was a real tigress in Wylie's rack, not getting much by way of satisfaction from the pansy she'd married in a moment of inattention—and he didn't want to have to give it all up just so this self-same pansy could go on gazing at his goddam fake lake.

But it wasn't an argument Wylie was going to win, he could see that now, so the hell with it, they'd just have to line the goddam lake with beefy security men the whole time Fairbanks was here, whether Brandon Camberbridge liked it or not, and hope for the best. In the meantime, there was no point pressing the issue any more, so Wylie shut his trap and squinted out at the tourists, imagining them all as armed desperadoes in disguise. Hmmmmm; some of those were awfully damn good disguises.

Wait a second. Wylie squinted more narrowly, this time for real. That fella there . . .

He did his quick draw after all, bringing up the walkie-talkie, thumbing Send, saying, "One to Base. One to Base."

Brandon, jumpy as a schoolgirl at a Hell's Angels picnic, said, "Wylie? What's wrong?"

"Base. What's up, Wylie?"

"Thayer," Wylie said, recognizing the voice through the walkie-talkie's distortion, "we got a doubtful on the east walk, just south of the lake, before the cottages."

Wide-eyed, Brandon whispered, "Wylie? Is it *him?* Which one is it?"

More importantly, the walkie-talkie said, in Thayer's voice, *"I got two guys right near there. What are they lookin for?"*

"Midforties," Wylie said, observing that lurker out there. "Six foot, one-eighty, Caucasian, light blue shirt, wrinkled gray pants. Hands in pockets. Hangdog look."

"Got it."

"Ten-four," Wylie said, and holstered the walkie-talkie with one smooth motion of his arm.

Brandon, meanwhile, who'd picked out the object of Wylie's attention from the description, was now staring at the lurker, who continued to lurk. "Wylie? *That* fellow? You don't think *he's* the one we're looking for, do you?"

"Not for a second," Wylie assured him. "No. What I think that fella is is a dip."

"Oh, come on, Wylie," Brandon said. "You see criminals everywhere. That out there is just your normal depressed family man, that's all."

"Then where's his family?"

"In the pool, maybe."

"He's hangin around this same area, I've been watchin him twenty minutes," Wylie said. "He isn't with nobody else. He is not a vacationer. He isn't a homeless, because he doesn't look at the money in the lake."

"None of that," Brandon said, "makes him a pickpocket."

"He's a undesirable," Wylie said, "let's just put it that way." And he nodded in satisfaction as the two beefy security men appeared, bracketing the lurker without appearing to notice him at all. "So we'll just move him along," Wylie said.

Brandon, frowning at the fellow out there on the curving sloping walk, surrounded by all the open-mouthed families in their gaudy vacation finery, sighed at last and nodded his concurrence. "He doesn't," he admitted, "look much like a customer."

43

When Dortmunder became aware of the two rent-a-cops in tan uniforms dogging his tracks, he knew it was time to go somewhere else. Surprising, though, how fast they'd made him. He'd thought of himself as looking like all these other clowns around here, moping along, trying to figure out where all the fun was supposed to be. Guess not.

In any event, he'd seen all he needed to see for now. The casino, the lake, the cottages where Fairbanks would be staying, the general lay of the land. So he yawned and stretched, he looked around like any innocent fellow without a care in the world, and he strolled away from the lake and the cottages, toward the main building and the casino and beyond them the Las Vegas Strip. And every time he happened to glance around, those two security men were still somewhere nearby.

Well, he'd been warned. He'd been warned three times, in fact, and all of them friendly warnings, given with his best interests at heart.

The first was last night, when he'd flown in from Newark, and walked through the terminal building at McCarran International Airport, ignoring the gauntlet of slot machines that seemed to snag one tourist in ten even before they got out of the building. Outside, in the dry night heat, he threw his suitcase and then himself into the next taxi in line in the rank, and said to the cabby, a scrawny guy in a purple T-shirt and black LA Raiders cap, "I want a motel, somewhere near the Strip. Someplace that doesn't cost a whole lot."

The cabby gave him the fish-eye in the rearview mirror, but all he said at that point was, "Uh huh," and drove them away from there.

Nighttime on the desert. High stars, wide flat dark empty land, and out in front of them the city, burning white. They rode in silence for a while, and then the cabby said, "Bo, a word of advice."

Dortmunder hadn't known he needed a word of advice. He met the cabby's unimpressed look in the mirror, that scrawny pessimistic face green-lit from the dashboard, and said, "Sure."

"Whatever the scam," the cabby said, "don't try it."

Dortmunder leaned forward, resting a forearm on the right side of the front seat-back, so he could look at the cabby's profile. "Say that again?"

"This town knows you, Bo," the cabby said. "It's seen you a thousand times before. They're fast here, and they're smart, and they're goddam mean. You think I come out all this way to haul a cab?"

"I wouldn't know," Dortmunder said.

"You are not a tourist," the cabby told him. "Neither was I. I come out eleven years ago, I figured, this is a rich town, let's collect some for ourself. I was down on the sidewalk with a shotgun in the middle of my back before I could even say *please.*"

"You've got me confused with somebody else," Dortmunder said.

"Uh huh," the cabby said, and didn't speak again until he stopped in front of the office of the Randy Unicorn Motel & Pool. Then, Dortmunder having paid him and tipped him more decently than usual, the cabby said, with deadpan irony, "Enjoy your vacation."

"Thanks," Dortmunder said.

The Randy Unicorn was long, low, brick, and lit mostly by red neon. When Dortmunder pushed open the office door a bell rang somewhere deeper inside the building, and a minute later a mummified woman in pink hair curlers came through the doorway behind the counter, looked him up and down, and said, "Uh huh."

"I want a room," Dortmunder said.

"I know that," the woman said, and pointed at the check-in forms. "Fill that out."

"Sure."

Dortmunder wrote a short story on the form, while the woman looked past him out the front window. She said, "No car."

"I just flew in," he said. "The cab brought me here."

"Uh huh," the woman said.

Dortmunder didn't like how everybody around here said *uh huh* all the time, in that manner as though to say, *we've got your number, and it's a low one.* "There," he said, the short story finished.

The woman read the short story with a skeptical smile, and said, "How long you plan to stay?"

"A week. I'll pay cash."

"I know that," the woman said. "We give five percent off for cash, and two percent more if you pay by the week. In front."

"Sounds good," Dortmunder lied, and hauled out his thick wallet. He was paying cash here, and his own cash at that, because the kind of credit card he could get from his friend Stoon might shrivel up like the last leaf of summer before this excursion to Las Vegas was finished. And although it was his own cash at the moment, it had in fact come originally from Max Fairbanks, one way and another, so it seemed right to spend Fairbanks's money to hunt Fairbanks down.

Also, the reason he was staying at a motel a little ways off from the Strip, rather than at the Gaiety, was because he knew Fairbanks knew he was coming, so any singleton guy checking into the Gaiety the next few days would be given very close observation indeed. In fact, pairs of guys together, or groups of guys, any combination like that, would be scrutinized right down to their dandruff, which was why none of the people coming out to help Dortmunder in his moment of need would stay at the Gaiety, but would all be around, here and there, somewhere else.

The mummified woman watched Dortmunder's wallet and his hands and the money he spread on the counter. He put the wallet away, she picked up the cash and counted it, and then she said, "It's none of my business."

Dortmunder looked alert.

"I wouldn't do it if I were you," she said.

Dortmunder looked bewildered. "Do what?"

"Whatever you're thinking of," she said. "You seem okay, not full of yourself or nothing, so I'll just give you some advice, if you don't mind."

"Everybody gives me advice," Dortmunder complained.

"Everybody can tell you need it," she said. "My advice is, enjoy your stay in our fair city. Swim in the pool here, it's a very nice pool, I say so myself. Walk over to the casinos, have a good time. Eat the food, see the sights. A week from now, go home. Otherwise," she said, and gestured with the handful of money, "I got to tell you, we don't give refunds."

"I won't need one," Dortmunder assured her.

She nodded. "Uh huh," she said, and put the money in the pocket of her cardigan.

So that was the second warning, and the third warning was this morning, in the cafe a block from the Randy Unicorn where he ate his breakfast, and where the waitress, at the end of the meal, when she slid the check onto the table, said, "Just get to town?"

"Yes," he said.

"Just a friendly word of warning," she said, and leaned close, and murmured, "Just leave."

And now, he's less than an hour at the Gaiety Hotel, Battle-Lake and Casino, and he's got security guards in both hip pockets. What's going on here?

It was a twenty-minute walk from the Strip back to the Randy Unicorn, through flat tan ground with more empty lots than buildings, and none of the buildings more than three stories tall. And back there behind him loomed those architectural fantasies, soaring up like psychedelic mushrooms, millions of bright lights competing with the sun, a line of those weird structures all alone in the flatness, surrounded by Martian desert, as though they'd sprouted from seeds planted in the dead soil by Pan, though actually they'd been planted by Bugsy Siegel, who'd watered them with his blood.

Walking in the sunlight through this lesser Las Vegas of dusty parking lots and washed-out shopfronts of dry cleaners and liquor stores, Dortmunder reflected that somehow, once he was out of New York City, he was less invisible than he was used to. He was going to have to move very carefully around this town.

When he came plodding down the sunny dry block to the Randy Unicorn, he had to pass the office first, with the rental units beyond it, and as he sloped by, the office door opened and the mummified woman stuck her head out to say, "Over here."

Dortmunder looked at her, then looked down along the line of motel room doors that faced onto the blacktop parking area between building and street. A silver Buick Regal was parked among the vehicles along there, nose in, probably in front of Dortmunder's room. It was quite different from the dusty pickup trucks and rump-sprung station wagons in front of some of the other units. Dortmunder couldn't see the license plate on the Regal, but he could guess. And he could also guess what the mummified woman wanted to say.

Which is what she said: "Some fella picked his way into your room awhile ago. He's still in there."

"That's okay," Dortmunder said. "He's a friend of mine."

"Uh huh," she said.

44

"Ah, the open road," Andy Kelp said, at the wheel of the Regal. (The license plates did say MD, as Dortmunder had expected, and were from New Mexico.)

Interstate 93/95, between Las Vegas and Henderson, was a wide road, all right, but with all the commercial traffic high-balling along it Dortmunder wouldn't exactly call it open. Still, they were making good time, and the Regal's air-conditioning was smooth as a diaper, so Dortmunder relaxed partly into all this comfort and said, "Lemme tell you what's been happening here."

Kelp glanced away from the semis and vans and potato chip trucks long enough to say, "Happening? You just got here."

"And everybody," Dortmunder told him, "makes me for a wrong guy. Like *that*. Like *that*." The second time he tried to snap his fingers, he hurt something in a joint. "Right away," he explained.

Again Kelp gave him the double-o, then looked back at the highway in time not to run into the back of that big slat-sided truck full of live cows. Steering around the beef, which looked reproachfully at them as they went by, Kelp said, "I see what your problem is, John. You don't have a sense of what we call protective coloration."

Dortmunder frowned at him, and massaged his finger joint. "What's that?"

"You'll find out," Kelp promised him, which sounded ominous. "When we get back from seeing this fella Vogel. But let's get this part squared away first." Shaking his head, weaving through the traffic in all this sunlight, Kelp said, "I hope he's got what we want."

"It would help," Dortmunder agreed.

— —
—

Dortmunder had phoned Lester Vogel from Vegas to introduce himself and get directions, and they found the place the first try, in a low incomplete tan neighborhood of warehouses and small factories in the scrubby desert, just beyond the Henderson city line. A tall unpainted board fence ran all around a full block here, with big black letters along each side that read GENERAL MANUFACTURING, which didn't exactly tell you a hell of a lot about what was going on inside there. However, when Dortmunder and Kelp got out of the Regal's air-conditioning and into Nevada's air, there was a smell wafting over that fence to suggest there were people somewhere nearby stirring things in vats with one hand while holding their nose with the other.

Kelp had parked, per instructions, next to the truck entrance to General Manufacturing, a big pair of broad wood-slat doors that looked just like the rest of the fence and that were firmly closed. Now they went over to those doors, banged on them for a while, and at last a voice from inside yelled something in Spanish, so Dortmunder yelled back in English: "Dortmunder! Here to see Vogel!"

There was silence then for a long while, during which Dortmunder tried unsuccessfully to see between the wooden slats of the door, and then, just as Kelp was saying, "Maybe we oughta whack it again," one side of the entrance creaked inward just enough for a bony dark-complexioned black-haired head to lean out, study them both briefly, and say, "Hokay."

The head disappeared, but the opening stayed open, so Dortmunder and Kelp stepped on inside, to find that the interior of General Manufacturing was a lot of different places, like an entire village of busy artisans in different sheds and shacks and lean-tos and at least one old schoolbus without its wheels. Various smokes of various colors rose from various places. Vehicles of many kinds were parked haphazardly among the small structures. Workers hammered things and screwed things together and painted things and took things apart. A number of trucks, mostly with pale green Mexican license plates, were being loaded or unloaded. In an open-sided lean-to off to the right, people stirred things in vats with one hand while holding their nose with the other.

The bony head that had invited them in belonged to a scrawny body in some leftover pieces of ripped clothing; judging from his size and boniness and the condition of his teeth, he could have been any age from eleven to ninety-six. After he'd pushed shut the door behind them and dropped a massive wooden bar over it to keep it shut, this guy turned toward Dortmunder and Kelp, nodded vigorously, flapped a hand in the direction of the schoolbus, and said, "Orifice."

"Got it," Dortmunder said, and he and Kelp made their way through this dusty busy landscape that would surely have reminded them of Vulcan's workshop if either of them had ever paid the slightest bit of attention in school, and as they got to the orangey yellow bus its door sagged open and out bounded a grinning wiry guy in a black three-piece suit, white shirt, black tie, and black wing-tip shoes. He looked like he was going to the funeral of somebody he was glad was dead.

This guy stopped in front of Dortmunder and Kelp, legs apart, hands on hips, chin thrust forward, eyes bright and cheerful but at the same time somehow aggressive, and he said, "Which one's Dortmunder?"

"Me," Dortmunder said.

"Good," the guy said, and squinted at Kelp: "So what does that make you?"

"His friend," Kelp said.

The guy absorbed that thought, then frowned deeply at Kelp and said, "You a New Yorker?"

Kelp frowned right back at him: "Why?"

"You are!" the guy shouted, and lit up like Times Square. "Lester Vogel," he announced, and stuck his hand out in Kelp's direction. "I used to be a New Yorker myself."

"Andy Kelp," Kelp said, but doubtfully, as he shook Vogel's hand.

Dortmunder said, *"Used* to be a New Yorker?"

Vogel did the handshake routine with Dortmunder as well, saying, "You lose your edge, guys. After a while. I gotta live out here now, this is access to the customers, access to the labor pool, access to the kind of air's supposed to keep these lungs from goin flat like a tire, so here I am, but I do miss it. Say, listen, Dortmunder, do me a— You mind if I call you Dortmunder?"

"No," Dortmunder said.

"Thanks," Vogel said. "Say, Dortmunder, do me a favor and say something New York to me, will ya? All I get around here is Mex, it's like livin in the subway, I hear these people jabberin away, I look around, where's my stop? East Thirty-third Street. But this is it, fellas, *this* is the stop. Dortmunder, say somethin New York to me."

Dortmunder lowered his eyebrows at this weirdo: "What for?"

"Oh, thanks," Vogel cried, and grinned all over himself. "You ask these people a question around here, you know what they do? They *answer* it! You got all this *por favor* comin outa your earholes. Sometimes, you know, I pick up the phone, I dial the 718 area code, I dial somebody at random, just to hear the abuse when it's a wrong number."

"So that was you, you son of a bitch," Kelp said, and grinned at him.

Vogel grinned back. "Kelp," he said, "we're gonna get al— Oh. Okay I call you Kelp?"

"Sure. And you're Vogel, right?"

"Waitresses around here," Vogel said, "they're all named Debby and they all wanna call *me* Lester. I sound like a de-odorant. Well, anyway," he said, still being cheerful in manner no matter how much he complained, "A.K.A. tells me I

can maybe help you boys, maybe so, and if I help you boys I'm gonna help myself, and that's what I like. So what can I do you for?"

Dortmunder pointed. "Those big tall metal canisters over there," he said. "They're green."

"You're absolutely right," Vogel said. "You're an observant guy, Dortmunder, I like that. I'm an observant guy myself, not like these laid-back putzes they got around this part of the world, and I'm observing you being an observant guy also, and I can see we're gonna get along."

"Green," Dortmunder said, "is oxygen."

"Right again!" Vogel cried. "Green is *always* oxygen, and oxygen is always green, it's a safety measure, so you don't put the wrong gas the wrong place, even though they got all these different fittings. We use oxygen here in a number of things we do, we got a supplier up in Vegas, the Silver State Industrial and Medical Gas Supply Company, they give us all this different stuff we got here."

"That's right," Dortmunder said. "You use some other gases around here, too."

"If it hisses out of a big torpedo-shaped canister," Vogel said, "we got it. I take it this is the area where you got an interest."

"It is," Dortmunder said.

"Well, come along, Dortmunder, and you come along, too, Kelp," Vogel said, starting off, not seeming to care that his shiny shoes were already getting dusty out here, "let me show you fellas what we got here, and you can tell me what you want, and then you can tell me what's in it for me."

45

Anne Marie undertipped the bellman, because she knew women are expected to undertip and she didn't want to call attention to herself. The bellman, seeing she'd lived down to his expectations, wrote her off as another cheap bitch, and had already forgotten her before he was well out of the room.

Once she was alone, Anne Marie went over to draw the drapes back from the room's all-window end wall, and there it was. The Gaiety Hotel, Battle-Lake and Casino. Well, no, not the casino, that part was somewhere down underneath her.

Twelve stories down. They had given her a room on what they called the fourteenth floor, because there are no thirteenth floors almost anywhere in America, and certainly none in Las Vegas. But they could call it fourteen all they wanted; it was the thirteenth floor, and Fate knew it.

And so, from here, thirteen stories up, Anne Marie looked out and down, and there was the Battle-Lake, looking more like a Battle-Pond, flanked by its bleachers, with the cottages beyond, all laid out like a model in a war room, ready for combat. A swimming pool was also out there, and a wading pool, and miniature golf, and miniature plantings, and many tourists, most of them far from miniature. From up here, the tourists looked like rolling blobs of Playdoh in their bright vacation colors.

Also from up here, the many many security people in their

tan uniforms stood out like peanuts in a bowl of M&M's. Looking down at them, watching their steady progress through the dawdling crowd, Anne Marie was convinced more than ever that the scheme was doomed.

The trip to Washington, on the other hand, had been a lark. It had seemed as though it would be a lark beforehand, and it had turned out to be a lark while it was going on, and John's friend May had been just the perfect companion for those times when Andy and John were off doing their thing. But when Andy had told her about *this!* When Andy had explained to her that they were all off this time to rob a casino in Las Vegas as a *diversion* from their attempt to get John's ring back, Anne Marie had understood, finally and completely, that these people were crazy. Bonkers. Nuts. Rob a Las Vegas casino, a place more determinedly guarded than Fort Knox, as a *diversion.*

I'm getting out of this, Anne Marie told herself. I am definitely leaving these March hares. But not quite yet.

The fact was, she did enjoy being with Andy, no matter how crazy he was. So, at least until everybody was in Las Vegas, and the *diversion* failed, and the whole crowd of them except her was carted off to jail, she would continue to pal around with Andy, and just watch the scene unfold. And at the same time she would do what was necessary to protect herself.

The reason was, she'd changed her mind about Court TV. It wasn't so much that she minded making an appearance on Court TV—that might also be fun, in a way—it was the eight-and-a-third to twenty-five years that would follow her appearance that she didn't care for. If there was one destiny open to her that was likely to be worse than marriage to Howard Carpinaw, it was a woman's prison for approximately a quarter of her life. No; not worth it.

So she'd taken steps. She had seen to it that, when the time came to cut loose from Andy Kelp and his lunatic friends, she could go ahead and cut, and be safe as houses.

First of all, she was traveling alone. Second, absolutely nobody on earth except Andy's friends had the slightest idea she even knew Andy Kelp. And third, before leaving New York she had written letters to two friends back in Lancaster, in both of them breaking the news that Howard had left her, and that she had stayed on in New York City a while to try to figure out what to do next with her life, and that she had now decided to come home but would spend a week in Las Vegas on the way. (Not that Las Vegas was exactly on the way from New York, New York, to Lancaster, Kansas. She was over-shooting Lancaster by about eleven hundred miles. But who's counting?)

So that's what would happen. She had come to Las Vegas, as announced, and she would spend a week, and then she would go home. And the fact that a major failed casino rob-bery—diversion!—would have taken place in the hotel while she was in residence would be no more than a coincidence, an exciting extra on her vacation to make up for the loss of her husband. After all, hundreds of other people would have been staying in the same hotel at the same time.

She unpacked, briskly and efficiently. Life had been one hotel room after another recently—this motel-box in the sky couldn't hold a candle to that terrific room at the Water-gate—and she'd become very adept at the transitions. Then, looking out the window once more at the near view of the hotel grounds and the far view of out-of-focus tan flatness and the distant view of low gray ridges at the horizon line, she wondered what she would do with herself in the quiet time until Andy reappeared.

The pool down there did look as though it might be fun. Normally, she'd be doubtful about the pool, because she felt she was about fifteen pounds overweight to be acceptable in a bathing suit, but from what she'd seen of the Gaiety's cus-tomers so far she believed her nickname around here would be Slim, so the pool it was.

She changed into her suit and packed a small purse, and was about to leave the room when the phone rang. It was—who else would it be?—Andy: "Hey, Anne Marie, I heard you were in town. It's Andy."

"Andy!" she said, being surprised on cue. "What are *you* doing here?"

"Oh, a little convention, the usual. I'm here with John."

"You want to come over?" she asked him. "Say hello?" And look out my window, of course, while you're here.

"Maybe later," he said, surprisingly. She'd expected them to want to *case the joint* right away. "Maybe tomorrow morning," he said. "We gotta get John dressed, a couple other things. Midmorning, okay?"

"I'll probably be somewhere around the pool," she said, with furrowed brow.

"See you then."

Anne Marie hung up and left the room and headed for the pool, to check it out. And all the way down in the elevator she kept thinking: Get John dressed?

46

"I don't know about this," Dortmunder said. "I don't know about those knees, to begin with."

"You brought those knees in with you, John," Kelp reminded him. "Look at the clothes."

It was very hard to look at the clothes, with those knees glowering back at him from the discount-store mirror like sullen twin hobos pulled in on a bum rap. On the other hand, with these clothes, it was very hard to look at the clothes anyway.

This was the end result of Dortmunder's having told Kelp, in the car on the way to Henderson, how everybody in this town seemed to gaze upon him with immediate suspicion. If he'd known that admission was going to lead to this he'd have kept the problem to himself, just resigned himself to being a suspicious character, which is in fact what he was.

But, no. Despite the absolute success of the meeting with Lester Vogel—that scheme was going to work out *perfectly*, he almost believed it himself—here he was, humiliated, in this discount mall on the fringes of the city, in front of a mirror, his knees frowning at him in reproof, wearing these *clothes*.

The pants, to begin with, weren't pants, they were shorts. Shorts. Who over the age of six wears shorts? What person, that is, of Dortmunder's dignity, over the age of six wears shorts? Big baggy tan shorts with *pleats*. Shorts with pleats, so that he looked like he was wearing brown paper bags from the supermarket above his knees, with his own sensible black socks below the knees, but the socks and their accompanying feet were then stuck into *sandals*. Sandals? Dark brown sandals? Big clumpy sandals, with his own black socks, plus those knees, plus those shorts? Is this a way to dress?

And let's not forget the shirt. Not that it was likely anybody ever could forget this shirt, which looked as though it had been manufactured at midnight during a power outage. No two pieces of the shirt were the same color. The left short sleeve was plum, the right was lime. The back was dark blue. The left front panel was chartreuse, the right was cerise, and the pocket directly over his heart was *white*. And the whole shirt was huge, baggy and draping and falling around his body, and worn outside the despicable shorts.

Dortmunder lifted his gaze from his reproachful knees, and contemplated, without love, the clothing Andy Kelp had forced him into. He said, "Who wears this stuff?"

"Americans," Kelp told him.

"Don't they have mirrors in America?"

"They think it looks spiffy," Kelp explained. "They think it shows they're on vacation and they're devil-may-care."

"The devil may care for *this* crap," Dortmunder said, "but I hate it."

"Wear it," Kelp advised him, "and nobody will look at you twice."

"And I'll know why," Dortmunder said. Then he frowned at Kelp, next to him in the mirror, moderate and sensible in gray chinos and blue polo shirt and black loafers, and he said, "How come *you* don't dress like this, you got so much protective coloration."

"It's not my image," Kelp told him.

Dortmunder's brow lowered. "This is *my* image? I look like an awning!"

"See, John," Kelp said, being kindly, which only made things worse, "what *my* image is, I'm a technician on vacation, maybe a clerk somewhere, maybe behind the counter at

I'd say not...

the electric supply place, so what I do when I've got time off, I wear the same pants I wear to work, only I don't wear the white shirt with the pens in the pocket protector, I wear the shirt that lets me pretend I know how to play golf. You see?"

"It's your story," Dortmunder said.

"That's right," Kelp agreed. "And *your* story, John, you're a working man on vacation. You're a guy, every day on the job you wear paint-stained blue jeans and big heavy steel-toe workboots—probably yellow, you know those boots?—and T-shirts with sayings on them, cartoons on them, and plaster dust like icing all over everything. So when *you* go on vacation, you don't wear *nothing* you wear at work, you don't want to *think* about work—"

"Not the way you describe it."

"That's right. So you go down to the mall, and here we are at the mall, and you walk around with the wife and you're supposed to pick up a *wardrobe* for your week's vacation, and you don't know a thing about what clothes look like except the crap you wear every day, and the wife picks up this shirt out of the reduced bin and says, 'This looks nice,' and so you wear it. And when we leave here, John, I want you to look around and see just how many guys are wearing exactly that shirt, or at least a shirt just like it."

Dortmunder said, "And is that who I want people to think I am?"

"Well, John," Kelp said, "it seems to me, it's either that, or it's you're a guy that, when people look at you, they think nine and one and one. You know what I mean?"

"And this," Dortmunder said, as he and his knees glared at one another, "is something else Max Fairbanks owes me."

47

When Stan Murch felt the need for temporary wheels, he liked to put on a red jacket and go stand in front of one of the better midtown hotels, preferably one with its own driveway past the entrance. It was usually no more than ten or fifteen minutes before some frazzled out-of-towner, vibrating like a whip antenna after his first experience driving in Manhattan traffic, would step out of his car and hand Stan the keys. One nice thing about this arrangement was that it wasn't technically car theft, since the guy did *give* Stan the keys. Another nice thing was that such people were usually in very nice, clean, new, comfortable cars. And yet another nice thing was that the former owner of the car would also give Stan a dollar.

Thursday afternoon, the eighteenth of May, while thousands of miles to the west Andy Kelp was dressing John Dortmunder in the dog's breakfast, Stan Murch drove away from the Kartel International Hotel on Broadway in the Fifties, at the wheel of a very nice cherry-red Cadillac Seville, and headed downtown to Ninth Avenue and Thirty-ninth Street, near the Port Authority Bus Terminal, where he was to meet Tiny Bulcher, the mountain shaped something like a man. There was a brief delay at that location, because Tiny was in the process of explaining to a panhandler why it had been rude to ask Tiny for money.

"You didn't *earn* this money," Tiny was saying. "You see what I mean?"

The way Tiny was holding the panhandler made it impossible for the fellow to answer questions, but that was okay; Tiny's questions were all rhetorical, anyway. "For instance," he was saying, for instance, "the money I got in my jeans this minute, where do you suppose I got it? Huh? I'll tell you where I got it. I stole it from some people uptown. It was hard work, and there was some risk in it, and I earned it. Did you earn it? Did you risk anything? Did you work hard?"

In fact, the panhandler at that moment was at some risk, and was working quite hard merely to breathe, for which Tiny wasn't giving him credit. And now some taxis honked at Stan, which made Tiny look away from his life lesson. He saw Stan there in the cherry-red Cadillac, patiently waiting, ignoring all those cab horns. "Be right there," Tiny called, and Stan waved a casual hand, meaning: take your time.

Tiny held the panhandler a little closer to give him some parting advice. "Get a job," he said, "or get a gun. But don't beg. It's rude."

Allowing the panhandler to collapse gratefully onto the sidewalk, Tiny stepped over him—displaying politeness—and walked around the cherry-red Caddy to insert himself into the passenger seat. "Quiet car you got."

"It's those cabs that are noisy," Stan told him, and drove away from there and on down to the Holland Tunnel and through it to New Jersey, and then deeper into New Jersey to an avenue of auto dealers and similar enterprises, among which was Big Wheel Motor Home Sales. Stan drove on by Big Wheel an extra block, and then pulled over to stop at the curb. "See you," he said.

"Stan," Tiny said, "I want to thank you. This is a roomy car. I'm not used to roomy in a car. I remember one time I had to make a couple people ride on the roof, I got so cramped in the car."

"How'd they like that?" Stan asked.

"I never asked them," Tiny said. "Anyway, I appreciate

you picking out this car, and I don't even mind the color. Just so it's roomy."

"We'll get roomier before we're done," Stan assured him, and got out of the Caddy to walk back to Big Wheel, where he got into a conversation with a salesman in which the salesman told some little lies and Stan told some great big lies, mostly about being a married construction worker off to different job sites all the time around the country, tired of renting little furnished houses here and there, deciding to get a motor home for himself and Earlene and the kids. So what've we got here?

"You're gonna love the Interloper," the salesman said.

— —
— —

So that was another lie. The Interloper was big, which was what Stan had asked for, but it was kind of tinny, and none of the individual rooms in the motor home were very big, and there was only one toilet. Stan and the salesman—who said his name was Jerry, which was probably true—took the Interloper for a spin, but it just didn't satisfy.

Next they tried the Wide Open Spaces XJ. It was also big enough, and it had a good-size living room and two small bathrooms, so Stan took that one for a spin, too, with Jerry again on the front seat beside him and a cherry-red Cadillac again trailing along in the outside mirror.

But Stan didn't like the way the XJ drove, big and boxy, like it would fall over any second, so back they went to the lot, where Stan rejected the Indian Brave because it wasn't self-contained enough; you had less than an hour of electricity available in the motor home, before you'd have to find a trailer park somewhere and hook up.

Then they got to the Invidia. Unlike most motor homes, which are either chrome or tan, the Invidia was a pale green, like fresh spring grass. It had three bedrooms, two baths, a good-size living room, built-in furniture that folded away to make more space, *plenty* of septic capacity, and all the water storage and electric batteries you could possibly want.

Off for another test drive, and Stan got happier and happier. The Invidia held the road well enough in city traffic that he felt he could probably let it out pretty good on the highway, if need be, big though it was.

They drove here and there, back and forth, and then Stan said, "What's that noise?"

"Noise?" Jerry looked startled. "What noise?"

"Something in the back, when we were stopped at that light. Lemme pull over here."

Stan stopped at the curb as a cherry-red Cadillac drove slowly by, parking just ahead. Jerry got out of the curbside door, while Stan dropped the ignition key out the open driver-side window. Then Stan got out, and he and Jerry went around to the back, where Stan tugged on the license plate—being a dealer plate, it actually was loose, but didn't really rattle—and tugged on the plastic housing for the spare wheel, and on the ladder going up to the roof, and finally said, "Well, I don't know what it could have been."

"Some other car, maybe," Jerry suggested. "Stopped there at that light."

"You could be right. Sorry about that."

They went back around to get into the Invidia again, and Stan found the ignition key on the driver's seat. When he palmed it, it was warm and waxy. He put it in the ignition, started the engine, and said, "Well, I don't hear it any more."

"Good," Jerry said.

Stan drove back to the lot, and assured Jerry he didn't have to see any more motor homes, he was pretty confident the Invidia was the one for him and his family, "though I'll have to clear it with Earlene, you know how it is. I'll bring her around on Monday."

They shook hands before Stan left. "See you Monday," Jerry said.

Well, no.

48

Well, it seemed to work. Dortmunder went here and there around Las Vegas, wearing this horrible clothing Andy Kelp had foisted on him, and nobody gave him a second glance. Cops drove by on the street and didn't even slow down. Hotel security people frowned right past him at boisterous kids. Citizens walked on by without snickering or pointing him out to one another as something that must have escaped from Toontown, and the reason for that, he could now see, was that most of them were dressed just as foolishly as he was. More.

In fact, the only comment he received, pro or con, was on Friday morning, when he came out of his room at the Randy Unicorn and the mummified woman was standing there, outside her office, squinting in the sunlight as though she'd just vaguely remembered that sunlight was bad for her, and when she saw Dortmunder in his new togs she looked him up and down, said, "Uh huh," and went back into her office.

The acid test came when Dortmunder and Kelp went over to the Gaiety. They walked around the Battle-Lake, and studied the cottages where Max Fairbanks would be staying come Monday, and while they were doing all that the *exact same* rent-a-cops never gave Dortmunder a tumble, didn't even recognize him from two days ago. It was amazing, this protective coloration stuff, simply amazing. Dortmunder said, "What if I wear this crap in New York?"

"Don't," Kelp advised.

They called Anne Marie's room from the lobby, but she wasn't in, so they wandered some more, looking at the casino, which was shaped mostly like a Rorschach inkblot. From the front entrance, if you came into the hotel and angled to the right you'd find the doors out to the pool and the Battle-Lake and the rest of the outdoor wonders, and if you went straight ahead you soon reached the broad check-in desk, with half a dozen clerks on duty, but if you angled to the left you entered a kind of cave, low-ceilinged and indeterminate and endless, with all the light you needed at any one specific spot and yet nevertheless an impression of overall darkness.

The first part of the cave was a ranked army of slot machines, brigade after brigade, all at attention, many being fed by acolytes in clothing like Dortmunder's, but with cups full of coins in their left hands. They were like sinners being punished in an early circle of Hell, and Dortmunder passed by with gaze averted.

Beyond the slots, the same room spread left and right, with the crap tables to the left, extending for some surprising distance, and the blackjack tables to the right. Following the crap tables leftward would funnel you back to the lounge, a dark room with low tables and chairs where drained holidaymakers dozed in front of a girl singer belting *your* favorites in front of a quartet of Prozaced musicians. If you went the other way, past the blackjack tables, you came to the more exotic dry-cleaning methods: roulette, keno, and, in a roped-off area staffed with men in tuxes and women in ball gowns, baccarat. The keno section was actually the back of the lounge, so you could continue on through and wind up at the crap tables again.

This was all one continuous room, without a single window. The ceiling was uniformly low, the lighting uniformly specific and soothing, the air uniformly cool and crisp, the noise level controlled so thoroughly that the shouters at the crap tables could hear and be excited by one another but would hardly be noticed by the intense memorizers at the blackjack tables.

In here it was neither day nor night, but always the same.

Dortmunder went through it feeling like an astronaut, far out in the solar system, taking a walk through the airless reaches of space, and he wished he were back on his native planet; even the protective spacesuit he was wearing, with its many colors and its white pocket, didn't seem like enough.

Eventually they found themselves outdoors again, where the nice bushy green plantings along the rambling blacktop paths at least were reminiscent of Earth. They roamed a bit more, breathing the airlike air, and then Kelp said, "There she is," and pointed to Anne Marie, swimming in the pool.

They went over and stood by the pool, crowded with kids of all ages, until she saw them; then she waved and swam over and climbed out, trim in a dark blue one-piece suit. "Hi, guys," she said. "This way."

They followed her around to her towel, on a white plastic chaise longue. She dabbed herself, then gave Kelp a moist kiss and Dortmunder a skeptical look, saying, "Who dressed *you?*"

Dortmunder pointed at Kelp. "He did."

"Get to know who your friends are," she advised.

Kelp said, "It's protective coloration. Before, people kept wanting to make citizen arrests."

"It seems to work," Dortmunder said.

"Good," she said. "I suppose you want to see the view."

"Yes, please."

They rode up in the elevator together, and Anne Marie unlocked her way into the room. Dortmunder immediately went over to look out the window, and there it was. The field of play, laid out for him like a diagram.

"I took some pictures," Anne Marie said, bringing them out. "Up here, and down there, too."

"I love your camera, Anne Marie," Kelp said, and went over to stand beside Dortmunder and look out the window. They contemplated the scene down there together for a minute, and then Kelp said, "So? Whadaya think?"

Dortmunder made shrugging motions with head and eyebrows and hands and shoulders. "We might get away with it," he said.

49

F riday night in New Jersey. The Stan Murch/Tiny Bulcher crime spree against the Garden State was getting into high gear. Having borrowed a different car—a Chrysler van, to give Tiny his roominess again—they had headed across the George Washington Bridge, to begin their outrages in the northern part of the state.

Between 9:00 P.M. and midnight, moving steadily south-ward toward the neighborhood of Big Wheel Motor Homes, doing each of their incursions in a different county to lessen the likelihood that the authorities would connect them all, they broke into a plumbing supply company and removed a pipe cutter, entered a major new building's construction site to collect the Kentucky license plates from front and rear of an office trailer there, and forced illegal entry into a drug-store to collect a lot of high-potency sleeping pills. The ham-burger they bought.

A little later that night, in the comforting darkness of a half-full parking lot behind a movie house half a mile from Big Wheel Motor Homes, waiting for the dobermans to go to sleep, luxuriating in the roominess of the van, and watching the rare police car pass with the occasional traffic, Tiny said, "I went out west once."

"Oh, yeah?"

Tiny nodded. "Guy from prison owed me some money,

from a poker game. Supposed to pay up when he got out. Instead, I heard, he went out west, worked in one of those places, whada they call it, uh, rodeo."

"Rodeo," Stan echoed. "With the horses and all?"

"Lots of animals," Tiny said. "Mostly what they do, they throw ropes on animals. People go out, pay good money, sit in the bleachers, you'd think they're gonna see something, but no. It's just some guys in dumb hats throwing ropes on animals, and then these people in the bleachers get up and cheer. It'd be like you'd go out to a football game, and the players come out, but then, instead of all the running and passing and tackling and plays and all that, they just stood around and threw ropes on each other."

"Doesn't sound that exciting."

Tiny shook his head. "Even the animals were bored," he said. "Except the bulls. They were pissed off. Minding their own business, they have to deal with some simpleton with a rope. Every once in a while, one of those bulls, they get fed up, they put a horn into one of those guys, give him a toss. That's when *I* stand up and cheer."

Stan said, "What about your friend?"

"He wasn't exactly my friend," Tiny said, and moved his shoulders around in reminiscence. When he moved like that, the joints down deep inside there made crackle sounds, which he seemed to enjoy. "They have all these extra guys there," he told Stan, "to open the gates and close the gates and chase the animals around, and this guy was one of them. I went over, I said I'd like my money now, you know, polite, I don't ever have to be anything but polite—"

"That's true," Stan said.

"So he said," Tiny went on, "gambling debts from prison were too old to worry about, and besides, he had all these friends out here with sidearms. So I could see he didn't intend to honor his debt."

Stan looked at Tiny's dimly seen face in the darkness here inside the van, and there didn't seem to be much expression in it. Stan said, "So what happened?"

Tiny chuckled deep in his chest, a sound like thunder in

the Pacific Ocean, one island away. He said, "Well, I threw a rope around *him,* tied the other end to a horse, stuck the horse back by the tail with the bowie knife I took off the guy— Did I mention I had to take a bowie knife off him?"

"No, you didn't mention that."

"Well, I did, and stuck the horse with it." Tiny made that distant-thunder chuckle again. "They're probably both still running," he said. "Well, the horse, anyway." Then he rolled his shoulders some more, made that crackle sound, and said, "Let's go see how the dogs are doing."

The dogs were doing fine, dreaming of rabbits. Tiny and the borrowed pipe cutter opened the main gate, and Stan went in with his new key and climbed up into the Invidia, which he liked just as much by night as he had during the day. He steered the big machine around the sleeping dogs, letting them lie, and then paused out on the street while Tiny shut the gate behind him so police patrols would not be alerted prematurely.

Tiny climbed aboard, looked around at the interior of the Invidia, and said, "Not bad, Murch, not bad."

"We call it home," Stan said, and drove away from there.

= =

They had one last misdeed to perform before finally leaving New Jersey in peace. At an auto repainting shop in yet another county, once they'd gone through the ineffectual locks, they picked up two gallons of high-gloss silver automobile body paint, an electric paint sprayer, and two rolls of masking tape.

After that, it was just a matter of picking up their passengers. Stan hadn't wanted to drive this big monster into Manhattan if he didn't have to, so everybody else was coming out, to be met at prearranged locations. First, he picked up the four who'd come over to Hoboken on the PATH train, saving some muggers there who'd been just about to make a mistake. Then he went on to Union City and gathered in the three who'd taken the bus over from the Port Authority ter-

minal through the Lincoln Tunnel. And finally he drove up to
Fort Lee, where he connected with the three who'd driven
across the George Washington Bridge in a car they'd found
somewhere.

From Fort Lee, it was nothing at all for the big Invidia,
green tonight but going to be silver by some time tomorrow,
with its new Kentucky license plates firmly in place, to get
up onto Interstate 80 and line out for the West, just one more
big highballing vehicle among the streams of them, all aglow
with running lights in yellow and red and white, rushing
through the dark.

"Home away from home," somebody said.

"Shut up and deal," said somebody else.

50

Sunday morning, across America. Rolling over the tabletop of Kansas, now on Interstate 70, here came the silver Invidia, containing Stan and Tiny and the ten other guys. Stan was now asleep in the back bedroom while Jim O'Hara drove, with Ralph Winslow clinking ice cubes in his glass beside Jim in the passenger seat. Tiny had sat in on the poker game, and was winning. He usually did win, but guys didn't like to refuse to play with him, because they knew it made him testy. So this bunch in the Invidia, alternating drivers and traveling day and night, expected to reach Las Vegas some time before dark tomorrow.

But right now, Sunday morning, in the sky over Kansas and the Invidia, a commercial airliner was sailing by, also headed west. It contained among its passengers Fred and Thelma Lartz, Gus Brock, Wally Whistler, and another lockman, who used to be called Herman X, back when he was an activist. Then, while briefly vice president of an African nation called Talabwo, his name had changed to Herman Makanene Stulu'mbnick, but when the rest of his government was hanged by the new government he came back to the States, and now he was called Herman Jones. He and the other four were on their way to Los Angeles, where Herman would select for them a nice automobile from long-term parking and Fred (that is, Thelma) would drive them tomorrow to Vegas.

Counting Dortmunder and Kelp and Anne Marie already established in Las Vegas, this meant a crew of twenty, four times Dortmunder's maximum. The result was, Dortmunder kept changing the plan this way and that way. His problem was, he didn't have enough for all these people to do, but he knew they all wanted to be part of the action. And, of course, they would all want part of the profit, as well.

As would Lester Vogel. Out there in Henderson, at General Manufacturing, on this Sunday morning, some of Lester Vogel's employees were at work on an unusual special order, preparing a consignment and loading a truck, to give A.K.A.'s pal John just exactly what he'd asked for. "I don't know, man," the workers told each other, shaking their heads. "*I* wouldn't do this." But then again, they didn't know how this special order was going to be used.

Sunday in Las Vegas. The wedding chapels and slot machines were busy. The sun was shining. Everything was calm.

51

M ax slept on the plane, in his own private bedroom aft, and didn't awake until the steward knocked, then opened the door to say, "Excuse me, sir, we'll be landing in ten minutes."

Max blinked, disoriented. "Landing where?"

"Las Vegas, sir. I'll have breakfast for you out here." And he bowed himself out, shutting the door.

Las Vegas. It all came back to him now, and Max sat up and smiled. Las Vegas. Here he would have meetings over the next two days in connection with his purchase of a partial stake in two small southwestern TV cable companies; and meetings concerning land of his along the Mexican border in New Mexico; and meetings concerning a few western politicians who could use his counsel, advice, and money. And here, *here,* he would rid himself once and for all of that goddamned burglar!

In coming here from Sydney, with a pause for a meal and a business discussion in San Francisco, Max had crossed twelve time zones, and had briefly moved backward in time from Sunday to Saturday, before returning to Sunday again in mid-Pacific. At this point, his body clock hadn't the foggiest idea what time it was, but he hardly cared. It was Sunday here in Las Vegas, some daylight hour of Sunday—harsh sun glared outside the small windows of his bedroom—and he had arrived ahead of the original schedule, at Earl Radburn's suggestion, to be sure the bait would be already firmly fixed inside the snare at the Gaiety before the mouse came to sniff the cheese.

Max washed and dressed, and soon went out to the main cabin, where the deferentially smiling steward ushered h̲i̲m̲ to the table set for one; snowy linen, china with his own ═══ symbol on it in the dark red known as garnet, one bright red rose in a cut glass vase, a sparkling tumbler of orange juice, the smell of toast, the pale yellow of a thin square of butter on a small white dish, red strawberry jam agleam in a shallow bowl, a folded white napkin with a slender garnet border. Lovely.

As Max settled himself into the comfortable chair, the steward poured his first cup of coffee and murmured, "Your omelette will be along in just a moment, sir."

"Thank you."

A second steward entered, with newspapers: the *New York Times,* the *Washington Post,* the *London Daily Telegraph.* They were placed on the table near Max's right hand, and then that steward withdrew.

Outside the window, the flat vista baked; gray runways and tan dead ground and low airport buildings in no color at all. Smiling upon this view because he was safely insulated from it, Max said to the remaining steward, hovering nearby, "What time is it here?"

"Three-twenty, sir. Your car will come at four. I'll just go get your omelette now, sir."

Things are looking up, Max thought, as he drank his orange juice. I can feel it. Las Vegas is where all the bad karma gets worked out of the system, and I'm on top of the world again. This is where it happens. Endgame.

He spread jam on toast, the cool knife in his right hand, and on the third finger of that hand the lucky ring glinted and gleamed.

═══

It wasn't a car that came for Max forty minutes later, it was a fleet of cars, all of them large, all except his own limo packed with cargos of large men. He couldn't have had more of a parade if he were the president of the United States, going out to return a library book.

His own limo, when it stopped at the foot of the steps from the TUI plane, held only Earl Radburn and the driver. Earl emerged, to wait at the side of the car, while half a dozen bulky men came up to escort Max down those steps, so that he corrected the previous image: No, not like a president, more like a serial killer on his way to trial.

The president image had been better.

But actually, Max realized, halfway down the steps from the plane, both images were wrong. It was all wrong. He stopped, and two of his guards bumped into him, and then fell all over each other apologizing. Ignoring them, Max crooked a finger at Earl, turned about, shoved through his escort—it was like pushing through a small herd of dairy cows—and went back up and inside the plane, where his breakfast-serving steward leaped up guiltily from the table where he'd been sprawled, finishing Max's breakfast and reading Max's newspapers.

Max ignored that, too, though in other circumstances he might not. Turning away from the red-faced stammering steward, now quaking on his feet, Max faced the doorway until Earl entered the plane, saying, "Mr. Fairbanks? You see something wrong out there?"

"I see everything wrong out there, Earl," Max told him. "We aren't trying to scare this fellow off, we aren't trying to make it obviously impossible for him to get anywhere near me, we're trying to *lure . . . him . . . in.*"

Earl stiffened, even more than usual: "Mr. Fairbanks, your security—"

"—is primarily *my* concern. And I will not feel secure until we have our hands on that burglar. And we won't *get* our hands on that burglar unless he believes he can at least make a *try* for me."

Earl clearly didn't like this. An enforcer to his toes, he had wanted to do by-the-book security here, without regard for the specifics of the situation. But he did at least recognize who was boss, so, with clear reluctance, he nodded once and said, "Yes, sir. What do you suggest?"

"Three cars," Max told him. "Two men each in the front and rear cars. You and I and the driver in the middle car. No one else. No cars out in front, none trailing along behind. No snipers on the roofs. No helicopters. No people on street corners with walkie-talkies. Earl, I want to arrive at the Gaiety in as normal a manner as possible, as though I didn't have a care in the world."

"Sir," Earl said. He nodded once more, permitted one small sigh to escape his thin lips, and exited to undo a whole spiderweb of security.

═ ═
═

Max still wasn't exactly making an anonymous entrance. They brought him in his limo around to the rear of the hotel, through the employee parking lot, and over to the high wall of shrubs shielding the hotel grounds from any view of parked unwashed automobiles. Max emerged from the limo at last to find himself in another dairy herd of bulky men in suits, who insisted on flanking him all the way through the gate in the shrubbery and across the paths and landscaping to the cottages, and thence around the secondary cottages, and at last to cottage number one, where they left him and, alone, he went inside.

All the drapes inside cottage one were firmly drawn, and all the lights switched on, as though he'd suddenly gone backward again into night through all those time zones. On their feet, waiting for him, were two men, one of whom he recognized, the other not. The one he recognized was his manager here, Brandon Camberbridge, a solidly reliable if unimaginative cog in the giant machine of TUI. The other, in tan uniform, bearing an expression of unassailable self-confidence, would be head of security here; the local Earl.

As the original Earl came into the cottage behind Max, shutting the door on the dairy herd, Brandon Camberbridge stepped forward, looking worried, pleased, attentive, nervous, and weepy. Such an excess of emotion seemed unwarranted—even Max wasn't *that* concerned about himself—but then all became clear when Camberbridge wailed, "Oh, Mr. Fairbanks, we *so* hope nothing will happen to you here at our beautiful hotel!"

"From your lips to God's ear," Max said, as he realized that Camberbridge cared more for the hotel than he did about his employer. By God, he thinks it's *his* hotel!

Max smiled on the man, while deciding in that instant to have him transferred at the earliest possible moment to some other territory within the TUI empire. There was, for instance, an older downtown hotel in Boston; that might be good. It isn't acceptable for employees to think of Max's properties as their own, it encourages the wrong kind of loyalty. "Good to see you again, Brandon," Max assured him, and, the man's fate sealed, pleasantly shook his hand.

"I want you to meet Wylie Branch," Camberbridge said, "head of security here at the Gaiety. I sometimes think he worries about the place almost as much as I do."

"I don't think I could," Wylie Branch said, with a western drawl. "I don't even think it would be fitting."

Branch and Max eyed one another, understood one another in an instant, and both of them smiled as Max shook the rangy man's hand, saying, "So you'll be keeping an eye out for me."

Branch grinned. "What I'll mostly do, Mr. Fairbanks," he said, "is try to keep out of your way."

"We'll get along," Max assured him, then turned aside to yawn largely in Camberbridge's face. "Sorry," he said, "it was a long flight."

"Yes, of course," Camberbridge said. "We should leave you alone to unwind. What time should we send the chef to prepare your dinner?"

"Nine, I think. A lady chef, I believe?"

Camberbridge blinked. "Yes, certainly," he said, with a brave smile.

"Have her phone me at seven," Max said, "to discuss the menu."

Camberbridge would have said something more, but Max yawned at him again, giving the man a full view of his long-ago tonsillectomy, and at last Camberbridge took the hint and, with the security men Earl and Wylie in tow, departed.

— —
═══
— —

It wasn't for sleep that Max had wanted to be alone—he'd just, after all, awakened after a long and peaceful slumber on the plane—it was for The Book. Since he'd made the decision to use himself to snare the bothersome burglar, Max had avoided the I Ching, almost afraid to know what The Book might think of his idea. In the two and a half weeks since that impetuous moment at the now-lost house in Carrport, Max had found doubt creeping into his mind, insecurity, no matter how hard he fought against it, misgivings, a sense that somehow, in taking the damn burglar's ring, he had not made a coup, but a mistake.

Not that he had done wrong, or, more accurately, not that he would care if he had done wrong. Many's the time in Max's eventful life he had done wrong, serious wrong, and never lost an instant's repose over it. No. What he felt somehow was that he had made an error, he had exposed himself to something unexpected, he had leaped before he had looked.

That wasn't like him. He was known for his impishness, for his surprising moves, but they were always grounded in his awareness of what was safe, safe for him. He didn't, because he no longer had to, risk all.

He hadn't known, in truth, that when he'd boosted that burglar's ring he was risking anything.

In any event, the time had come. He was here now, in place, waiting for the burglar. The die was cast, it was too late to change his mind. Now he could consult The Book.

His luggage had been brought here when his plane had first landed, while he breakfasted, so that his clothing was now neatly stored in closet and dressers, and the briefcase containing The Book awaited him on the pass-through counter between the cottage's living room and kitchen. Opening the briefcase there, Max took out The Book and the small leather Hermes cuff-link box in which he kept the three pennies.

These he carried to the conversation area of the living room, where he sat on the sofa, readied hotel pen and hotel pad on the coffee table, and tossed the coins six times onto a copy of the in-hotel magazine, to lessen the clatter they made.

The lines in a hexagram are built from the bottom up, and this time Max threw 8, 7, 8, 9, 7, and 8. And there was his personal trigram again, Tui, at the top. With what below?

He consulted The Book, and the trigram below was K'un, the Abysmal, or Water, and the name of the hexagram was Oppression (Exhaustion), and Max's heart sank as he looked at that name. So The Book *really* didn't approve.

Well, he might as well get on with it, read what The Book had to say. He did understand, somewhere below the level of belief, that much of the interchange between the I Ching and himself was dependent on his own interpretation of often ambiguous statements, so what could he find for The Book to say about his current situation?

K'UN—OPPRESSION (EXHAUSTION)
The Judgment
Oppression. Success. Perseverance.
The great man brings about good fortune.
No blame.
When one has something to say,
It is not believed.

Well, that's not so bad. Is it? Success and perseverance and the great man bringing about good fortune; it certainly sounds as though The Book approves his current scheme. It even says there's no blame for Max's little peccadillo that got him into this situation.

On the other hand, what's this business about having something to say, and not being believed? What could he want to say to anybody in this matter? And who is it who refuses to believe?

And why should Max give a damn if anybody believes him or not?

Well, let's move on to the Image, and see if it gets any clearer.

The Image
There is no water in the lake:
The image of EXHAUSTION.
Thus the superior man stakes his life
On following his will.

Yes, of course! Nothing ambiguous there. Max had *always* staked his life on following his will. And on that special night, not quite three weeks ago, in Carrport, on Long Island, it had been Max's will to possess this ring. Yes! The Book approves.

Is there more? In the second half of the I Ching there are further comments and explanations; Max turned to that part and read:

Miscellaneous Notes
OPPRESSION means an encounter.

So. This time at last we will meet, the burglar and I. And . . .

Appended Judgments
OPPRESSION is the test of character.
OPPRESSION leads to perplexity and thereby to
success. Through OPPRESSION one learns to
lessen one's rancor.

And even that made sense. *Rancor* was certainly an accurate word—if an odd one—to describe Max's feelings toward the burglar who had stripped the Carrport house and reduced Lutetia's New York home to bare bones and made off with fifty thousand dollars from the Watergate apartment, and it was certainly true that once Max had the son of a bitch in his grasp, that once the burglar was well and truly on his way to prison for the rest of his unnatural life, his rancor would lessen. His rancor would *disappear,* is what it would do. His rancor would be replaced by sunshine and glee. The last sound that damn burglar would hear, as he was hustled off the Gaiety's property into durance permanent, would be the boom of Max's laughter, vengeful and free.

And what else did The Book have to say? Again, as in every time when he'd thrown the coins on this particular question, there was only the one changing line, this time the nine in the fourth position, which read,

> He comes very quietly, oppressed in a golden carriage.
> Humiliation, but the end is reached.

Well, wait now. *Who* comes very quietly in a golden carriage? The plane that had brought Max here, he supposed that could probably be thought of as a golden carriage. But had he been oppressed?

Well, yes, actually he had been, in that he was still oppressed by the thought of the burglar out there, prowling after him. So that's what it must mean.

It couldn't very well be the *burglar* in a golden carriage, could it? What would a burglar be doing in a golden carriage?

Again Max went to the further commentaries in the back part of The Book, where he read,

> "He comes very quietly": his will is directed downward. Though the place is not appropriate, he nevertheless has companions.

I have companions. I have Earl Radburn and Wylie Branch and all those bulky security men. I have the hotel staff. I have thousands and thousands of employees at my beck and call. The place is not appropriate because a person in my position shouldn't have to stoop to deal personally with such a gnat as this, that's all it means.

And that's why there's humiliation in it, the humiliation of my having to deal with this gnat myself. But the end is reached. That's the point.

Come on, Mr. Burglar. My companions and I are waiting for you, in our golden carriage. The end is about to be reached. And who do *you* have, to accompany you?

52

At Nellis Air Force Base, just a few miles northeast of Las Vegas, at some time in the evening hours of Monday, the twenty-second of May, somebody broke into a seldom-used storage building and removed a dozen cartons, all alike. The objects inside these cartons had never been used, and it was unlikely anyone in the Air Force would ever use them, so nobody noticed the theft right away, and in fact it would probably never have been noticed at all if it were not for the inventory the Air Force was required to take on this base every year at the end of September. By then, of course, the stolen objects had long since been used and discarded.

There were other thefts during the evening hours of that Monday night in May in the general Las Vegas area, all of which were discovered and reported to the authorities long before the end of September, but not soon enough to alter events. The Finest Fancy Linen Service, for example, of North Las Vegas, which provides cloth products for several of the Strip hotels, ranging from room-service napkins to croupiers' pocketless trousers, was burglarized for eight freshly cleaned tan uniforms with shoulder patches and other markings to identify them as used by the security personnel at the Gaiety Hotel, Battle-Lake and Casino. Also, a large hydraulic-compacting garbage truck was liberated from Southern Nevada Disposal Service, a private trash contractor with several Strip hotels as its customers. In addition, five new cars, fresh from the factory, were boosted from a Honda dealer in the city, and equipped with license plates lifted from cars in McCarran Airport's long-term parking lot.

One of these recently acquired Hondas was later that evening driven by Fred Lartz (Thelma at the wheel) with Stan Murch and Tiny Bulcher as passengers, both of them wearing dark blue coveralls, down to Henderson, where the Lartzes let them out next to General Manufacturing. There they found awaiting them the truck previously loaded to their specifications by Lester Vogel employees, with a lie freshly painted on both doors that read,

R&M
INDUSTRIAL
&
MEDICAL
GAS SUPPLIES

This misinformation was done in the style of the actual R&M, a legitimate outfit up in Las Vegas with a variety of regular customers ranging from hospitals and dentists to factories like General Manufacturing to Strip hotels. This truck was then driven north, back to Vegas, by Stan, with Tiny beside him.

The rear of the Gaiety, like all the hotels along the Strip, contains a loading dock where food and drink and other supplies are brought in, and access to this loading dock is controlled by a guard in a guard shack with a red-and-white bar which should always be kept down to block access, but which is almost always kept up instead because there's never been any reason to keep it down, and it's an irritation to have to keep raising and lowering the damn bar every time the butcher arrives, the baker arrives, the linen service arrives, the vintner arrives, the oxygen supplier arrives, on and on.

Yes, the oxygen supplier. The casino part of each Strip hotel is widespread, but it is also low-ceilinged and window-less, so that its air supply, except out at the very edge of the slot machines near the check-in desk and the main entrance, is completely artificial. It is air-conditioned, of course, with temperature and quality controlled from an air room near the rear of the hotel, next to the kitchens and very close to the loading dock. But air-conditioning isn't all. Each night between midnight and 8:00 A.M., the controlled air delivered from this room to the vast casino area is sweetened with just a little extra oxygen, to make it a richer air than human beings normally breathe on the planet Earth. This richer air makes people feel more awake, happier, more energized. Because of this, they don't feel like going to bed, not quite yet. They feel like staying up, playing at the tables just a little longer, trying just a little harder. Who knows? Luck might turn.

The Las Vegas casinos are vacuum cleaners, designed for only one specific purpose: to suck the money out of the customers' pockets, purses, savings accounts, insurance policies and cookie jars. To this end, between midnight and eight every morning, just to squeeze a little extra out of the civilians, they sweeten the air.

At the Gaiety Hotel, Battle-Lake and Casino, the company that supplies the oxygen in the tall slender green canisters, like World War II torpedos, is R&M, which delivers once a week, usually on Tuesday. The fresh canisters are lined up at one end of the loading dock, from where hotel employees wheel them on dollies back to the air room. The empties are wheeled out and stood at attention near the full ones, to be taken away next time by R&M. When the R&M truck arrives at the guardshack every week, the driver waves a yellow manifest at the guard, which the guard doesn't bother to read, merely waving back, and the R&M truck drives through, to make its delivery and pick up the empties.

And so it happened tonight. Monday instead of Tuesday; not a big deal. Stan slowed as he approached the guardshack and waved a yellow sheet of paper that looked a lot like a manifest, unless you were to actually hold it in your hand and read it, when it would turn out to be an advertising flyer from a local SavMor Drug Store. If the guard behaved as he always did, merely waving them through, fine. If he decided, either because he was a new guy on this job or because Monday after all is not Tuesday, to look at the manifest, then Stan would show him the other thing he had with him, which was a Glöck machine pistol. Stan would flash the truck lights twice while he and the guard discussed the fine points of the Glöck, and then Jim O'Hara, in a crisply dry-cleaned Gaiety security service uniform exactly like the guard's, would emerge from the nearby parking lot to take over the guard's duties for the rest of the night, while the guard would spend a no-doubt restful period of time under Tiny's feet on the passenger side of the truck before being tied up and left in a location where he would most likely be found by kindly people before anything really bad happened.

Fortunately for the guard's blood pressure, however, none of that was necessary. The familiar name on the side of the familiarly shaped slat-sided truck, the familiar green canisters strapped upright in the back, the familiar yellow sheet of paper waved in the familiar fashion, were enough; the guard waved them through.

At one end of the loading dock there was a small office with a window facing out over the concrete platform where goods were unloaded from the trucks. The older heavier security guard at the small desk inside that office was there to receive deliveries, to call the right employees in the hotel to come sign for stuff and pick up stuff, and also generally to discourage pilferage. This guard saw the normal R&M truck make a U-turn and back up against the loading dock. He saw the driver and the driver's extremely burly assistant get out of the truck, hike themselves up onto the platform, and wave in his direction. He waved back, and phoned the air room: "The oxygen guy's here."

"What? Tonight? It's Monday!"

"They're here," said the guard in the office. "They're unloading now."

"Shit," said the guy in the air room. "Nobody tells me anything. Okay, be right out."

Meanwhile, Tiny and Stan used the dolly in the truck and

one of the ones on the platform to offload the new canisters and then to load onto the truck last week's empties. But then they went even further, loading onto the truck the unused oxygen canisters from last week as well.

Toward the end of this operation, a fussy-looking guy in shirtsleeves came out onto the dock from inside the hotel and crossed to the R&M truck, where he said, "How come you're here tonight?"

Stan said, "We just do what they tell us."

"Well, lemme see the manifest."

"Let us just finish this," Stan said, as he and Tiny continued to move yesterday's full canisters onto the truck.

The fussy-looking guy frowned. "Aren't those full?"

"We just do what they tell us," Stan said.

"But why take away full ones?" the guy asked, as two uniformed security men, being Jim O'Hara and Gus Brock, joined them on the platform.

"Listen," Tiny said, "lemme show you something. Come over here."

He gestured for the guy to come onto the truck, which the guy did, frowning at all the canisters, saying, "Nobody tells me anything."

"Well, *I'm* gonna tell you something," Tiny promised. "This place is being robbed."

The guy continued to frown for a couple seconds, and then he stared at Tiny in horrified understanding. He spun around to the two security men, as though for aid, but when he looked at their faces his understanding grew and became even more horrifying.

Tiny said, "Comere, look at me, *we're* the ones having a little talk here."

The guy turned back to Tiny. Through his fright, he now looked confidential, as though he wanted to convince Tiny, and only Tiny, about some important fact. "I can't get into the money room," he whispered. "Honest to God."

"Don't you worry about it," Tiny told him. "I'm here to help, see? My pal's gonna drive this truck away, and I'm gonna wheel one of them tanks inside, with you and those two guys in uniform over there, and we're all gonna go to the air room. You with me so far?"

"I don't know what you—"

"You *with* me?"

The guy gulped and nodded. "Yes, sir," he whispered.

"The four of us and one tank," Tiny went on, "we're gonna go back to the air room, and nobody's gonna get hurt or bothered or not a thing like that. *Or,* plan two, I hit you with a hammer here, and you lay down in the truck, and my partner drives the truck away with you in it, and the two uniforms and me go to the air room without you. Up to you."

The guy stared at Tiny, fish-eyed. He didn't seem to know what he was supposed to say.

So Tiny helped: "This is called an option situation," he explained. "Option one, you cooperate. Option two, you get hit on the head with a hammer. Up to you."

"Cooperate," the guy whispered.

"Option one. Very good."

It was excellent, in fact, and the option they'd been hoping for, since Dortmunder's research had never managed to show them exactly where the air room was. Certainly, they'd have been able to find it eventually, knowing it couldn't be far from either the kitchens or the loading dock, but it certainly did make life easier to have cooperation from this bird dog, who obediently preceded Tiny and Jim and Gus into the building and along the maze of basement corridors, Tiny wheeling the canister.

The air room looked a lot like a television studio's control room, being a long narrow space with a lot of equipment along one wall and a few chairs at tables facing the equipment. The four people in the room barely looked up when their fellow worker and the two security guards and the burly guy in the blue coveralls with the canister on the dolly joined them, but then Jim O'Hara said, "Gents, could I have your attention for a second?"

They all turned away from their dials and meters, eyebrows raised, polite.

"Thanks, gents," Jim said. "What I have to tell you is, the hotel is being robbed."

They all reacted. One of them even jumped to his feet. A different one cried, "Robbed! Where? Who?"

Jim showed them his sidearm. "Us," he said.

Gus showed them *his* sidearm. Calmly, he said, "We are dangerous and desperate criminals here, and almost anything is likely to set us off into a frenzy of bloodletting, so I'd keep a tight asshole if I was you boys."

One by one, the technicians—for that's what they were, technicians, not cops or commandos or kamikaze pilots—raised their hands. One by one, Tiny had them lower their hands to be cuffed behind their backs. Then Tiny helped them into seated positions along the rear wall, and stood over them to say, "I don't see any reason to tie up your ankles or put gags on you or shoot you dead or give you concussions or nothing like that, do you?"

They all shook their heads, and Tiny gave them an approving smile, which they didn't seem to find all that encouraging.

There was an oxygen canister hooked up to the equipment at the far end of the room, but since it was now barely 11:30 at night, that part of the equipment wasn't switched on. So Jim made sure the valve on that canister was screwed down shut and then he unscrewed the connector from the hose to the canister, and he and Gus wrestled the canister out of the way so Tiny could put the new one in its place.

One of the technicians, sounding very scared, said, "What is that? Is that oxygen? What is that?"

Gus looked at him, briefly. "What do you care?"

The technician couldn't think of an answer, so Gus went back to what he was doing, which was putting the old canister on the dolly.

"Be back," Tiny said, and wheeled the old canister out, planning to return with another of the new ones.

Gus looked up at the clock on the wall above the dials and meters; still not 11:30. "What the heck," he said. "Let's give everybody an early treat." Then, having learned all about this stuff in a heating and air-conditioning course in prison, he turned on the oxygen equipment, adding it to the mix. "A special treat," he said, and turned the regulator all the way up.

Through the system the new mix began to make its way. Through the ducts, the pipes, inside the walls, silently breezing out of the modest registers and inhaling just as silently through the returns, circulating through all the sections of the casino, circulating through the cashier's cage and the counting room behind the cashier's cage and the money room behind the counting room, not circulating through management's offices or security's offices or the kitchens or the lobby or any of the basement areas, but certainly circulating through the rest rooms off the casino, and through the lounge, and even moving upstairs to circulate in the dark room where the spotters sit, hired to look down through the one-way glass in the casino ceiling, to watch for cheats, for larcenous employees and card counters and all those other misguided individuals who have not grasped the central concept that the casino is supposed to take it *all*.

Through all those spaces the new richer mix of air circulated, silent and persistent. Richer now, not with the oxygen normally laced into the mix, but with something chemically not that much different, a combination of oxygen and nitrogen called nitrous oxide. Or, to give it its familiar name, laughing gas.

53

Just around the time the mixture of cooled air and laughing gas began to fill the public areas of the Gaiety Hotel, Battle-Lake and Casino, the last airplane for the day from the east was coming in to a landing out at McCarran International Airport. A pair of Las Vegas policemen, in uniform, had driven out especially to meet that flight, and they stood patiently to one side until they saw their man. They'd never seen him before, and he hadn't waved at them or done anything else to identify himself, and he was dressed in ordinary civilian clothes, and he was in a crowd of two hundred deplaning passengers, but there was no doubt in their minds. He was their man, all right. A cop can always tell a cop.

They approached him, where he was walking along with that stiff-legged weariness that follows long plane rides, carrying his battered black soft suitcase, and one of them said, "Detective Klematsky?"

"Bernard Klematsky," he told them. "Nice of you to come out to pick me up."

"Our pleasure," one of the cops said. "I'm Pete Rogers, and this is Fred Bannerman."

There was a round of handshakes, and Bannerman said, "So how's New York?"

"Not much worse," Klematsky said, and they all chuckled.

Rogers said, "You wanna go pick him up?"

"Nah," Klematsky said. "He isn't going anywhere. My flight back isn't till nine-thirty in the morning. Let him have a good night's sleep, and let me have a good night's sleep, too. We can go over, oh, I don't know, say about seven in the morning."

"You'll have a different escort, in that case," Rogers said. "Me and Bannerman will be sound asleep in each other's arms at seven in the morning."

Klematsky blinked, but then he nodded and said, "Uh huh."

Bannerman said, "We'll drive you to your hotel."

"Thanks," Klematsky said.

54

Max prowled his prison. It *was* a prison, complete with guards, and he didn't like it at all, even though he'd sentenced himself to this plush incarceration, and even though the term of imprisonment was to be very short; by tomorrow evening, he'd be out of here, one way or the other.

Not the other, please. *One* way, and one way only: With the burglar in custody, in jail, or in the morgue. The fellow had to make his move while Max was still here in Las Vegas, he just *had* to.

In the meantime, Max prowled, from the large L-shaped living room to the big square bedroom with its big square king-size bed to the slightly smaller second bedroom with its own compact bathroom and with, at the moment, Earl Radburn napping as neatly as a corpse atop the bedspread; and on to the completely furnished gleaming white-and-chrome kitchen with its sink currently full of dirty glasses and cups, and around to the pleasingly pink large bathroom with all the mirrors and all the little bottles and boxes of sundries: shampoo, hand and body lotion, bath gel, hair conditioner, shoe polish, shower cap, toothpaste . . .

Irritated, Max slapped the tiny bath gel bottle back onto the bathroom counter, and glowered at himself in the wall-length mirror. In his boredom, he was reading the little bottles' labels again. Again!

The business meetings he'd scheduled here had gone well, better than might have been expected under the circumstances, but now they were done, and he was still here, and there was nothing to do, nothing to do. Fuming, restless, struck livid by ennui, Max paced back out to the living room, where the four uniformed guards continued to sit murmuring together in the conversation area, and the drapes remained resolutely closed against the outside world.

Max hated that, the shut drapes. He'd argued against it, pointing out that the idea here was to let the burglar *know* he was actually present in this cottage. So why not let him *see* that Max was present? But Earl Radburn had said, "I've been thinking about this problem, Mr. Fairbanks, and I've been thinking what *I* might do, if I was the fella we're looking for. It's always a good idea to put yourself in that other fella's place. And it seemed to me, if what I wanted was that ring on your finger there, and if I could see you through a plate-glass window, I just might decide to fire a high-powered rifle through that window, and put a bullet in your head, and count on stripping that ring off your finger in the subsequent confusion." While Max had blanched at this idea—the bullet in the head was just too graphic an image—Earl had gone on, "Now, I'm not saying this fella's the kind that might do such a thing, or not. I'm just saying, if *I* was that fella, that's one of the possibilities I'd consider."

So the drapes would stay closed. Every once in a while, a battle would take place out there on the Battle-Lake, unseeable beyond the drapes, and during the period of explosions, and the roaring of the crowd, Max and his guards would pace more restlessly than ever inside this prison, the guards with hunted looks, their hands hovering over their sidearms as the cannonades sounded all around them. But other than during those battles, there was no way to tell for sure that there was anything at all in the entire world outside this apartment. They might as well be on an asteroid in the asteroid belt, the last human beings in existence.

A knock on the door. Max at once removed himself to the kitchen doorway, feeling ashamed of his caution, but knowing nonetheless that caution was his only friend at this moment. One of the guards crossed the room to cautiously—caution was everybody's friend in this cottage—open the door.

A murmur of voices. The guard stepped back, and a dapper black fellow in a tux came in, with a clipboard in his hand and a gold nametag reading JONES on his left lapel. "Evening, sir," he said, with a broad toothy smile and a slight bow of the head in Max's direction.

Max grimaced in return. Evening? It was after midnight, and nothing had happened yet. He could almost wish this was the burglar himself, or at least one of his friends.

"Housekeeping," the guard explained to Max, unnecessarily.

"Just checking," the fellow from Housekeeping said, still with that broad smile, "to be sure everything's all right."

"Everything's," Max said savagely, "hunky-dory."

"Well, we'll just look around," the fellow from Housekeeping said. "With your permission, sir?"

"Go ahead," Max told him, and moved out of the kitchen doorway, so the fellow could go in.

The guard had already returned to his conversation in the conversation area, and now Max went over there to say, "You recognized him, did you?"

The guard had just resumed his seat on one of the sofas, but now he stood and said, "Sir?"

"The fellow from Housekeeping," Max said. "You recognized him."

"No, sir," the guard said. "Why would I recognize him?"

Max only now looked at the shoulder patch on the guard's uniform, and realized it did not say Gaiety Hotel, Battle-Lake and Casino, it said *Markus Plaza*, which happened to be a shopping mall owned by TUI outside Phoenix, Arizona. So he was part of the extra security force brought in for the occasion.

Max now looked more carefully at the other guards' uniforms and shoulder patches. He said, "None of you work here at the Gaiety?"

"No, sir," they said. "No, sir."

"So you won't recognize bona fide employees of the Gaiety," Max said.

"Well," the first guard said, "they have to show us ID."

"Did that fellow show you ID?"

"His nametag, sir." The guard, who was himself black, cleared his throat and said, "Uh, the guy you're waiting on, he's white, isn't he?"

"Well . . . yes."

"So," the guard said, and shrugged.

"But why," Max demanded, "aren't there people from the Gaiety in here, who know what the other employees look like?"

The guards looked at one another. One of them said, "Mr. Fairbanks, sir, we couldn't take over for them. We wouldn't know their jobs. We're extra security on account of you, so we're assigned to you."

"The people outside as well? Around the perimeter?"

"Yes, sir," they said. "Yes, sir."

Max frowned deeply, thinking about this. He wanted to blame Brandon Camberbridge, accuse the man of keeping the most knowledgeable guards for his *hotel* instead of using them to protect the boss, but he did understand the orders would have come from Earl, and it did make sense to keep the hotel staff at its normal duties. "If a white person tries to get in here," he said, "*check* his ID."

"Yes, *sir,*" they said. "Yes, *sir.*"

Max walked back over to the kitchen doorway, and looked in. The fellow from Housekeeping was washing the dirty dishes in the sink. Looking over toward Max, his inevitable smile now apologetic, he said, "Won't take a minute, sir. This should have been taken care of."

"Very good," Max said. He was pleased to see someone who took an interest in his work.

"I'll be back a little later with the supplies you need," the fellow said. "For now, I'll just finish up in here, check the bedrooms and baths, and be out of your way."

"There's someone asleep in the second bedroom."

"I'll be as quiet as a mouse," the fellow promised, and flashed that big smile again as he stood over the sinkful of soapy water. "I'll be in and out of there, he'll never even know I'm around."

55

It was such a temptation to make off with the sleeping guard's handgun, but Herman resisted the impulse. He was here on reconnaissance only, and would be coming back later, so pilfering pistols would not be a good idea.

Herman Jones, formerly Herman Makanene Stulu'mbnick, formerly Herman X, finished stage one of his reconnaissance, thanked Max Fairbanks for his patience, and was ushered out of the cottage by the same brother who'd admitted him. Two more guards, one a brother and one not, escorted him from the cottage to the main path, where he thanked them for their courtesy, assured them they'd see him later, and moved jauntily away, toward the main building of the hotel.

For Herman Jones, subterfuge at this level was child's play, was barely deception at all. Back in the old days when he'd been actively an activist, when he'd been X and most of his jobs had been selfless heists to raise money for the Movement, so that he barely had time left to steal enough to keep his own body and soul together, he'd constructed an entirely false cover life to live within, full of nice middle-class friends of all races who believed he was something important and well-paid in "communications," a word that, when he used it, sometimes seemed to suggest book publishing, sometimes the movies or television, and sometimes possibly government work.

Later, when he'd been in politics in central Africa, vice president of Talabwo, a nation where your Swiss bank account was almost as important as your Mercedes-Benz and where the only even half-educated person within five hundred miles who was *not* trying to overthrow the president was the president, and where if the president went down the vice president could expect to share with him the same shallow unmarked grave, Herman had learned a level of guile and misdirection that Americans, had they been able to observe it, could only have envied.

So now that he was home, no longer devoted to turning over the proceeds of all his better heists to the Movement (mainly because the Movement seemed to have evaporated while he was away), and no longer having to deal with politicians and army men (most of them certifiably insane) day and night, Herman was ready to turn his hard-earned expertise to for-profit crime.

Which was why he was here. He'd only worked with John Dortmunder twice before, but he'd enjoyed both jobs. The first time, he'd been brought into the scheme by Andy Kelp, whom he'd met in the course of various non-Movement enterprises, and the scheme was an interesting one, in which they'd stolen an entire bank, which had given him plenty of leisure time to work on the vault. The job hadn't wound up to be an absolutely perfect success, but the group had been nicely professional and the experience basically a good one. The second time he'd been included into a Dortmunder job, it had been a scam, a little favor like this current one, but with less potential return.

Pilots say that any landing you walk away from is a good landing, and Herman's variant on that was, any crime you walk away from unhandcuffed is a good crime. With that criterion, all of Herman's experiences with John Dortmunder had been good ones.

So now he was back in the States, and he wanted people in the profession to know he was here, he was available, and that's why he'd phoned Andy Kelp. Then, when Andy'd told him what was going down here, and why, he could see it was a caper he had to be part of. However large or small the profit on this one, it would get him noticed in the right places. "Herman is back," people would say to each other after tonight. "As good as ever."

No no no. They would say, "Herman is back. *Better* than ever."

≡

The night outside the cottages was dark, and very lightly populated. The children among the hotel guests were presumably all tucked into their beds at this point, watching television, while their parents and the other adult customers of the Gaiety roamed the casino or sat around in groups in the coffee shop, telling each other how much fun they were having. Outside, the dry desert air was cooler at night, almost pleasant, but the only human beings to be seen, here and there on the paths and walkways, were hotel employees and extra security personnel. And, of course, a number of robbers.

Striding away from cottage one in the shadowed darkness, exuding the confidence of a supervisory employee on official business, clipboard prominent, Herman made his way to cottage three, diagonally to the right rear of cottage one, and at the moment—as at most moments since the high rollers left—unoccupied. (Cottages five, six, and seven, even farther back from the Battle-Lake, currently housed the imported extra guards.)

So many hotels and other such places no longer have actual keys for their many doors. They have electronic locks instead, that respond only to a specific magnetic impulse. All the old skills of the lockman, with picks and slugs and routers and skeleton keys, have gone by the board. But technology is there to be mastered, and mastered it shall be. The card Herman now inserted into the slot of the front door of cottage three had not been supplied by a hotel check-in clerk, but had come from the criminal workshops of New York City. This card was an alien, a wily seducer, a cuckoo in another bird's nest, and the instant Herman slid it into the slot that little green light went on, and the door fell open before him.

Cottage three was a bit smaller than cottage one, and had the faint chemical smell of a place with wall-to-wall carpet after it's been shut up for a while. Herman moved briskly through the place, turning on lights, making notes on his clipboard, doing small adjustments here and there. At the end, he left the small light on in the kitchen, the one under the upper cabinet that merely illuminated a bit of the white Formica counter beside the sink.

At the door, because he wasn't going to give his magic card away, Herman paused to take a roll of duct tape from inside his tuxedo jacket, tear off a length, and attach it to the edge of the door over the striker to keep it from locking. Spies, political agents, and other amateurs put such tape on a door horizontally, so that it shows on both front and back, and can be noticed by a passing security person. Herman ran the tape vertically, which did the job just as well while remaining invisible when the door was shut.

Having made cottage three ready, Herman marched off and this time made his way around the Battle-Lake along the path illuminated by low-wattage knee-high flower-shaped fixtures. Beyond the lake, he approached a guard standing next to the walkway with his hands clasped behind him, observing the late-night stillness with the satisfied look of a man who likes peace and quiet for their own sake. This guard, however, was not actually a guard at all, but was another associate of John Dortmunder's, named Ralph Demrovsky; he too wore a uniform copped earlier this evening from Finest Fancy Linen Service.

When Herman approached, Ralph smiled and held his right hand out. Herman took no notice of him, but somehow, as he strode by, the clipboard left his hand and wound up in Ralph's. And then, as Herman moved on through tree shadows between lighted areas toward the main building, his right hand brushed across the front of his tux jacket, and when next he moved into the light the nametag was gone from there, and he was now merely a handsome black man in a tux, surely a guest of the hotel, though better dressed than most these days. Still, there are always *some* well-dressed hotel guests in Las Vegas, even in these latter times, people who maintain the standards and joie de vivre of the good old days of mob bosses and Arab sheiks.

Herman entered the hotel not as though he owned it, but as though he were thinking of buying it. He strode past the open coffee shop and the closed boutiques and around the check-in desk, where things were very quiet at the moment, with only one clerk on duty. To get to the elevators, he had to skirt the edge of the slot machine area, and surreptitiously he sniffed a little, to see if he could tell anything about the air, but of course he couldn't. And from the look of the few people he could see in among the slot machines, it hadn't started to take effect as yet.

Well, there was plenty of time.

Herman took an elevator to the fourteenth floor, and walked down a hallway chirping with the chatter of many television sets behind many closed doors. He was on his way to Anne Marie's room. A nice lady, he thought, he being a connoisseur in that area. If Andy Kelp needed a lady, then that was probably the one he needed. However, Herman would keep his opinion to himself. He did not intrude into other people's love lives unless he had hopes of becoming a participant therein, and neither Andy Kelp nor Anne Marie Carpinaw interested him in that way, which was probably just as well.

Rap-a-de-rap; rap, rap. The agreed-upon signal. The door opened, and it was Anne Marie standing there, giving him a skeptical look. "Room service," he suggested.

"Come on in," she said, and he did, and she shut the door behind him, saying, "Took you long enough."

"Well, you know how it is, ma'am," he said, playing along. "We get awful busy down there in the kitchen."

"That's all well and good," she said. "But there's no *telling* how upset I'd be, if it happened I'd ordered anything."

"Thank you, ma'am, I'll tell the manager you said so," Herman said, grinning at her. Then he turned away to see Dortmunder and Kelp both in chairs over by the window, looking out at the night. Dortmunder was in a guard uniform, Kelp dressed like a bank examiner in black suit, round-lensed black-framed eyeglasses, and navy blue bow tie with white polka dots. Herman could see their backs in the room and their fronts reflected in the window they were looking out. He said, "There's nothing out there."

They turned at last to look at him, with glazed eyes, like people who've been at the aquarium too long. Dortmunder said, "That's what I'm hoping for."

"Nothing out there," Kelp explained.

"A quiet night," Herman assured them, and went over to also look out the window.

Fascinating. By night, the hotel grounds became a sketch outline drawing of itself, the little flower-shaped lights becoming dots of amber against the black, defining the paths, drawing a pointillist line around the Battle-Lake, marking off the cottages. The only truly illuminated area was the pool; its underwater lights were kept on all night, creating a strange blue-green bouillon down there, its surface shadowed, its depths cool and crystal clear. Being the only center of light made the pool look much closer than it really was, as though you could open this window here and jump right in.

Herman looked until he realized he was about to become as mesmerized as Dortmunder and Kelp, and then he backed away from it, shook his head, grinned at the other two, and said, "What are you trying to see out there, anyway?"

"Trouble," Dortmunder said.

Kelp explained, "If anything goes wrong in the caper, we'll know it from up here."

"And," Anne Marie said, "they'll get *out* of here."

"Absolutely," Kelp assured her.

Dortmunder said, "Red lights coming from out there," and waved in the general direction of employee parking and Paradise Road, the parallel street behind the Strip.

Kelp showed a walkie-talkie. "Any problem," he said, "I warn the guys, and John goes to get his ring."

"And I turn off the light," Anne Marie said, "and I was asleep in bed here, all by myself, the whole time."

"Poor you," Herman said, with a little smile.

She gave him an oh-come-on look.

"Plan two," Dortmunder explained.

"Plan six or seven, actually," Kelp said. "And how are *you* doing, Herman?"

"Just fine," Herman assured them. "John," he said, "you got that rich man *extremely* worried. He's like a cat on a hot tin pan alley."

Dortmunder, interested, said, "You got in there all right?"

Herman did his big toothy yassuh-boss smile: "Jess as easy," he said, "as fallin off a scaffold." Reverting to his former persona, he said, "I rigged one kitchen window and one bedroom window so they look locked but you just give them a tug. I sussed out the circuit breaker box; it's in the kitchen, the line goes straight down. There's no basement under those buildings, just concrete slabs, so the line must go through conduit inside the slab. Give me pen and paper and I'll do you a drawing of the layout inside there."

"Good," Dortmunder said.

The room's furnishings included a round fake-wood table under a hanging swag lamp—some styles are so good, they *never* go away—which Dortmunder and Kelp had moved to make it easier for them to see out the window and hit their heads on the lamp. Now, while Kelp turned his chair and pushed it close to that table, Anne Marie produced sheets of hotel stationery and a hotel pen. Herman sat at the table, hit his head on the lamp, stood up, moved the chair, sat at the table, and did a very good schematic drawing of the cottage, using the proper architectural symbols for door, window, closet, and built-in furniture pieces, like toilet and stove.

As he drew, Herman described the look of the place, and as he finished he said, "There's four uniformed guards inside, four outside, but they're not from the hotel, they're imported."

"Extra security," Dortmunder commented.

"Extra, yeah, but they don't know the lay of the land." Herman put down his pen. "I got cottage three ready," he said. "Door's open, one little light in the kitchen so's you can find your way around."

"I should go there now," Dortmunder decided. "You John the Baptist me," meaning Herman, looking more presentable, should go first, to be sure the coast was clear.

"Fine," Herman said, and got to his feet, not hitting his head.

"And I'll keep watch here," Kelp said. "Anne Marie and me."

Dortmunder looked one last time out the window. "Gonna get exciting out there," he said.

Herman grinned at the outer darkness. "I'd like to be here to watch it," he said.

"No way," said Anne Marie.

56

There are no actual *slow* times in Las Vegas, not even in August, when the climate in and around the Las Vegas desert is similar to that of the planet Mercury, but the closest the city and its casinos come to a slow period is very late on a Monday night, into Tuesday morning. The weekenders have gotten back into their pickup trucks and campers and station wagons and vans and gone home. The people who'd spent a week or two weeks left the hotel last night. The people who are just starting their week or two weeks in funland didn't get here until late this afternoon and they're exhausted; not even extra oxygen in the air will keep them up their first night in town. Conventions and business conferences, which last three or four days, start in midweek and end by Sunday.

So on Monday night, particularly into Tuesday morning, is when the casinos are at their emptiest, with the fewest tables open, the fewest dealers and croupiers and security people around, the fewest players. On this particular Monday night, Tuesday morning, by 3:00 A.M., there were barely a hundred people in the whole casino area of the Gaiety Hotel, Battle-Lake and Casino, and they were all giggling.

None of the Dortmunder crew were in with the gigglers, not yet. Tiny Bulcher and Jim O'Hara and Gus Brock, cause of the giggling, remained on duty near the air room. Not inside it; the air room was also on the sweetened air line. Tiny and Jim and

Gus hung around the basement corridors, keeping out of other people's way—not that many other people wandered around down here late at night—and from time to time checked on the equipment in the air room, where the technicians were now all fast asleep, with smiles on their faces.

In cottage three, Dortmunder sat in the dark living room, looking out at the lights behind drapes of cottage one; Max Fairbanks hadn't gone to bed yet. In their fourteenth-floor crow's nest, Kelp and Anne Marie looked out the window at the night and discussed the future. Herman Jones, now in chauffeur's cap, sat at the wheel of a borrowed stretch limo near the front entrance of the Gaiety, ready to be part of the general exodus should trouble arise.

Across town, on a dark industrial street near the railroad tracks, Stan Murch napped in the cab of the big garbage truck borrowed from Southern Nevada Disposal Service. Out of town, up by Apex, in a wilderness area off a dirt road leading up into the mountainous desert, Fred and Thelma Lartz had parked the Invidia, in which at the moment Thelma was asleep in the main bedroom, lockman Wally Whistler was asleep in another bedroom, and Fred and the other lockman, Ralph Winslow, and the four other guys aboard were playing poker in the living room, for markers; they'd settle up after the caper.

Who else? Ralph Demrovsky, in guard gear, patrolled the dark paths in the general vicinity of the cottages. And three other guys, dressed all in black and holding pistols in their hands, stood in the shrubbery at the rear of the main building, near an unmarked door that opened out onto a small parking area. This parking area held an ambulance, a small fire truck, and two white Ford station wagons bearing the logo of the Gaiety security staff. The unmarked door beside them led into the security offices, where at this moment five uniformed guards were yawning and giggling and trying to keep their eyes open. "Jeez," one of them said. "I don't know what's the matter with me tonight."

"Same thing's the matter with you every night," another one told him, and giggled.

The guy who was supposed to be watching the monitors—

fed by cameras pointed at the front entrance, at the side entrance, at various spots within and without the hotel, a whole bank of monitor screens to watch for stray movement—that guy gently lowered his head to the table in front of him and closed his eyes. His breathing became deep and regular.

"Jeez," said the first guy again. "I need some *air.*"

That made all the others, except the sleeper, laugh and chortle and roll their heads around.

The first guy lunged to his feet, staggered, said, "Jeez, what's the *matter* with me?" and moved, tottering, to the door. "I'll be back," he told the others, and opened the door, and then, true to his word, backed directly into the room, blinking, coming somewhat more awake, as the three guys dressed in black pushed their way inside, guns first, one of them saying, "I was beginning to wonder when one of you birds would come out."

A second guy in black pointed his pistol at the seated guards, and snapped at one of them, "Stay away from that button! Your foot moves over by that button, I'll shoot your knee off!"

These guards were professional, highly paid, three of them ex-cops and the other two formerly military police. Normally, they would have caused a great deal of trouble for any three wiseguys with guns blundering in here. But tonight their reaction time was nil, their coordination was off, their brains were wrapped in cotton and their bodies in bubblewrap. Before the guard sitting near the emergency button could even *think* about moving his foot over to press that button—which would send alarms both to police headquarters and to the manager's office behind the check-in desk—he'd been roughly hustled out of his chair and over against the wall, with his friends, including the sleeper, who was very rudely awakened indeed. All five of them were briskly disarmed, and then, blinking, open-mouthed, fuzzy-brained, they stared at their captors and waited for whatever would happen next.

"Uniforms off," one of the guys in black said.

The guards didn't like that, not at all, but the guys in black were insistent, so off came the trimly pressed shirts with the pleats, and the shiny gun belts. More difficult were the trousers;

all five guards had to sit on the floor to remove their pants, or they would have fallen to the floor and possibly hurt themselves.

There was a locked gunrack full of shotguns and rifles and handguns along one wall, with a heavy barred gate locked across the face of it. The guys in black forced the guards, now in their underwear, feeling foolish and ill-used but unable to stop the occasional giggle at the sight of one another, to sit on the floor under this gunrack. Then they were trussed, ankles and wrists (behind back), with duct tape, and more duct tape was looped under their armpits and through the bars of the gunrack gate, so they wouldn't be able to crawl across the room; toward the emergency button, for instance.

"Let's move this along," said one of the guys in black. "I'm beginning to feel it."

"Jeez," the first guard said, shaking his woolly head, body hanging there suspended from the gunrack by duct tape. "What's goin *on* here?" he wanted to know.

The guys in black were stripping out of the black and into the uniforms. One of them paused to say, "Oh, don't you know? It's a heist goin on here."

One of the other guards, the one who hadn't managed to get to the button, tried to snarl, "You won't get away with this," but the threat came out softer than he'd intended, almost caring, and was further diminished by a loud snore: the sleeper had returned to sleep. All of which should have made the failed snarler mad, but somehow it didn't. He chuckled instead, and shook his head, and grinned at the heisters now zipping up the uniforms. "You're crazy," he told them, and laughed. So did the other still-awake guards.

"That's okay," one of the heisters said. He had the extra uniforms and their own former clothing wrapped in a big ball in his arms. "See you later," he said.

Which the still-awake guards—now down to three—found very funny indeed. They were still laughing as the heisters went out and the door swung shut behind them, leaving the guards in their underwear alone on the floor in here with nothing but the air-conditioning.

57

It's quiet out there. Too quiet.

That's what Earl Radburn told himself, as he patrolled the general area of the hotel, moving around the Battle-Lake, the pools, the tennis courts, the outside bar (shut for the night), the parking lots, the main entrance. He never went into the casino or the coffee shop or the lounge; there was nothing in there of interest to him. What was of interest was outside, was somewhere around cottage one, was one insane but determined burglar aimed at Max Fairbanks.

But where was he? Earl *knew* the fellow was around some place, he could feel it, like a tingle on the surface of his skin, as though all his pores were breathing in, smelling the villain out there. But where?

Quiet; too quiet. Earl saw his own guards here and there, saw the hotel's security people, other hotel staff around and about. He saw the bored doorman at the main entrance, saw the black chauffeur in the stretch limo waiting for the last of the high rollers, saw the parked cars in the employee parking lot around back and the guest parking lot to the left of the entrance, and the nonresident visitor parking lot off to the right of the entrance, and *nothing* was suspicious. That's what was so suspicious about it all; nothing was suspicious.

The local head of security, Wylie Branch, had gone home at midnight, stating his opinion that nothing would happen in the middle of the night, and his intention to be back on duty "bright-eyed and bushy-tailed," as he'd phrased it, at six in the morning. Which was all well and good for Wylie Branch, but Earl Radburn knew you could never be sure, never be absolutely sure, *what* would happen, or *when*. This was the burglar's last clear shot at Max Fairbanks. Would he wait till morning to make his move? Earl didn't believe it.

But where was the fellow? Earl roamed and roamed the territory, moving constantly back around the cottages, then out again, moving, moving, questing, like a hunting dog that's lost the scent. And it remained quiet out there. Too quiet.

He walked again around the side of the hotel toward the front, one more time, and saw the big motor home just turning in from the Strip, bowing and nodding up the entrance drive to turn rightward, toward the nonresident visitor parking lot. There seemed to be a woman driving it, in a hat.

Earl watched the big vehicle move across the nearly empty lot, the only moving vehicle in sight. It came to a stop over there, and Earl turned away, aiming his attention elsewhere. He walked past the front of the building and saw the doorman seated beside the entrance on a little stool, half asleep. The stretch limo was still there, the patient chauffeur at the wheel; he gave Earl a friendly wave, and Earl waved back. Poor fellow; had to wait out here hour after hour. And here it was, almost four in the morning.

Earl turned back, retracing his steps, looking this way and that, and his eye was snagged by that motor home. The woman was still seated there, at the wheel. Nobody had got out of the motor home, though its lights were on inside, behind drawn shades.

Why would a motor home come visiting at four in the morning? Why would it stop, and nobody get out of it?

Hmmmm. Earl strolled over that way, seeing that the woman's hat was one of those tall things with fruit, like a salad. She was just sitting there, as patient as the chauffeur, hands on the wheel.

Was she waiting for somebody who was supposed to come

out of the casino at this hour? Waiting, like the limo driver? Earl's curiosity was piqued. A sixth sense told him there was something meaningful about this motor home. He walked closer to it, wary, watching this way and that, watching the door in the side of the thing, waiting for it to open, but it didn't.

The woman finally did turn her head to smile down at him when Earl stopped beside her window. "Hello, there," he said.

The window was closed, and probably she couldn't hear him. She smiled, and nodded.

Mouthing carefully, raising his voice a bit, Earl said, "Who are you waiting for?"

Instead of answering, the woman smiled some more and pointed backward, gesturing for him to walk along the side of the motor home. He frowned up at her, and also pointed down in the same direction: "Down there?"

Her smile redoubled. She nodded, and made rapping motions in the air with one fist, then pointed down along the vehicle again.

She wanted him to go down there and knock on the door. All right, he would, and he did. The woman, and her smile, and her hat, had made him less suspicious than before, but still just as curious. He knocked on the door, and a few seconds later it opened, and a smiling guy in T-shirt and brown pants stood there, saying, "Hi."

Earl said, "You folks waiting for somebody?"

"We are," the guy said.

"Who?"

"You," the guy said, and brought his hand out from behind his back with a Colt automatic in it. "Come on in," he invited.

58

It was just a horrible night for Brandon Camberbridge. His hotel, his beloved hotel, under siege, full of strangers, *mercenaries*. Nell not here to console him, and the big cheese over there in cottage one acting as though he blamed Brandon for something. Blamed *Brandon!* For what? For loving the hotel?

He couldn't follow his normal routine tonight, he just couldn't. Normally, he was out and about, everywhere in the hotel, smiling, greeting, nodding, encouraging the staff, beaming on the beauties of his paradise, circulating all night as the great hotel sailed like a wonderful ship through the darkness, himself out and about until his bedtime at four in the morning, like the captain of the wonderful ship, walking the decks, feeling the great hum of it, alive beneath his feet.

But not tonight. He couldn't stand to be out there tonight, the tension, the strange faces of the imported security people, the knowledge that the big cheese was brooding in cottage one, *festering* in cottage one.

No, no, Brandon couldn't walk the deck of his great ship tonight; the hotel had to sail without him, while he sat here in his office, the control center of it all, waiting for disaster to strike.

For a while, he'd phoned security every now and then, just to check in, but at 11:30 Wylie Branch had come on the line

304 Donald E. Westlake

and had been *extremely* sarcastic: "Let my boys do their job," he suggested. "Anything you need to know, they'll be in touch. They got your number, believe me."

So for the last four and a half hours he'd just *been* here, listening to a local news radio station, trying to go over old paperwork, waiting for the phone to ring. What's happening? Has the war started? Has the disaster struck?

Four A.M. Time to go to bed, though Brandon seriously doubted he'd get much sleep tonight. Still, he ought at least try to maintain his normal schedule; it wouldn't help anybody if he were to come down with a bug tomorrow, would it? So, at 4:00 A.M. exactly, he switched off the news station—grateful that he'd heard no news at all about the Gaiety—and left his office.

Brandon's managerial office suite was directly behind the check-in desk, but his primary route in and out was via a short corridor to a door that opened onto the public space around the corner from the main desk, between that and the coffee shop, and facing the glass doors out to the pool area. Coming out here tonight, he wasn't surprised to see no one in the coffee shop or walking by; 4:00 A.M. on a Monday night was always very slow. But he ought at least look in once on the guests in the casino, just to reassure himself with a faint echo of his normal routine, so that's the direction he turned.

There was no one visible at the desk, but that was also normal. No guests would be checking in at this hour, and if anyone did have a question they could press the bell on the desk and the young woman from the office behind it would step promptly out to be of service.

Brandon walked on by, and saw no one at all at the slot machines, which was slightly unusual. Slot players have more staying power than any other human beings on the planet. Reflecting on that, he walked on by, just peripherally registering the fact that two players *were* there, crumpled on the floor in front of machines, cardboard cups of coins spilling from their limp hands, when his attention was drawn horribly to the sight of four people *unconscious* at a blackjack table.

Good God! The dealer and three players, all sprawled on the half-moon-shaped table, dead to the world. And beyond them, another table, three more sleepers.

Brandon stared. He couldn't believe his eyes. People were sleeping on the crap tables! They were sleeping on the floor! They were sleeping—

Were they sleeping? Or were they . . .

Poison! Thoughts of botulism, death from his own kitchens, scrambled in Brandon's brain as he hurried forward to the nearest table. Oh, please be alive! *Please* be alive!

They were alive. Their arms were warm. Several of them were snoring. They were alive, they were merely asleep.

"Wake up," Brandon said, and prodded the nearest dealer, a heavyset middle-aged man, who kept right on sleeping. "Wake *up*," Brandon insisted. "What's going *on* here?"

But the man would not wake up. Brandon stared around, and it occurred to him he could see none of his guards, none of the security people, not a uniform in sight. Where were they all? What's happened to everybody?

Along the wall to the right of the blackjack tables was a plain unmarked doorway, leading to a curved hall with walls papered the same dull green as this part of the casino, and a floor with the same dull red carpeting, the hall angling away out of sight, featureless, uninviting. This hall led to the day-room, as it was called, which was a small private place where security people could take their breaks. Coffee and tea and pastries were available in there, and chairs and sofas for the guards to sit on, put their feet up, rest from the hours of standing around that was the main ingredient of their jobs. Bewildered, growing frightened, apprehensive of what he might find, Brandon crossed to this doorway, hurried along the curving hall, and came into a room full of sleeping guards, sprawled in furniture and on the floor all over the room. And every one of them lashed wrist and ankle with duct tape.

"Oh, my God!" Brandon cried, and off to the right a guard in the security uniform, who had been seated with his back to the entrance, stood up and turned around and said, "Well, hello, there."

Brandon thought he would faint. He thought he'd have a heart attack, or at least a humiliating accident in his underwear. He didn't know *which* element was the more bewildering and the more terrifying: the pistol that was being pointed at him; the gas mask on the guard's face; or the muffled metallic sound when the guard spoke, the voice coming through that horrible mask, the mask like a parody of an elephant's head, gross and inhuman.

"I—" Brandon said. "Uh—" he said. His hands moved, accomplishing nothing.

A second guard—no, a second interloper, in a guard's uniform—also stood and pointed his gun and his gas mask at Brandon. "Room for one more," he said, and he had the same muffled metallic voice as the first one.

Brandon said, "What's *happening?* What are you *doing?*"

The first gas mask turned to the second gas mask and said, "You notice how they all ask that? I would of thought it was obvious what was happening, but they all wanna know."

There were rest rooms beyond the coffeemaker, and from the men's room now came a third man in security uniform and gas mask, who looked at Brandon and then at his friends and said, "What have we got here?" (These were the three who'd recently dealt with the staff in the security offices.)

Brandon thought, *Not in my hotel.* You can't destroy my hotel, whatever the big cheese may think. This isn't a toy! I have to be strong, he thought, I have to get my wits about me, I must establish authority here. He said, his voice quavering only slightly, "I am the hotel manager. I am Brandon Camberbridge, and you are—"

"That's nice," the first one said. "That's a nice name. Come sit down here."

"I demand," Brandon said, "to know—"

The second one said, "Brandon Camberbridge."

Brandon blinked at him, at that horrible gas mask. "What?"

"Sit down or I'll shoot your knee." (He said that to every-body.)

I must argue with them, Brandon thought, I must protest, but even while thinking that, he was nevertheless moving forward, unwillingly but obediently placing himself in the chair indicated, unwillingly but obediently allowing them to tie his wrists and his ankles with duct tape.

"See you later," one of them said.

"Where are you going?" Brandon demanded, with increasing hysteria. "You aren't going to burn it down, are you? Why are you wearing those *things* on your face?"

They laughed, fuzzy metallic horrible laughs, and one of them leaned forward close enough for Brandon to read the Air Force markings on the boxlike thing at the bottom of the hose-snout on the front of the mask. "It's the latest style," said that nasty twangy voice, like a robot singing a country song.

They all laughed again, and headed for the doorway. "Pleasant dreams," one of them said, and then they were gone.

Pleasant dreams? Was that supposed to be funny, some sort of sadistic comedy? Did they really think he'd be able to *sleep?* Here? Under these circumstances?

Wide-eyed, Brandon stared around at the sleeping guards. Sleeping. Gas masks.

Oh.

It turned out he could hold his breath for under three minutes.

"I'm not really sure," Anne Marie said, "we're supposed to be together, you and me."

"Well," Andy Kelp said, looking out Anne Marie's window at the quiet of the Gaiety grounds, "who knows? I mean, I'm not sure either. But do you think this is the time to ask the question?"

"Well, maybe not," Anne Marie said.

T he deal was, Dortmunder had organized the heist, and he would participate in any profit from it, but he had no part to play in the actual operation itself. This was another of the advantages of having a string of twenty instead of a string of five.

Of course, Dortmunder had not only organized the job, he'd also made it possible. This entire casino/hotel had changed its normal operations, had introduced a lot of uniformed personnel who didn't know the territory and didn't know one another and weren't known by the regulars, had shifted their whole emphasis from guarding the casino to guarding this single individual in cottage one, and that made the robbery possible. Without Dortmunder, this caper couldn't fly. So he could be left alone to do his own little transaction, and would make his move in the confusion following upon the—successful, they all hoped—completion of the main event.

Four-ten A.M. The lights behind the drawn drapes in cottage one had finally switched off twenty minutes ago, but Dortmunder continued to sit in his own semidark in cottage three and watch. There wasn't a chance he would fall asleep at the wrong time tonight, he was too keyed up, he was too ready, he *knew* this was the end of it. Tonight, he would get back his lucky ring.

So all he had to do was sit here and watch that cottage, to

be sure that nothing happened to change the equation. He didn't want Fairbanks to sneak out under cover of darkness, or sneak reinforcements in, didn't want any changes that he didn't know about. So he'd just sit here, and watch, and meantime the heist would go down.

Four-ten A.M. The side door of the Invidia opened and six men stepped out, five of them dressed as guards and carrying under their arms small cardboard cartons that used to be in a storage shed at Nellis Air Force Base. The sixth was dressed as a Gaiety doorman, which came as something of a surprise to the actual doorman when this group approached him, showed him a variety of weapons, and explained he was going to be replaced for a while.

In the limo, Herman saw the group coming, and was pleased that the time was finally here. He'd been getting bored inside this vehicle, with nothing to do but think about the good old days in Talabwo, not getting killed by his nearest and dearest political friends.

The substitute doorman sat where the original doorman had been seated, and fixed his face into an identical expression of brain-dead somnolence. The five pseudo guards with the boxes under their arms escorted the original doorman into the casino, where more surprises awaited him, including three men in gas masks who took him into the guards' dayroom and hog-tied him with duct tape. The five new guards, who included the two lockmen, Ralph Winslow and Wally Whistler, put on gas masks of their own from those cardboard cartons they'd been carrying and proceeded through the sleeping casino to the cashier's cage at the back.

Herman got out of the limo, leaving his cap on the seat. He also entered the casino, but veered off the other way, around the unmanned check-in desk and into the empty coffee shop, and out its interior door to the bare concrete corridor leading to the kitchens. The kitchens were open for business, for room service or any food the customers in the lounge might want—though on this particular night there hadn't been any orders from the lounge for quite some time—but the kitchen staff paid no attention to the black man in the tuxedo who marched with such confidence through their territory. Out of the kitchen Herman went, and past the garbage room, and veered right into the hallway where Tiny and Jim and Gus were loitering.

Who looked at him with relief. "About time," Tiny said.

"The song begins," Herman told him.

The four of them went off to the loading dock to relieve the guard in the little windowed office there of his duties, Jim taking his place, and then did the same service for the guard at the vehicle barrier, Gus taking his place. Tiny and Herman escorted the two now unemployed guards back to the air room, where they were immobilized and placed next to the sleeping technicians.

Across town, Stan awoke, yawned, stretched, and started the garbage truck.

Wally Whistler and Ralph Winslow bypassed several alarms to unlock their way into the cashier's cage, where the three cashiers on duty slept peacefully. The two lockmen worked together, cursing quietly inside their gas masks, to countervene even more difficult locks and alarms to get from the cashier's cage back to the counting room, where the cash intake was constantly counted and sorted and stacked, and where the two employees with the rubber fingers on their fingers slept like babies amid messy piles of unsorted greenbacks. And finally, just as difficult as the door to the counting room, was the door to the money room, where the metal shelves were lined with trays containing the neat stacks of money; but they got through that one, too.

And now the lockmen were finished, at least in here. They made their way back out to the main casino area, past doors carefully propped open, and the other six guys in gas masks nodded and went on in. Wally and Ralph walked away through the casino, tossing their gas masks under blackjack tables, and went back out the front door, giving the OK sign to the doorman on their way by, who grinned and forgot for just a second to look stupid.

The six now in the counting room and the money room

took black plastic garbage bags out from under their uniform shirts and began stuffing them with money.

Wally and Ralph made their way to the Invidia and entered it, and from inside came a small but rousing cheer. Then Wally and Ralph came out again, each carrying a big plastic gallon bottle of spring water, and they walked from the parking lot around the side of the casino, past the swimming pool and the kiddie pool to the Battle-Lake, where they found Ralph Demrovsky pacing slowly along, looking exactly like a cop on the beat. Wally and Ralph grinned at the other Ralph, and then went on about their business, while Ralph Demrovsky turned and made his deliberate way to the cottages, paused on the path between cottages one and three, and took off his hat. He scratched his head, and put his hat back on.

Dortmunder, in the window of cottage three, lit a match and blew it out. Then he checked the glowing numbers on the dial of the watch he'd borrowed for this evening's work.

Ralph Demrovsky strolled back to the Battle-Lake, in time to see Wally and the lockman Ralph reunite, neither now carrying a bottle of spring water. Ralph Demrovsky took a little machine from his pants pocket, pressed a button on its top and tossed it into the lake, where it floated inobtrusively. Then Wally and Ralph and Ralph all strolled off to the Invidia and climbed aboard. Laughter sounded from within. Then the door opened, and an extremely trussed and irritated Earl Radburn was carried out and laid gently on the tarmac between two parked cars, his head cradled by his hat. His eyes shot sparks, but nobody seemed to care.

Herman had some doors to unlock. The first led from a corridor near the kitchens to a side corridor that angled around behind the casino to a second door that needed his services, which led to the casino manager's office, where the night-shift manager slept cozily, head on desk. There were two other doors in this office. The one leading via the manager's secretary's office to the casino floor was not locked, nor was it of interest. The other one was of interest, since it led to the cashier's cage.

This last door was the only one Herman had to deal with while breathing tonight's enriched air, though he wouldn't be in here long enough to feel any real effect. The knowledge, however, did make him a little nervous and caused him to slip slightly and take a few seconds longer than he should have, which annoyed him. He thought of himself as cooler than that.

When Herman opened this last door, it was to find the six guys in guard uniforms and gas masks standing there waiting for him, now all holding full and heavy black plastic bags. There were muffled greetings, and Herman led the others back the way he'd come.

In the security offices, the monitors showed all this activity, none of which disturbed the sleepers at all, though the two recently inserted guards, being still awake, did stare at the monitors, and at one another, goggle-eyed.

Stan Murch steered the big garbage truck onto Gaiety property and around back, where Gus waved from his post at the barrier. Stan waved back, drove on in, made a U-turn, backed up against the loading dock, and Herman and the six guards came out. All the plastic bags and all the gas masks were thrown into the back of the garbage truck. Jim and Gus joined Stan in the garbage truck cab, and he drove them away from there.

Most of the people who'd come here in the Invidia, except the substitute doorman, went back to the Invidia, and Fred and Thelma drove them away.

The three guys who'd dealt with the security offices joined Herman and they walked through the hotel and past the check-in desk, and the other three went on out the front door while Herman paused at the house phones, dialed Anne Marie's room, and let it ring once.

Anne Marie's phone rang once. She and Andy Kelp turned away from the window. "I'm off," Kelp said.

"You must be," Anne Marie told him.

They kissed, and Kelp said, "Will I see you in the city?"

"I'll phone you."

"Okay."

He left, and she went back to the window, to look at the nothing outside and think some more, while Kelp took the elevator down to the lobby and stepped outside. The limo waited, with Herman at the wheel, in his chauffeur's cap. The side windows of the limo were shaded dark, so nothing could be seen inside there. The doorman came over to open the door for Kelp to get aboard, which he did. Then the doorman got aboard after him, and pulled the door shut behind him. Herman put the limo in gear, and it hummed away into the night.

Five minutes later, Dortmunder looked at his watch. "They're done by now," he told himself, and went over to the cottage phone. He dialed 9 for an outside line, and then dialed police headquarters. "I want to report a robbery," he said.

61

Max dreamt of Elsie Brenstid, the brewer's daughter. She still loved him, but she wanted him to drink warm beer. Then the phone rang. Odd; it was an American phone, not British. Then there were excited voices, disturbances somewhere, and Max opened his eyes. The burglar!

Where am I? Las Vegas, the Gaiety, cottage one, waiting for the burglar. Dark in this bedroom, the door outlined in light. But all the lights in the cottage had been switched off when at last he'd come to bed, too exhausted by tension to stay up any longer.

He'd been sleeping in most of his clothes, having taken off only pants and shoes. Now he hurried back into both, listening to the raised voices outside. What was going on? Was this the burglar, or wasn't it? Why didn't somebody come in here to tell him what was happening?

Max hurried from the bedroom, just a second before the bathroom window behind him was pushed open and a dark figure, made cumbersome by what he was wearing, climbed cautiously inside.

The scene in the living room was utter confusion. His guards moved this way and that, bumping into one another, hands hovering near holstered sidearms, as they stared at doors and at draped windows, waiting for who knows what. Other guards jittered in the open doorway, looking stunned;

the darkness beyond them was full of running people and voices shouting.

On the telephone in the conversation area was Earl Radburn, looking both messier and more furious than Max had ever seen him. The messiness he remarked on first, because Earl was always so *neat,* so inhumanly perfect in his appearance. But look at him now, grease-smeared, pebble-dotted, dirt-daubed. He looked as though he'd been rolling around in *parking lots,* for God's sake.

And as filthy as he was, that's how angry he was. Enraged. Yelling into the phone, demanding action, finally slamming the receiver down, spinning around, glaring at Max, *shrieking,* "Well, this is what we get!"

"What we get? Earl? What's going on here?"

"The casino was robbed!"

Max couldn't believe it. Robbed? The *casino?* Stunned, he looked down at his right hand, and the ring was still there, where it was supposed to be. It was still there.

So what could have gone wrong? "Earl? Robbed the casino? Who did? And what on earth *for?*"

Acidly, Earl said, "For the money, if you ask me. Probably two million, maybe more."

"The money? But— But it was this *ring* he was after!"

"*That's* the goddam beauty of it," Earl snarled, and with some astonishment (and resentment) Max realized that Earl Radburn was mad at *him,* at Max Fairbanks, at his employer! "You've got us all," Earl snarled, "bending ourselves out of shape to keep an eye on *you* and that goddam *ring,* and that's just the chance those sons of bitches needed! It couldn't have worked out better if you were *in* it with them!"

"Which he was, of course," said a voice from the doorway.

Max turned, blinking, trying to absorb one astonishment after another, and be damned if it wasn't that insane New York City policeman, Klematsky, whatever his name was. Walking in here, bold as brass, with a pair of Las Vegas uniformed cops behind him.

Max shook his head at this new wonder, saying, "What are *you* doing here?"

One of the Las Vegas cops said, "You've got yourself a strong gasoline smell out there."

But nobody listened to him; there was too much else going on. And particularly what was going on was Detective Klematsky, who came over to Max, smiled in a knowing fashion, and said, "Been busy, haven't you? Up to your old tricks."

"What now, Klematsky?" Max demanded. "I have no time for you and your nonsense now, this hotel has just been robbed."

"Which you'll be telling us all about, a little later," Klematsky said. "Or was *this* robbery, while you were actually in residence here, *another* of your coincidences?"

"What? What?"

"I was going to get here a little later this morning," Klematsky went on. "I didn't figure the local department to wake me at four-thirty, but that's okay. Max Fairbanks, you are under arrest for grand theft, filing false statements and insurance fraud."

"What? What?"

"Here is the warrant for your arrest," the insane and implacable Klematsky went on, "and here is the extradition from a Nevada judge. Come along, we'll have a nice little cell for you to wait in until our flight back to New York."

"Get your hands off me! You're out of your mind!"

Max flailed around, not wanting to be touched, and inadvertently bopped Klematsky on the nose. Klematsky, no man to be trifled with, reached for his blackjack.

And that's when the Battle-Lake caught fire.

62

If all those trees and shrubs and ferns around the Battle-Lake had been real they probably would have contained the fire to some extent, since it hadn't been that big a fire to begin with, and real plant life does contain some percentage of water. But they were plastic, all those green leaves and fronds, those brown stems and trunks, they were plastic, and they burned like blazes.

The desert wind is sometimes strong, sometimes light, but it's constant. The wind wasn't particularly strong tonight, but it was very dry, and it had no trouble wafting shreds of burning plastic flowers and burning plastic leaves across to the cottages, which were made of wood.

In the chaos and confusion, Detective Klematsky tried desperately to keep hold of Max Fairbanks, but it was impossible, particularly after the lights went out. Max moved around in the increasingly smoky darkness, with that acrid petroleum smell of burning plastic, afraid he was doing irreparable damage to his lungs, when all of a sudden, seeming almost to appear out of the bedroom, there was a fireman in front of him, illuminated by the burning lake, dressed in firehat and smoke mask and heavy black rubber coat and heavy black boots. At once he grabbed Max by the arm, his muffled voice professional but urgent as he said, "This way, sir. Let's get you out of here."

"Oh, yes! Thank you! Out of here!"

"Clear the way," ordered the fireman, and they moved through the milling guards, while the crackle of the fire grew louder. The cottage roof had caught.

Somewhere in the darkened rooms, the crazed Klematsky was crying, "Where is he? Where's Fairbanks? Don't let him get away!"

I have to get away, Max thought, blundering forward out the cottage door, clutching to the fireman who was guiding him by the arm. I have to get away, I have to find a phone and find a lawyer. I need a lawyer, two lawyers, maybe ten lawyers, to protect me from that utterly mad detective.

"This way," said the fireman's muffled voice. "The fire's spreading. This way."

"Yes, yes, let's get away from here."

The fireman led him down the path between the cottages, and Max could see that two more of them had now caught fire. This whole part of the hotel complex would burn to the ground soon, if the fire department didn't get to work on it, didn't start hosing it down.

From far away, the sound of fire engine sirens screamed, coming closer.

The fireman led Max through the gate in the hedge, into the employee's parking lot, floodlit at night. "Thank you, thank you," Max babbled, as the sirens got closer. "You saved me—"

Wait a minute. The fire department is still on its way, it hasn't got here yet. Who is this fireman?

Even as Max formed that question, and even as he instantly knew the answer, the false fireman spun around at him in the middle of the employee parking lot, under that garish white light. Grabbing for Max's right hand, he bellowed, "Give me that ring!"

"You!" Max cried. "You're the one!" And he whacked the false fireman across the head, which only hurt his left hand when it struck the smoke mask.

"Give me that ring!"

"No! You've ruined everything, you've destroyed—"

"Give me the ring!"

"Never!"

Max, inflamed by the injustice of it all, leaped on the false fireman and drove him to the blacktop. They rolled together there, the false fireman trying to get the ring, Max trying to rip that mask off so he could bite the fellow's face, and Max wound up on top.

Straddling him. Winning, on top, as he always was, as he always would be. Because I am Max Fairbanks, and I will not be beaten, *not* be beaten.

You didn't expect *this,* did you, Mr. Burglar? You didn't expect me to be on top, did you, holding you down with my knees, ready now to give you what you deserve, kill you with my bare hands, rip this mask—

"YOOOOOOOOUUUUUUUUUUUUUUUUUUUUUU!!!!!!"

Startled, Max looked up, and here came Brandon Camberbridge, tearing across the parking lot, running full tilt and screaming like a banshee: "You! You destroyed my hotel! My beautiful hotel!"

"I've got him," Max started, to reassure the man, but it was *Max* that Brandon attacked, hurtling into him headlong, tackling him, the two of them flying over and over across the parking lot, away from the cause of it all, the false fireman, the burglar. The burglar! Him! Over there!

Max tried to say so, but Brandon was strangling him, pummeling him, beating his head on the blacktop. Max shrieked, and Brandon shrieked louder, and they clawed at one another, and Max felt himself blacking out.

"Excuse me."

The calm voice stopped them both. They turned their heads, and the fireman was there, hat gone, mask dangling from the left side of his face. "This is mine," he said, and reached down, and plucked the ring off Max's limp finger. "Thank you," he said, and straightened. "Carry on," he suggested, and walked away across the parking lot, and Brandon grasped Max by the throat and screamed terrible words into his nose.

By the time many hands arrived to drag Brandon free and help Max to his feet and pound his back until he started breathing again, the burglar, of course, was long gone.

And so was the ring.

63

There were about three days a year, all of them in June, when the sun, if the sun were shining at all over the island of Manhattan, could angle down and shine into the living room of Dortmunder's apartment on East Nineteenth Street. Thursday, June 8, two and a half weeks after the Las Vegas spectacular, it happened again, at a time when Dortmunder chanced to be present in the living room, still not quite having decided what to do with himself today. The sun shone in through the window near the sofa, bounced off the end table by Dortmunder's right elbow, and reflected itself in the gray face of the TV set. Becoming aware of that unusual light, Dortmunder put his right hand out to catch the ray, and turned the hand back and forth, watching how warm and yellow everything looked. Then he opened the drawer in the end table and took out the ring.

Still the same ring. Shield-shaped top with those little glittery lines on it. Dortmunder held the ring in the ray of sunlight, and gave it a good long look.

Funny. He hadn't worn that ring once since he'd got it back, just never exactly felt like it. On the plane home, it had been in his pocket, and ever since, it had been in this drawer here. Now he looked at it, and thought about it, and he was just about to put it on when the phone rang. So he put the ring on the end table in the sunlight and leaned over the other way to pick up the phone and say, "Yeah?"

"A.K.A., John."

"Oh, A.K.A. How you doing?"

"Well, I'm fine. Remember the Anadarko family?"

"No," Dortmunder said.

"John, would you *like* to remember them? That deal's comin alive again, same as before."

May walked by the doorway, home from work, carrying her daily bag of groceries from the Safeway, headed for the kitchen. She and Dortmunder nodded to each other, and Dortmunder said into the phone, "I don't think so, A.K.A."

The whole idea of rememorizing life on Red Tide Street in Carrport just didn't appeal. Also, there was the fact that he was flush these days. After expenses, the return on the Las Vegas trip had worked out to just over seventy-two thousand dollars a person, which was a lot more than Dortmunder was used to realizing from a job. In fact, most of the time, just getting *himself* out of a heist with not too many rips and tears and dog bites was what he considered a good return on investment, so this was a pretty nice feeling to have, being flush. He didn't *need* to remember the Anadarko family for five hundred bucks, so why do it? "Sorry, A.K.A.," he said. "I'm in semiretirement at the moment."

"Well, I understand what you're saying, John," A.K.A. said. "I'll get somebody else. I just thought, you know, you went down that road the once."

"That was enough for me," Dortmunder said, and hung up, as May came in, empty-handed. "How are things?" he asked her.

She sat down, said, "Whoosh," and said, "Ah. The feet do get tired."

"I told you, you know," he said, "you could quit there for a while."

"Then what do I do with my day? There's all these people working there, John, they've got lives you wouldn't believe, they're like soap operas, that's what we talk about all day, I wouldn't want to miss any chapters. So I'm okay, John. Is that the ring?"

"Yeah," he said, picking it up, turning it again in the sunlight. "I was just looking at it."

"You don't wear it."

"I don't," he agreed. "That's what I was thinking about. Now, you know I'm not superstitious."

May knew he *was* superstitious, deeply superstitious, but she also knew he didn't know he was, so she said, "Uh huh."

"But this was supposed to be the lucky ring, right?" He looked at it, and shook his head. "And what happened the first time I put it on? Bang, right out of the chute, I got caught, I got arrested. It wasn't till Max Fairbanks stole the thing from me that I started to get some luck. Good luck, I mean. And once *he* had it, look what happened to him."

"He's still in trouble," May said, "and he doesn't have the ring any more. It was in today's paper."

Dortmunder frowned. "For what? They don't still think he set up all those robberies, do they?"

"That's kind of on the back burner," she told him. "What it is, he's one of those guys, he could go along for a long time, pull a lot of stuff, get away with it all, because nobody ever looked close. Now they're looking close. He's gonna be in jail the rest of his life, for stuff that doesn't have anything to do with the robberies. They just started the cops looking."

"Well, it couldn't have happened to a nicer guy," Dortmunder said, as Andy Kelp walked in, saying, "You mean me?"

May said, "We were talking about Max Fairbanks."

Dortmunder said, "*Why* don't you ring the bell?"

"I don't want to startle you," Kelp said. "What I was wondering, you wanna go out to the track?"

Dortmunder looked at May, who spread her hands and said, "It's your money, John."

"At the moment," Dortmunder said. "Maybe I'll go and just watch."

Kelp said, "Is that the ring?"

"Yeah. We were just looking at it."

"I never saw it," Kelp said, and picked it up, turning it in the ray of sunlight. "Doesn't look like such a big deal, does it? How come you don't wear it?"

"Well, here's what I think," Dortmunder said. "I think it used up all the good luck it ever had keeping Uncle Gideon solvent. I think the only luck it has left is the other kind."

"Oh." Kelp put it down, and went over to sit in the chair by the TV, saying, "So what are you gonna do? Give it away?"

"If I find somebody I really don't like," Dortmunder said. "Otherwise, it can just stay in the drawer there." And he put it back in the drawer, away from the sunlight.

May said, "John, it's all right with me if you want to go to—" and the phone rang.

"Second," Dortmunder said, reaching for the phone, wondering if this was A.K.A. again, having failed to find another Fred Mullins, but Kelp said, "John, no, that's me."

Dortmunder looked at him. Kelp pulled a small telephone out of his pocket, a thing that folded together to become hardly anything at all. Opening this machine, putting it to his face, he said, "Hello?" Then he smiled all over. "Hi, Anne Marie," he said. "What's up?"